The Restorers

Steve Pillinger

Book Two of
The Mindrulers
series

© Steve Pillinger 2019

Cover design and illustration on p. 162 by
Cathy Helms, Avalon Graphics LLC.

Illustrations on pages 21 & 123 and maps by Steve Pillinger.

Scripture quotation on p. 292 taken from the Holy Bible,
NEW INTERNATIONAL VERSION®, NIV®
Copyright © 1973, 1978, 1984, 2011 by Biblica, Inc.®
Used by permission. All rights reserved worldwide.

ISBN: 978-0-6399077-3-4

Although some of the characters in this book were inspired by real people, they remain entirely fictitious, and any identification made with actual persons is the reader's interpretation, not the author's intention.

Note also that the theological speculations in this book represent the characters' attempts to understand the situation in which they find themselves, and do not necessarily reflect the beliefs of the author.

Readers may notice in this book that pronouns referring to God are not spelled with capitals (he, him, his, etc.). This does not imply any disrespect for God. It simply follows the example of most English versions of the Bible.

Other titles in this series:

The Mindruler
The Strongholder

Praise for this book:

"I loved the first novel, *The Mindruler*, but this novel takes the story to even greater heights! It is the best adventure I've read—with great moments of spiritual truth and reality, and a tantalizing finish (complete with a twist)." *Caleb, UK.*

"The pacing was fast and effective throughout, and the last few chapters kept me up past my bedtime on a work night wanting to finish." *Gordon Deane, UK.*

"There were times when I cringed, times when I yelled, and times when my heart sang while reading *The Restorers*. ... I recommend this book for Christians who enjoy a large-scale fantasy where God is not relegated to the position of a bit-player on the world stage." *Christine, USA.*

"Kudos to Steve Pillinger! He's given us an even more amazing sequel! I can't wait to see what book three holds, but I know I want this series to be more than a trilogy!" *Stan, USA.*

"Having marveled at the well-polished writing and carefully constructed characters and world-building, I was honestly surprised to discover that this book was not published by a mainstream publishing company. In fact, so long has it been since I have read a book so well-written, edited, and with such moving and relevant spiritual themes, I would almost say that the "mantle" of Christian literature has a new owner." *R. Gilbert, USA.*

Praise for The Mindruler:

"The rich setting and world-building of this novel drew me in and enticed me to keep reading from the beginning. ... I would recommend this book for readers who enjoy vivid world-building and portal fantasy with a bit of grit." *Bridgett Powers, USA.*

"One thing I really like is the characters. They're not the usual flat and stereotypical heroes – they feel real, flawed and quirky, like they could be your own grandmother, over-enthusiastic friend or rebellious cousin." *Jennifer, UK.*

"Excellence on an epic scale!" *Donald S. Meador, USA.*

Praise for The Strongholder:

"A stunning end to a riveting series. Highly recommended." *Fiona Veitch Smith, CWA Historical Dagger shortlisted author for* The Jazz Files, *UK.*

"I found *The Strongholder* deeply engrossing and very moving too. The best of the three books in *The Mindrulers* series, leading to a very satisfying finale." *Adriana, South Africa.*

"Steve Pillinger has woven together a great adventure filled with tender, moving moments, unforgettable characters, spiritually powerful scenes, and a great finale to the Restorers' saga! This novel (and the series) stays with you!" *Sean, UK.*

Table of Contents

To my family
who played the game,
inspired the story, read the drafts,
and kept me writing.
This is your book!

Acknowledgments

This book has taken shape over many years, with helpful input from many people. Those who have been there from the beginning are my family, and many of the characters and events took shape during the happy hours we spent playing the 'Family Game'. You know that this story is yours as much as mine.

Then there are my 'beta testers'—the intrepid band of friends who read my half-baked drafts and made constructive comments. Thank you for your perseverance!

Among these special mention must be made of the Beardlings, my fellow-writers in Thame, Oxfordshire. Andrew and Victor, you so often put your fingers on the exact issue that needed correcting; our sessions of coffee, laughter and helpful criticism have improved the story immeasurably.

To Fiona Veitch Smith, whose penetrating and insightful critique transformed a slightly rambling story into a book worth publishing—I can only say a deeply heartfelt thank you!

Last, in pride of place, is my wife. She ruthlessly slashed excess verbiage, transforming my writing style. The movie-like 'scenes' she pictured provided seminal ideas that enriched the plot time and again. It is no cliché to say that this book could not have been written without her.

Who's Who

Alanya	Dûrian name of Lannie Catterick, Restorer (Dûrion) and website designer (UK).
Bishop Harlon	Dûrian Head of State and Hearth (Church). Kept under house arrest by Bishop Shambor.
Bishop Shambor	Bishop Suffragan, *de facto* ruler of Dûrion and of the Dûrian Hearth (Church). Also Mind-ruler and head of the Cult of Gadesh.
Danîsha	Dûrian name of Denise Thompson, Restorer (Dûrion) and retired teacher (UK).
Destor	'High Walker' or leader of the Galeronden.
Dorbians	Intelligent wolf-like species living to the far north of Dûrion, whose emissary is Gwargif.
Father Martin	A.k.a. Dr. Martin Fellowes, Vicar of the Round Church of Leston in Oxfordshire.
Fira	Former Lieutenant in the defeated Rebel forces, who joined the Restorers in *The Mindruler*.
Frengor	'Visionary' or head of the Travelling Order of Lightist priests, who assists and supports the Restorers.
Galeronden	Autonomous Dûrian clan living in remote settlements in the Tallissôr Mountains.
Garset (Captain)	Lightist officer in the Dûrian armed forces who turned a blind eye when the Restorers entered Stillárre in *The Mindruler*.
Gelmion	Dûrian name of Gil Denbigh, former Bishop's Guard (Dûrion) and university lecturer (UK).
Gil (Denbigh)	English name of Gelmion.
Gwargif	Wolf-like Dorbian emissary who befriended Danîsha in *The Mindruler*.

Jomel	Former prostitute in the Temple of Gadesh, rescued by the Restorers in *The Mindruler*. Cousin of Perrely.
Kindler Mâron	Kindler of Sûrilane and *barây* (chess) companion of Bishop Harlon.
Lannie (Catterick)	English name of Alanya.
Lishet	Nist's retarded brother.
Nist	Large lady, head of the network that smuggles victims of Shambor's oppression to temporary refuge among the Galeronden.
One, the	Short for the One Creator God: All-powerful God in whom Lightists believe.
Ongaret	Travelling priest, personal assistant to Frengor.
Perrely	Young Dûrian girl of noble family, Jomel's cousin, who joined the Restorers in *The Mindruler*. Shiván's sweetheart.
'Pure Company'	Captain Garset's army company, four hundred strong, all of whom are followers of the Light.
Prince Orrénne	Son of the One Creator God.
Shîrin and Cârin (Shîr and Câr)	Twins, wisecrackers, and former rebel soldiers who joined the Restorers in *The Mindruler*. (Also nicknamed Shere and Khan.)
Shiván	Dûrian name of Steve Harston, Overguardian (Dûrion) and university student / CU Chairman (UK). Perrely's sweetheart.
Strongholder, The	Chief Initiate of the Cult of Gadesh, Ruler of Mindrulers and Lord of Selmion.
Tarlion	Garset's Second-in-Command in the Pure Company.

Maps of Dûrion and the Dûrai Region

Key to Map symbols and shadings

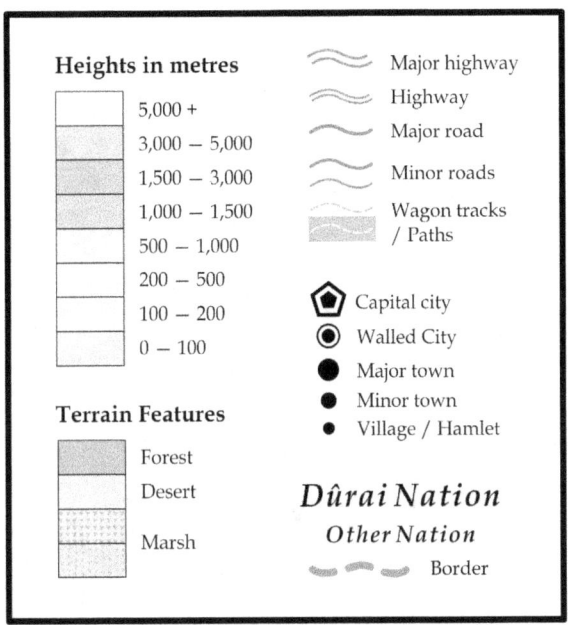

Heights in metres

	5,000 +
	3,000 – 5,000
	1,500 – 3,000
	1,000 – 1,500
	500 – 1,000
	200 – 500
	100 – 200
	0 – 100

Terrain Features

Forest

Desert

Marsh

~~~ Major highway

~~~ Highway

~~~ Major road

~~~ Minor roads

Wagon tracks / Paths

⬠ Capital city

◉ Walled City

● Major town

● Minor town

• Village / Hamlet

Dûrai Nation

Other Nation

~~~ Border

Note: The **Dûrai Nations** are Dûrion, Selmion, Thrinar, Marûvin, Pandiar and the city-state of Calardane.

The primary Dûrian unit of distance is the *aldor* (plural *aldoret*), which is equivalent to approximately one and a quarter kilometers or three quarters of a mile.

Map 1:
The Dûrai Region

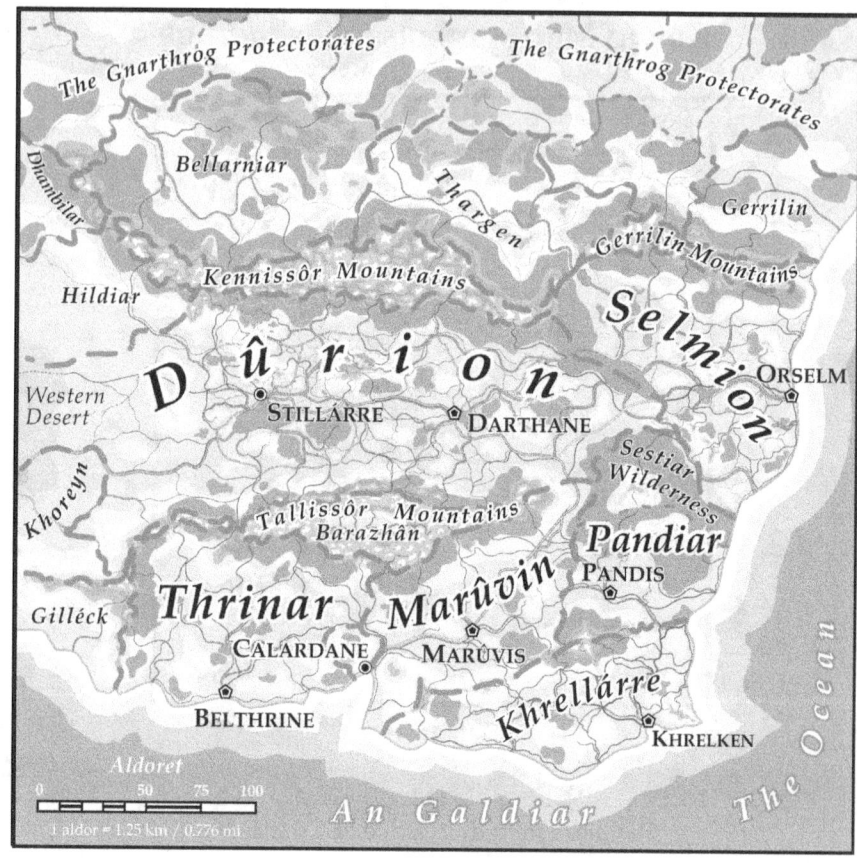

Map 2:
Central Dûrion

The Story So Far...

Steve Harston (**Shiván**), Lannie Catterick (**Alanya**), Denise Thompson (**Danîsha**) and Gil Denbigh (**Gelmion**) are stranded in a country called **Dûrion**, which they discover is on a different planet. Unable to return home, they become involved in the Dûrians' struggle for freedom from their despotic ruler Bishop **Shambor** and the cult of the **Mindbenders**, which he secretly heads, whose reign of terror includes abusing the Dûrians' innate telepathic abilities by mentally enslaving those useful to them.

The four foreigners are joined by a handful of Dûrians, including **Fira**, **Shîrin** and **Cârin**, former soldiers in the recently-defeated rebel army; and **Perrely**, a young noblewoman. Through Perrely they learn that they are in fact the long-awaited **Restorers of the Way**, prophesied in the Dûrian scriptures. They are also amazed to discover that the religion of the majority of Dûrians is so similar to Christianity that they can only regard '**Light-ists**' as fellow believers in the One true God.

Shiván, Alanya and Danîsha gradually accept their rôle as 'Restorers'; but Gelmion – an agnostic – goes his own way, and through the machina-tions of Perrely's cousin **Jomel**, a temple prostitute, ends up enslaved to **Dhelgor**, the Mindbender of Stillárre.

Indirectly assisted by the **travelling priests** and their leader **Frengor**, Shiván and his friends succeed against all odds in freeing Gelmion. In the process Shiván kills Mindbender Dhelgor. The mental vacuum when his mind-control is abruptly removed causes all Dhelgor's enslaved Guardsmen to 'freeze' – a condition that is fatal without specialised care. The city of Stillárre descends into lawlessness. In the chaos Shiván and his group rescue the prostitute Jomel – who has had an encounter with the One Creator God.

Meanwhile Bishop Shambor has flooded the area with troops to capture those who caused this disaster. The Restorers manage to escape from Stil-lárre – but now they need to find a way through Shambor's dragnet ...

Chapter 1: *Unexpected seizure*

"*AAAAH!*"

The anguished cry jerked Shiván out of a dream in which Bishop Shambor was having him whipped for criticising his new purple socks. He sat up abruptly. There were exclamations and rustles of movement from the others in the bushy hollow. A faint light filtered through the trees from the planet's two moons, revealing pale faces looking around for the source of the disturbance.

"*Aaaaaah– aah!*"

"Gil!" Lannie's voice exclaimed. Shiván yelped as a hard knee crunched his leg. Red-haired Lannie taking the shortest route.

"Keep Gelmion quiet!" Lieutenant Fira hissed.

"He's gone into spasm! Help me —"

Shiván's heart sank as he joined the scramble through the feathery fronds of the ground-cover to get to the tall academic arching up off the ground. Each upward jerk was accompanied by a drawn-out howl of agony.

"No! Don't hold him down, Shivvie!" Danîsha spoke urgently, her motherly face drawn with anxiety. "Just stop him hurting himself — grab his legs."

Shiván pinned down Gil's legs and Lannie and Trooper Cârin held an arm each, while Cârin's twin and comrade-in-arms, Shîrin, stood guard at the edge of the hollow. Fira slapped a thick cloth over Gil's mouth, anchoring it to the ground on either side with her hands. The sound immediately diminished. Danîsha warned her anxiously not to smother him. "I won't," Fira growled, green eyes sharp in her narrow, hawk-like face. "I did this often enough in the Rebellion."

They waited without speaking for the seizures to pass.

Until yesterday everything had gone like a breeze, Shiván thought wryly. After killing a Mindbender and setting off a French revolution in Dûrion's second city of Stillárre, they'd slipped through the Bishop's fingers and hopped on a passing boat. A favourable wind had blown them to the eastern shore of the lake, where they'd scuttled like mice through the grass to the Forest of Janulane.

1

Then those pesky patrols started popping up. He'd been leading the group south-east towards Dhembis, as Frengor and the travelling priests had advised, when they started getting diverted this way and that by troops of green-coats hunting them in the forest. Shambor was throwing out a wide dragnet. After giving the last patrol the slip, they'd accidentally stumbled out of the trees near the village of Barveck — way to the north! And now this.

Gil's convulsions began to ease off. With a final heave and cry he collapsed. Fira removed the cloth and sat back on her heels.

"Gil!" Lannie took his head in both hands, leaning over him. He stared up blankly.

"Gil! Are you okay?" No reply.

"Alanya —" Fira began in a weary voice.

Lannie looked round at them, her eyes brimming. "It's the same thing that happened to me when I was mindbent, isn't it?"

Fira nodded grimly. "Mindlock."

"But he's been fine!" Lannie protested, her tears flowing freely. "He's been walking and running, and in the last couple of days he's even started talking again! Why should the mindlock hit him *now*?"

"Because the *teméyn* has finally worn off. It's only been the drug that's kept him going."

"You mean, all this time he's been high on teméyn?" Lannie sounded indignant.

"That's what happened to you, too," Shiván reminded her. "In your case we hadn't outed the Mindbender, so you didn't freeze. But you still went through this jerking and stuff — only much sooner, because you'd had a lot less of the drug pumped into you."

"And now Gil's unable to move, like I was?" Lannie lifted his arm a short way. It was completely limp. When she let it go it fell unresisting on to his chest. She buried her face in her hands. She had every right to, Shiván thought. She alone, of all of them, knew exactly what Gil was going through.

Shiván squatted beside her. "Cheer up, Lannie. That's how you broke free, remember? It'll be the same for Gil. Without the drug all this mindbending stuff can't last. He'll break the mindlock and be his old superior self again — just like you."

"Well, thanks." At least there was a glimmer of amusement in her red-rimmed eyes.

"And you're the best person in the world to help him do it quickly."

"I suppose so." She heaved a deep sigh. "Thanks, Shivvie."

"But what are we going to do now?" Perrely asked anxiously. As always the young noblewoman's winsome face looking into his made Shiván's heart skip a beat. But no time for that now.

He cleared his throat. "That's the thousand *demeril* question. Sorry to say it, Lannie, but Gil could stay this way for weeks, even a month according to what Frengor and the travelling priests told us. We have to get him to a safe place, soon. We have to find that woman in Dhembis that Frengor mentioned — um … what was her name? — who helps people in trouble with the Bishop."

"Nist," Fira supplied.

"Yes, her. And that's going to be hard, because Gil's a big lad. He'll need two to carry him — we'll have to take turns. That'll slow us down a bit."

"A lot, with all these patrols after us," Fira muttered. She glanced at the twins, Shîrin and Cârin, who were keeping watch at either end of the bushy hollow. Shiván was struck again by how lithe and cat-like they looked as they stood poised for action. Both their heads suddenly snapped round at a rustle in the undergrowth, their large Dûrian eyes even wider in their olive-skinned faces. They relaxed when one of the small, spotted squirrel-like creatures dashed across the clearing.

"We'll have to make Gelmion a stretcher," Danîsha said.

Fira looked sceptical. "That would be hard to run with."

"It would be easier than two people carrying him, dear."

"All the way to the mountains?" Lannie exclaimed. "We'll never make it!" She sounded desperate. Tear-streaks glinted on her cheeks in the increasing light. Dawn was coming. They had to decide quickly.

"I don't think we have much choice," he told her.

"Yes, we do." A new voice spoke. They all turned and looked at Jomel, the former temple prostitute and cousin of Perrely's, who they'd rescued in Stillárre. There was scepticism in Fira's sharp glance, which turned to incredulity as the slim, dark-haired cultist girl outlined her alternative. Shiván smiled. "I like it!"

"Shiván, we can't do that!" Fira declared. "It's reckless and irresponsible. What if we're seen? We won't be the only ones to suffer!"

Danîsha also looked doubtful, but Perrely was wearing her devil-may-care mischief-making grin. "It'll be the quickest way to reach the mountains — and we won't have to carry Gelmion!"

That brought a wan smile to Lannie's face. It faded as she asked, "But will they agree?"

"Of course they will," Jomel assured her. "They'll do it for me."

"Shiván, I hope you're not going to go along with this madness," Fira snapped. "We'll be out in the open, where any of Shambor's soldiers or spies might notice us."

"But only for a short while!" Jomel said. "We'll get to Dhembis a lot sooner than if we have to carry Gelmion past all Shambor's patrols in the forest."

Fira glared at the young woman. Shiván thought wryly that once, not long ago, Fira had been the group leader — and a good one, too, as a former rebel officer. But then, in that strange Dûrian changing of *shiláyet* or personal 'auras', the leadership had passed to him, though he was younger and less experienced. It couldn't be easy for her to accept; and yet, like her fellow-Dûrians, she did. It was built into their minds and culture.

"I'm sorry, Fira," he said, "but I think Jomel's right. It *is* a risk, but one worth taking."

Fira huffed and said no more. 'Neesh also looked at him doubtfully. But it was decided. They'd follow Jomel's plan.

* * *

The ruler of Dûrion awoke to a vague sense of loss. Bishop Shambor sat up abruptly on the wide bed with its dark blue covers. There was a moan from the young woman beside him. He ignored her. What was wrong? Suddenly it hit him. *Gelmion was gone !* He swore loudly, and the girl jerked awake.

"What — ?"

"Shut up!" She subsided, hugging her naked breasts and staring at him fearfully.

Swinging his legs out from under the covers, he sat on the edge of the bed and swore again. Where Gelmion should have been, there was an empty void in his mind. The teméyn had worn off, and he'd lost contact. It had happened sooner than expected. He wiped a hand over his mouth. That was a large dose he'd made Gelmion take just before he was 'rescued'. But he was a foreigner, and you could never be sure with them. If only his troops had been in time to catch them as they left the ship in Palderen—or at least to prevent them reaching the forest! But with uncanny timing they'd hit the gap between the first detachment he'd sent and the second. His hastily-dispatched cavalry squadron had arrived too late.

Flisht! How much more trouble could such a small group of rebels cause? But then, they weren't ordinary rebels, were they? They claimed to be the Restorers of the Way, the long-prophesied rescuers sent by the One Creator God, who would banish the dark cults and fill the land again with his Light. Old fears from a distant childhood rose up in him as he clutched the edge of the bed. The Restorers could not fail. They could not be diverted or destroyed. They had the power of the Creator behind them, and in the end they would destroy *him...*

Nonsense! Shambor shook his head to dislodge the pernicious fears. He'd left those superstitions behind him decades ago. As he sat there breathing heavily, fear gave way to anger. How dare those charlatans defy him so blatantly? They'd killed a Mindbender! Destroyed an entire slave network! Thrown a whole city into chaos! Then slipped through his fingers into the Forest of Janulane. And if they *were* the Restorers, who had brought them here? Who had opposed him and taken their side from the start? Who had *prayed* them into existence?

That traitor would be hearing from him today.

He turned and smacked the girl's rump—hard. "Get out!" With a little scream she leapt from the bed, scrambled to pull on her nightdress, and ran from the bedchamber.

It eased his feelings a little.

* * *

At sunrise Jomel, her cousin Perrely, Shiván and Shîr set out for the village. This was where she'd so desperately wanted to go last night, but it had taken Gelmion's seizure to persuade the others. Now, instead of being the rescued victim, beholden to everyone else, she would be the rescuer, helping them out of a desperate situation.

Of course her parents still needed to be persuaded... But they'd do it, she was sure. As cultists they hadn't supported the Rebellion, and they would be taken aback to find a rebel soldier in the party. And of course her other two companions were Lightists, who believed in the One Creator God and his son Prince Orrénne. *I suppose I'm a Lightist too now,* she thought. It gave her a strange feeling. But cousin Perrely was one of them, and they loved Perrely and her family; so her support should overcome any remaining doubts.

They soon reached Barveck, which was not much more than a staging post on the Stillárre–Janulane highway – an inn surrounded by a cluster of thatched houses. People were just beginning to stir. There was light and movement in the inn kitchen, but the courtyard that fronted on the highway was deserted. They hurried across it to the main entrance.

A surly porter in his off-duty tunic let them in. Money changed hands, and he stomped away muttering darkly about disturbing guests at this unseemly hour. They waited in the small public reclining room. It was rather plain and unadorned, but the hangings on the walls were new, with a fashionable diamond design in green and gold.

Jomel ran a hand over her long, tangled hair. The four of them had spruced up as best they could, but they still looked as though they'd been rolling in the grass. She was only too aware that the other three were wearing battered peasants' sandals; and their clothes…! What would her parents think? Shîrin's rebel military cape was crumpled, his brown hair hastily – and ineffectively – smoothed. Shiván's green shift was a mass of creases under his robe, which was too short for him; and his blond thatch stood out in more ways than one: he was a head taller than the rest of them, like all the foreigners except Alanya.

But Shiván's wild hair matched his sparkling blue eyes. He wasn't her type, but she could see the attraction that had snared Perrely. Her cousin's short flaxen locks with their silvery highlights looked best cared-for; but her dark blue travel robe was badly creased. Her expressive, bluey-purple eyes were fixed on Shiván.

After what seemed like an age, a voice could be heard approaching. It spoke in a broad Selmian accent. Jomel's heart leapt.

"So why it is that a good man cannot sleep his sleep, I am not understanding."

"They said they couldn't wait, Master Taboru," the porter whined.

"A good excuse they'd better have for their impatience! Never have I – "

A short, knobbly man with an unkempt shock of grey-black hair, sticky-out ears and a truculent expression came marching round the corner. He had a blue robe thrown roughly over his night clothes. Jomel had never been so happy to hear his broken Dûrian speech. She stopped him short by leaping up and throwing her arms around him. "*Babu!*"

"Jomel?" He held her away from him to examine her face. Bewilderment turned to delight. "Child!" She found herself sobbing in his tight embrace. "Child, child, it is *you* again! In more ways than one you are back." She nodded, savouring the familiar smell and feel of him.

Finally they let go of each other. Her father harrumphed and wiped his eyes. "But Jomel, what do you here? Stillárre, this is not!" Then he saw Perrely. "Niece, you too! It is a morning for surprises." He embraced her and planted a kiss on each cheek.

Jomel introduced Shiván and Shîr as friends who, with Perrely, had saved her life. Daddy's bushy eyebrows shot up, shock spreading slowly over his features as he took them in. "But we can't talk here," Jomel said hurriedly, glancing at the porter hovering in the background.

With an effort he recovered himself. "You are right. We go to our rooms. Here, you—" He tossed the porter a coin. "You did right waking me. Go and do right somewhere else." The porter muttered his thanks and disappeared.

As they headed up the stairs, Jomel clutching her father's hand, he told her small items of family news, including their visit to Uncle Thandor in Janulane, which they were now returning from. Jomel was delighted to hear that her brothers and sister were here with her parents. She would get to see the whole family.

They entered the front suite, which covered the entire width of the inn's third floor. In the reclining room off the suite's entrance hall, where tall windows overlooked the courtyard below, the décor was shades of blue—dark 'Bishop's blue' floor cover, faintly striped pale blue wall hangings, and silver light trees. Daddy moved forward to loop back the window hangings, but Jomel gently stopped him with hand on his arm.

A door opened, and the tall figure of Jomel's mother entered wearing a slightly rumpled house robe, her dark hair coming loose

7

from its pins. "Taboru, what—" Then she saw Jomel. She gave a cry of amazement as Jomel launched herself into her arms.

After a long mother-daughter hug, Mum turned and embraced Perrely warmly. Then she faced the two men and suddenly paused, her eyes widening as their two very different *shiláyet* hit her. Mum had always been highly sensitive to the *shiláy*—the mental and emotional aura that every person radiated. The foreigners apparently couldn't feel it: Jomel found it hard to imagine such blindness. But she knew that to her mother the former rebel trooper Shîrin reeked of his anti-establishment sympathies; and as for Shiván... well, she still vividly remembered her own shock when she first encountered the foreigners' utterly alien shiláyet, like a blaze of brand new flamboyant colours assaulting her senses, screaming out their individuality and self-assertion.

As Mum took an involuntary step backward Jomel hurried to the rescue. Placing a hand on Shîr's shoulder she said, "This is Shîrinor, mother: he fought with the rebels, but he's now helping our group. We'll tell you all about it in a moment." Mum recovered herself enough to clasp his arm in the high Dûrian handshake. "And this is Shiván, our leader. I owe my life to him and his friends."

With a wide-eyed glance, Mum went through the motions of greeting Shiván. As she and Daddy continued their stilted introductions with Perrely's help, Jomel breathed a sigh of relief—initial contact had been successful. She slipped out of the reclining room to look in on her three brothers and her little sister, who were asleep in the bedrooms behind. Her heart swelled with joy. Not long ago she'd thought she'd never see them again.

When she came back they all settled on recliners, and she started telling her story. The colour drained from Mum's face when she told them she'd been chosen by the Cult of Gadesh as a human sacrifice. She glossed over her affair with the Mindbender of Stillárre, which had led to the death sentence; but described her utter despair, and her encounter with the One Creator God. That led to an awkward silence from her cultist parents. But when she told them of the daring rescue Shiván, Perrely and the others had pulled off, snatching her from a hostile mob in the Stillárre market square, Mum and Dad were outspoken in their relief and gratitude—and full of questions.

"How is it that in the city there was such disorder? That the mob could kill the priest of *Gadesh*?" Daddy was frowning, his eyebrows bristling.

"We heard there was trouble in Stillárre," Mum added, "but we didn't know it was that bad."

To explain, the two Lightists had to tell their side of the story: how they had set out at night to rescue their companion Gelmion — another foreigner, even taller than Shiván (Mum's eyes widened) — who had been mindbent and drafted into the Bishop's Guard. How this same Gelmion, while under the Mindbender's control, had captured Perrely and another of their companions, Fira — who had then been imprisoned in the Guardhouse. How they'd entered the Guardhouse at night through building works at the back, and Shiván had fought Mindbender Dhelgor, who'd been trying to rape Perrely, and kicked him through an upstairs window. Mum and Dad gasped at that, and shook their heads in amazement that the Mindbender had been killed by none other than this young man Shiván, who was sitting in front of them looking embarrassed.

Daddy leaned forward and tapped Shiván on the knee. "If this is true — and it must be, because Jomel is here! — then me, I am glad. I congratulate you! A man of great evil was Dhelgor. And I thank you." Clasping hands, he raised Shiván's arm high. "You have saved my daughter's life. On that I can place no price. I am in your debt, always." Shiván nodded and looked uncomfortable. Perrely was gazing at him shiny-eyed. They were so obvious, those two.

"*But* —" Daddy pursed his lips. "There will be trouble. Bishop Shambor, he will not lose a Mindbender easily. The Cult of Gadesh will not lose a victim easily. No, they will not. They will search." He sat shaking his head slowly.

"Taboru!" Mum exclaimed, her eyes widening. "Then Jomel is in great danger — and the others. We must do something!"

"Berenel, be peaceful," he said, patting her hand and looking worried. "We will work something out —"

"It's all right," Jomel said quickly. "Shiván and Perrely have a plan. Tell them, Shiván."

Shiván told them that they'd been given a contact in Dhembis who could find them somewhere to stay that was out of the Bishop's reach. Daddy nodded, hope dawning on his face. "I have heard there are such places in the south. Yes. Yes, this is good. But Dhembis, it is a long way. How will you get there?"

"Well, we were thinking of travelling through the forest, but we started running into these patrols..."

"Patrols?" There was new alarm in Mum's voice.

"It's okay, we got away — " Perrely reassured her.

Mum's hands flew to her cheeks. "Dear gods!"

" — but our companion, Gelmion, went down with a, er, sickness last night. So he can't walk now, and ..." She paused, looking at Jomel.

"... We wanted to ask if we could borrow the two carriages. I saw them last evening," she said in a rush. "We came out of the forest on that hill above the village, and they were standing in the inn courtyard. We didn't want to involve you in our troubles, but during the night Gelmion got sick. He's too heavy to be carried all the way to Dhembis... Please? We could be in Dhembis tonight, and the coachmen would drive back tomorrow. It would only mean one extra day at the inn..." She stared pleadingly at her parents.

"Child — of course!" Daddy agreed at once, as she'd been sure he would. "This is the least to do for you and your friends. Your life they have saved, and now you all are in great danger. We are happy we can help — yes, Berenel?"

"Yes, of course." Mum's approval was wholehearted, too. Jomel breathed a sigh of relief. Her pleading had worked. Mum might otherwise have objected for fear of drawing the authorities' attention. She felt a sense of satisfaction that she'd been able to ensure her parents' agreement. It would not only enable them to escape, but would enhance her status in the group.

They all embraced, then Perrely, Shiván and Shîrin left to fetch the rest of the group from the forest. Daddy stomped downstairs with them to send for the coachmen and have the carriages prepared.

She had just a few more precious minutes to enjoy with her family.

* * *

Lannie kept looking round anxiously as they entered the village from the forest. This was the point where they were most exposed. They had tied Gelmion's arms so he couldn't slip, and Shiván and the twins were carrying him almost doubled up between them. The others walked close, forming a human hedge. Lannie's every nerve was on full alert, but fortunately not many folk were about yet. Fira wore a dark scowl as if to intimidate anyone who glanced their way. "Watch while we're travelling to see if any vehicles follow us," she muttered in an undertone.

Two small, enclosed carriages were standing in the courtyard. They were tricked out in green and white, the paint and brassware gleaming. Coachmen sat on the open front seat; and between the shafts of each carriage were three pairs of *sinélle* — the sandy-brown dog-like creatures with narrow, foxes' faces who could pull vehicles at great speed in the central fast lanes of the highways. Their legs were long, and their shoulders and hindquarters powerful. Lannie was fascinated to see them up close.

"Those sinélle will get us to Dhembis in no time — it'll be an exciting ride!" Perrely said beside her, apparently unaffected by Fira's fears. Then Jomel appeared at the inn entrance with a short, ungainly man and a statuesque woman wearing a rather severe expression. Her parents, presumably. Perrely grinned at Lannie before hurrying over to join them.

Hmph. Lannie felt she could do without exciting rides. She hoped Gil wouldn't be too shaken up by the journey. If he was, there would be nothing he could do to help himself, or even let anyone know.

They bundled Gil into one of the carriages. Lannie arranged him as comfortably as she could in a corner, and sat next to him to prevent him slipping. She closed the window shutters on his side. It was a relief to have him out of sight with no questions asked. She spoke to him quietly, explaining what was happening. Her own terrible isolation during mindlock was still a vivid memory.

Eventually all the greetings and thankyou's were said, and the others clambered aboard. Lannie saw Danîsha struggling into the neighbouring carriage with her *bellaril* — the large guitar-like instrument she played so well. Fira helped her with it and climbed in after her.

Despite its awkwardness, Lannie was profoundly glad 'Neesh's bellaril had survived through all their adventures. Its ability to 'freeze' the Bishop's forces made it worth its size in gold. Her hand dipped into the pocket where she kept her *bess* — the turquoise, cowry-like shell that enabled her to speak to people at a distance —

11

the only mobile phone in Dûrion. Her mind briefly skipped back to the day when they'd discovered the bess and bellaril, along with Gil's magnifying glass, in Carreck Manor—the ruined castle where they'd first stayed in Dûrion. Later Shiván had been given the Blade of Darthane, a sword famous in Dûrian history. They'd little realised then how often these prophesied 'instruments' of the Restorers of the Way would prove their value in the days to follow.

Shiván and Perrely boarded the two outside seats at the back of Danîsha and Fira's carriage—Perrely wanting to make the most of her 'exciting ride', no doubt. The coachman lowered a protective hand bar over their laps. Lannie's own carriage rocked to the sound of happy laughter as Shîrin and Cârin sprang on to the rear perches. With a scowl Lannie grabbed Gil to prevent him slipping. By now a few passers-by had stopped to watch their departure.

Finally Jomel joined Lannie and Gil inside, and her mother passed in a bulky food hamper. That was thoughtful. Jomel leaned down and gave her mum a kiss of thanks. More embraces with her younger brothers and sister followed, till the last farewell had been said. The family stepped back, with Jomel waving furiously from the open window.

There were abrupt shouts from the coachmen, and with a sudden lurch they were off.

* * *

He stood among the bystanders watching the carriages pull out of the courtyard. "*They're just leaving,*" he said in his mind.

"*Where to?*"

"*I heard Dhembis mentioned.*"

"*How many passengers?*"

"*Eight. Three men and five women, looking rather scruffy. They loaded a couple of large packages as well.*"

"*And the party that arrived in the carriages yesterday?*"

"*Returning to the inn. Waiting for the vehicles to be sent back before continuing their journey.*"

"*And their final destination was…?*"

"*I heard them say Stillárre last night.*"

"*Good. Your report will be passed on to his Dominance.*"

Chapter 2: *Driving to Dhembis*

"THIS IS FUN!" Perrely cried, throwing her head back. Shiván grinned at her enjoyment. The plaited hairstyle she used had come apart in the wind, which was blowing a golden stream of hair all over her face. They sat high on the rear of the coach facing backwards, clinging to the hand bar and watching the Dhembis highway uncoil behind them. The few carts and riders travelling at this early hour dwindled rapidly in their wake.

Shiván found himself marvelling again at these amazing Dûrian highways, with their smoothly laid surfaces and six lanes—three in each direction—for pedestrian, slow and fast traffic. They were in the central fast lane heading south, and he reckoned their little carriage must be barrelling along at all of twenty-something miles an hour—not much by earthly standards, but here it felt like seventy. The only vehicles faster than theirs were the small one- or two-person chariots—'racers', Perrely called them. They were also pulled by the large, dog-like sinélle, who flowed sinuously along the road at high speed.

"You know, I saw these sinélle on the highways before," he said, "when I still thought Dûrion was some backwoods country under our own 'sky' back home. I just put 'em down as weird local animals. It was meeting Gwargif—the speaking wolf—that made me revise that idea from the bottom up. There are *no* creatures under our sky, apart from us, who can talk."

"Then our sky is richer than yours!" Perrely said with a grin. "We have three different speaking peoples. It's even written in our Book."

"Three! Which is the third, then?"

"I'll tell you. In the Book it describes how the Creator fashioned from the dust of the ground a male and a female of each of the three races under Malane, and taught them how to live in peace and harmony with one another, and with him. For a while this worked—"

"Wait, wait. What do you mean, 'under Malane'? What is Malane?"

"Malane is the name of our sky."

He blinked. "It's not 'Dûrion', then?"

She laughed. "Many Dûrians would like to think that. No, Dûrion is just one country under the sky—quite a small one. The whole sky, we call Malane. Don't you have a name for your sky?"

"Um, well, I suppose we would call it Earth. Or the earth."

Perrely turned a wind-swept stare on him, brushing aside strands of hair. "'*Soil?*'" she said incredulously. "You call your sky 'soil'?"

He gave a short bark of laughter. "Yeah, we're all upside down over there. No, it's just that we don't call the whole thing the 'sky', we call it..." He stopped, at a loss for words. God had enabled him and his companions to pick up the Dûrian language amazingly quickly when they first arrived, and they'd been improving ever since; but this was one of those times when he just ran out of vocabulary. "Ah... forget it. Let's just use the English word: 'Earth'."

"Ur... Urrith?" she tried tentatively.

"That's the one."

She shook her head. "What a strange language you have. Anyway, as I was saying, for a while the Creator and his creatures dwelt together in harmony under Malane: one couple lived in the open plains; another, in the woods; and the third in the mountains. But then Gadesh started whispering to the three wives, and the wife of the plains-dweller began to covet the easily-plucked fruit on the trees of the forest; the wife of the forest-dweller envied the many clever implements of the mountain folk; and the wife of the mountain-dweller desired the easily-milked cattle on the plains. They therefore nagged their husbands, until all began stealing from one another. The Creator's heart was so saddened by their disobedience, that he withdrew his protection and left them to fend for themselves. Therefore each couple raised their hands against the others: they fell into wickedness and strife, and suffered floods and famine and diseases; and from then on all creatures under the sky were estranged from their Creator."

"Wow." Shiván nodded appreciatively. "We have a story like that in our Book, too." He told her about Adam and Eve, and for a while they discussed the similarities and differences. Then he asked, "But you haven't told me—who are the third race of speaking people under Malane?"

She grinned at him mysteriously. "If we're going up into the mountains, we may meet them soon. But not too soon, I hope. They are called the Grûzhack. According to the legends, they are terrible ogres forty hands high who eat people alive. But fortunately for us, they keep themselves to themselves. They live in a hidden valley deep in the Tallissôr Mountains."

"If they invite us for a meal, remind me to turn them down."

"If they come anywhere near, I'll remind you to run!"

"Yikes! I get the picture."

"So, coming back to the sinélle. If they were different from anything you have on Urrith, why didn't you realise straight away that you were under a different sky?"

Rats. He didn't really want to discuss their home planets right now. He had something rather more romantic in mind. But there was a mischievous glint in her eye. Was she teasing him? "Is this what you want to talk about? Earth and Malane?"

"Yes. Don't you?"

Double rats. "Not in the least, but if the lady commands..." He attempted an elaborate bow and slipped off his seat. He managed to grab the hand bar, his feet flailing for a footing on the curved wheel guard below. There was a volley of angry Dûrian from the coachman. Shaking with laughter, Perrely hauled him up by the scruff of his tunic.

"See what happens when you don't take things seriously. Now sit still and answer my question."

He made a big play of gasping for breath, wiping his brow, and straightening his robe. "I think I'll be okay, thank you. What was the question again?"

Before Perrely could reply they had to hold tight as the carriage slowed and swung off the highway on to a bumpy side road. Following instructions, the coachmen were stopping for a break at an inconspicuous spot. The two vehicles came to a standstill at the edge of a field, shielded from the highway by a small stand of trees.

Everyone climbed out, Danîsha groaning as she straightened up. "Oh, it's good to stretch my legs! I'm not made for such cramped spaces."

"You should have sat up on the roof, like us," Shiván said as he and Perrely jumped to the ground. "Plenty of legroom there!"

Danîsha chuckled and shook her head. She opened her mouth to speak, but Fira cut in first. "What, so she could fall off, as I saw you almost did? Really, Shiván! You ignored sensible advice to follow this risky plan, with four of us in full view on the outside of the carriages — and then by your childish behaviour you do everything in your power to draw attention to us!"

"Oh, oops. Hadn't thought of that." He glanced at Perrely, who was giving Fira an unfriendly stare.

"Well, think of it now! There was no vehicle chasing us, thank the One, but what if you'd fallen off the carriage? Others would have stopped to help — and they'd immediately have felt your foreign shiláy! One word of that to Shambor, and we'd be done for." The lieutenant's accusing eyes bored into him.

It was a disturbing picture. "Um, not so good. You're right, Fira. We'll restrain ourselves." He glanced at Perrely, who gave an unladylike snort and left to help Jomel unpack the food hamper. Shiván sighed and walked under the trees to the small glade where the others had settled themselves. He found a seat on the soft grass beside 'Neesh.

The older lady chuckled as Fira strode off to where the twins were sitting on the other side of the glade. "That was a well-deserved ticking-off, I would say. Fira's probably giving Shîr and Câr a dose of the same. They got a bit wild, too."

"Yes, they did," Lannie said darkly. She was sitting beside Gil, who she'd propped up against a nearby tree. "They kept rocking the carriage, and it was all I could do to keep Gil on his seat."

"Well, looks like Fira's giving them what-for," Shiván said, watching the twins' hangdog expressions as Fira harangued them across the glade. "Where would we be without the good lieutenant to keep us in line?"

Just then Jomel called, "Come and help yourselves!" and everyone moved over to where her mother's goodies were spread out on a pristine white tablecloth.

"There's plenty of choice!" Jomel told them. She pointed to the different foods in turn: there were buns; cheese from the *arbilet* or bovine deer; its much riper cousin *grûn* cheese, from the great beasts of burden that pulled carts on the Dûrian roads; a bowl of wrinkled *sheyet*, like walnuts; another of salted *sûlinar*, the small, crunchy legumes; two large bowls of gleaming golden berries. "And for the main course," Jomel continued, "we have sliced beef, venison pasties —"

"*Meat?*" Fira exclaimed.

"Oh!" Jomel gasped, her face blossoming red and her hand flying to her mouth. "We forgot! Lightists don't eat... meat... do they?" Her voice dwindled as she looked round guiltily at the shocked Dûrian faces.

"Oh, we eat *meat*," Shîr hastened to assure her. "As long as it doesn't come from an animal."

"Or a person," Câr added.

"Most of it is meat. We can't eat it," Fira declared. "We'll divide up the buns, cheese and other food."

"Mother had to plead with the inn cook for the meat!" Jomel declared, her embarrassment turning to annoyance. "She paid double for the pasties!"

Shiván looked at Danîsha. She nodded. "'Neesh and I will have the meat," he said. "We eat it at home under our sky – and we haven't had any for a long time. It'll be a rare treat for us."

"Oh, thank you!" Jomel exclaimed, and began pushing all the meat plates their way. Perrely and Lannie looked askance at Shiván, and he grinned at them. Couldn't keep everyone happy. Lannie was a vegetarian, like the Dûrians. But he was going to enjoy those pasties...

They sat under the trees and ate their casual midmeal. Jomel helped Lannie feed Gil some of the *tilin*-bean soup her mother had put in a flask especially for him. To their relief he was able to swallow.

Half an hour later Shiván and Perrely were back on their high perches, suitably warned and bracing themselves against the hand bar as the sinélle picked up speed toward their destination, the town of Dhembis.

On one side, a couple of aldoret away, the Forest of Janulane was a brooding presence. About the same distance on the other side the River Eller glinted in the hazy sunshine. Between the forest and the river lay a belt of lush farmland, mainly vegetables and fruit orchards. Beyond the river stretched wide swathes of ploughed land waiting for next year's crop of wheat.

Shiván thought the countryside was beautiful. But he thought even more of Perrely's hand in his when they let go of the bar. It was great having this short time alone together. He grinned at her. Her expressive face lit up in a smile, and she put out her tongue at him. She really was like no other girl he'd met. Praise the One she didn't feel bound by Fira's stricter code. Fira scowled darkly whenever she saw their hands entwined. But then, Shiván thought, Fira scowled darkly at a lot of things. Sometimes she was right; but if you let yourself be guided entirely by Fira's scowls you'd live a pretty restricted life.

"You still have a question to answer!" Perrely exclaimed, grinning at Shiván. "Why didn't you Urrith people realise much sooner that you were under a different sky?"

Shiván heaved an exaggerated sigh. "Oh, that one. Let me think..."

He stared up at the sky for a long moment. Then he turned to her and grinned. "Okay, well, there were a lot of small things that we couldn't miss — like the sinélle, the different trees and plants, the way you can feel a person's shiláy, your brighter hair colours — we don't have purple, orange or that greeny-yellow colour — and so on. And there were a lot of things we would have expected to see on Earth that we *didn't* see here...

"But I'll tell you two things that really threw us. The first was all those English items we found at the castle — at Carreck Manor. We kept remembering them and thinking we *must* be somewhere on Earth. I found my copy of our Book there. It seemed too hard to believe that those things had somehow found their way to a different sky. Of course, we didn't know then that the Founders of Dûrion also came from Earth, hundreds of years ago..." He stared with unseeing eyes at the highway receding behind them. It still seemed too hard to believe sometimes. He pulled his mind back to the present.

"Then there were all the similarities between our two skies. You mustn't forget that. When you come to think of it, our skies are *very* similar. For a start, we can breathe your air and drink your water."

Perrely had been watching him gravely. Now she said, "Surely that must be so under all skies that have living creatures."

"Well, yes, maybe." *Perceptive comment*, Shiván thought. Water and oxygen were basic building blocks of organic life. "But what really blows my mind, is how similar to us you Dûrians are! You have two arms, two legs, ten fingers and ten toes. Your faces are arranged like ours. Even your animals run about on four legs, like ours do. "

"But why is this surprising? Doesn't your Book tell you that you were made in the Creator's likeness?"

"True. 'God created man in His own image.'"

"If he did that on your world, why wouldn't he do it on ours? Isn't his likeness the same everywhere?"

"True! If you put it that way, it makes sense." He suddenly realised how brainwashed he'd been by the science fiction novels he'd read on Earth—which delighted in portraying creatures on other planets that were as gruesomely different from human beings as their authors could dream up. This opposite truth from the Bible had never occurred to him.

"Also," he went on, fired by the new idea, "the first writing in our Book says that when he'd finished creating everything, 'God saw all that He had made, and it was very good'. Which means it could hardly be improved on. And being God, he would never make anything less than the best! So he used the same 'pattern' on every sky where he created life."

"Exactly." She nodded indulgently.

"But wait—what about your other two speaking races here on Malane?"

"*Under* Malane. What about them?"

"Well, I haven't seen the Grû-zits, or whatever you called them—"

"The Grûzhack."

"Right. But I've seen a Dorbian, and he doesn't look at all like us."

"Oh, Shiván, but they do! You haven't looked closely enough. Their hands are like ours, although they run on them—they have special pads for that; but they have free-moving fingers and thumbs and can make things and build houses, just like we can. Their faces—if you look behind the hair you can see they're very much like ours..."

"So you're saying the Dorbians are just a different variety of humans?"

"Yes!"

"O-kaaay... Well, it's true that when explorers under our sky first discovered people who looked very different from themselves—people with dark-coloured skin and so on—at first they weren't sure if they were human. But when they found they could speak and make things, they had to accept that they were."

"There you are."

"And what about the Grû-whatsits?"

"They're human too. They're bigger, and to us they look ugly —
but we probably look ugly to them."

"OK. So the Dorbians and the Grû-zits…"

"Grûzhack."

"They're like the different human races we have on Earth. Except that we don't have any speaking races that run around on
four legs like animals."

"Well, I'm sure the One has made many other variations under
Urrith that we don't have here."

"*On* Earth. Yeah, that's true. Haven't seen any black faces here —
or red or yellow ones."

"You have black, red and yellow people on Urrith?" Perrely stared
at him in shock.

"Well, usually not absolutely black, and not *bright* red or yellow;
but their skin is a lot darker, redder or yellower than ours is. But
they're human, like us: their blood is red, like ours and yours; and
they can speak, they can use tools, they're intelligent, they have
feelings, they know right from wrong, they live in organised socie-
ties… So many similarities. Just like your Dorbians and Grû-zhack.
As you said, God's basic pattern stays the same. Even here under
Malane."

"Which is why we look like you," she concluded. "Except that, of
course, *we* look much prettier." She grinned, inviting contradiction.

He gazed at her soulfully. "I have no argument with that."

"Uhh, Shiván!" she exclaimed in exasperation, turning away and
shielding her face with a slender hand.

Chapter 3: *Large lady*

THE OLD BISHOP OF DÛRION SMILED.
He lifted the cover off his hidden
game piece. "Ladder," he said.
"*Heyss!*" his companion exclaimed, staring at the board. "I
could have sworn it was Cavalry."
The young Kindler looked up at
Bishop Harlon, his turquoise eyes
sparkling as he smiled. "You've
done it again, your Radiance — I
can't stop you breaching my Cita-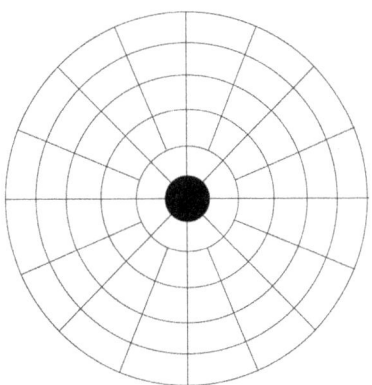
del." He reached out and lifted the miniature tower from its circle
at the centre of the board. Opposing blue and cream carved figures
dotted the spiderweb field radiating out from the Citadel. They began collecting them up.

Harlon dropped the last trooper in the box and stretched. The
sleeves of his blue satin house-robe slipped down his mottled arms.
Barây — the spiderweb. His only recreation these days. Young Mâron
didn't stand a chance, really. But he always lost graciously. Harlon
brushed a lock of silver hair from his eyes. By unspoken agreement
they left the small table with its circular board and opposing stools,
and stretched out on recliners before the fire.

The flames and hot coals bathed the room in a warm, flickering
glow, aided by a couple of free-standing light trees with their many
little lamps on upturned branches. The faded browns and reds of
the upholstery and hangings had an old, comfortable, well-used
look — rather like their owner, he thought wryly. Eighteen years
he'd been here now. He preferred it to his other apartment at the
Bishop's Palace, out on the nearby downs — though there he could
get some exercise on the episcopal estate.

He sighed. Palace or Cathedral, both were prisons. He'd never
have kept his sanity without Mâron's weekly visits. And those of
the previous leader of the worshipping community in nearby Sûrilane, old Kindler Gannor. He and Gannor had been friends for
many a long year. He'd been delighted when Mâron had taken up

the visits after Gannor passed beyond. Sometimes Mâron brought others along—old friends, faithful Lightist Elders, even parishioners from his Hearth, the Sûrilane house of worship.

Apart from those golden occasions, the only people he ever saw were Shambor, various Cathedral flunkeys, and the occasional foreign dignitary when Shambor saw fit to let him exercise his rôle as Head of State. That was a joke they all laughed at, though never to his face. He detested the hypocrisy.

"Have you heard the news from Stillárre?" Mâron asked.

"No, of course not. You are my eyes and ears. Tell me."

"Mindbender Dhelgor has been killed."

"*What?* By whom?"

Mâron's lips quirked. He swept back his mane of blond hair. "Officially, a popular protest got out of hand. There was widespread unrest. The Stillárre Guardhouse was breached, and the priest of Gadesh got lynched by the mob."

"Light! But unofficially—?"

"There are many stories. A Thrinari plot, black magic, even a sorceress weaving webs of music! Only one explanation makes sense, though."

"Which is...?"

"The true Restorers."

"Blessed Prince. Do the people believe that?"

"There's a lot of confusion. But the travelling priests do. They're preaching openly that the Restorers have come."

Harlon sat, his eyes unfocussed on the fire. Six years ago it was now. He vividly remembered kneeling in his private chapel with a leaden heart, Mâron beside him, and declaring before the One Creator God those words he had never thought to utter. The Entreaty of Need. A solemn plea for divine intervention on behalf of the nation, that could only be made by the Bishop of Dûrion himself. Since then he and Mâron had continued to pray, and in small ways to act, as the Light led them to that goal.

"They are truly here, then," he murmured, half to himself.

Mâron smiled warmly. "I believe the Entreaty has been answered, your Radiance. Those initial indications have now been confirmed. "

"Thanks to the part *you've* played."

Mâron shrugged. "A very minor rôle. My uncle is the one who has done most to set them on the right road."

"Ah yes. You told me Frengor and the travelling priests had actually met some of them."

"They did. Uncle Frengor was convinced they fulfilled the prophecies. 'A disturbingly foreign shiláy' was the phrase he used. He'd never come across any people who could more fittingly be described as 'strangers and loners'. I think we can safely accept that they are the ones we were expecting."

"Have you heard from Frengor recently?"

"Not since the episode in Stillárre. I wouldn't be surprised if he were somehow involved in that—"

They both jumped as the outer door banged violently open. A figure in blue and red came storming into the room. Blue was the robe. Red was the face.

"*You!*" A quivering finger almost jabbed Harlon's nose. Shambor planted himself with his legs astride in front of the fire, looming over him. The glow of the light trees revealed his heavy features contorted with fury. "You're behind this, aren't you?"

"Behind what, your Serenity?"

"Don't play games with me!" A foot lashed out, and the barây table went flying, blue and cream pieces scattering throughout the room. With a pang Harlon hoped none had fallen in the fire. It was an antique set, impossible to replace.

"You know what I mean! You did it, didn't you? You made it all go wrong!"

Harlon's steady grey eyes surveyed the fermenting ruler of Dûrion. "What has gone wrong, Shambor?" he asked quietly.

"*You know!* Don't keep asking me questions! *I'm* the one in charge. *I* ask the questions!"

Harlon couldn't help glancing at Mâron. The young man's eyebrows were raised.

"Of course you do. Forgive me," he soothed.

"*Forgive you?* Oh no, never. But I'll make you plead for forgiveness. You'll go down on your knees and beg me for mercy. Oh, yes! For all you've done to me." A finger stabbed at Harlon's face. Shambor was breathing heavily, his eyes wide. "I'll make you sorry! You think you're so high and mighty, but I'll make you see how miserable, deluded, naïve, and pathetic you are. You'll *weep* for the way you forced me to—" He broke off. His eyes hooded over. Without another word he walked away. The outer door slammed.

There was a long moment of silence. Mâron was the first to break it.

"*Forced* him?" he murmured. His eyebrows were high.

Harlon shook his head, perplexed. "As if I could force him to do anything!"

"Has he raved at you before?"

"No, not this way. You've heard him gloating over me, making snide comments, ordering me about. But never a hysterical outburst like this."

"The trouble in Stillárre must have hit him hard. And he thinks you're behind it."

"Which is irrational. That worries me, Mâron."

They were silent for a while.

"He sees you as a threat," Mâron said.

"Then why doesn't he mindbend me?"

"The old question. As you've often told me, he *could* have done so eighteen years ago."

"The old answer: he was proud of having overthrown me by other means, and wanted to keep it that way. Besides, once I was a prisoner I was no threat to him."

"Not so. I think he's always seen you as a threat. He knows how popular you are. What happened in Stillárre has reminded him."

"I pose no danger to Shambor."

"That's not how *he* sees it. We must ask for the One's protection." The young man's face was concerned.

Harlon nodded. They prayed together, then got up and began collecting the scattered barây pieces.

* * *

Shambor struggled to compose himself. Sitting at the blackwood desk in his reception chamber, he wiped a hand over his mouth. He shouldn't have flown off the handle like that. He'd almost given away— certain things that he shouldn't.

On the other hand, Harlon deserved it. If only he knew... Shambor's thoughts went back to his tortured childhood. Always being pushed. Never good enough. The son of a Lightist father with high ambitions for him in the Hearth. Nothing he did ever seemed to please him. An only child, sent away at a tender age to a Hearth School in a distant town. He'd thought his mother understood him, but then, when he'd confided to her the exciting new horizons that were opening up, she had turned out as bad, or worse. He closed his eyes at the bitter memory. He'd been dominated, rejected, betrayed.

And now Harlon was doing the same. *Harlon* had raised him to be Bishop Suffragan. He had handed over the day-to-day running of the country to him. He'd said, 'I trust you, Shambor, to make Dûrion a nation to be proud of'. Then, when he'd started doing just that, Harlon had complained and objected and thrown up endless hidebound Lightist scruples, until he'd been forced to set him aside where he could no longer interfere. He'd tried to include him, to convince him of the high spiritual principles of the Realm of the Mind… but he'd rejected both it and him.

Even after his influence in the state had been neutralised, Harlon had continued to oppose him at every turn. He'd written that encyclical letter that triggered the Rebellion. Now, somehow, he was supporting these upstart 'Restorers'… Rejecting him, betraying him, undermining him! Despite the fact that he, Shambor, had shown Harlon nothing but consideration and forgiveness. Why, he even still allowed those weekly barây sessions with Mâron, because he knew how much they meant to the old man.

A terrible thought hovered at the edge of his mind. He should do away with Harlon altogether. Then he'd really be in charge.

No. He couldn't. Not *that*, on top of…

Then he must mindbend him. Should have done it long ago.

No!

He stood up from the blackwood desk and began pacing up and down between the recliners in his reception chamber, his hands clasped behind his back. He'd sent his secretary Estaron away. He needed to think.

Forget Harlon and his machinations. He'd take care of him in due course. More to the point was this present disaster. Gelmion mindlocked. He and his companions vanished. And the on-going mess in Stillárre, with civil unrest still simmering and the entire local network shattered.

But it was the loss of the foreigners that infuriated him. Stillárre would recover. A new Mindbender had been appointed, and troops were restoring order. *But those so-called Restorers had to be found!* He mentally sifted through the conflicting reports he'd received. They'd been seen galloping through Bostane on horseback.

They'd been sighted among a gathering of Kindlers in Janulane (but had subsequently disappeared). Two sinélle carriages had been taken over by a large party at Barveck. Four foreigners had been apprehended in Chale—though they'd turned out to be an indignant party of merchants from the distant land of Anáricar, who'd had to be soothed and compensated.

All the reports might turn out to be red herrings. Nevertheless he would ensure that each one was followed up. He distance-spoke all his Mindbenders, authorising them to offer a large reward for information leading to the capture of the four foreigners.

* * *

"Oh, Shiván, cut it out!" Lannie snapped.

Danîsha shared Lannie's feelings. The four foreigners had been sitting in this little inn bedroom since midday yesterday, while their Dûrian companions scoured the town of Dhembis for anyone who'd heard of a woman called Nist. That was the unusual name Frengor, the leader of the travelling priests, had given them as their passport to a safe hiding place.

Shiván was perched on the window ledge, crooning softly as he stared out of the small unshuttered opening. When he heard Lannie's exclamation he turned towards them and let his voice rise in a muted crescendo with outflung arms as he reached the climax of the song. Then he grinned and said, "What's the matter, don't you like good singing?"

"Yes, I do. That's the point," Lannie shot back.

"Ouch! Okay, if I'm not appreciated, I'll shut up." His exaggerated pout fought a losing battle with his grin. Danîsha couldn't help smiling. Ah, what a wonderful thing, young love. Nothing could get Shiván down these days.

A few moments later his fingers started drumming a rhythm on the window ledge.

"Shiván!" Lannie snapped.

"Hmmm?"

"Stop that! Sit *still*, for goodness' sake!"

"Yes, ma'am! Whatever you say, ma'am!" He threw her a casual salute and a cheeky grin.

"Idiot!" Lannie smiled in spite of herself. She relayed the event to Gil, who was lying stretched out on one of the beds with his eyes open. As always, he made no response.

At least Shiván lightened up this interminable waiting, Danîsha thought. They'd been here here since daybreak, and it was now almost noon. The sinélle carriages had reached Dhembis at about midday yesterday, and the coachmen had found them this unobtrusive inn away from the market square. Praise God for the cash they'd 'liberated' from the Stillárre Guardhouse after Shiván had killed the Mindbender! She couldn't think of it as stealing. That money had been extorted or stolen in the first place. Now it was being used to start righting those wrongs.

She sighed, and shifted on the edge of her bed to try and get comfortable. She was finding all this sitting without a proper backrest tiring; but she refused to lie down like an old lady. For a brief moment her thoughts went back to her comfortable cottage in England, and a pang of longing shot through her for her lost home and family. Her youngest grandchildren, Ellie and Anthony—how big they must be now! Would she ever see them again?

Well, it was no use fretting over what couldn't be changed. If all went well they would soon reach the safety of the mountains. From the carriage the snow-clad peaks to the south had looked so serene and enticing. Her thoughts went back to their time at Carreck Manor, on the slopes of the northern mountains. That had been a true home from home. Gone, now. Most of those early friends killed. Including dear young Teynel, the twelve-year-old Dûrian girl who had adopted Danîsha as the grandmother she'd lost—only to be savagely slaughtered by the mindbending monsters who oppressed this beautiful land. She absently fingered Teynel's small wooden comb in the pocket of her shift—the comb she'd prised from the dead girl's hair that terrible day in the Manor basement.

The door burst open and they all jumped. It was Perrely and Shîrin, looking excited.

"We've found someone!" Perrely announced, her face flushed. Shiván leapt from the window ledge. For a moment Danîsha thought he was going to embrace her, but he stopped short just in time.

"His name's Carmelet," Shîr said. "Big, black-haired fellow. He was at the fourth inn we visited. We were asking about Nist, and he was there having discussions with a client. He's a local merchant," he explained.

"He was glaring at us while we were asking around," Perrely chipped in, "so we didn't bother to speak to him. Then when we left —"

" —he came out after us," Shîrin resumed. "Light, what a tongue-lashing he gave us! Said we were jeopardising the whole operation, whatever that may be. But he calmed down like a patted deer when we said that Frengor had told us to ask for Nist."

"We started to explain why we needed to see her, but he shushed us."

"Said he didn't want to know. It was enough that Frengor had sent us."

"He'll come to the inn after the midmeal, when the others are back —"

" —and take us to Nist!"

"She's in a nearby village — Jarmenis, I think — so we need to be ready to travel, *if* she accepts us."

The little village of Jarmenis was about seven aldoret south of Dhembis — five and a half miles. Carmelet led them on a stiff uphill climb along the tumbling River Mardhem, with snow-capped heights soaring up ahead of them. Danîsha was puffing by the time they crested the last ridge. Her lot was easy, though. The three men were red-faced from coaxing a handcart up the rough country path. They'd bought it off the innkeeper, and hidden Gil in it on some bedding, covered by an assortment of extra robes and clothing — and the bellaril.

They paused on the crest to catch their breath. A short way ahead on a small plateau she saw the thatched cottages of the village, clustered around the usual circular white Hearth. To the right the river bubbled over some attractive falls on its journey down to Dhembis. When she looked back the way they'd come, she gave a sigh of pleasure. The town was spread out below with its green-tiled roofs and neat, well-kept streets. Beyond, across a broad tract of farmland, was the Forest of Janulane; and to the north-east lay the wide, hazy valley of the River Eller. All was bathed in the golden glow of the setting sun.

Carmelet called them to order and they trudged wearily on towards the village, dragging the handcart.

They entered the single street as the villagers were returning from the fields. Many nodded to Carmelet, and several of the men silently took over the cart. They brushed aside Shiván and Shîrin's surprised thanks with a brief grin. Danîsha wondered how many other weary refugees they had welcomed this way. It seemed a well-oiled routine.

Carmelet led them to a sizeable cottage at the far end of the village, and drummed on the door with his fingers.

"*Coming!*" a deep voice boomed.

The tall door opened, and Danîsha involuntarily stepped back, along with the others. There were several gasps. The largest woman she had ever seen loomed in the doorway, filling it completely. Dressed in a workaday blue tunic and leather skirt, she looked like a man—apart from the substantial battlements in front. She was almost as tall as Gil, and enormous in all directions, with no trace of fat. A disorderly mop of dark greeney-blond hair surrounded a large, square face tanned to a rich brown from the outdoor life. Vivid green eyes assessed them under narrowed lids, testing their shiláy. Her hands were on her hips.

"So, Carmelet. What are *they* running from?" she demanded in a resounding baritone.

Chapter 4: *Mountain accident*

THE CHILD LAY CURLED UP on the thin straw of his cell, exhausted from weeping. He didn't know what he'd done wrong. It must have been something horrible—so horrible that they could never stop punishing him.

His mentor—grim, terrifying Faranu—had told him today was his birthday. He'd promised him a special treat—Nurse Olôra could be with him all day! He'd waited and waited and waited. But she hadn't come. He whimpered as he lay hugging his bony shoulders. Olôra, the one warm, safe place in his life. It was his birthday. And she hadn't come.

Long ago, he knew, there had been Ammi and Baaba. They had hugged him, like Olôra. They had also punished him when he did wrong. Baaba could get very cross. But nothing like Faranu. One day the whole family had gone on a journey, and the wagon had slipped. It had gone over the edge. That was the first nightmare. He remembered screaming inside the tumbling vehicle—then a terrible crash. Ammi's body, bent over a rock, leaking blood. Baaba all sort-of crushed. Shakhere shouting to him. Then the other men came and Shakhere fought them, but they took him away from Shakhere.

Had he made the wagon fall? Had he killed Ammi and Baaba? Was that why he was being punished?

They'd brought him here, to Sel-mee-on. The strange place of the short people—though the grown-ups were still much bigger than him. When he'd screamed for Ammi and Baaba they'd whipped him. That was the second nightmare, when the punishment began. Faranu had put him in a dark room with no light till he was quiet.

His mentor had brought other children to the echoey stone building where his cell was. He was allowed out to play with them. But they were horrible. They showed him he was different—ugly. They put a shiny thing in front of him, where he saw their faces, and his own face. Theirs were smooth and pink, their eyes were straight, and they had short, light-coloured hair. His face was white and wrinkled, his eyes slanted downward, and his hair was long and black. They laughed and kicked him. He fought back, and Faranu grew angry. He held him and cut his arms. It had hurt so much. He had screamed and screamed. That was the third nightmare.

Then Olôra came and comforted him. Faranu kept hurting him, and Olôra comforted him. But not today. Not on his birthday.

Footsteps echoed in the corridor, coming towards him. He knew that quick, light tread. Olôra! Joy flooded him, and he leapt up. There she was, with her blue tunic, purplish hair and friendly face — she'd come after all! Only... she wasn't smiling. Ice touched his heart. She was leading another small boy by the hand. Her face was hard and cold. What was wrong? The gate clanged as the two entered his cell.

"Olôra?" He took a few steps toward her, arms open to be held.

"Get away from me, you ugly boy!" He froze. Tears pricked his eyes. A deep pain grew in the pit of his stomach.

"I've found a real boy, now. This is Randoru. Look at him. His face isn't all wrinkled like yours. His back is straight. He can talk properly. Say hullo, Randoru."

"Hullo, ugly boy!" Randoru and Olôra looked at each other and laughed. She hugged him.

"So I won't be wasting time on you any more." With a scornful glance she and her proper boy left.

He stood staring after her, arms hanging at his sides. Then he sank to the straw, clasped his knees, and squeezed his eyes shut. He began breathing in long, tortured gasps. With each breath a desolate keening filled the empty corridor.

* * *

"Lishet, bring chass!" Nist bellowed. There was a muffled response from the back of the cottage. "Sit, sit, sit!" she barked at the rest of them, pointing to a motley collection of chairs, stools, and a long settee in the spacious living room.

They sat. Nist enthroned herself in an outsize armchair in a corner of the room, and surveyed them. Carmelet and two others stretched Gil out on the settee, but Lannie's attention was riveted on the enormous woman who effortlessly dominated the gathering.

"Foreigners!" she declared in her deep voice. "So — why do you need to be rescued?" She was looking at Shiván. It was this shiláy thing again: she'd detected he was the leader.

Shivvie cleared his throat. "Frengor, the leader of the travelling priests, told us to look for you. We, er, had a little trouble with the authorities in Stillárre, and we need somewhere safe to stay until they get over it."

Nist's eyes narrowed. "Hmmm," she rumbled. "A 'little trouble'? I hear the whole of Stillárre was thrown into chaos and Shambor has been combing a wide area for the perpetrators. They wouldn't happen to be you, would they?"

Shiván quailed under her penetrating gaze. "Well, ah— yes."

"I see. It's a miracle you escaped. What under the sky gave you the idea that your little rag-tag band could take on Mindbender Dhelgor and the Bishop's Guard?"

Lannie frowned. She saw Shivvie's eyes harden. "Frengor and the travelling priests believe we are the Restorers of the Way. The 'strangers and loners' foretold in your Book."

A slow smile touched the edges of Nist's mouth. It widened, and a rumbling chuckle began deep down inside. It rose up, building as it went, till the whole cottage shook to her laughter.

"*You!*" she exclaimed, wiping her eyes. "Ha-ha-ha-haa. Restorers of the— ha-ha. A youngster, an old lady, a smart miss, and an invalid! You're going to rescue Dûrion? With a grand army of five? No wonder you want to hide in the mountains! Ha-ha-haa."

Lannie's ears were ringing from the sheer volume of the laughter, but she fixed Nist with an unfriendly stare. A smart miss, eh?

"Have you heard what actually happened in Stillárre?" she asked sharply, cutting across the continuing rumbles of mirth.

Nist's chuckles subsided. "A Mindbender got what was coming to him."

"We did that. Shiván here killed him."

The large lady's eyebrows rose and she surveyed them for a moment, her gaze moving from Lannie to Shiván and back. "Hmmm," she said at last. "Your shiláy indicates that you're telling the truth. Well, well. Then you hardly need my help."

"Well, *he* obviously does," Lannie said, pointing to Gil.

"You're the Restorers, and you can't take care of one casualty?"

Lannie's impatience boiled over. "We're being hunted by the Bishop's forces, and we have a sick man to look after, who can't even walk! We killed the Mindbender of Stillárre to rescue our friend, and yes, it was a miracle we slipped through all Shambor's patrols and got to Dhembis — because we'd heard you help people in need. Or is that no longer the case?"

"I help people in need. Not the Restorers, who can look after themselves."

"We happen to be both."

"Ha-ha-ha. Have it your way. All I see is another bunch of people on the run." She turned back to Shiván. "Now. Explain to me. Why should I help you poor, helpless Restorers?"

While Shiván repeated their story in detail, a tall, gangly man with a bright red face, straw-coloured hair and a beaming smile shambled in. He was carrying a tray with six cups of chass. He hesitated on the threshold and gazed around. The smile became tinged with puzzlement. Nist saw him and uttered an explosive "*Chahh!*" of annoyance.

"Lishet, you might as well carry your head on the tray for all the good it does you. Can't you *count* the guests before making the chass?"

The man nodded solemnly. "Yes, yes, you're right Nist. That was silly of me." He did his counting, head bobbing and lips moving silently, while Nist tapped her foot.

When he'd gone Nist declared crisply, "My brother is a well-meaning idiot. Continue, Shiván."

Shiván told the rest of the story, and everyone eventually received a mug of chass.

Nist said she'd have to think about their request. Arrangements had already been made for their accommodation overnight, and they were ushered out to various cottages. Tomorrow was Anderil — a welcome day of rest. By evening they would know their fate.

* * *

Danîsha hung on grimly to the pommel of the small camel-horse's saddle, nestled between the two humps. They'd warned her downhill was worse than up. Without the poise of an experienced rider you couldn't sit upright, or the swaying motion would topple you. The only alternative was this undignified posture leaning forward, your backside heaving in harmony with the animal.

They'd been riding for almost four hours now, with two short breaks. At least they were heading into the mountains. Ahead of her on the steep forested slope the handcart was jolting along, strapped to two horses. Lannie was immediately behind it, watching over Gil. At first she'd wanted to keep stopping to adjust his position, but after a brusque word from Nist the man assigned to the cart simply ignored her.

It was a large party. Some would be going all the way, to help them over the difficult bits. 'Nursemaid duty', Nist called it. They would also help carrying Gil—because about halfway up the going apparently got too difficult for horses and carts. Carmelet, as he bade them farewell yesterday, had explained that there was no well-travelled route to wherever Nist was going. She never followed the same path twice, to avoid making a trail for the Bishop's forces to follow. Sure enough, not far outside the village the track had petered out, and since then they'd been weaving to and fro from hill to valley to forest; but always steadily climbing higher.

Suddenly they emerged from the trees on to a small field over-looking a deep ravine, and Danîsha gasped. All other thoughts were wiped from her mind. To their right a mountain reared up to unimaginable snow-covered heights; and to their left across the ravine stood another mountain. Ahead of them, peak piled upon peak in an incredible grandeur of forests, plunging gorges, massive rocks, sheer cliffs, and blinding sheets of pure snow—all appearing through veils of tenuous mist that kept shifting to reveal tantalising glimpses of further glories beyond. She stood wide-eyed, drinking in the sheer beauty of the scene.

There, sitting on the sparse upland grass, they ate their cold midmeal. Danîsha shivered, pulling the fur coat she'd been given tighter around her.

When they'd eaten, half the escorts left with the horses and the handcart; and the rest of the party set off on foot. Two of Nist's people carried Gil on a stretcher along the narrowing lip of the ravine. Before long they had to turn up the side of the mountain, climbing widely-spaced rocky ledges like a giant staircase. Danîsha was soon puffing from the exertion.

Gil's 'bearers' had strapped the heavy fabric of the stretcher around him like a body bag, only his face protruding. Removing the poles, the stocky, bull-like man at the front put his arms through the top two loops of rope, leaving his hands free to assist in climbing. With help from above and below he hauled Gil up the stair-like ledges. Nist's brother Lishet followed behind with the bellaril fastened to his back. His slow thought processes didn't affect his agility: he leapt up the rocky ledges as nimbly as the rest.

They continued, making their way laterally along a steep slope that plunged toward the gorge. Far below was a glimpse of white water and the distant roar of a mountain river. Lishet was walking just below Danîsha—in case she lost her footing, she was sure. Finally they reached a more level stretch through a pine forest, and she could breathe again.

Up ahead she could hear Shiván talking to Nist. She hurried to catch up with them.

"…you'll be staying with the other refugees," Nist was saying in her booming voice. "*If* the Galeronden accept you."

"The Galer— Who are they?"

"Frengor did keep you in the dark, didn't he?" Nist shot them both an amused glance. "The Galeronden are an autonomous Dûrian clan living in these mountains."

"Autonomous?"

Nist nodded. "Ever since Shambor's Edict of Religious Tolerance, six years ago. There was unrest all over Dûrion. Destor—that's the High Walker of the Galeronden—"

"Their leader?" Shivvie asked.

Nist gave him an amused sideways glance. "Yes. You'll answer to Destilor Banneralt when you get there. If he says no, some or all of you will be tramping down again with me the day after tomorrow. Anyway, after Shambor's Edict, Destor revoked Galeronden allegiance to the Bishop of Dûrion, destroyed all the paths, and cut off contact with the lowlands. A year later the Rebellion broke out. Soon there were so many displaced people, I pleaded with him to take in refugees. He agreed—not easily—to give temporary sanctuary to people like yourselves escaping the Usurper's forces. That means you can stay until your places are needed by others."

"Would we be able to remain over the winter?" Danîsha asked, chilled at the thought of being driven out into the snow.

"Probably. The Galeronden are not heartless. However, *that* young lady—" She jerked her head towards Jomel, who was flashing a pert smile at Cârin up ahead "—that young lady will have to mind her manners. Destor will not be happy about taking in a cultist. Her behaviour is not what the Galeronden will expect."

Danîsha's heart sank. The Galeronden must have an even stricter code of behaviour than the Manor community. They would have regarded what Jomel was doing — smiling, and fluttering her eyelashes — as only mild flirting, lacking any physical contact. She sighed. A battle clearly lay ahead there.

A different battle lay ahead right here and now. Danîsha groaned as they came out of the trees and she saw the leaders swarming up an almost vertical rocky slope.

* * *

Gil's right leg was trapped at an awkward angle under his left inside the stretcher bag, and his mind struggled to shift it. But as always, no matter how much he strained and heaved, nothing happened. At last he gave up and suffered till it went numb. The whole problem was, these louts carrying him were paying no attention to Lannie. The previous journeys had only been endurable thanks to her constant care. A wave of gratitude welled up in him — and was immediately tinged with guilt. She'd been so good to him; but she had no idea how unfaithful he'd been to her.

Jomel. It had been an unpleasant shock when *she'd* been added to the party — though the unselfish part of him was glad they'd rescued her from the terrible death of human sacifice. A death that *he* would have suffered if her original plan had succeeded. As far as he could tell, she'd said nothing about that — unless maybe to her cousin Perrely. But Jomel was part of the group now; which meant that sooner or later the truth would come out. He only hoped he'd be able to speak in his own defence when it did. He couldn't bear the thought of Lannie turning against him — especially not while he was still mute and helpless.

But all that paled into insignificance beside the overriding fact that he was finally free of the Mindbenders! First Dhelgor, then the overpowering presence of Shambor himself. It had been a shock, to say the least, when he'd found himself transferred to the Mindruler of Dûrion during those last days in Stillárre! That mocking voice in his head. Evil personified.

Yet he'd miss the sense of power he'd enjoyed in the tightly-knit structure of the Bishop's Guard. What they did was abominable, but they had an efficiency and a driving sense of purpose that was lacking in his new freedom. What was he now? A Restorer of the

Way? That's what the others believed. He uttered a mental snort. He could just see himself, a knight in shining armour crusading against the infidel to defend a narrow-minded belief system!

Mindbending, though, was unspeakably evil. The rape of a person's inner integrity. *That* he could crusade against. The enemy wasn't the problem. It was the new "us" that he couldn't identify with. He was in limbo—neither on one side, nor the other. But it was only a matter of time before he broke the mindlock. Then he'd be truly free. Then he could decide whether to stick with these 'Restorers', or risk striking out on his own again, with all the attendant dangers—which he now knew only too well. If he could just persuade Lannie to join him...

Ouch. The stretcher was suddenly put down. Lannie came and stood by him while the poles were removed. "Bit of a climb ahead, Gil," she murmured. His heart sank. Those were the worst parts, being yanked upward in a near-vertical position while his eyes saw with ghastly clarity just how far he could fall.

With a sudden jolt they began to climb. Another man followed below, easing the stretcher bag over outcroppings. He gritted his teeth as his limbs started protesting. Then, about thirty feet up, there was a ripping sound beside his right ear. He slipped sideways. The front man cried out and tried to turn. He slipped further, saw a broken rope loop swaying beside his shoulder, and realised he was only being held by one corner of the stretcher bag. Confused shouting broke out, the man below trying to grab his feet, while the man above teetered dangerously on the narrow ledge. Then the stretcher broke free and with a silent yell of terror his fears were realised.

* * *

Lannie screamed. Gil was tumbling helplessly down the cliff. She leapt forward with some crazy idea of catching him, but at the last moment his foot struck a rock and the stretcher pivoted outward away from the cliff. It hit a bush, turning over, and Gil landed on his back. He lay limp in the stretcher bag, his chalk-white face staring up at the sky. Lannie was there in an instant, bending over him and feeling gently for broken bones. Praise God! He seemed to be in one piece.

Nist's brother Lishet came charging up. He had a flask in his hand, and before she could stop him he was pouring the contents into Gil's open mouth. "No!" she cried, trying to push him away.

"It's all right. This is good medicine. It will make him better," the simple fellow told her, nodding earnestly. He paused long enough to allow the coughing victim to swallow.

"Lishet!" Nist bellowed. Then she saw what he was doing. "Oh, split the man. It's his cordial again."

"You know it helps, Nist."

She gave Lannie a resigned look. "Let him do it. It won't hurt. It's a cordial he gets from the Care House in Dhembis. It keeps him calm. He thinks it can cure anything."

"But it can, Nist! Remember when Camilay burnt herself? And Fennior—"

"All right, all right! I'm sure it'll help Gelmion. But that's enough now."

Lishet reluctantly re-corked the flask and carefully wiped Gil's face with a corner of his tunic. Lannie heaved an exasperated sigh. She was beginning to see why Nist was short with her brother.

Others had crowded round now, and they opened Gil's stretcher bag. A careful examination revealed no injuries. The front man, who was nursing his right arm, nodded at Lannie. "That was a Light-given escape. He'll have a few bruises, but he's done better than I have."

"That was a close one, Lannie!" Shiván looked serious. "They say it was a frayed rope. Nist actually apologised. Good thing the fall was broken. If it had happened just a few yards further over…"

He left the sentence unfinished. Lannie glanced at the yawning ravine to their left and shuddered.

* * *

They finally reached the settlement of Galeron with great relief late that afternoon. It lay in a wide saddle of land between the mountains, and as they approached they passed clearings in which crops had obviously been grown, though most had now been harvested and only bare soil remained. All around the clearings stood a tall pine forest, and beyond the tilled area they began to see rustic wooden dwellings dotted among the trees.

At last they reached a central clearing where fires were burning with cooking pots over them, and the tantalising aroma of food welcomed them. They sank down gratefully on the logs provided while Nist and her party went to report in.

Map 3:
The Galeronden Area

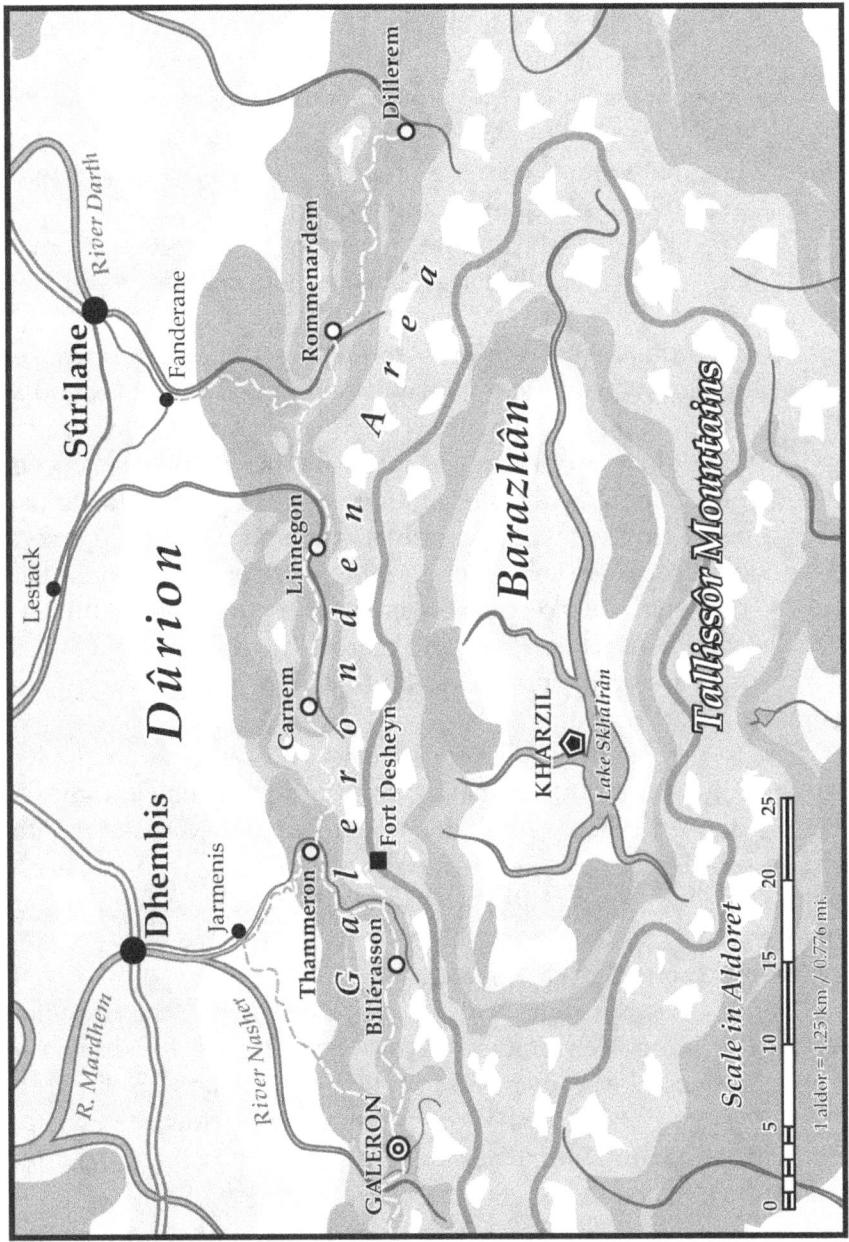

Chapter 5: *Refugee Restorers*

"THE RESTORERS are a bag full of wind!" a great ox of a man shouted from the back of the wayside chapel. There was a chorus of groans, cheers, and impatient shushings from the rest of the crowd.

"Then you'll get blown away, my friend!" Frengor shot back, his beard bristling and eyes sharp in the deeply-lined face. "Because believe me, that wind is coming. When it does, will you blow with it, or against it? It'll sweep this country clean!"

"Yah, just like the Rebellion was meant to!" a bitter-faced woman called out. "And where did *that* get us? Whole families wiped out, an' all fer nothing!"

An old woman sitting nearby rounded on her. "Oh, *hush* yer snivelling, Jinny." She stood up, hands on hips, and glared round at the country folk filling the plain wooden benches in the little building. "When did the priests ever speak for the Rebellion? *I* never heard Frengor, or Ongaret here, or Lannet—" she pointed to various of the purple-robed travelling priests scattered among the crowd "—*I* never heard 'em telling us to join Armanet and Dôrion. Did *you?*" There was a silence, punctuated by uncomfortable shufflings.

"*Did* you?" she asked Frengor, eyebrows high.

Every crease on the priest's walnut-like face was grinning. "No, Feréldy, never!"

"There, you see? *We* believed Armanet and Dôrion were the Restorers, and *we* sent our husbands, sons and daughters to fight wi' them. I don't say they weren't good men, but they were not the Restorers—and the priests never said they were! Now Frengor here is telling us about the real Restorers, and I want to hear him. Wi'out noise from *you*, Gallor, or *you*, Jinny!"

With a resounding sniff she sat down.

"Feréldy has the right of it!" Frengor declared. "The Rebellion was *not* the One's Restoration. But my dear friends, I want you to know that your loved ones did not die in vain. The Rebellion prepared the way for the true Restorers, who are even now among us!"

"Did they kill the Mindbender of Stillárre?" a young man cried out, his eyes gleaming.

Frengor stood silent. A deep hush settled over the crowd. "If they did," he said slowly, "it was only a small beginning. Because there is one thing they still lack." In his mind's eye he saw a gold rod topped with a silver circle, gleaming in the sunlight. Now, alas, long lost.

"What's that?" the young man asked.

"The Ambon of Sûrilane."

There were assorted exclamations of amazement and disbelief. "The Ambon's been lost for hundreds of years!" "How could they find it? So many have failed!" — and "Why would they need *that?*"

"Because that great emblem of our faith will prove their claim. This is the main reason we of the Travelling Order did not support Armanet and Dôrion: they did not raise the Ambon. The scripture says clearly, *They will lift high the Rod of Truth to summon the faithful; they will raise it above the altar of darkness, and release my captive people.* My friends, we believe the Rod of Truth is the Ambon of Sûrilane. As you know, it was first used by the Founders of Dûrion as their battle standard. Wherever they raised it followers of the Prince flocked to them — and the truth prevailed. Today, in Dûrion, untruth prevails! The black cloud of Gadesh is blotting out the Light of life. The Rod of Truth must be raised again!"

"But how will we know it's the real Ambon?" Jinny asked sceptically. "Anyone could smarten up an ordinary ambon from the front of a Hearth building, and claim it was the Ambon of Sûrilane. Who's to know otherwise?"

Frengor pointed a finger at her. *"Because it will summon you.* I don't know how — I only know that it will. And *this* is how you will recognise the true Restorers — when you find yourself summoned by the Ambon of Sûrilane. Then you must give any service you can, endure any hardship, suffer any pain, fight any fight, to restore the Way of the One Creator God!"

"Not a lot *I* can do," Feréldy muttered.

"For the first time you're wrong, older sister!" Frengor cried. "What can Feréldy do?" He opened his arms, appealing to the crowd.

"Pray!" someone called out.

"Yes! Can you pray, Feréldy?"

Her old face broke into a crooked smile and she nodded.

"Then pray! And what can *you* do?" He pointed at the young man.

"Fight!"

"Then fight! And what can *you* do?" His finger picked out a young mother.

Flustered, she stammered, "I— I suppose I could cook, or—"

"Then cook! We will not all be called to fight, but to do whatever we can. Until then—pray! All of you. Pray for the true Restorers. They are here—strangers and loners with the instruments of cleansing, exactly as foretold in the Book. The One is preparing them. They *will* find the Ambon. *Will they find us ready?"*

The majority were with him now. "*Yes!"* came the roared response. Gallor, Jinny and a few others maintained a sceptical silence. Well, there would always be those for whom seeing was believing. But their time would come. Of that Frengor had no doubt.

* * *

"A bit like our first meal with the Dûrians—remember?" Shiván grinned at Danîsha. They were perched on one of the many logs surrounding the cooking fires, among a crowd of Galeronden and Dûrian 'refugees'. It was bitterly cold, but the flames and the heavy fur coats they'd been given kept them warm. Trees arched over the dining circle on all sides, with a central gap open to the sky. Stars winked on and off through the swirling columns of smoke, and they caught occasional glimpses of the two moons and the 'Ring of Orrénne', that amazing circle of stars in the centre of the sky. All around the hollow, thatched wooden buildings could be seen among the trees—the 'lodges', as they called them.

Shiván savoured his mouthful of stew. Bear, someone had told him it was. Lip-smacking good stuff. Lannie, on the next log, had a face like a lemon, though. The news that they would be staying with meat-eaters had left the lady unamused. The Galeronden, bless their cotton socks, had some vegetable mush simmering for newcomers. Evidently it was not up to lowland standards.

'Neesh surfaced from the stew to answer his question. "Good heavens," she said, "this is not at *all* like that first day. Then we were still... shell-shocked. We didn't know where we were, and we couldn't understand a word of the language. We didn't even know if they were friends or enemies! Here at least we know what's going on... more or less."

"Hah!" Shiván laughed. "I'm glad you added that. I can hardly follow these bearded mountain men, unless they talk sl-o-o-o-w-ly and clearly, like that fellow who met us—what was his name? Garmen."

"What are you saying?" Perrely asked. They'd been speaking in English. He translated.

"Yes, the Galeronden are hard to understand," she said. "But then, they don't talk much, do they?"

Shiván looked around. She was right. About a dozen of those present were refugees, but half the chatter was coming from them—with the other half from Shîrin, Cârin and Jomel. The tall, blond Galeronden with their braided hair and high cheekbones were quietly concentrating on their food.

Sensible folk. He dipped his spoon into the delicious, spicy stew. Beside him Perrely stirred her vegetable gruel and sighed.

A shadow fell across Shiván's bowl. A craggy-faced Galeronden was standing in front of him. "When tha hast eaten, Destor will see thee." At least, that's what it would have sounded like in English, he thought, once he'd disentangled the antiquated words.

"Thank you, Garmen." The man nodded, unsmiling, and left.

"Now to face the interrogation," he muttered, scooping up the last of the stew. "I hope I can understand the questions!"

He found Garmen again, and the Galeronden led him to a small lodge where a bright blaze crackled in the central stone fireplace. An old man sat on one side of it, and Garmen ushered Shiván to a well-shaped and surprisingly comfortable wooden chair facing him. Garmen muttered a few words and left.

Shiván found himself looking into a pair of keen grey eyes in a deeply wrinkled face, with thick, white hair pulled back into a braid, and a luxuriant beard and moustache. So this was Destor. He was swathed in a robe of the browny-green homespun many of the Galeronden wore. A small silver ambon hung on a chain around his neck, and there was a silver bracelet on each arm.

Destor smiled, his whole face lighting up. "Welcome to Galeron, young man." His voice was surprisingly deep and strong. And praise God, he spoke normal Dûrian!

"Now, tell me why you wish to stay with us. Nist has told me a few things. I would like to hear the rest from yourself."

Shiván gave him the simple version. They'd run foul of Shambor's forces in Stillárre, and since then had been fugitives. One of their number had fallen ill, and they urgently needed a safe place where he could recover.

Destor nodded. "Your friend who is ill, he is a foreigner, is he not? Like yourself and two others in your group. But unlike you he has not entered the Light." He paused, his sharp grey eyes boring into Shiván's. "Why are you here in Dûrion? And what have you done to anger Shambor the Usurper?"

Rats. No glossing over. "We are not here by our own choice. At first the four of us just wanted to find our way home. Then various things happened — Alanya was mindbent by Shambor — " Destor's bushy eyebrows shot up " — and local friends began to believe the four of us were the Restorers of the Way promised in your Book." He held the old man's gaze.

"Nist mentioned this. But you say Alanya was enslaved by the accursed Mindruler himself — and she escaped?"

"Yes."

"How did she achieve that remarkable feat?"

"By engaging in spiritual warfare. She denied his power to darken the mind of one who has been born again into the Kingdom of Light."

The old man stared at him for a long moment. Eventually he said softly, "You answer well, young man. And there is the light of truth in you." He continued more briskly, "What about the young female cultist? How did she come to join your party?"

"Jomel is a cousin of Perrely, the other young woman in our group. As we were escaping from Stillárre we found Jomel on the point of being executed by the mob. So we rescued her."

"I see." Destor sighed. After a pause he continued, "We are a people faithful to the Way of the One. Since we turned to him we have never tolerated cultists in our midst. It is a lot you ask."

Shiván was silent.

Destor shifted in his seat. "Tell me, then. On what do you base your claim to be the promised Restorers of the Way?"

"Well, as I said, we had no idea at first that we were fulfilling prophecy. So in a way, we haven't made this claim. Others — Dûrians — have made it for us. Mainly because they see us as the prophesied 'strangers and loners'; and because we have the *nestilar* spoken of in the Book."

"You have the instruments?"

"Well, we found four objects in the first place we stayed. I found a copy of the Book in our own language; Alanya found a bess; Danîsha a bellaril; and Gelmion a two-handled glass. People said those corresponded to the prophecy of the instruments: the Sword of Light, the Shell of Hearing, the, er, Strings of Truth; and the Glass of Seeing. They've already shown their power — at least, the bess and the bellaril have."

"And do you have the Ambon of Sûrilane?"

"Umm, no, but our first priority will be to search for that."

Destor smiled sadly and shook his head. "So you do not have it. Yet that is the principal mark of the true Restorers: *They will lift high the Rod of Truth to summon the faithful; they will raise it above the altar of darkness, and release my captive people.* No, Shiván. Until you can show me the lost Ambon of Sûrilane, I will not accept any claim that you are the Restorers."

He leaned forward, his grey eyes glinting under the bushy white eyebrows. "Dûrians have swallowed too many plausible lies in recent years, Shiván. All the things you mention are impressive — but so also seemed Armanet and Dôrion's claims when they first raised their standard. And now we have hundreds of refugees to feed and house. No. Until *every* prophecy is fulfilled — and especially that of the Ambon — we cannot accept any further claims."

"Then I suppose we'd better leave," Shiván said bleakly.

"Not at all! You have satisfied me that you are sincere — though sincerely wrong. You are welcome to stay among our refugees over the winter, provided they will accept the cultist girl. But I will recommend it, and I'm sure either Billérasson or Carnem will take you in. They are our two nearest settlements given over to the refugees. Here in Galeron, you understand, we can only provide temporary accommodation. But as it happens a family has just moved out, so you may use their lodge for the next few days. After that you will have to move on. But we will find a place for you. You are in need. We will not turn you away."

* * *

Lannie sat cross-legged on a cushion beside the rough-hewn settee on which Gil lay. The others were out and about, getting to know people and helping to prepare the evening meal. She'd slipped back to keep Gil company.

She glanced round the interior of the wooden lodge that had been assigned to them. It was raised off the ground on thick pillars made of sawn-off tree trunks. A wooden stairway outside led up to the only door. Inside was a large room with a masonry column in the centre. This contained the two-sided fireplace, and continued as a chimney up through the thatched roof. Bedrooms led off on either side. It was plain, but a lot more comfortable than she'd expected. And it was a safe place for Gil to recover.

Lannie's thoughts went back to their journey up here, and nightmare memories flashed across her mind of Gil tumbling down the cliff. Shîrin and Cârin, who'd washed him last night, reported that he had quite a few bruises to show for it. Poor simple Lishet was convinced his magic cordial had healed Gil. He'd given him another dose this morning, and declared he would stay on for a few days to make sure Gelmion was really getting better. Nist had agreed with an exasperated sigh. Oh, well. It did no harm.

"Don't give up, Gil," she said softly for the umpteenth time, holding his hand and staring at his still profile. "Keep reminding yourself that the Mindbender is dead! He no longer has any power over you!" It was hard to keep on talking to someone who never responded. But she remembered only too well the terrible loneliness she herself had suffered while mindlocked.

It was getting dark. She got up, stretched, and lit the wall lamps with a sliver of kindling from beside the fire. Then she closed the window shutters. Immediately the living room became a magical place, lit by the steady light of the night-oil lamps and the warm, flickering glow of the fire. Gil, lying still and straight on the settee, looked like a dead knight being prepared for burial in some secret mediaeval sanctuary. She shivered to banish the thought as she sat down next to him.

"Shiván says we'll be staying in one of the other Galeronden settlements, Gil. We'll be going there — "

Gil's arm slipped off the settee, landing on her lap. She absently put it back, staring into the fire.

"We'll be going there in a few days. It'll be wonderful to get properly settled —"

The arm flopped down again. She lifted it, glanced at Gil, and froze. His head had moved! Hadn't it been straight? Now it was inclined towards her. He was looking at her! No, she was imagining it.

"Gil?" she whispered.

He blinked.

"Did you do that deliberately? Did you blink? Do it again!"

She sat staring into his eyes. Disappointment welled up as nothing happened. Then, in slow motion, he blinked again.

"*Gil!* Oh, Gil, you're doing it! You're breaking free…!" Tears trickled down her cheeks. She clasped the hand that had been trying to reach out to her. He slowly blinked again. She stroked his hair, her heart bursting.

"Gil, this is fantastic! I've prayed so hard for you to come out of the mindlock quickly. And it's only been… what? Five days? Frengor said it could take a month! Have you been doing what I said — denying the Mindbender's power over you?"

Slowly he blinked again.

"I'll take that as a Yes!" She bent and kissed his forehead. "Keep on doing it! Don't stop. Then you'll soon be back to normal. Oh, this is so great! I have to tell the others. Just wait — I mean — I'll be back soon!"

Squeezing his hand, she dashed out of the lodge. The cold air knifed into her. But she hardly noticed it. She charged down the forest path leading to the central cooking hearth. She passed other lodges scattered among the tall, pine-like trees. Some were grouped around smaller hearths where families were preparing the daymeal. They stared, but she ran on through the gathering dusk.

She found Perrely and Jomel first, peeling a bucketful of tubers. "Gelmion's started moving again!" she gasped.

"Alanya, that's wonderful!" Perrely exclaimed, her face lighting up. "We must go and see him." She glanced at Jomel, whose face was down, continuing with her work.

A few minutes later the whole group was crowding into the lodge, congratulating Gil. Lishet was there too, telling everyone that he'd known his cordial would make Gelmion well again.

People kept asking Gil to blink, but she put a stop to that. She knew what an effort it took to make sluggish muscles work while coming out of mindlock. With a final volley of encouragements they all straggled out to return to the daymeal preparations.

All except Jomel, she suddenly realised as she sat down again beside Gil. Jomel hadn't come. She'd hardly reacted at all when told the news. Which reminded her that even in the few days after they'd escaped from Stillárre—before Gil had been struck down with the mindlock—the cultist girl had seemed to avoid him.

That was strange. Could Gil and she have met while he was a Guardsman in Stillárre? The thought chilled her.

She'd have to ask Gil about it when he could talk again.

Chapter 6: *Grûzhack fortress*

IN STILLÁRRE, TWO GREY-CLOAKED GUARDSMEN sat holding their silver, shell-shaped helmets under one arm in the stately entrance hall of the Domicile, headquarters of the Travelling Order throughout the Dûrai lands. One tapped a foot on the marble floor. The other stared grimly at the scattered black leather recliners and glittering light trees. They appeared not to appreciate the elegant décor.

Brother Ongaret smiled inwardly as he returned to them after a fairly extended absence. "The Visionary will see you now. Please come this way."

Shooting him filthy looks, the Guardsmen stood and straightened their tunics. It was a wonder they hadn't protested more vocally. The new Bishop's Guard had used a heavy hand to restore order in the troubled city.

Ongaret led the Guardsmen up a curving staircase to the upper floor, where he plucked the door chime at the office of the head of the Travelling Order. After a moment there was an answering chime from within. He opened the door; but before he could usher their guests in, he was brushed aside. "Lieutenant Harbion and Trooper Condet," he announced to their backs. Ongaret smiled to himself as he closed the door and returned to his duties. Visionary Frengor was more than capable of dealing with impatient Guardsmen—not to mention the Mindbender who would be watching through their eyes.

Inside, they marched over to the short figure in a purple robe who was sitting at a *shey*-nut writing table. The Lieutenant announced, "I have a message for you from His Radiance, the Bishop of Dûrion."

The weathered, deeply-lined face looked up and a pair of calm brown eyes surveyed them. "Do you, indeed," he murmured. "That is a pleasant surprise, and most welcome. Take a seat." He gestured to a couple of comfortable brown leather recliners.

His visitors remained standing. "The Bishop requires you—"

"Excuse me." Frengor leant back in his chair to get a better view of the tall Lieutenant. "You did say this message was from His Radiance, Bishop Harlon of Dûrion?"

A sneer touched the Guardsman's aquiline features. "No, it is from the ruler of Dûrion, Bishop Shambor."

"Oh, from His Serenity the Bishop Suffragan. I see."

The Lieutenant took a deep breath before continuing with a smouldering eye. "His Radiance requires you to appear before him in Darthane to explain why your priests have been disturbing the people."

Frengor's eyebrows shot up. "Disturbing the people! Dear me. That's a serious matter. How have we been disturbing the people?"

"By spreading false rumours about these so-called Restorers of the Way."

The Visionary frowned. "My dear man, they are 'so-called' because that is what they are. One should call people by their proper names, don't you think?"

"Your priests have not done so. They have been teaching that a group of foreigners styling themselves 'Restorers' are the true Restorers prophesied in the Book, though scholars deny any basis for such an interpretation. His Radiance demands to know why you are propagating this false doctrine, which is dividing the people and encouraging his enemies. He requires your presence in Darthane at once, to give an assurance that all such teaching shall cease forthwith."

" 'Shall cease forthwith'," Frengor murmured. "Well, well. This is clearly a very important matter that needs to be discussed at the highest level." Every wrinkle on his face lit up in a broad smile. "Please ask Suffragan Shambor to inform His Radiance Bishop Harlon that unfortunately I cannot get away at the moment, but I would be only too happy to discuss this with Bishop Harlon the next time he's in Stillárre."

The Lieutenant stared at Frengor, his face slowly reddening as the triple insult sank in. He turned, and the two Guards left without a word.

*   *   *

Gil and Lannie walked slowly together along a forest path just outside the settlement of Galeron. Gil sniffed the pine-like scent of the trees, Lannie's hand entwined in his own. It was so good to be moving about in his own strength again!

"I can't believe how quickly you've recovered!" Lannie said. "It's only been a few days, and here you are, walking and talking almost normally already."

"Glad you said— 'almost'," Gil replied haltingly. "Not fluent— yet."

"No, but you're getting there! I took just as long, but I was mindbent for a much shorter time."

"Followed— your example. Told my body— I was— in charge again." Gil felt his eyes blink a couple of times.

Lannie gave him a radiant smile, and his heart lurched. She was looking utterly desirable today, with her green shift and golden yellow scarf showing under the partly-open outdoor coat. *One day soon...*

"It's hard, isn't it?" Lannie was saying. "I had to keep telling the Mindbender—who turned out to be Shambor—that he was a liar, and at first I didn't really believe it; but the more I said it, the more God convinced me it was true. Was it like that for you?"

"Something like— that. It was hard. But thank you— again— for all your— help." Getting better slowly had been a challenge, he thought. But not speaking or moving at all before then was the hardest. How would he have managed without Lishet and his... cordial?

Lannie smiled again, and they walked on at a gentle pace. Like his speech, Gil's walking was jerky; but with these leisurely strolls he made sure it improved every day. Above the trees the sun was shining, and it broke through here and there with little dappled patches lighting up the pine needles.

After a while Lannie turned to him. "Did you know Jomel in Stillárre?"

For a moment Gil went cold and struggled to find an answer. This was the question he'd tried to prepare for. *Can't deny it, in case Jomel one day tells her side of the story...*

"Not well. I met her— at the Temple of Gadesh. Was sent there— as part of— my duties."

"Oh, I see. Did you know she was going to be killed as a human sacrifice?"

Gil blinked. "No, didn't."

"I've noticed that Jomel avoids you. And she didn't come with everyone else when you started breaking out of the mindlock. Was there some trouble between you two?"

Gil sent up a silent plea. Then the words came. "Well, she— er— threw herself— at me. You know— the dashing Bishop's Guard… Didn't like it when I— turned her down."

It went well. Lannie's sympathy was sweet in his ears.

* * *

"Darinor," Shiván said, turning to the tall, dark-haired refugee leader walking beside him. "What can you tell us about the terrible ogres that are supposed to live in these mountains? The Gû-… What were they, Perrely? The third race you told me about."

"The Grûzhack."

"Yes, them. What are they like, Darinor?"

They were following a well-trodden path eastward from Galeron to Billérasson, the next settlement, now entirely populated by refugees. It had been agreed they would spend the winter there. Events had moved quickly over the past week: Gil had rapidly regained speech and movement; and as soon as he was able to walk normally Destor had sent for Darinor to escort them to their new homes.

The saddle of land between two mountains where Galeron lay was fairly wide, and at this point they were still able to walk abreast through the forest. Behind them 'Neesh was talking to Fira; then came Lannie and Gil, still catching up on missed time; then Jomel and the twins, chattering and laughing together as always. Another pair of Billérasson refugees, Hillet and Delmior, followed as rearguard.

"Well, for a start," Darinor said, "the Grûzhack live higher in the mountains."

"They don't come visiting lower mortals like us?"

"You'd better hope not."

"Hmmm. Right. But what do they live on up there? Ice and snow?"

Darinor grunted in amusement. "No, they live in Barazhân."

"And what might that be?"

The others behind them had moved in closer to listen.

"Their Hidden Magistry. It's a deep valley among the high peaks. The Galeronden say it's a broad land, with farms and towns and all. But that's hearsay: no outsiders have ever seen it."

"They don't allow people in for a holiday, or anything?"

"Hah! No. They keep their own people in and other people out. They have forts in the mountains all round. You can see one from Billérasson."

There was an exclamation from behind, and Shiván turned to see Shîr and Câr staring wide-eyed at the refugee leader. "There's a Grûzhack fortress near you?" Shîrin gasped.

"Yes. Fort Desheyn. It's on a mountainside nearby."

"*That* I'd love to see! From a distance," he quickly added as a rebuke flashed in Fira's eyes. "We've heard the Grûzhack are great warriors. Some say they use dark magic..."

"And others say they have powerful weapons," Cârin finished.

"They can afford them, with their evil wealth," Fira muttered sourly.

"Evil wealth?" Shiván asked, puzzled.

"They control the teméyn trade," Perrely said softly.

"What! How can they do that, stuck away in the mountains?"

"Their hidden valley is the only place it grows."

"Oh! So they actually *produce* the stuff?"

"They do," Darinor nodded. "The foul weed grows in Barazhân, and the Grûzhack turn it into a powder and sell it to all the lands. That's how they've built their wealth."

"But then... Why aren't there roads everywhere up into this Grûzhack valley? How can the Galeronden remain hidden from Shambor, when this country lies between Dûrion and the place he gets his teméyn from?"

It was Fira who answered. "There are only three roads through the high peaks into Barazhân. One is from Marûvin in the southeast; the other from Thrinar in the south; and the third from the Thrinar Pass between Thrinar and Dûrion. That's how teméyn reaches our land."

"The Grûzhack guard all the roads strongly," Darinor added. "In the past many have tried to invade their land to gain control of teméyn. None have succeeded. If anyone approaches bearing arms they attack without hesitation."

"I've been told they're enormous creatures," Perrely said, "as much as forty hands tall. Is that true?"

Darinor chuckled. "Those are the tales they tell in the lowlands. I haven't seen one, but the Galeronden say they're broad in the shoulder and have faces like Gadesh, but are certainly not ogres. The tallest is no more than twenty-two hands."

Shiván worked it out. A hand was about four inches. That came to more than seven feet. *Whoa!* Broad, too. He wouldn't want to meet a Grûzhack down a dark alley.

Just then the path narrowed as it climbed off the saddle of Galeron and rounded the slope of a mountain. The group became strung out and Shiván found himself in the middle, following Shîrin, Cârin and Jomel. Perrely was beside him. He took her hand.

A peal of laughter rang out from Jomel, and she slapped Cârin roguishly on the wrist. Darinor glanced back at them with an expression of distaste.

Perrely sucked her breath in – the Dûrian equivalent of clicking the tongue. "Oh! I must talk to her again. She should not be doing that, she knows the Galeronden and the refugees have only accepted her on sufferance."

"Not only them," Shiván muttered. "Fira, too. The kind of looks she's been giving Jomel could shrivel a Mindbender."

"I know. She can never forget that Jomel was a temple prostitute. And Jomel doesn't help, the way she carries on with those twins!" Perrely glared at the back of her cousin's coyly tilted head.

"It's just as well the refugees don't know her full story yet. Why is she playing up like this? At first she seemed genuinely thankful to the Prince for rescuing her."

"She *is* genuinely thankful. She's learnt that the One Creator God is more powerful than Gadesh. She's seen his Light, and she's drawn to it. But she knows nothing yet about how to live in the Light."

"So, put her with a couple of handsome young fellas, and she falls back into old habits."

"Exactly."

"Tough that we've had to bring her into a conservative community like this, with these strict taboos against all the kind of stuff she's used to – like flirting, and – "

"Holding hands," a sharp voice added from behind.

"Oops. Didn't know you were listening, Fira."

"No one has said anything against holding hands!" Perrely snapped, clasping Shiván's more tightly and turning to glare at the woman behind.

"They don't have to say it. Haven't you seen the way people look at you?"

"Fira, there's nothing in the Book against an unmarried man and woman spending time together or holding hands. But there is quite a lot against passing judgment on others."

"It's the refugees' judgment you should be concerned about, not mine."

"We are, and I don't believe they disapprove as much as you think."

"Maybe you'll find out one day soon."

"Maybe we will."

With a final backward glare at Fira's stern, hawk-like face, Perrely marched on, breathing heavily. She was still clutching Shiván's hand tightly. Well. That was a new side of her. He hadn't realised she could be so… assertive.

He looked back. "But meanwhile we'll think about what you've said, Firey."

Perrely gave him an indignant glare and dropped his hand.

* * *

After many ups and downs — but nothing like the hazardous rock-climbs of their journey to Galeron — they began passing the first outlying lodges of Billérasson. Around some of them there were clearings with bare soil, the crops now harvested. Finally they came into a large open area at the centre of the settlement, and Shiván gasped as his eyes rose higher and higher to take in the snow-capped peaks that towered up on three sides. Billérasson sat on their lap, looking out to the north-west over a dim and hazy Dûrion far below the tumbled forests.

"What a view!" he muttered. Up here the sun was bright, the air sharp and cold. Perrely had told him (before the episode of the hand-holding), that this glorious, brief season of Goldshine would soon be over; then they'd have the dark misery of winter to endure. Better enjoy this while I can, he thought, with a pang of sadness. Soon after the exchange with Fira, Perrely had left him to detach Jomel from the twins. They hadn't spoken since.

One of the refugee ladies led the women off to find accommodation, and Darinor turned to Shiván. "The midmeal will be ready in about an hour and a half. You can get settled in the meantime, or — "

he swung an arm, taking in the large settlement " — take a look around. Make yourselves at home. From tomorrow you'll need to play your part in the last of the harvesting and hunting to stock up for winter."

"We'll be glad to."

Darinor nodded and walked off.

Shiván glanced around. Shîrin and Cârin were talking animatedly with Hillet, one of the rearguards on their walk over here.

"Shiván!" Shîr called as he approached. "Hillet here has been telling us about that Grûzhack fortress Darinor mentioned. He says he could take us to have a look — just over that hill." He pointed to the south-east. "What do you think?" His eyes and Cârin's were gleaming.

Suddenly the alternative of hanging around the settlement held little attraction for Shiván. "Sounds fun! Can we get there and back before the midmeal?"

"Easily," Hillet replied. He had a shock of wild red hair and a broad grin. "It'll take about an hour."

"Well, Darinor did tell us to take a look around. Maybe we should invite the women as well..." He glanced around.

Shîr shook his head emphatically. "Nah, they're too busy choosing lodges and looking at bedding and cooking arrangements, and for me — anything will do. But a Grûzhack fortress? That's something you don't see every day! What do you say?"

"Yes, I'm in!"

As they set off Shiván felt a twinge of sadness that Perrely wasn't with them. It was the sort of thing she'd normally have jumped at, and she wouldn't have gone off with the other women. That business about holding hands must have bitten deep.

As they followed a south-easterly path through the forest, the lodges began to thin out. Before they left the settlement altogether, Shiván noticed that all the outlying homes were newly-built. Billérasson had expanded rapidly in recent years — thanks to Shambor.

Suddenly, to his surprise, the forest path came out on to a road. Not a cart track, but what had once clearly been a broad carriageway of well-laid stones — like the Dûrian highways, though only half the width. Now the edges were eaten away, and it was covered with greenery and full of potholes.

"Hillet! What's this? Fira told us there were no direct roads between the Grûzhack territory and Dûrion."

"The Galeronden say it's the old teméyn road to Dhembis."

"But that would run right past Billérasson! With my own ears I heard Fira say there was only a road to the west—to the Thrinar Pass."

"This road goes nowhere," Cârin said, pointing back the way they'd come. Now he saw that the old carriageway dwindled into rubble just below where they'd joined it.

"They say it was destroyed many years ago," Hillet told him, "when the Founders cut off the teméyn trade. At that time the Grûzhack built a new road westward, and they've never needed to restore this one."

"I see. The more I hear of your Founders, the better I like them!"

They walked carefully along the crumbling road. When it began to wind around the hill Shîr had pointed out earlier, Hillet branched off heading upward. After scrambling over boulders and through close-knit trees for a while, he brought them to a halt at the entrance to a rocky overhang. There he turned to face them. His expression was serious.

"From here we'll see the fortress clearly. But we have to be careful. Go on to the ledge slowly, then stand still. Don't make any sudden movements. The Galeronden warned us that the guards at Fort Desheyn can see a long way."

With these ominous words he stooped under an overhanging branch and led them on to the ledge.

And there was the Grûzhack fortress. It sat, square and stark, on the bare cliffside opposite, maybe a mile distant. A road had been cut into the rock face, running in both directions from the fort. To the east and to the south they could glimpse sections of it winding away into the further ranges. The fortress's massive walls and towers appeared to be the outer façade of a much larger structure that had been delved into the mountainside.

Small figures could be seen moving slowly along the walls at different levels. They had short vertical lances strapped to their backs. All the parapets had gaps at regular intervals. In the gaps were dark circular shapes that looked vaguely familiar. There was a quick flash of light from one of the towers that also tugged at Shiván's memory.

"Incredible," Cârin murmured, awestruck. "Why are all those soldiers guarding this fort in the middle of nowhere? Are they afraid you or the Galeronden might attack them?"

"Not much danger of that," Hillet chuckled. "No, from what I understand the Grûzhack guard all possible entrances to their Hidden Magistry. They don't trust any outsiders. The Galeronden say this is only a small fort. The ones guarding the teméyn roads are a lot bigger."

There was another quick flash of light, and Shiván suddenly remembered where he'd seen that before. In the same instant it hit him what the round shapes were—and those lances on the soldiers' backs. He also remembered Darinor's comment about the Grûzhack attacking first and asking questions later. His jaw dropped and his eyes widened. He felt horribly exposed. They had to get off that open ledge.

"We must leave," he said quietly.

"But we've only just got here," Shîrin protested. "That's the most amazing—"

"We must leave. Now. Very slowly—back to the forest."

Hillet's eyebrows were raised, but his urgency had its effect. After they'd all made their adagio exit they crowded round him where he sat under the trees.

"What in the Prince's name got into you?" Cârin demanded, annoyed.

"Can our revered Overguardian not stand the sight of a Grûzhack fortress?" Hillet said, staring at Shiván quizzically.

He paused till they quietened down. Then he said softly, "There were weapons there that I recognise. Like ones under *my* sky. You don't have them in Dûrion. They are deadly. And if you've been up here before and haven't been seen, you've been very lucky. Which is why we must return to Billérasson *now*, under cover of the forest."

They argued, of course, but left in the end, still unconvinced. There was no way he could have explained properly.

Because, unless he was very much mistaken, the Grûzhack had cannon. And muskets. And those quick flashes came from telescopes catching the sun as they swept the valley.

Chapter 7: *Shattered hope*

IN A TEMPLE IN SELMION, Mindbender Faranu and his colleague stood at the door of the underground cell, engaged in the silent communication of their kind. The emaciated child lay naked on a pile of dirty straw in the corner. His ugly, ridged face twitched as he dreamed, and he uttered intermittent high-pitched whimpers.

The other Mindbender's nose wrinkled, and his mental tone was tinged with disgust.

"How often do you clean him – and the cell?"

"Oh, just enough to prevent disease. The stink adds to the mental pressure."

"Ah. He's not mindbent. Why?"

"I don't want him in my mind!" The two grey-robed men smiled thinly. *"Besides, natural reactions are best."*

"Well, he looks a miserable specimen. Sensitive mind, though. I can see why you chose him. Where did you pick him up?"

"He was found in Marûvin, squalling beside the teméyn *trail. Parents' wagon had fallen into a ravine. Both were dead. That was just after the Strongholder made the appeal for subjects. Mindruler Nagôr recognised his potential, and sent him."*

"He's starting to achieve that potential. An impressive demonstration this afternoon. Clever idea, building up his hopes by promising the nurse and then dashing them."

"The goal is to keep him oscillating between hope and despair. That produces the best results."

"So I see."

* * *

"Garion."

Bishop Shambor started as the sudden mental presence scattered his thoughts. Only one person in all the lands dared mindspeak him by his childhood name: the man who was *his* Mindbender. He sat up straighter in the plush leather seat as his carriage rolled past the Forest of Janulane on its way to Dhembis.

"Strongholder."

"Have you dealt with those upstarts?"

*"Not yet, Strongholder. But I know where they are, and it's just a mat-
ter of time."* He felt a surge of relief that this query was coming now
and not a few days ago, when he'd been at his wits' end.
"I hope so, because I had thought to make you my Second."
"That – would be a high honour, your Supremacy."
"Make sure you get your house in order quickly."
"I will, Strongholder."
"Good."

The vibrant, youthful presence with its pent-up energy faded from
his mind, and he slumped back in the seat. He always needed a few
moments to re-gather his scattered thoughts after these encounters.
The new Strongholder was the youngest – and the most powerful –
ever elected.

Then a slow smile spread across his heavy features. The Strongholder's Second-in-Command! *That* was a prize he'd hardly dared
hope for – especially given the age difference between them. Heir
Apparent to the supreme ruler of the Cult of Gadesh throughout the
Dûrai lands! Of course, actually to become Strongholder he would
need to outlive the man, and to be elected by the Holders' Table, the
ruling council of Selmion. But Strongholders often died young; and
as designated Second he would be the front-runner in the election.
Imagine holding ultimate power over every mind in the five Dûrai
nations – and beyond! He stared unseeing out of the carriage window, the smile still tugging at his lips.

After a while his mind wandered back over the years, remembering all he'd suffered as a trainee Mindbender in Selmion – a young
lad alone in a foreign land, without family or friends. That was after
he – after the – ... He didn't want to think about the traumatic end
to his childhood in Dûrion.

What a long way he'd come since then! His parents, who had so
oppressed him with all their expectations and criticisms, would never appreciate it. They'd rejected him, but *he*, the reject, would become
the most powerful man in all the Dûrai nations. As Strongholder of
Selmion he'd command the Mindrulers of Dûrion, Thrinar, Marûvin
and Pandiar. Though, of course, *she* would never know... A familiar
anguish twisted his gut, and he dropped the thought.

As the endless green wall of the Forest of Janulane rolled slowly
by in the mellow afternoon light, his mind went back to the travelling priests. He'd been fuming over Visionary Frengor's defiance

before the recent welcome interruption. Not only was that jumped-up roadside tramp openly promoting the Restorers' cause, but he'd added insult to injury — refusing the summons of the *de facto* ruler of Dûrion, suggesting he was a mere lackey of Harlon's, and openly challenging Harlon's house-arrest!

Frengor was hiding behind the legal fiction that the head of the Travelling Order, which was active in all lands, did not answer to the Bishop of Dûrion. He was also relying on the enormous respect the travelling priests commanded among the common people, assuming this would discourage any drastic action against them.

But the arrogant priest hadn't realised those days were past. The Strongholder's words confirmed that Dûrion was moving out of its ancient Lightist straightjacket. No one could be allowed to stand in the way of that. It didn't need drastic action. A slow smile spread on his heavy features. Something much simpler would do. Sooner, rather than later, those priests would get what was coming to them.

Satisfied with his solution to that problem, his thoughts turned to recent developments in Dhembis, the town he was now approaching. Very encouraging they had been. Mindbender Jastor was to be congratulated on the efficiency of his local spy network. A report had reached him about a group of foreigners appearing in the nearby village of Jarmenis. They had come there on foot from Dhembis — but they'd travelled to Dhembis itself in two fine sinélle carriages.

As soon as he'd heard that, he'd remembered that earlier report about a rag-tag bunch of travellers taking over some carriages in the village of Barveck, beside the Forest of Janulane — where the would-be Restorers had last been seen. *Those* carriages had set off for Dhembis …

Now he was coming there himself to take charge. Two hundred infantry — all skilled woodsmen — were following on foot.

It was the mention of Jarmenis that had clinched the matter. Jarmenis, as he well knew, was the gateway to Galeron. What a perfect hiding place *that* would provide for four runaway Restorers! Remote. Inaccessible. Full of discontented refugees ripe for any cause that aimed to overthrow his regime. Oh yes, those traitors thought they'd covered their tracks, but he'd long known of the clandestine traffic in human flotsam that made its way through

Jarmenis. Until now he'd ignored it. Good riddance — let others be burdened by those who rejected his rule.

All that was about to change.

* * *

Fira was appalled at what Shiván was telling them, though she could barely understand it. Tubes that burst into flame and shot great rocks at you! It sounded like something out of a children's ogre tale. Yet despite the twins' laughter, the fun-loving foreigner showed no glimmer of a smile. That was enough for Fira.

"Did you know about these Grûzhack weapons?" she asked Darinor.

The refugee leader had joined them for the daymeal. All around them on the logs surrounding the cooking fires well-wrapped members of the refugee settlement were sitting, and a cheerful babble, punctuated by children's squeals, filled the chilly evening air.

Darinor nodded slowly. "The Galeronden told us about their small shooting-sticks. But not the large ones. Nor the far-seeing glasses."

"If their weapons are so powerful," she said, "aren't you afraid the Grûzhack may some day decide that you and the Galeronden are a nuisance, and come down and destroy you?"

"Not really." Darinor smiled. "I don't think we are important enough to them. Unless an armed force approached the fort, they would ignore us as they've always done." He looked at Shiván. "Your caution was commendable, but I don't think you need have worried."

"There! That's what *we* said," Cârin crowed.

Shiván shook his head, unconvinced. Fira was inclined to agree with him. Weapons like the ones he'd described made her uncomfortable. Very uncomfortable.

"And Shambor would never be so stupid as to send an armed force up there," Perrely added, "because that would threaten his teméyn supply."

Fira noted the unhappy look Shiván gave Perrely, and the way she ignored it. The girl was making him suffer for her own folly about holding hands. Well, they'd stopped doing so now, thanks to her earlier warning. She hoped Shiván would have the guts to stand up to Perrely.

* * *

Perrely shivered and pulled her fur coat tighter. The evening chill was beginning to bite. Her thoughts were as gloomy as the dark trees whose shadows now filled the eating circle.

Darinor had left, and Shiván was sitting a little way off, talking to Danîsha. Perrely felt miserable now that she'd behaved so childishly. That only happened when she was in the wrong — and she'd at last accepted that she *had* been wrong about holding hands among these conservative refugees. If only it weren't blunt, abrasive Fira who'd pointed it out! That woman always brought out the worst in her.

But as she sat alone on a log, something that had happened long ago was coming back to haunt her. She'd suppressed the memory in the pleasure of Shiván's company; now it would no longer be denied. As a young girl on the threshold of womanhood, she had pledged her life to God alone for prayer and service. She'd had no thought of marriage, simply assuming that her love belonged entirely to the Prince of Peace. That was how she'd continued to think of herself… until she met Shiván.

He was like no other man she'd come across. His heart, like hers, was wholly given to the Prince. He was light-hearted, funny, yet utterly sincere. His deepest desire was the same as hers — to love the Creator with all his heart, soul, mind and strength. His calling was the same as hers — to see Dûrion restored to the Way of the One. And he loved her.

Surely they belonged together? They could help and encourage each other along the difficult road ahead. Her heart yearned for that. She longed to join their lives into a fragrant offering to the Prince. And yet… Wasn't this just how Worldruler Gadesh, master of lies, presented his detours to the follower of the Way? *See how much more attractive* this *road is — and it goes in exactly the same direction!* But only for a while. Then it began leading you astray — or to a disastrous dead end.

There were practical considerations also. She also knew that one of the Inglish Founders, Jemmet dos Simion, had married a Dûrian woman — but they'd had no children. Did that mean physical intercourse was not possible? Would Shiván want children, and be disappointed if she couldn't give him any? And what would happen when — if — the Restorers completed their mission? Would Shiván return to Inglan? If he did, would she be able to go with him? Was this what the One was calling her to — to spend the rest of her days under an alien sky? And the alternative — that Shiván stayed in Dûrion. Was that part of *his* calling?

She stared ahead of her with unseeing eyes. They would have to talk about this. And *she* would have to find out whether marriage to Shiván was God's way for her — or an alluring detour of the Worldruler's.

* * *

A few minutes later, as everyone was getting up to return to the warmth of their lodges, Shiván came to her and pleaded for a chance to talk things over. She agreed at once, and followed him away from the central hearth to a place where they could speak privately.

Shiván stopped in a secluded spot beyond the lodges where the moonlight shone through a gap in the trees. It was a perfectly clear evening — so wonderful after the endless overcast of the previous season, Raingold. The first moon was full in the sky, the second just rising above the tall trees. The Ring of Orrénne could be seen, faint but clear, directly overhead. Everything was very still. Not a twig moved. The silence of the night was emphasised by the distant laughter around the cooking fires.

He turned to face her. There was a sadness in his eyes that made her heart lurch. He took both her hands in his.

"Perrely, I'm sorry. You were trying to stand up for us, and I let you down."

She shook her head. "I was wrong. Fira was right."

His face cleared. "Do you really think so?"

"Yes."

"Then how would it be if — " He faltered as his eyes seemed to devour hers. "If we held hands just when we're alone together — like this." He stopped. His hands felt so warm around hers.

"But not... when we're with others?" she whispered.

"That's right."

An age passed as they stared into each other's eyes. She was about to tell him she agreed, when an intensity gathered in his face, and the next instant she found herself engulfed in his arms. For a moment she was filled with ecstasy. Then she suddenly realised what was happening—Shiván was embracing her! And they were not betrothed!

With a gasp she broke free and stepped back, horrified. He stared at her, his face filling with uncertainty. They stood frozen for a moment.

"I'm sorry— I didn't—" He stopped.

It dawned on her that he knew no better.

"Shiván," she said, "embracing before we're betrothed is— is like—" She struggled for the right description. "It's like saying you want to dishonour me. To… to force me." She coloured at the crude words.

"*Omigosh.*" He looked stricken. "Perrely, I'm truly sorry. I had no idea—"

"It's all right. I know that's not what you meant."

"So— You're saying that we can't hug or… or kiss, unless we're betrothed?"

She nodded. A smile began to spread on his face, and she said quickly, "No, Shiván! It's not that easy. I'm not ready. And I don't think you are, either."

* * *

Shiván was fighting a growing sense of bewilderment as he stared at Perrely. She seemed to be blocking him at every turn. Yet he knew she felt the same for him as he did for her.

"Perrely, I love you. I've never felt about anyone the way I feel about you. I—"

"Is that all that matters? Our feelings? What about God? Doesn't *he* have a say?"

"Well— Yes, of course, but— Surely he wouldn't have brought us together otherwise."

She smiled. "That's a pathetic argument, and you know it." Her voice took on an urgency. "Shiván, have you thought about the future if we marry? First of all, when? Now? We have such an uncertain road ahead. We don't even know if we'll both live to see the Way of the One restored in Dûrion."

"No, but we could encourage each other in the process."

Her eyes dropped. "Yes, we could," she murmured. She heaved a shaky sigh, and looked up again at him, tears glinting in the moonlight. "Shiván, I long for that as much as you do. But we don't need to be married to encourage each other. And say we do live to see the evil conquered in Dûrion. What then? Will you go back to Urrith?"

The question caught him by surprise. "I— Well, I don't know yet. I guess we've all assumed that the One will send us home when our job here is done, but… we have no idea how or when."

"So, if we were married — would I be able to come with you?"

"I don't know! But Perrely, I love you! I'll stay in Dûrion with you if that's the only way."

She shook her head gently. "You can't be sure of that. I love you too, Shiván, but even if one of us *could* go and live under the other's sky, that's not a quick, easy decision!"

"We could work it out!"

She sighed, and nodded. "But there's also the question of — children. Would you want children, Shiván?"

He rolled his eyes. "For the One's sake, woman, we're not even betrothed yet!"

"No. But it's not a small thing, Shiván. I don't know about Inglan, but here in Dûrion men have abandoned their wives because they were not able to bear children. I doubt if we could have any, coming from different skies. Would you feel sad — disappointed — if it was just you and me, no little ones?"

"Of course not!" He stared at her, baffled. They loved each other! Why was this so hard?

She gazed back at him, tears trickling down her cheeks. "Shiván, it's easy to think we're sure now, when we feel so strongly about each other. I'm afraid—" Her voice faltered. "Afraid we'll make snap decisions, based on our feelings, and later discover they were the wrong ones. I want to be sure, Shiván. I want to know that this is what God wants. I don't know that yet." She took a deep, shuddering breath. "Can we pray about it? Each of us, separately? Keep asking our Father if this is what *he* wants, until he gives us a clear, definite answer?"

He looked at her for a long moment. Then at last it came to him. He'd been thinking of Dûrian betrothal as being like 'starting a relationship' back home — the time when it became legitimate to hold hands, kiss and hug. To be 'with' someone. Marriage came later, if at all. But reading between the lines of what Perrely was saying, that's not how it must be here in Dûrion. It seemed as though betrothal was a binding agreement—the first stage of marriage. There was nothing before that. No being 'together'. That made sense of why Perrely's thoughts were already on all the implications of marriage, while he'd barely gone beyond wanting a little more physical contact.

His eyes softened as he took in the deep earnestness in her purple eyes, the moon's white fire lancing through the trees to lighten her golden hair, the silver of the tearstains on her face. He ached to reach out, touch her cheek, stroke her hair, hold her. But he couldn't.

"Yeah, okay," he said softly. "Let's do that."

"You really mean it? You'll seriously ask the One if marriage is what he wants for us?"

"I will. Definitely. But can we be friends in the meantime?"

A faint smile touched her lips. "You mean, like holding hands when we're alone?"

"Yeah, like that."

She nodded slowly. "Alright. But nothing more."

His heart soared. They walked back to the lodges in silence, hand in hand.

* * *

Shiván used every spare moment during the next two days for prayer. He saw Perrely slipping off alone into the woods as well. The more he prayed, the more sure he became. God had brought them together, and they belonged with each other.

There were the obvious things: their shared longing for reality with God; the compatibility of their personalities; their joint desire to serve and encourage others; their common goal here in Dûrion; and the certainty all their friends felt that they were made for each other. But those were not what convinced him. The clincher, for him, was the peace that descended on his heart whenever he spoke to God about it. It was as if God himself was smiling at him, saying, "It's okay, I've given you your heart's desire. It's right to love Perrely."

The only minor chord was that when he smiled at Perrely she didn't always smile back.

On the third evening he made his way between the lodges to the quiet spot under the trees where he and Perrely had spoken before. He pulled his coat tighter—it was cold away from the fires.

He walked up and down the little glade while he thought and prayed. *Please God, make Perrely just as sure as you've made me!*

There was a rustle of foliage, and Perrely appeared in the glade. She came up close, and he could see that her cheeks were tear-stained. Coldness settled in the pit of his stomach. No. Oh no. This couldn't be.

She took hold of both his hands. "I think the One has given me an answer," she whispered.

"What is it?" His voice came out in a croak.

"When I was a young girl, Shiván, I met Prince Orrénne. I loved him so much, because he'd first loved me." The tears flowed freely down her cheeks. "I gave my life to him for prayer and service. My love belonged entirely to the Prince of Peace. Then I met you. And I loved you, too…" She faltered and dropped her eyes. There was a blade cutting into Shiván's heart. She seemed to gather all her strength to look up at him again.

"But now — He's shown me that I belong to him only. My path is a single one, to be a woman of prayer. Your love for me —" She swallowed, and continued unsteadily, "Your love is a gift beyond price. I'll always treasure it. Right now — our lives are entwined together in the One's tapestry. But later the threads will — separate."

Her voice broke on the last word, and she looked down, her shoulders shaking, still clasping his hands tightly.

Shiván was devastated. Nothing had prepared him for this. The blade in his heart had cut all the way through. He tried to speak, but nothing came. He stared at Perrely's hair, held her hands. It was all he could do.

Chapter 8: *A new line of thought*

SHIVÁN AWOKE WITH A JERK from the worst nightmare he'd had in many years. His clothing was drenched with sweat, he was panting, and there was a deep pain that clouded his thoughts.

As he lay in the dark it dawned on him that it wasn't a dream. It had happened. Perrely had told him they could never be married. She was called to be a woman of prayer—alone. The light in his life had gone out.

Self-doubt came flooding in. All these days had he somehow not been 'in tune' with God, just following his own desires? Yet he wasn't aware of having wandered away from God. He'd spent time with him every day—praying, and reading the old, worn King James Bible; he'd shared constantly with the Prince—with Jesus.

He knew he desperately needed to pray now; but he couldn't. He'd prayed already, and God had given his answer. It was an answer that had cut through to the very heart of him. Now he could only lie here, eyes closed, not thinking, just suffering the aching sense of loss.

After a timeless interval, the down-to-earth urgency of a full bladder asserted itself. He started the slow, careful roll out of the Galeronden hammock, then stopped. Something was wrong. He felt around him with his hands. The surface he was on yielded to his body, but it wasn't a hammock. It was flat, and softer. The covering over him was no longer a bearskin, either. What the heck…?

He levered himself up and carefully swung his feet over the straight edge of the thing he was lying on. They came down on a soft, furry surface. Now he knew that reality had slipped a cog. The floors of Galeronden lodges were plain boards.

He sat on the edge of whatever-it-was, letting his eyes adjust to the dim glow from the window. He gradually made out that instead of shutters, there was a thick cloth hanging in folds over the window. He glanced round the room. No other sleeping bodies. He was alone in here! He felt a sudden wave of fear.

A roaring noise began in the distance and raced rapidly nearer. He leapt to his feet in terror. A bright light swept over the window cloth, briefly illuminating the whole room. Then the light disappeared and the noise dwindled. And suddenly everything clicked.

His heart still racing, he reached for the bedside lamp. His fingers fumbled till they found the tiny knob and pressed it. It lit up—all on its own! Imagine that, a lamp without a flame.

He sat down on the... yes, it was a bed, with a soft mattress—and looked around the room. *His* room, in the small house he shared with two others. It was unbelievable. He was back in England, just starting third year at university. On the wall facing him were several open shelves bending under the weight of books. He walked over, feeling he was in a dream, and picked one up at random. *Practical Ethics Applied*. He riffled through it. Had he once taken this stuff seriously? A different life, a different person.

Before Dûrion—and Perrely. The pain crashed back.

* * *

He collapsed on to the edge of the bed. His eyes closed as the agony of her final words swept through him again. After a few moments he opened them, feeling a wetness on his cheeks which he angrily wiped away. Self-pity wouldn't solve anything. He looked around bleakly—at this room from a past life, a life that wasn't real any more.

Or was it? Was *this* the reality, and had Dûrion just been a dream?

Everything within him screamed *No!* Dûrion and all that had happened there filled his mind. Of course it was real.

But you had to admit appearances were against it. Here he was, in his bedroom, just where he'd been when he fell asleep and *thought* he woke up in a Dûrian forest three months ago—or was it last night?

His eyes wandered round the dimly-lit room. Last night? Then why were his memories so foggy? Why did everything look strange and somehow... *alien* to him? The upright chair in front of the desk was too broad and squat. The book shelves... you didn't dump books casually on a *shelf*, you put them in a bookcase! The jeans and underwear lying on the floor ("Slob!" he muttered) looked awkward and hard to get into compared to the loose Dûrian clothing he'd got used to wearing...

His eyes fell on his blue pyjama sleeve, and he froze. *That's not a pyjama top!* It was a shift, the body-length garment all working Dûrians wore. He felt the finely-woven fabric between his fingers—

tattered and frayed in places, but still serviceable. It was made from *hilminay*, the Dûrian textile plant whose fibres were woven into thread and retained their bright colours—no dye needed.

That clinched it. He had been in Dûrion. It was no dream. Maybe *this* was the dream…

He sat up wearily. He pinched himself. Ouch. He rubbed his hands on the duvet, clasped his fist round the lamp stand. It all *felt* real. He sat on the strange chair, opened the lid of the laptop and turned it on. It took as long as usual to boot up—then there was his desktop, with the date at the top right corner. Thursday October 15th. Oh, okay: that would be the day after he fell asleep in his clothes. So no time had passed here, though he'd spent almost three months in Dûrion. He shook his head. Too much to process.

For one final reality-check he went down the corridor and turned on the shower. The water was wet. It heated up and became delightfully warm. He dropped his Dûrian tunic to the floor, climbed into the shower cubicle, and luxuriated. The feel of hot water pelting his skin was one he hadn't enjoyed for a long time, and it was too intensely physical not to be real.

Back in the bedroom he slowly got dressed in a clean white T-shirt and jeans. So both Dûrion and this were real. They were not dreams. Somehow God had brought him back to Earth—in the same immediate and impossible way he'd sent him to Dûrion in the first place.

What about the others—Lannie, 'Neesh and Gil? Had God sent them home, too? Surely not. That would mean their mission in Dûrion was finished—and they'd barely started. Well… He was at the university, where Gil was one of his lecturers—and he had a lecture with him on Friday, didn't he? He'd find out then if Gil had also come back. And if he hadn't, it was unlikely any of the others had.

He sat on the chair, staring unseeing through the window as the sky slowly lightened. *Am I back permanently now? No, I can't be. But I have no choice in the matter. Either God will send me back, or he'll leave me here. Do I want to resume this old student life? No! I want to be in Dûrion with Perrely…* The pain surged back. Pictures of the two of them together flashed on his mind's eye, gradually shifting into scenes of all that he and Perrely and the other Restorers had been through.

With them came another painful thought. *I'm their leader — the Overguardian. Can I even go back now? How can I still be an effective leader, when I completely misread God's intention for Perrely and me? I prayed and then interpreted what I wanted as his answer — a classic newbie mistake! I should know better than that by now.* The words of the prophet Isaiah echoed in his head: "'For my thoughts are not your thoughts, neither are your ways my ways,' declares the LORD."

Maybe God has sent me home because I'm no longer fit to be the Overguardian. Maybe right now another 'stranger and loner' has arrived to fulfil the Lightists' prophecy... A deep hurt throbbed in his heart.

He urgently needed to pray. He lifted his arms in the Dûrian fashion — but he couldn't concentrate: his mind and heart were too full of conflicting currents. In the end he could only ask God to show him *why* he'd sent him back to Earth.

He lowered his arms. Okay. One thing at a time. This was real, not a dream. He had to live, here and now, despite the pain.

He pushed his ragged Dûrian clothes under the bed, and downed cornflakes and tea as day broke. Still no sign of his housemates. By rummaging for course schedules from his old life, he worked out where he was meant to be today.

His hair was the lopsided result of Cârin's unskilled hacking, so he called in at a barber en route to the university. Then he spent half an hour in the library before his first lecture. He found a modern Bible, opened it at the ribbon, and found himself reading Psalm seventeen, verse eight: *Keep me as the apple of your eye; hide me in the shadow of your wings.* Tears pricked his eyes. Maybe this was God's intention. He'd carried the wounded bird to a safe place, where he could rest in the shadow of his father's wings.

But when I'm rested, will you let me return? Will I ever see Perrely again? While I'm here, will I hear you when you speak to me — or will I make up my own 'answers to prayer'? Do I have a whole lot more learning to do before I can go back? The questions ate away at Steve's heart as he made his way slowly to the lecture hall.

The lecture went by in a haze. He couldn't have said what it was about. Several students greeted him, reminding him that his name over here was Steve. He replied mechanically.

As he came out of the lecture, he almost bumped into a familiar figure with black hair sticking up on end, a narrow, beak-like nose, and a remarkably thin face.

"Steve!" the fellow exclaimed. He grabbed his arm. "Just the man I was looking for! We've got an emergency on our hands." Steve struggled to remember the guy's name. He was in the CU—the Christian Union—and they knew one another well. His eyes were wide, his thin face registering maximum shock.

"I've had an email from Accord," he continued breathlessly. *'E' male from a cord?* "They want to use the James Hall for a series of meetings early next term. They need it every day for a week!"

Things finally clicked into place. This was Roger Husted, Secretary of the CU. 'Accord' was the rival interdenominational Christian group on campus—founded two years ago by dissatisfied CU members. Now there was a full-scale emergency because Accord wanted to use the hall the CU had booked for their own activities, including their main weekly meeting.

No... not now. I can't handle this now. "Later, Rog, okay? Gotta rush." He pushed past the gaping secretary and hurried off to his next lecture.

When he came out from that, Rog was waiting for him. "Sorry, Steve, this really, you know, it c–can't wait much l–longer!" His eyes were wide and he was stuttering with agitation. "Aren't you, you know, at least going to c–call a c–committee meeting?"

Steve closed his eyes. *Dear God, do I really have to deal with this? I can't!* "Rog, sorry, I'm just not in a good place right now." He took a deep breath. He had to give the guy something, or he'd expire on the spot. Today was Thursday. Right. "Next week, okay? Call a committee meeting for Monday afternoon."

"Um... That's a bit... I mean..." Then, staring at Steve, he began nodding rapidly. "Yes, yes, fine, committee meeting on Monday at five p.m. I'll tell everyone that right now you have some urgent— stuff—to..."

"Great, thanks Rog." Steve walked off, feeling the secretary's unhappy gaze on his back.

*   *   *

Steve somehow survived the rest of Thursday and Friday. At Gil's lecture on Friday a junior colleague took his place. "Dr. Denbigh's in a meeting" was the only reason given. *Sounds thin. But it means Gil definitely hasn't come back from Dûrion, at least not yet: 'cos if he had, he'd be here looking for me.* Steve heaved a sigh. *So. I'm the only one who's been sent home...*

By the end of Friday friends were pestering Steve to know why he was so down, and he'd had to fend off several CU committee members jabbering anxiously about Accord's request. He was deeply grateful for the weekend.

Meanwhile the pain of Perrely's rejection — and of her absence — and of his own failure to discern God's purpose — ate deeper into his heart. On Saturday he stayed in his room all day, despite good-hearted attempts by his housemates to draw him out. On Sunday he couldn't bring himself to go to church. He tried to pray, but it was as if God had dumped him here and left him to stew in his own juice.

As the quiet Sunday hours passed, a new fear raised its ugly head. He could feel it happening within him: the slow, inevitable slide down into the pit of depression.

No! That plague of his past life was *over!* The incident at school when he'd used his martial arts to seriously injure an older boy... that was finished and done with! The depression that had dogged his life since then — along with his fear of ever again causing injury — ... Dûrion had dealt with them! When the Mindbender of Stillárre had been on the point of raping Perrely, he had used his martial arts to kick the depraved despot through a third floor window. That had broken his fear of causing injury in a just cause. Since then he'd enjoyed a new sense of freedom, a new lightness of spirit, that he knew was due to more than just being in love. The old, recurring fear of sliding down into despair was gone.

Except that now it was back.

Steve sat at the table in his bedroom staring out at the street below, a half-finished burger and mug of tea beside him. The sun was setting, and people were coming home, chatting and calling out happily to one another after a day of relaxation. *Dear God, don't let me fall into depression again. Show me a way out!*

He slowly got up, leaving his unfinished supper, and collapsed on to the bed. *Safer to sleep than to think...*

He woke up disoriented. The room was dark. For a tiny fraction of a second he thought he was back in Dûrion. Then the pain crashed in — but with it, something new. A spark of defiance. *No, I*

will not *give way to depression again. God enabled me to defeat it once —*
he'll do so again!

He shivered. He was lying on top of the duvet. He turned the
light on and checked the time. Six a.m. — he'd slept solidly for twelve
hours. That couldn't be bad. He got up, grabbed a change of clothes,
and took a steaming shower. Back in his room with a fresh cup of
tea, he felt — almost — like a new person.

He sat at the table sipping the warm beverage and watching the
outside world slowly brighten. As he did so he thought and prayed.
One Creator God, you brought me here from Dûrion. And you put me in
Dûrion in the first place. Help me understand why I'm here, and what you
want to teach me.

So, what's pulling me down into depression? he thought. The old
hopelessness tugged at him, but he thrust it aside. *Is it that Perrely's*
rejected me? No, it's not only that. It's because I prayed and prayed about
it, and I was absolutely positive God was saying Yes, that we were meant
to be together — he felt himself choking up, and willed himself to concentrate. *But I got it wrong! I took what I wanted as God's answer, and —*

Did you?

The gentle question — definitely not from himself — threw everything he'd been thinking into disarray. *I — What? Yes, I did! I — What*
do you mean?

What if it was Perrely who got it wrong? Not you.

No, Perrely couldn't have got it wrong! She's so much more spiritual,
so much closer to you than me —

Is she? You know about these things, do you?

Shiván's eyes widened and he sat with his mouth half open, di-
gesting this new idea. Perrely was younger than him. Young and
idealistic. A few years ago she'd had an amazing encounter with
God, in which he'd given her new life and a special ministry of
prayer — and all her ideals centred around that. Falling in love with
Shiván felt to her like a betrayal of those ideals, as she herself had
said — and now, perhaps, she was making the exact same mistake
he thought he'd made, only in reverse: rejecting what she wanted
as not coming from God, when in fact he delighted in giving his
children their hearts' desire.

There's no way I can be sure that's what happened. This might just be
more wishful thinking… But the voice in his head — God's voice —
had some convincing arguments. As he thought about it he real-

ised that, given their personalities, Perrely was just as likely to have made that mistake as he was.

"Thank you, Father!" he breathed.

Well, this opens up a whole new line of thought. Maybe Perrely will realise she's wrong. Maybe I'm not such a washout as a Christian after all. Maybe I have learned a thing or two in Dûrion...

"Please God, if this is true, send me back to Dûrion!"

First there's something you need to do.

??? "...Oh. You mean, this stupid CU thing?"

Shiván had the strangest impression that God was smiling. *Yes. This CU thing.*

"But it's so unbelievably trivial! It'll split the committee, as it's always done since the whole Accord thing started. Pete, Shelley and Tom will be up in arms if anyone suggests giving them our booking. But Jo and Rich and that lot will see it as a heaven-sent chance to mend relations. Things will get heated, and... Lord, I just don't think I can handle it!"

I made you President of the CU for a reason. And I sent you to Dûrion for a reason. You've been learning to lead there, because you've been listening to my voice. Now, because of Perrely, you've started to doubt if you're hearing me correctly. Are you willing to trust me – to take a leap of faith – here and now?

Shiván took a deep breath. "OK, Lord. Let's do it the Dûrian way. I'm listening..."

─────────────────────

Chapter 9: *Blindsided*

SHAMBOR REACHED DHEMBIS in the early evening, and made his stately procession through the streets to the Guardhouse. A crowd had been laid on to cheer. Staying at the Guardhouse was a break with protocol (which specified either the Elder's residence or the Hearth guesthouse). But to *sarrákh* with protocol! His business here was military.

Mindbender Jastor had provided him with a large apartment in the Guardhouse from which to direct the expedition to Galeron — and a luscious young adherent to keep him company. For a while that evening he allowed her to distract him; but, as always, he failed at the crucial moment. Frustrated, he ordered her out. Otherwise he'd have to mutilate her, and that was a last resort.

It was always the same. He could never find release without inflicting pain. Yet he knew it need not be that way. Even after all these years he felt a pang of longing as his thoughts went back to Yestel. He savoured the name. It had only been a brief liaison with that attractive, independent-minded young woman, but he'd loved and deeply respected her — and it had worked. Then she'd discovered his darker side, and everything had come to an end. He longed to find such a woman again. But these days it was always either a soft, compliant Gadeshite, desperately anxious to please; a slutty prostitute; or a terrified prisoner who could only be forced.

Next morning Shambor summoned Mindbender Jastor to transfer control of the spy who had discovered the foreigners' escape to Jarmenis. He was a 'sleeper' — one who had been commanded hypnotically to forget his connection with the Mindbenders. He himself, therefore, didn't know he was a spy — which effectively disguised his shiláy. But his sense-impressions were fully available to his controller. What's more, he was actually a member of the subversive network that smuggled so-called 'refugees' to the Galeronden area. He was like a hidden peephole into their activities. And when needed, he could be 'woken' and put to good use... which Shambor intended to do.

He smiled at the thought. The sleeper's information had reached him too late to catch the foreigners before they left Jarmenis — but the sleeper would guide Shambor's two hundred infantry up into the mountains after them. He would also keep the Mindruler informed of developments, and pass on his instructions via the mindlink.

The problem was that the Bishop's Guard could not take part in this little jaunt. Shambor had learnt his lesson from events at Carreck Manor and Stillárre, where the old woman's instrument — her bellaril — had frozen his Guards, and even himself, with the appalling purity of its music. Much as it galled him to admit it, those would-be Restorers had the upper hand over his mindbent troops. But they were ordinary flesh and blood. Pit them against similar flesh and blood with superior weapons and training, and their mind-tricks wouldn't help them.

Jastor arrived — a gaunt, sallow-faced, superior-looking fellow with purple-black hair. Shambor distrusted him. His obligatory kowtowing to the Mindruler was perfunctory. A faint smile crossed his lips when Shambor demanded control of the sleeper. He wondered why — and found out as soon as the transfer was complete.

"What...! But he's — How can I work with this idiot?"

Jastor shrugged, barely hiding his amusement at Shambor's discomfiture. "He's the ringleader's brother — and the only one we can trust to guide the troops to Galeron."

"Get me one of the other Jarmenis villagers! There's no way I can use this fool."

"With due respect, Mindruler, they are all fanatics. They will kill themselves rather than be taken captive."

Shambor stared at him for a long moment, breathing heavily. "Very well. Get out."

With an elaborate bow the Mindbender left. Shambor turned to the weary task of making Lishet dom Brûnor's body play a rôle that his mind could never comprehend. With great difficulty he got the fool to slip away unseen and climb a small hill from which he had a good view of the village below.

Early in the afternoon, watching through Lishet's eyes, he saw the two hundred woodland troops entering Jarmenis. To his annoyance, despite their stealthy approach they were seen coming, and the villagers all suddenly fled different ways into the surrounding hills — including the ringleader, Lishet's sister Nist. It was all he could do to prevent Lishet following her without damaging his fragile mind. Well, her escape was a minor annoyance. Their operation was at an end, in any case. The troops bedded down in the village for the night.

Jastor supplied a more experienced devotee that evening. Shambor returned her the next morning in a rather damaged condition.

As he sat down for his dawnmeal the assault force set out for Galeron, guided by Lishet. Here the miserable idiot's active participation was essential: only he knew the way. Shambor calmed his abject terror by telling him his sister was there, and he'd soon be with her.

The plan was to capture Galeron first — since that was the gateway to the Galeronden settlements — and then to strike fast for Billérasson, where he'd learnt from Lishet the foreign fugitives now were.

Those little birds would soon be in his hands.

* * *

Later that Monday morning Steve looked for Rog, and found him in the library. He and the tall, thin secretary went to a nearby café where they could talk.

"I've given it some thought, Rog, and I think we can sort out this Accord situation today."

Rog blinked. "Really? Just like that?"

"Yes, I think we can. Do we have a quorum for the meeting this afternoon?"

Rog nodded. "Eight. More than enough."

"Great. And in Accord's email, do they say what kind of meetings they're planning?"

"No. Only that their original venue has fallen through, and could we see our way, etcetera, etcetera. It's from Dave Bartlett, their Chairman."

Steve nodded. He knew Dave. "Okay."

They chatted a little longer until Rog had to leave for a lecture. Steve stayed on to have an early lunch — his uncertain meals over the weekend had left him with a hearty appetite, and he thoroughly enjoyed the novel taste of macaroni cheese, peas, and orange juice. He daydreamed of Perrely as he ate, imagining her winsome face as he'd last seen her up in the Dûrian mountains, wrapped up tightly against the cold. He silently shared with God the longing that filled him to see her again.

When he'd finished he went out in search of Dave Bartlett, the chairman of Accord. He eventually ran him down in one of the college common rooms. They had a useful chat.

Five o'clock came. Steve deliberately arrived at the committee room a couple of minutes late. When he entered there was a loud babble of argument around the long table in the centre. The hawks and the doves were at each other already.

"*Order!*" he bawled. In the sudden silence he took his seat at the head of the table. "Okay, guys, we have some issues to discuss. Shall we pray?" Taken by surprise, heads automatically bowed and eyes closed. He briefly asked the Creator God to guide their discussions. There was a pause as people waited for more, then they began looking up. Eyebrows were raised — maybe at the brevity, maybe at the lack of any hallowed clichés.

"Hey, Stevie, were you under the sunlamp last night? You're as brown as a jacket potato!" This from tall, aquiline Phil, who valued his tan.

"No, didn't I tell you? I won a holiday in the sun, all expenses paid. Now listen — I guess you all know why we're here."

Pete jumped in at once, the intense expression on his pale face even sharper than usual. "Yes, and let's have none of this ridiculous talk of agreeing to Accord's request. I think it's — "

Shiván raised a hand. "All in due course, Petey, all in due course. First I'd like to take the opportunity while we're all together to have a very quick discussion about those outreach meetings we were considering for the summer term."

There was an immediate outcry. Everyone wanted to deal with the main item on the agenda, the Accord request. Steve held his ground.

"Bear with me, okay? Just bear with me. This won't take long. We need to agree on the basics, that's all. We can appoint a subcommittee to work out the details."

Eventually they simmered down and sat with folded arms to humour him.

"Right. First of all, we've already agreed, I think, on the need for direct evangelism, with large public meetings in a central venue?"

There were some nods and a few half-hearted comments. No one wanted to waste time on this.

"A show of hands — all who agree?" Every hand went up.

"Good. So — we're talking about a week of meetings, right?"

"Oh, come on, Steve — that's normal! Why are we going over all this?"

"Just getting it straight, Phil, for the record." He glanced across at Rog, who as usual was rattling away on his laptop taking down the minutes. "Hands?" All hands rose. "Okay. Now, for a theme. We don't have to discuss this in detail now, but here's an idea — how about loneliness? Something a lot of people struggle with. With a slogan like, say, *Are Friends in Need A Dying Breed?* Could be a good lead-in to discuss deeper things."

Despite themselves the committee members warmed to the suggestion, and comments flashed to and fro before Steve applied closure.

"Okay, enough on that — the subcommittee can thrash it out. Last question — the speaker. Just a few quick suggestions, that's all."

Several names of prominent Christian speakers were mentioned. Steve cut any discussion short, insisting that Rog merely list possibilities for the subcommittee to consider. He himself suggested the well-known Christian celebrity, Larry Ormond. There were some doubtful faces, but most nodded, and Ormond was added to the list.

"Great! That covers it, I think — except for the subcommittee. Any volunteers?"

Phil and Jo raised their hands; and with a little persuasion Shelley was added.

"Right! Thanks, people. Now we come to the main reason for this meeting."

Someone muttered "At last!" and there were a few chuckles. Everyone sat up straighter. Pete jumped in again.

"I'd like to say straight off that Accord has no right — "

"Hold it, Petey. I want to ask someone in to address the committee."

Pete stopped, mouth still open.

"An outsider?" Phil asked, frowning.

"Yes." He walked to the door and said over his shoulder as he went out, "Dave Bartlett of Accord."

There was a babble of shocked comment as he went to fetch Dave from the next room, where he'd agreed to wait while Steve laid the groundwork.

Silence fell as he escorted Dave into the committee room; but Pete was red-faced, building up steam for a protest. Steve did some quick bud-nipping.

"Dave has agreed to come and put Accord's request in person, which I think is very decent of him. He's our guest, and whatever people may think—" he let his eyes rest on Pete "—let's hear him out courteously. Over to you, Dave." He motioned to his own chair, and took a seat some way down the table.

The Chairman of Accord was a solid, thickset man with short brown hair, a determined chin and a confident smile. He flashed it round the committee room now. "Thanks for allowing me into the lion's den, if you'll forgive the expression." His face sobered. "We all know Accord and the CU have had their differences. I'm sure many of you feel the faults are mainly ours, and many of our committee feel the opposite. But having said that, whose side are we all on? I think you'll agree we're all on Christ's side. There's something more important than our differences, and that's getting *his* work done. That's why I'm here this afternoon."

The hawks stared, stony-faced.

"Okay, now about these meetings. We've had them planned for a long time as an outreach initiative, and we've already been building up towards them in our small groups. Quite a few non-Christians are interested. We were going to meet in St. Botolphs Hall, but they've just discovered a major structural defect—cracks in one of the roof joists—and all public meetings have been cancelled. So we've got everything arranged, leaflets printed, speaker laid on, and nowhere to meet. We approached the university and the Students' Union, as well as nearby churches, but there's nothing big enough that's available every lunchtime for a week. That's why we've had to come to you. James Hall is the only possibility left. Believe me, we wouldn't dream of disrupting your regular meetings if this weren't absolutely our last hope. We're basically throwing ourselves on your mercy. If you can't help us, the fixture will have to be scratched."

He let his earnest gaze linger on the committee members, then turned to Steve. "Thank you." He stood to leave.

"Half a minute, Dave." The Accord chairman sat down again. "Can you tell us a little about these meetings? You said it was an outreach initiative. What sort of theme do you have? And who's your speaker?"

"Our theme is loneliness, with the slogan *Friends in Need: A Dying Breed?* I'm sure you're aware how many lonely people there are on campus, despite all the artificial 'friendship' and forced camaraderie. We want to bring this out into the open, as a stepping stone towards discussing deeper issues. Our small groups have been having discussions and socials on this theme already, and like I said, there's been an encouraging response from non-Christians.

"For our speaker we've managed to get Larry Ormond. He gave a talk in my home church last summer about how people think celebrities must feel on top of the world, surrounded by admiring fans — when actually they're some of the loneliest individuals around. He's a great speaker, very dynamic and convincing. It was quite something that we could book him for a week; but now — Anyway, I'd better leave you guys to your deliberations. Thanks again, and God bless."

He gave them his smile again, and walked to the door. Steve waved farewell and returned to the head of the table. There was total silence in the committee room.

It was tall Phil who broke it. "Why," he murmured, staring at the ceiling, "do I get the feeling I've been set up?"

Jo uttered a peal of laughter, which set off Rich and most of the committee. "Steve, that was brilliant," Jo gasped. "Talk about being blind-sided! There we were, agreeing to the theme, and the slogan, and the speaker — " She broke into laughter again.

" — which Accord were already using!" Rich finished. "How can we say we disapprove of them now? We *almost* planned exactly the same series of talks!"

Pete finally found his voice. "Just because we might have planned the same talks, doesn't mean we have to approve of Accord, or give them our booking!"

Steve sat back and watched the game play itself out. The hawks were fighting a losing battle, and they knew it. They wouldn't easily forgive him, but that was the price of leadership. Eventually he called for a vote, which the doves won by five to three. Accord would get their hall.

As they left the room, Phil gave him a measuring look. "Have you been studying Napoleon's Seven Secrets of Success, Steve? Where'd you learn a trick like that?"

"Oh, here and there, Phil. Here — and there."

* * *

Shiván felt a great weight lifting from his shoulders as he walked down the road to his shared house. He'd listened to God, and he hadn't misheard him. He *could* still lead. Even through the pain.

God would send him back to Dûrion soon, he knew that. His time there wasn't over. And probably, as with his arrival here, his return would take him back to the moment he had left. That seemed to be the way his father handled these things—so there were no awkward absences on either world. That was okay by him, except... he'd be right back in the situation where Perrely had just rejected him. How would he deal with that? She'd been so certain... He'd have a long talk with her, helping her to see—

No. I will show her when the time is right.

But Lord, surely if I just—

Trust me.

Yes, Father.

_____

Chapter 10: *Decoy*

A CALL OF NATURE woke Shiván in the early hours. He sat up — and immediately began wobbling to and fro alarmingly. His arms flailed about, trying to grab on to something, and then with a loud cry he landed on the hard wooden floor. And burst out laughing.

"What is… happening?" Gil demanded jerkily from the corner.

"Hero," Shîr said peevishly, "has no one told you falling out of a hammock is *not funny?*"

"He's a man without honour," Câr declared. "He wakes the whole lodge and then laughs at us."

"No, no," Shiván gasped. "Not laughing at you — at me. I'm so happy to fall out of a Dûrian hammock!"

In the dim, pre-dawn light Shiván saw Shîr and Câr exchange a glance and shake their heads. "Perhaps we can throw you out of the window," Câr said. "Then you'll be even happier."

"Everyone, shut… up!" Gil said grumpily. "Get back to… sleep."

Later at the dawnmeal Shiván saw Perrely sitting alone on one of the logs surrounding the communal fire. He went and joined her. She looked up at him, and his heart lurched at both the beauty and the pain in her face. Dark shadows underlined her red-rimmed eyes. He ached to stroke her cheek and take her in his arms.

"Shiván… This is hard enough without you… staring at me!" She drew a tortured breath and turned away from him.

"Can we still be… friends?" he asked gently.

She looked at him again, then turned her eyes down to the untouched plate of gruel in her hands. "Yes, of course. It's just that… right now…" Her voice trailed off and she bent forward over the plate, her shoulders shaking.

Shiván longed to say more, to urge her to rethink — and re-pray — her decision; but his instructions were otherwise. His heart breaking for her, he rested a hand for a moment on her shoulder before slowly standing up and walking off to join Shîr and Câr.

* * *

A couple of days later in Billérasson Danîsha woke, as usual, before dawn. She'd trained herself to do that here in Dûrion, where she missed her little bedside alarm clock. She manoeuvred herself out of her comfortable Galeronden hammock and wrapped herself warmly in several layers. She still gasped, though, when the cold air hit her on the front doorstep. It was dark, with just a faint glimmer of light to the east; but she knew the way well enough.

Carrying the bellaril, she walked through the settlement and forest to the spot she'd found on a hillside overlooking the track to Galeron. She made herself comfortable on the carpet of dry pine needles and laid the bellaril beside her. When the sun came up there would be a glorious view over western Dûrion that she never tired of. This was her private place, where she could worship the One who had made it all.

Today was Anderil, so there would be a hearthtime later. But first she needed space to be alone with God herself. In the pocket of her robe her fingers stroked the handle of Teynel's comb as she quieted her mind.

She thought about God's greatness, displayed so graphically in the majestic mountains and deep silence all around her. He was the Alpha and the Omega, the beginning and the end. He had created everything: that included *all* worlds. He had brought her into Dûrion, and he knew what he was doing. He had his own plans for her — plans to help and not to harm her; plans to give her hope, and a future. And not just for her own benefit: she was God's workmanship, created to do good deeds which *he* had prepared in advance for her. It was such a comfort to know that the Creator of the universe had a path laid down for her to follow, good deeds prepared that only she could do. She thanked him, then rejoiced silently in the awareness of his enfolding love.

Her thoughts turned to the others in their group. Dear Gil, constantly improving. He could do just about everything for himself now. She asked her father, the One Creator God, to take care of him. The One had made Gil. He could heal him — and even more importantly, bring him out of his darkness into the light of new life.

Then Jomel came to mind. She shook her head. That girl was really asking for trouble. Somehow she seemed quite unaware, despite many warnings, of how provocative her behaviour was toward the twins. She asked God to enable her to understand.

Then there were dear Shiván and Perrely. How her heart ached for those two. There was sorrow in Shivvie's eyes whenever he looked at Perrely, and the girl seemed desperately unhappy. It was clearly more than a lovers' tiff, and she wished she knew what the trouble was. She'd invited Perrely to talk about it, but she'd shaken her head, her eyes filling with tears. Well, their heavenly Father knew. She asked him to help them sort it out.

Ah, the sun was rising at last in its full splendour! The golden morning light flooded across Dûrion. What a joy this season they called 'Goldshine' was—and how appropriately named. The forests glowed a rich, velvety green, and distant Lake Stillárre was a glistening aquamarine jewel on the bosom of the land. The first birds began to twitter. Her heart full of praise, she lifted the bellaril—but then the full dawn chorus broke out, and she revelled in the song of birds and the murmur of human voices.

Human voices?

With a shock she realised that was exactly what she was hearing, mingled with the birdsong. Subdued, but clear—and not far off. She put down the bellaril, frowning. Who was out here at this time of the morning? The inhabitants of Billérasson, those who were up, would be busy with their morning chores.

She peered through the trees toward the track from Galeron down below. Yes! Just there, a group of people was standing. She moved to get a better view, and clapped a hand over her mouth to stifle a gasp. They were wearing green capes with a silver edging—Dûrian infantry officers! Now she heard other sounds, further away—the soft crunch of boots approaching, the creak of leather, the muted noises of a large column of soldiers moving up as quietly as they could.

"We'll strike as soon as everyone's assembled. Beldior, you will secure the perimeter. Not a man, woman or child is to escape, you understand? Tarragon, search the houses for any trying to hide. Haldet—"

She didn't wait for more. *Dear God, help me!* She scrambled to her feet as quietly as she could and picked up the bellaril. No point using it against these soldiers, of course: the bellaril had no effect on non-mindbent troops. She'd learnt that in the Stillárre market square when she'd played it and been arrested by a similar troop in infantry green. Escape was the only option: she had to warn the others at once!

She hurried along the ridge above the track, thanking God for the trees that hid her and the springy layer of pine needles that deadened her footsteps. The ridge path rejoined the Galeron track. There was no sound of movement behind her—but for how long? She came to the outskirts of the settlement and started to run.

She reached the men's lodge and burst in. Shiván was sitting in a chair with a faraway look, nursing a cup of *benoriss*, the Galeron-den version of chass.

"Shiván! Everyone!" she gasped. "Wake up!"

Shiván jumped to his feet, spilling his drink. "What is it, 'Neesh?"

"I saw soldiers!" she panted. "They're coming—ordinary troopers, not Guards! We must warn Darinor—" As she struggled to describe what she'd seen, the doors of the sleeping quarters opened and Shîr, Câr and Gil appeared, questions on their faces and lips.

Shiván wasted no time. "Quick! The Bishop's troops are here. We have to escape. The bellaril won't help, because they're not mind-bent. Get dressed, and we'll call the rest of the women. And warn Darinor." Shiván grabbed the Blade on the mantelpiece and began strapping it on.

On the point of dashing back to dress, Shîr turned. "Where will we go?"

"Probably the next settlement—Thammeron. We'll see what Darinor says. Hurry!"

They all pulled on their coats and slung their travel pouches over their shoulders before hurrying off to the women's lodge on the other side of the settlement. A rich military oath escaped Fira when she heard the news, while Jomel uttered an earthy exclamation that sent Lightist eyebrows shooting up. The women dressed quickly, and in a few moments they were all heading for Darinor's lodge near the dining circle.

They found the refugee leader already up. Without preliminaries Shiván said, "Shambor's soldiers are here. Danîsha's seen them—they may arrive any moment."

Darinor stood and strode towards them at the door, his face settling into grim lines. "Then we evacuate. Your group can accompany the able-bodied to Thammeron. Our young, old and infirm will use the hidden refuges nearby. Help me rouse the settlement!"

* * *

Perrely's heart was in her mouth as they hurried out of the lodge after Darinor. They reached the dining circle, where Danîsha waited with Gelmion while the rest of them scattered through the settlement to rouse the lodges. In a few moments the place was in an uproar, with people running in every direction collecting children and belongings. Darinor posted a lookout on a hill overlooking the Galeron track.

Before long Shiván and the others returned, and they all clustered together in the centre of the dining circle.

"Brindion!" Darinor shouted. A tough-looking man with a pock-marked face and prominent hooked nose came over. "Gather all the able-bodied folk here and lead them to Thammeron. Tell them they may need to continue on to Carnem if Thammeron also evacuates." His eyes strayed to the Restorers' group. "Farewell, and the Prince be with you! " He strode off.

Perrely looked at Shiván. He was staring into the middle distance with narrowed eyes. What was he thinking? They'd hardly spoken since the morning after she'd told him they could never be betrothed. She missed him desperately. There was a cold emptiness inside that his warmth had once filled. So often now she cried herself to sleep. She had moments of terrible doubt, when she wondered if she'd thrown away a lifetime's happiness for a misguided ideal. Yet... At other times she felt a strong conviction that she'd chosen to be with the Prince, and he would never leave her or forsake her. Was that her own imagination? She just didn't know.

Small groups of residents started coming into the dining circle and were gathered together by Brindion. Hillet and Delmior arrived with their older children, and struck up a low-voiced conversation with Shîr and Câr. Fira broke in abruptly. "Troopers, come with me! This evacuation is taking too long. We need to get people going." She set off towards the nearest lodges. The twins muttered apologies and hurried after her.

"Fira—wait!" Shiván called. She stopped and stared at him. "Come back! I have a different idea."

"Shiván, you're wasting time! You heard Darinor—we must get the able-bodied to Thammeron as soon as possible!"

"Just a moment! I need a brief word with Hillet here..."

Muttering under her breath Fira returned, the twins trailing after her. Shiván took Hillet aside a short distance and spoke to him in a low voice. Hillet uttered an exclamation and stared at Shiván wide-eyed. They talked a bit more, and he calmed down. A wide grin appeared on his cheerful face. Perrely stared, intrigued.

Suddenly there was a drumming of footsteps, and they all leapt up. The lookout charged into the hearth area, followed by a crowd of residents. "They're coming!" he panted. "Over a hundred and fifty armed soldiers. They'll be here any moment!"

"Follow me!" Brindion shouted, and turned to set off in a north-easterly direction towards Thammeron. But Shiván yelled at the top of his voice, "*WAIT!*"

They all froze. "If the soldiers follow you to Thammeron, you'll bring trouble there." He swept out the Blade of Darthane and held it aloft. "*Anyone who can run, stay with me!* We'll lead them a different way, to allow the rest to escape!"

Doubtful glances were exchanged. "To Thammeron! Darinor's orders!" Brindion roared. "Shiván, this is madness!" Fira barked. But a young refugee man stepped up to Shiván. "I'm with you!" There were cries of agreement, and over a dozen more joined them. Perrely's heart filled with pride.

"To Thammeron!" Brindion bellowed, and set off at a trot. The majority followed.

"Shiván, we need to *go* with them!" Fira exclaimed, her face thunderous.

"Gil, Danîsha, Jomel, Alanya—you go." Shiván commanded. "Fira, you, Shîr and Câr stay with me. *Don't argue!*"

Jomel quickly embraced Perrely before hurrying off after Brindion's crowd with the other three. They soon disappeared among the trees. Fira's eyes shot flame and her lips tightened to a thin line—but she stayed. Shîr and Câr stared at Shiván with a new respect. Perrely almost laughed. She glanced round, and was thrilled to see that their group numbered over twenty.

"What now, Hero?" Shîrin wanted to know.

"Now we get ready to run. Those soldiers will be tired—but we're rested. The instant we're sure they've seen us, we'll be off. Cârin and Perrely, I'd like you in the lead with me and Hillet. Fira, Shîr and Delmior, will you be our rearguard?" They nodded. "I hope you know what you're doing," Fira muttered, her eyes still burning.

"Which way will we go?" one of the new arrivals asked.

Shiván hesitated a moment. "We'll dash about a bit, get them confused. Just follow me."

The man frowned. "But how will we escape?"

"Don't you worry about that," Hillet said. "Shiván knows what he's doing." There were murmurs of agreement. The questioner nodded, and was silent.

Perrely smiled at Shiván. His face brightened for a moment, then he turned away.

At that moment everyone heard the rumble of approaching boots.

"Don't move till I give the signal!"

The first of the green-caped figures appeared on the Galeron track where it approached the central hearth, about two hundred strides away. Everyone round Shiván stood poised to flee. Other infantrymen became visible, moving at a weary jog.

Suddenly Shiván leapt towards them, brandishing the Blade of Darthane. The gleaming metal flashed in the sun. "*I am Shiván* Aténnelor, *Overguardian of Dûrion! You will never capture me!*"

The Billérasson refugees gaped at him. There was a scattered uproar from the soldiers, who stumbled to a halt, milling about in confusion. "*Run!*" Shiván yelled. He dashed off with Hillet between the lodges to the south-east, away from the Thammeron track. The others sprinted after him. Behind they could hear shouts and the thunder of boots as the green-coats took up the pursuit. *Dear Prince, bring us through this!* Perrely prayed.

At first they had little trouble keeping ahead of the soldiers. But once they'd left the settlement, the going became more difficult. The path wound between trees and boulders. The troops began to gain on them.

"We must — branch off soon," Cârin panted. "Otherwise we'll reach the — old road. Can't run — on that."

"Have to," Shiván said.

Cârin turned to him, disbelief on his face. "Shiván, you're not—!"

"I am."

"But that's— that's not— that's brilliant!"

"Thanks."

"If we can — make it. How do we—"

"The hill."

"Right!"

The disjointed conversation washed over Perrely. She needed all her attention for running. Something about it bothered her, though.

A clash of swords broke out behind them. Her heart sank. *Father, help Fira, Shîr and Delmior!* Everyone redoubled their speed. The sword-strokes stopped.

Then they suddenly broke out on to a crumbling stretch of stone paving. The 'old road'! How had Cârin and Shiván known about it?

"*Hurry!*" Fira's voice from behind.

"*Watch your footing!*" Hillet shouted. They sprinted up the overgrown carriageway, dodging bushes. Perrely's leg suddenly went down into a pothole, and she crashed to the ground. By the One's gift nothing was broken. Hands helped her up and she ran on. There was a yell from behind. Someone else had fallen. Distant cries arose from their pursuers. The road would also slow them down, thank the One.

The crazy trip to see the Grûzhack fortress! That must be how Cârin and Shiván knew about this road—and why Hillet had led them here. Then— *Oh, no! Oh, dear Prince, no!* Did Shiván realise what he was *doing*?

A thickly-wooded hill rose up beside the road. They rounded a bend. Ahead was a brighter light where the forest ended. The road ran on into the sunshine, but Shiván blocked the way. He was directing everyone up the hill. He grinned at her as she scuttled under the low-hanging branches. The others were hurrying on over the soft carpet of pine needles. She waited, crouching behind a tree where she could see Shiván.

"*Go, Shiván!*" It was Fira, calling out in an intense undertone from some distance away. "Don't wait! They're close behind!"

More people scrabbled frantically past under the branches. Shiván trotted back the way they'd come. Perrely craned her neck till she could see him slipping an arm under Shîr's shoulder. Fira was supporting him on the other side. The left side of his tunic was soaked in blood, and he was a bad colour. She dashed out and helped them pull him under the overhanging branches.

They were only just in time. Moments later running boots crashed by, and they waited, huddled under the pine foliage, until all their pursuers had passed.

"You go on up, Shiván," Fira whispered. "I'll stay with Shîrin."

He hesitated, then took Perrely's hand. She smiled uncertainly, but went with him. They climbed halfway up the wooded hill to where the others were sitting on the ground catching their breath.

A volley of muted thanks and questions met Shiván. He raised an open palm for silence.

"We don't know if it's worked yet. You may hear some strange sounds. Don't be afraid. Just wait here."

She was sure she must look as puzzled everyone else, but he beckoned, and she followed him a short distance. He held a low branch aside for her, and said "Crawl through. Be very quiet, keep low, and stay absolutely still." There was an open ledge beyond. Hillet and Cârin were squatting a little way along it. She crawled towards them, and turned to face the valley. Shiván followed.

Below them faint voices could be heard. She peered over the edge, and saw small figures in green capes milling about between the main forest and smaller patches of woodland scattered along the base of the hill.

"They're trying to find where we've got to," Cârin murmured with satisfaction.

"But what if they look up!" she gasped.

"They'll have other things to worry about soon," Shiván said softly. "Look at the cliff opposite. I don't think they've seen it yet."

She raised her eyes and saw the fortress built into the stark rock face. Figures were hurrying to and fro on the parapets. Groups were clustered about the strange dark circles that appeared at intervals. She felt a shiver of fear at the alien sight.

"They'll be making a charge soon," Cârin said. "That'll wake the Bishop's boys up!"

"No, something else will happen first. Get ready for a loud noise! Lie flat!" He pressed a hand on Perrely's back.

Hillet quickly flattened himself, but Cârin gave Shiván an exasperated look. "You know, sometimes you talk the most amazing —"

His words were cut off by the loudest bang Perrely had ever heard. They all leapt in shock, and Cârin tumbled forward, his hands saving him at the very edge.

" — sense!" he yelped.

With the explosion had come a burst of flame from one of the round holes in the Grûzhack fort, followed by a brief whistling noise. Soil and stones erupted from the ground on the old road between the green-coats and the forest. Several soldiers fell down, and there were yells of terror. They began stampeding the opposite way.

BANG!

Perrely's body jerked again, even lying flat. Another of the round holes spat flame. This time destruction fell in the midst of the leading wave of fleeing soldiers. In a chaos of screams and shouts they surged back the other way, leaving a pile of heaving and groaning comrades.

Then all the other holes in the fort began erupting. Green-coats were screaming and falling everywhere. Perrely could hardly believe her eyes. This was a horror beyond her imagining. And Shiván said they had such weapons under *his* sky? A haze of blue smoke hung over the valley, and through it she saw scattered survivors scampering for their lives back into the forest.

"They won't get away," Cârin said grimly. "Look."

He pointed to the east, where a road from the fort met the old forest road. A column of soldiers in teal-coloured tunics was jogging down into the valley, each with a short metal lance protruding above his left shoulder. Even at this distance, Perrely could see that they were bigger than Dûrians. They were all slightly hunched over, as though their backs were bent. They had black hair down to their shoulders, and their skin was unnaturally pale. What was it Darinor had said? 'Faces like Gadesh'. She had no desire for a closer look.

"This is where we get off the ledge," Shiván said.

She was only too happy to comply.

Chapter 11: *Catastrophe*

SHAMBOR WAS FUMING. Those fools had gone haring off after Shiván before he could get Lishet to stop them. It should have been obvious to a one-eyed *grûn* that this was a decoy. That theatrical challenge, flourishing the sword! The other alleged Restorers had escaped with the rest of the inhabitants—and that lump of a Lieutenant had left barely enough men behind to garrison the village, let alone send out search parties! They were forty men short already after leaving a garrison in Galeron. The local inhabitants had disappeared into the surrounding mountains, and he was happy to leave them there.

He strode up and down the thick maroon floor-cover, hands clasping and unclasping behind his back. He was oblivious of the plush leather recliners or the inlaid occasional tables in the apartment Mindbender Jastor had given him. The opulent midmeal that had been sent up had turned to ashes in his mouth. If those incompetents let the Restorers slip through his fingers *again*, he'd hunt every last one of them down and make them die slowly.

If only he'd been able to send the Guards! There would have been no mess-up like this if he'd been inside the commander's mind. As it was, he couldn't even see what was happening on the chase, because that pathetic idiot Lishet was too worn out physically and emotionally to go with them. He'd pushed him to the limit to keep up with the hardened troops. Now all he could do was lie weeping on a bed. Shambor had a magnificent, tear-streaked view of the inside of a thatched roof.

Soon even that disappeared as the exhausted man fell asleep. Let him recover his strength. As soon as those fools returned with Shiván he'd send them off after the other foreigners, and he wanted Lishet's eyes and ears with them.

He poured himself a goblet of mulled wine and settled down on one of the recliners. He always tried to avoid idleness, because of the unwanted thoughts that arose. But now he had no choice. He didn't dare get involved in other things at this critical juncture.

Time went by. The darkness gathered in him. He looked around the luxurious apartment. He had to find *something*. There! A small decoration—a stuffed bird in flight. He fetched it from its shelf on the wall. It was a *galénne*. The body was about three finger-widths long, each wing a hand's breadth. The iridescent feathers shimmered in the light. It was skilfully mounted on a narrow rod rising from a wooden base, which from a distance one hardly noticed. With wings extended and head streamlined in a downward swoop, it looked exquisitely real.

He wrenched the bird from its stand. Cradling the body between his fingers, he ripped one wing off. Then the other. His lips were compressed and his eyes hard. He tried to twist the head off, but the dry, preserved body was too fragile. It collapsed under his hands, falling to the floor in a litter of feathers, tiny bones, and crumbled stuffing. He picked up the wings, and with violent movements ripped the feathers off.

He sank back on the recliner. *I have power,* he declared to himself. *I am stronger than all who oppose me. I will seize these Restorers and crush them!*

As always, a reply from the distant past echoed faintly in his mind: *Not by power, nor by strength, but by the One's Light.*

"No!" he exclaimed aloud. "That's empty Lightist claptrap!" A picture rose before him. Himself at a tender age, looking up proudly from a dead bird at his feet. Horror spreading across Mama's face. "*No, Gari!* That's not being strong, that's being cruel and… horrible!" It was like a slap in the face. Then Mama taking him on her lap. The long explanation, ending with those dread words quoted from the Lightist scriptures: "Garion, *we* do things *'not* by power, *nor* by strength, but by the One's Light.'"

Arrant nonsense. A feeble excuse made by those who had no power. What supernatural abilities did those pathetic Lightists ever display? Could *they* control another's mind? Could *they* speak to one another over a distance? Could they even do such trivial things as raise winds, control animals, or arouse love in another? Of course not.

Well, the Restorers had powers, of a sort. But theirs were channelled through those instruments — and they were limited. Pit them against non-mindbent troops, and they were as helpless as unarmed civilians. That had been proved this morning, when they'd fled instead of fighting. But once he got hold of their instruments, he could find out how they worked and use them himself. They might secure his position as the Strongholder's Second. Certain rivals could be seriously inconvenienced... He smiled as his mind ranged over the possibilities.

No, Mama, you were wrong. The One's Light never gave anyone power. Power is something you take for yourself.

He'd done so. As a schoolboy in early puberty he had discovered real power and seized it. Then Mama had found out. She'd tried to stop him, and— He groaned and clasped his hands over his eyes to blot out the picture. Fire, darkness and despair. The end of his Dûrian childhood.

A distant shouting disturbed his morbid thoughts. He sat up, disoriented. Was there trouble in the Guardhouse? No, this was what Lishet was hearing, up in that mountain village. He focused on the sleeper, saw him struggle groggily to his feet and stumble out of the lodge.

Figures were pelting towards them, covered in dirt and grime. Tattered capes still hung from some shoulders. *Great Gadesh!* Were these the troops who'd set out after Shiván?

"Run!" they were yelling to their comrades guarding the settlement. *"The magicians are coming! Run for your lives!"*

Magicians?

Lishet turned and broke into an ungainly sprint to catch up with the rest of the garrison. "What happened?" Shambor made him shout. "Shut up and run!" was the reply.

In fury Shambor had Lishet scream, *"Stop, at the Bishop's command!"* They kept on running.

Gesh! What in the dark god's name had Shiván *done* to them? He sat transfixed on the recliner. This was a disaster.

The whole company was sprinting out of the village back along the track to Galeron. Through Lishet he managed to do a rough count. *Heyss!* Of the hundred and sixty he'd sent to Billérasson, only about forty remained. Shiván had wiped out three quarters of his force? *That was unthinkable.* 'Magicians'. Had he found some new instrument?

Dire predictions from childhood echoed in his mind. *The Restorers will rebuild the Way of the One. They will come in his power. None can stop them.*

Nonsense! Mumbo-jumbo. Nothing more.

The tattered soldiers were running like men possessed. Something had terrified them to the very bone. Lishet could never have kept up if Shambor hadn't released every last drop of energy in his body.

"*They're coming!*" It was an agonised shriek.

Lishet glanced back. On a crest behind, large figures in teal-coloured tunics had appeared. In rapid, co-ordinated motion they knelt down and pointed sticks at them. What in all —

Crack! Crack-crack!

The sticks spat flame. A sharp pain seared Lishet's leg. He and Shambor yelped in unison. Lishet crashed to the ground. There were screams as others fell. Lishet stared in disbelief at a gaping hole in the back of his right thigh. He tried to stand and howled in agony. He fell back and gibbered with terror as the teal-coated soldiers slung the sticks over their shoulders and came loping down the track towards them. They drew short swords as they ran.

Shambor's mind was in turmoil. These huge warriors were not Shiván's! He registered a maelstrom of fleeting impressions: hunched backs, long hair, deathly white skin; thick, corded legs; heavily-ridged faces, piercing black eyes under down-slanted lids; lips drawn back in a feral snarl…

GRÛZHACK!

No. Oh no. Great Gadesh, no. Those imbeciles, those blithering idiots, had stirred up the Grûzhack!

Lishet soiled himself as one of the hulking brutes loomed over him. "*Nist!*" he screamed. A sword flashed and swept down. Shambor cried out at the sudden agony. Then everything was dark.

He lay stunned on the recliner, trying to grasp the magnitude of this catastrophe.

"Your Dominance! Are you all right?"

Mindbender Jastor was bending over him.

"Yes. Yes, I'm fine." His voice sounded weak in his own ears. He sat up and said firmly, "A touch of indigestion, Jastor. I'll be all right." He waved the man away.

As soon as the door had shut he buried his head in his hands. Forget any hopes of becoming the Strongholder's Second. He'd provoked the Grûzhack. He might even have started a war. Whatever happened, he'd jeopardised the precious teméyn supply — not only for himself, but also for the Strongholder and all the other Mindrulers.

The thought that the Grûzhack must also have slaughtered Shiván and his would-be Restorers was cold comfort.

* * *

Shiván and those with him had had rather a dismal time since the battle yesterday noon. The initial euphoria had quickly worn off, and boredom had set in. They had nothing to do but wait. The men took turns keeping watch on the hillside ledge—but there had been no sign of the Grûzhack column returning. They hadn't dared go back to Billérasson until they knew the coast was clear.

But now they couldn't wait any longer. They moved cautiously through the forest towards the settlement. Shiván's head snapped round as a twig cracked. This was dangerous—but they had to find out. Somewhere in front of them Cârin and Gromon, one of the refugees with woodland skill, were scouting the way ahead.

Everyone had speculated anxiously about what might have happened. Fira—after what for her was a handsome apology for doubting Shiván earlier—had declared categorically that the Grûzhack would chase the Bishop's men all the way back to Galeron if necessary—and leave garrisons both there and in Billérasson in case of further attacks. The anxious refugees had thrown up every counter-argument they could think of. Tempers had become frayed.

They'd had a cold, supperless night huddling together under the trees, covering themselves with dry pine needles. Several were coughing this morning, and Shîr's colour was not good. He'd taken a heavy sword stroke to his left thigh. They'd bound it up as best they could with strips torn from people's tunics. He was managing to hobble along now with a couple of the refugees supporting him; but his face was pale and beaded with sweat. He'd need to rest soon.

The Grûzhack troops had finally returned to the fort around mid-morning. That should have been good news—except that there were too few of them. They'd counted over a hundred setting out yesterday; only twenty-four had come back. That supported Fira's prediction. There was gloom and despondency in the refugee ranks. They had to find out for sure. In any case, they needed to pass Billérasson to reach to the next settlement, Thammeron, where Lannie, Gil, 'Neesh and Jomel were—hoping it hadn't also been captured. Shiván didn't want to think about that. He walked warily on, placing his feet with care.

There was a sudden rustling of bushes, and Cârin appeared with Gromon. They were both out of breath. Shiván held up a hand, and everyone halted.

Câr spoke the words they'd all been dreading: "The Grûzhack are guarding Billérasson." A soft moan of despair rippled down the line. "We saw 'bout fifteen," Gromon added. "But there may have been more." He was a tall, gangly man with fair hair and close-set blue eyes.

"Then where can we go?" someone asked with a tinge of hysteria. "The track to Thammeron runs through Billérasson!"

"We must find another way," Fira declared.

"Okay, let's all sit down." Shiván motioned them to an open space between the trees. He took a seat on a rock where he could keep an eye on everyone. Perrely was staring at him anxiously. "Hillet and Delmior, will you keep watch, please." The two men nodded and moved out.

"Now—let's consider our options. Could any of you from Billérasson get us to the Thammeron track by a roundabout route?"

A medley of replies was followed by discussion and argument. The upshot was that there was no easy shortcut. Just outside Billérasson the Thammeron track crossed a ravine. There was a rope bridge. As Fira pointed out, the Grûzhack would probably have found that and be guarding it—or they'd have destroyed it. As the ravine ran way up into the mountains, there was no quick way round it.

Still, it was their best hope. There was just a chance the Grûzhack might not have gone far enough to find the bridge—though Fira shook her head over that. But they had to try for it.

They set off, slowly and warily, following Cârin and Gromon as they skirted the settlement along faint paths through the forest.

* * *

Shiván was at his wits' end. They'd been struggling all afternoon to reach the Thammeron track, without success. The rope bridge over the ravine had been guarded by the Grûzhack, as Fira had predicted. Cârin and Gromon had reported seeing a dead Galeronden on the Thammeron side, with a bloodstained hole in his back.

They'd tried another route that one of the locals thought he knew—but it had petered out. For the last couple of hours they'd been following the ravine up into the mountains—hoping against hope for a fallen tree or some other way of crossing. No such miracle, and the ravine only seemed to get wider, with a small river rustling at the bottom. He stopped beside a large rock.

"What now, Hero?"

Shiván ground his teeth. He knew Cârin wasn't mocking him, but that was how it felt. He was no hero. He just did his best, like anyone else. Sometimes his best wasn't good enough — but God knew that. Only that experience with the CU back in England had kept him going this far.

"Time to pray," he said.

They all crowded round and raised both hands in the Dûrian attitude of prayer. "Creator God, help us," Shiván said. "You know we're lost, and Shîrin is injured. Please help us across this ravine."

Others echoed his prayer. Perrely asked healing for Shîr. In jerky sentences Fira committed their loved ones to the Prince's protection. Then someone started softly singing a well-known worship song — and Shiván felt his spirits lift as the clear Dûrian voices joined in muted harmony, declaring their love to the Creator of the universe who had sent his son to die for them.

Then he heard a voice from the sky.

Chapter 12: *Voice from the sky*

THE CHILD WAS YANKED ABRUPTLY out of the water barrel. He took a deep gasp of air, coughed and spluttered, then began screaming. After a few moments he felt himself once more being thrust down into the barrel. *No! Not again! I'll be good! I'll never cry or make a fuss again...*

The icy water closed over him and terror flooded his senses. He struggled frantically, but an iron hand was gripping the harness on his back. He opened his mouth to scream, and choked as the water rushed in. Just as he thought he must be dead he was hauled to the surface again.

A third time. Now a dull despair seeped through his mind. His mouth opened, water filled it, and as his body thrashed he resigned himself to death. Almost at once he was jerked up into the air.

"... no good," he heard his mentor Faranu mutter angrily to the strong man holding him. Tears joined the water trickling down his face. He knew he was no good. He'd never be good enough. He'd killed his Ammi and Baaba, and must suffer forever.

"Oh, my poor child!" A large, motherly woman enfolded his wet, shivering body in a thick cloth and took him from the strongman. "Nanny will look after you now. That horrible man, trying to *drown* you! We'll get you dressed warmly, then you'll be just fine."

She took him to his cell and pulled two layers of clothing on him. Then she held him close and began rocking him gently as she crooned a soothing lullaby. It felt so good to be held again. Olôra hadn't come back, but now Nanny was here. He relaxed in her arms.

As he lay there he heard Faranu as from a distance: "... and now the reverse. But never in a field situation, you understand. The timing is crucial." He didn't understand. But it didn't matter. He was warm and cared-for. Until next time.

* * *

Many leagues to the north — far beyond Dûrion and the surrounding lands — dark green *khargiz* trees stretched unending across the hills and valleys in every direction. Their soft needles absorbed sound, and the deep, peaceful silence was broken only by the chatter of small streams and occasional birdcalls.

Some might have found this country desolate: yet the traveller's heart rejoiced as he ran steadily on. He knew every tree, every rock, every hillside: they bore the welcome scent of home. For two hands-full and four sunrises he had been travelling, and in just a few more he would be there. The thought of his own fragrant Hishray — wife, lover, friend — filled him with joy. And his little ones! He repeated their names for the sheer delight of them: Hreldaz, Gishrin, Sykhar, Khelris, and tiny, wriggling Barkhim.

But beyond the joy lay a sadness and an excitement. A sadness, because he would not long enjoy the heart-light of home. Only three hands-full of days, perhaps, then he would have to leave again. But an excitement, because he — Gwargif — had found the Warriors of Light that the priests had smelt! They had told *Bankhez*, Eldest of the people, that they scented the arrival of the long-promised Lightwarriors far in the south. The time has come, they declared, for the People of Light to go to war for the Shining One. The *Hrarkhoneyl* — the Great Legion — should be mustered! Every warrior of every clan — more than ten hundred-hands! — must run south to fight for the Warriors of Light.

Bankhez had been doubtful. He had sent Gwargif and two other warrior leaders all the way to the land of Doorin to sniff out these Lightwarriors. Many of the Clan Fathers felt they were following a dead trail. But there, amid deep darkness, he had found *Mylendel*, Warrior of Song! And later he'd met *Hrarborgh*, Father of Warriors, *Karkhendel*, Warrior of Hearing, and *Sheyrendel*, the Prayer Warrior. He'd smelt their light, and knew they were sent by the Shining One. What a thrill it would be to bring this news to Bankhez and the Clan Fathers' Council! He had no doubt that, at the priests' urging, they would muster the *Hrarkhoneyl* at once, despite the lateness of the year. The darkness he had smelt in Doorin could not be allowed to spread further.

His grey-white, wolf-like form flowed smoothly over the carpet of needles as he ran tirelessly on. In the hills ahead, he knew, was another of his people's supply caches, where he'd find preserved meat and dry tubers, along with fireclay and firesticks. He was looking forward to a hot meal.

His thoughts turned affectionately to Mylendel, the Warrior of Song. When her fingers ran over those golden strings, she made music from the Shining Place that set the heart alight. During their short time together they had truly become a pack-pair. She had befriended him, and he had protected her during the black days when her friends were killed. He wondered how she was managing without him. She'd been so slow to accept that she was a Warrior of Light! That had come as a surprise. She—and the others— had much to learn. No need to mention that to the clan fathers. The Prince of Light himself would train them, of that he had no doubt. One day soon they would summon the People of Light to fight for them, and Gwargif would be with the Great Legion when it responded.

But now, Hishray was waiting. He lengthened his pace.

* * *

"Shiván!"

In the hills above Billérasson Shiván looked up, startled. Who was calling him? He glanced all around—even up. Answer to prayer? Voice from heaven?

The others in their tired, bedraggled group stared at him. "What's the matter, Hero?" Cârin wanted to know. "Been stung by a fly?"

Then it came again. *"Shiván, can you hear me?"*

Alanya! She'd found them with the bess!

"Yes, Lannie, I can hear you."

"A fly that talks Inglish," Câr remarked.

"It's Alanya."

"Alanya's a fly?"

"Lannie, where are you?"

"In Thammeron. Where are you?"

"You're using your shell—the bess?"

"Of course, idiot."

Perrely caught on. "Alanya's talking to him through the instrument the One gave her—the bess!"

"Then she has the voice of a fly. I can't hear a thing."

"Hush! Don't distract him."

"Ah—Alanya's bess has found us. That's good," Fira commented, her intense gaze riveted on Shiván.

"Where are *you, Shiván?"*

"Somewhere near Billérasson. We've been trying to get to you, but the Grûzhack are guarding the bridge, so we can't cross the ravine."

"The Grûzhack*...? Never mind, tell me later. Praise God you're alive! I'll see if I can find – ... Gil, can you call one of the Galeronden? We need help to guide Shiván...* Her voice faded.*"

"Alanya is finding someone in Thammeron who can tell us how to get there."

There were some exclamations of relief, against a background buzz of confusion over the one-sided conversation.

Lannie came back on the line. *"Gil's looking for one of their foragers who really knows the mountains well. 'Neesh sends her love. Are you all okay? What happened to Shambor's men? How have the Grûzhack got involved?"*

Shiván filled her in. It felt weird talking into thin air with no phone in his hand. Then Lannie began having interruptions.

"What? Yes, I'm talking to Shiván, our leader. How? With this shell. No, he's not in the shell, you silly man... He's near Billérasson. They can't – ... No. No! ... STOP LAUGHING AND LISTEN!!"

"Ouch!" Shiván clasped his ears.

Cârin sucked in his breath. "Flies like Alanya pack quite a sting."

After a few minutes' silence Lannie's voice came again, sounding weary but determined. *"Right. These fools have all had their little laugh, now they say they'll humour me. If you describe things you see around you that they would know but we wouldn't, they may even believe I'm not making it up. So fire away."*

A complicated exchange followed in which Shiván described their surroundings as best he could, and Lannie relayed his words to the Galeronden.

"Okay. Their eyes are wide and they're jabbering away at each other. They've recognised the place you're describing. Alright. Just wait – " There was an audible Lannie-like sigh of exasperation. *"Now they believe us, so they want to know if you've seen anything of their messenger. They sent a messenger to Billérasson this morning, and he hasn't come back."*

"Oh. Sorry, Lannie, bad news. Two of our folk saw a Galeronden lying on the Thammeron side of the rope bridge. He'd been shot in the back."

"Shite. I'll tell them, but there'll be wholesale mourning, so it may take a while..."

It was ten minutes before Lannie called Shiván again. *"Okay, your guides are back. Just a minute... They're saying you won't reach a crossing point before dark. But there are some caves where you could spend the night..."*

Soon they were trudging up towards a line of cliffs, guided by Lannie's voice in Shiván's ear. They found the caves, which were dry and accommodated them easily. They also contained stores of basic dry food, water and firewood for stray travellers. After thanking the One for answered prayer they ate and drank before lying down, huddled together for warmth. Most were soon asleep despite the hard ground.

* * *

"Keep the rope tight!" Fira rapped out as Shiván and those above paused for a moment. The group was clambering slowly up the rocky wall of the ravine. It was even steeper, more overgrown and treacherous than the way down into it had been. The air was bitterly cold, and an involuntary shiver shook Fira's body as she grabbed the 'rope' to keep Shîrin from falling backward. She and several others had contributed extra items of clothing that they'd knotted together to make the makeshift support that was tied under Shîrin's arms to help him climb.

How they could have done with some real rope! They could have done with a lot of things, but they hadn't known what lay ahead the morning Shambor's soldiers arrived. Shiván's decoy had certainly disposed of Shambor's troops, but it had left them cut off by the Grûzhack and struggling up a cliff right now with an injured man! Shiván was brilliant at spur-of-the-moment solutions, but she preferred thorough long-range planning herself.

Shîrin groaned as he was jerked forward again. Delmior and Cârin steadied him with their hands from behind.

Above them Shiván was still listening to Alanya's voice in his ear, pointing out where to go. *That* was something to be thankful for. They would never have found this route across the ravine without Alanya and her bess — and the Galeronden of Thammeron. But it wasn't easy. Last night had been their first proper meal in two days, and they were all tired and weak. One false step... She glanced to her right, where a chasm of cold air stretched down to the white water gleaming far below amid grey pebbles that were massive boulders. She shuddered and concentrated on the upward path.

At last they reached the top where the path continued level, hugging the rocky shoulder of the mountain. Next to it was a fall into nothingness.

After a rest, strung out along the path, they continued. Jagged rocky stairways alternated with near-vertical downward slopes, narrow cliffside ledges with slippery stepping stones across mountain torrents. By the One's enabling they somehow got Shîrin across each obstacle.

It was early evening by the time they finally trudged into Thammeron. The whole settlement was there to welcome them, food had been kept warm, and Shîrin was hurried to a waiting bed where his wound was tended. Alanya was looking almost as exhausted as they were, but she gave Shiván a weary hug, and brushed aside their thanks for rescuing them with her bess. The cultist girl Jomel warmly embraced Lady Perrely, and led her away to the dining circle; and Danîsha, or *Mâra*—'Auntie'—as the younger women called her, was almost weeping with relief to have them all back.

Fira heaved a sigh of relief. Despite her uncertainty at times about Shiván's leadership, it was good to have their group together again.

Chapter 13: *Adrift on the mercies of God*

CAPTAIN GARSET DON TEMBOR of the Bishop's Own Infantry Legion gave the men of his company a cheery wave as he deserted the army. They waved back with broad grins. "See you later!" Tarlion his Second called. Garset was dressed in mufti—an old grey townsman's tunic that they'd dug up from somewhere, with a coarse-spun brown robe. On his feet was a pair of unspeakable cracked leather sandals that Trooper Jembet had found in a ditch. Oh, well. He'd get new ones soon.

Other members of the Legion waved as he passed. It was an open secret that Garset was deserting, a wanted man.

He made his way along the track that led to Chale, the nearby town. The Legion had taken a rest stop in a field beside the Janulane–Dhembis highway. The day was overcast, and there was a chill wind—precursor to the end of Goldshine and the beginning of Winter. Garset found it invigorating. He inhaled deeply. It was a long time since he'd walked alone—though he'd always been something of a loner as a child. He revelled in the crisp, no-nonsense breeze, the bare arms of the fruit trees in the orchards lining the track, the sense of getting back to basics. He would enjoy his freedom—until Tarlion and the rest of the 'Pure Company' caught up with him.

It was a complicated situation. It had all begun with the incident three weeks ago at the Westgate of Stillárre, when the Restorers of the Way had impersonated one of his patrols. He still believed that's who they'd been. 'Strangers and loners'. He'd never regretted letting them into the city, even though he and his officers were later arrested by the Bishop's Guard. But then the Restorers had turned up miraculously in the Guardhouse and set them free, just before all the chaos broke out in the city.

But now the Guard were trying to get hold of him again. A few days ago the Legion had received a change of posting, to Dhembis—something about border clashes with the Grûzhack. Hard on the heels of that his legionary commander, Legate Melleron—an upright man—had told him the Stillárre Guard was demanding he be handed over to them on a charge of treason. The charge had actually been brought by Guards from other towns who had been assisting Mindbender Dhelgor before his death. They had heard from their late comrades in the Stillárre Guard how Garset had let the Restorers through the city gate.

News of the charge had provoked widespread outrage in the camp (not only from his own company, who were all dedicated Lightists). He had been humbled by this support from others who did not share his Lightist principles. Legate Melleron had responded that he, too, was unwilling to send a popular officer to the Guardhouse. But these days the Bishop's Guard had the final say.

The Legate had therefore taken advantage of their new posting to Dhembis to work out a small subterfuge. Garset's transfer to the Guards had been delayed, ostensibly due to the confusion of having to leave Stillárre at short notice. Melleron had sent a regretful note to the Mindbender of Stillárre when already en route to Dhembis, saying that Garset would be handed over at their destination. In view of the serious nature of the charge, he'd told them, Garset had been stripped of his rank and was travelling under escort. His Second, Tarlion, had been promoted as Captain in his place.

Then he'd quietly suggested that Garset 'desert' en route to Dhembis. To soothe the powers above, an entire company of four hundred men—with scouts and cavalry—would immediately be dispatched to search for him. His own company. In due course, when the Bishop's Guard were baying after other victims, they would find him. Then they would return to the legion—with Garset—and the matter would quietly be forgotten. He would continue as Captain in all but name.

Garset had had little choice but to accept this solution. He couldn't see how his death at the hands of the Bishop's Guard would serve the One's purposes; and the Legate's willingness to go to such lengths, even putting his own career at risk, avoided that. So here he was, doing something he'd never thought possible—deserting his legion.

Half an hour's walking brought him to Chale—a neat little green-roofed country town. With coins from his belt-pouch he treated himself to midmeal at an inn. Then he set off south-east for Sûrilane. The nameless crowds of a large town would be a natural place for a deserter to go to ground—and besides, he had relatives there. On the well-travelled Sûrilane road he would immediately stand out as a loner — and therefore an outcast from society, legitimate prey for any group wanting to increase their workforce. He'd either have to find a group of Lightists to join, or leave the road and travel under cover. But one way or another he would reach Sûrilane.

He had plenty of time to kill. Today was the twenty-eighth of Nargand. Act Two of their little charade — when the Pure Company ran him to ground in Sûrilane — was not scheduled until about the seventh of next month. In the meantime they would ostensibly be hunting high and low in all the intervening villages.

Garset sighed. What had the country come to, when soldiers like himself — who only wanted to give honest, God-fearing service — were reduced to such subterfuges. He wondered what had become of those Restorers; and whether they were up to the task. That leader of theirs had been very young. But they'd shown plenty of initiative — killing the Mindbender and turning Stillárre on its head! Foolhardy, perhaps, but it had achieved their goal of rescuing their companions. And one day soon, ready or not, they would summon all who loved the One Creator God to take up arms with them against such rank offences as the Bishop's Guard. Would he be there when that summons came?

If he was, he had no doubt where his allegiance would lie. There would be no more subterfuges.

* * *

Bishop Harlon started as his outer door slammed. Only one person entered his apartment that way. He steeled himself as the large blue-robed figure strode into the room. Shambor seated himself in an upright chair and stared at Harlon, who was lying back on a faded red recliner in front of the fire. Shambor's lips were compressed.

"Do you know what's happened now?" he demanded.

"No, Shambor. I'm sure you'll tell me."

"Those so-called 'Restorers' of yours have brought the Grûzhack down on us."

"What!"

"Yes, I thought that would make you jump. We lost half a company, and those barbarians are on the rampage among the Galeronden."

"Dear Prince!" Harlon's heart went out to Destor and his people. "A bit late for prayers, isn't it? The damage is done. We may have a war on our hands. Does that please you? Are you happy that your latest lot of Restorers are bringing yet more trouble on the Dûrian people?" His voice rose, his eyes glittering with anger. "When will you be satisfied? The Rebellion was not enough, was it? When will enough Dûrians have suffered, enough blood have been shed? *When will you stop meddling and let me build a strong, free country?*"

"Shambor, look at me. I am a weak old man. I can do nothing. *You* are the ruler, you can do as you please."

"Not with you going behind my back and stirring everyone up against me!"

"When have I done that? *I* have no contact with the Grûzhack."

"You prayed for those fake Restorers to come. I know about your pathetic 'Entreaty of Need'! Praying against me, trying to raise up others to replace me!"

"Shambor, you talked about a strong, free country. In Dûrion today only the rulers are strong and free."

"*So I need to be replaced? Is that it?*" he screamed, his face mottled with rage.

Harlon stared at him in silence.

Breathing heavily, Shambor jabbed a finger at him. "You even have those mongrel priests yapping that the true Restorers have come!"

"If so, that's their own conclusion. I had nothing to do with it."

"No? You didn't put them up to it? You had nothing to do with the disaster in Stillárre, or stirring up the Grûzhack? Then you can say so publicly. Yes! I want you to send round an encyclical letter denying the rumours these priests have been spreading."

Harlon sighed. "I can't do that. I prayed that the Restorers would come, and I hope the rumours are true."

"You defy me to my face! You openly declare that you support my enemies!" He stood up abruptly, his features contorted. "You appointed me to run the country. You said you trusted me. But it's always been the same, hasn't it? You've *never* really trusted me, have you? I've never been good enough. Never measured up to your high standards, never—" He stopped suddenly.

Harlon saw a glint of moisture in the tortured eyes. His own heart felt as though a great stone were weighing it down. "I'm sorry," he said.

Shambor's face began to crumple. He turned and walked rapidly from the apartment.

Harlon stared with unseeing eyes at the place where he had been. A terrible suspicion was growing in his mind.

* * *

That night Shambor had the nightmare again. Fire and smoke against the dark sky, a terrible roaring, his mother's agonised screams. Standing at a distance watching the results of his handiwork, while others vainly tried to quench the blaze. Emptiness, helplessness, the end of his world.

He awoke sweating, his own hoarse cry echoing in his ears. He waved the anxious attendants away and tried to swallow water from a goblet that shook in his hand.

The Realm of the Mind had been like a glittering new world full of promise and delight when he was a young lad on the threshold of puberty. His parents had sent him as a boarder to the Hearth School in Sûrilane, where he'd made friends with Barlesh, a Selmian boy. Barlesh had invited him to his home one weekend, and he'd attended the family's secret Gadeshite rites. The Cult of Gadesh was the state religion of Selmion, but it was banned in Dûrion, along with all the other cults. Fascinated, Garion—as he was then known—had eagerly soaked up all he could of the new religion. He became an adherent of Gadesh, forswearing allegiance to his parents' God.

In his first year at school he rose swiftly in power and status among the followers of Gadesh, being admitted as a devotee despite his youth. Later he learnt that he'd deliberately been targeted by the Selmian Initiates—the cult rulers—as the one to return Dûrion to their Master's control. A Dûrian born and bred, son of a Lightist Kindler—he was the perfect candidate. Naturally he'd become rather arrogant, which had alienated not only Barlesh, who was furiously jealous; but also his other schoolmates (who knew nothing of his involvement in cultism). Garion didn't care, though—he was special, he was favoured, he was superior to them all!

But Mama had realised, hadn't she? She must have felt the change in him. She'd somehow found out that her son—the son of a Kindler!—was involved in cultist worship. Had she visited the school after he came home for the holidays? Had she learnt about

Barlesh and his family's Gadeshite connections? He would never know. But one evening she had confronted him when Father was away, and asked him point-blank if he'd been worshipping Gadesh.

Unable to lie to his mother, Garion had blurted it all out—the bright new world he'd discovered, the ability to do supernatural things, to control events, even to read people's minds! He'd so longed for her to understand. But she hadn't. He'd seen the darkening of her shiláy with anger and revulsion. In hard, flat tones she'd told him he'd never return to that school. He'd never attend another Gadeshite meeting. His father would be told when he returned home, and from this moment he was under strict supervision. He was to go to his room at once. He'd protested, and she'd slapped him.

Alone in his room he couldn't face the collapse of all his dreams. His anger mounted against his parents, whose minds were so confined by their narrow religion that they wouldn't even *try* to understand something different. Now at a single stroke they would cut off all his bright prospects. From being a rising star in the Gadeshite community, he would revert to being the wayward son of a Lightist Kindler, always falling short of his parents' expectations.

He'd marched to the door, determined to confront his mother. It was locked. His anger had boiled over. She was treating him like a disobedient child! *Him*—who had powers at his command she knew nothing of. He'd stood in his room, legs apart, concentrating on her parlour down the second-floor passage, where she always retired after the daymeal. Inside the parlour there was a key in the door and a fire in the grate. He'd caused the key to turn, locking the door, then sent it sailing into the fire. He'd raised a breeze in the room and coaxed the fire to a blaze. He heard his mother's cry of alarm. That was okay. Let her find out the hard way that her son was not to be trifled with.

He'd opened his bedroom window and climbed out on to the furnace-house roof below. He'd go to the woods and watch, and when the fire died down he'd stroll in through the front door and tell her he'd done it. As a lesson, to show her he wasn't a child to be ordered about. He was a person with powers, to be treated with respect. He *would* return to school, and he *would* worship Gadesh.

Only the fire hadn't died down. It had grown and spread beyond his control. He'd watched in horror, hearing his mother's despairing screams. He'd tried to run in and open her door, only to be beaten back by the flames. He'd remembered too late that her parlour was an inner room, without a window. There was no one else in the house. He'd tried to move water from the kitchen tank by his power, but the tank had ruptured, spilling its contents uselessly on the floor. He had power to start a blaze, but not to stop it.

Neighbours had come running, and he'd fled to the woods on the hill. There he'd heard the last of his mother's screams as the house became a raging inferno. He'd watched, empty eyed, while it burned to the ground.

His mother was dead. He'd murdered her.

* * *

Frengor couldn't sleep. He tossed and turned on his narrow bed for an hour before giving up the struggle. Something was nagging at his mind, and he had to get to the bottom of it.

He got up, pulled his sandals on, smoothed his sleeping tunic, and went and stood at the window of the small second floor bedroom, looking out over the city. He murmured, "Father God, are you trying to tell me something?"

He waited quietly for the answer. It came, not in words, but in a series of clear certainties. Severe hardship was descending on the Travelling Order and the Domicile—it was approaching at this very moment. They needed to gather their few possessions and leave—now. It would be long before they could return. But to survive they had to exercise a little godly discretion.

He sighed. He'd suspected it might come to this—just not so soon. He pulled on his robe and walked from his bedroom to the Visionary's office down the corridor. In a corner of the office a rope hung. He tugged on it repeatedly, and the alarm bell began its dismal tolling.

In a few moments Brothers Ongaret and Lannet came bursting into the office in their night clothes. Frengor began issuing crisp instructions. "Make sure everyone's up. We're leaving—maybe for good. Tell the brothers to pack one change of clothes, their copy of the Book, and any small valuables. But no one is to get changed yet." The two priests' eyebrows rose. "They must take their travelling clothes and their packed travel pouches down to the back door."

He turned to the younger priest. "Lannet, get some of the novices to help you. Take everyone's things out of the back door and stack them as best you can in the lane behind the garden wall, so they can't be seen. Also gather some food in the kitchen—bread, honey, dry supplies—and firesticks and fireclay—and put as much as you can in two carry-sacks. They can also be stacked in the lane." To Ongaret he said, "When the younger brothers are organised, help the seniors."

With wide eyes the two priests nodded and dashed off. The Domicile soon filled with noise as bleary-eyed priests fumbled to obey their Visionary's orders.

Frengor heaved another sigh. This was going to be tough, especially for the older priests who seldom travelled the roads these days. He went to a waist-high cupboard and rummaged at the back. He pulled out a small leather bag that clinked, and slipped the long leather cord over his head so that the bag hung out of sight under his clothing. Then he quickly gathered the Order's most important documents, slipped them in a leather folder and added it to his travel pouch. In a few moments he joined the stream of priests heading for the back door with their travel clothes and pouches. He fended off anxious queries with a smile and a brief word of reassurance.

An hour later everything had been stacked in the lane with a couple of novices guarding it. Frengor addressed the priests milling about in the entrance hall. "Thank you, brothers! We are now ready to leave when the time comes. But it has not come yet! Please, all go back to bed now and try and get a little more sleep." Amid exclamations of surprise and some doubtful glances, the priests headed back upstairs. Frengor nodded at Lannet and Ongaret to join them.

Silence slowly descended. Frengor sat on one of the recliners in the entrance hall, praying and waiting.

Perhaps three quarters of an hour passed before his wait ended. There was a distant clump of booted feet drawing closer; then a mellow tone from the front door chime. *"Open in the name of his Radiance the Bishop of Dûrion!"*

Frengor smiled and remained where he was. God his father and protector had not misled him. After another sixth of an hour had passed, filled with progressively more rapid chimes and loud banging, he walked over and opened the door. A familiar, burly Guard lieutenant stared at him with burning eyes in a red face. What looked like a full cohort of a hundred Bishop's Guards was clustered behind him in the street.

"Yes?" said Frengor.

The lieutenant took a breath and his face cracked into a mocking smile. "Well, well! Now you yourself are opening the door to me, Visionary. Last time you made me kick my heels for over half an hour before graciously agreeing to see me. How times have changed!"

"Lieutenant Harbion. To what do we owe the displeasure of your company?"

The lieutenant's face flushed a deeper red. "Oh, my company will be the least of your displeasures. Out!" He pointed to the street. "You and all your vermin priests. This building and everything in it now belongs to the Bishop of Dûrion. You will leave at once."

Frengor's eyebrows rose. "At once? That's a little high-handed, isn't it? In case you hadn't noticed, it's the middle of the night."

Harbion smiled again. "Nevertheless, those are my orders. You are to leave immediately, in the clothes you are wearing, without any removing any other items of the Bishop's property."

A collective groan arose from behind Frengor where a crowd of priests had gathered.

"But surely," Frengor protested, an anxious frown creasing his forehead, "you can't be suggesting we leave in our *night* clothes?"

"I'm not suggesting, priest, I'm ordering you. Now go!" The Lieutenant's arm pointed to the door. Frengor and his priests shuffled out into the dark and icy street, while the Guard company jeered and followed their lieutenant into the Domicile.

"Farewell, 'Travellers'," Harbion shouted after them from the entrance portico. "Now you can finally live up to your name!" The door banged shut on his raucous laughter.

More than a hundred scantily dressed priests stared shivering at the closed building—home to many of them for most of their lives. A hundred others were away on their travelling rounds.

"Come, brothers," Frengor called. He set off at a slow, dejected pace. They rounded a corner into the main street, where the Domicile was out of sight. Then he urged everyone to hurry to keep warm, and took them down an alley and through several byways that led to the lane behind the Domicile. Lannet and ten others ran

ahead and helped the novices on guard there to carry all their belongings back to the main group, moving as quietly as they could.
The priests quickly pulled on their travel clothes, and Frengor had
to shush the many exclamations of relief.

"Now to find some shelter, if it's in the One's plan." He led them
to the market square, a dim purple tide flowing down the darkened
streets. No shutters opened and no voices called out. They turned
down a side street that ran beside the ancient Hearth building. This
was where Kindler Varlion lived. Surely he would help them.
Frengor banged on the door of a tall townhouse with his staff.

After a short delay the door opened slightly and Varlion's narrow face appeared in the gap. He gasped when his flickering torch
revealed a street full of purple robes.

"Kindler, may the Light find you."

"And lead you," came the conventional response in a rather tentative voice. Varlion opened the door a crack wider. He was wearing
a pale blue night robe, and his long features looked even more anxious than usual.

"Forgive us for disturbing you, but we find ourselves in a difficult position. The Bishop's Guard have just expropriated our Domicile."

"I— ah— That is most unfortunate."

"You could call it that. Kindler, we are your brothers in the faith.
Would you allow us to shelter in the Hearth for a few hours? Just
until we make other arrangements."

Varlion's eyes ranged over the sea of purple robes, and he licked
his lips. His face took on a hunted look.

"I'm sorry, Frengor," he whispered. "That's not— possible."

Frengor frowned. "Why not? We won't disturb anything. And I
promise you we'll be gone before sunrise."

"It's not that... It's just—" His eyes took on a pleading look.
"They warned me, Frengor. The Guards. They came yesterday. They
said I wasn't to offer you any help, not even a crust. I daren't—"

Frengor's heart went out to the man. The Guards had probably
threatened him with imprisonment, torture, the rape of his wife
and daughters—all the usual.

He nodded. "I understand." He reached out and clasped the
man's shoulder. "The Guards have their power. Our God has his.
The One bless you and keep you, Varlion!"

Relief flooded the Kindler's face. "You're a good man, Frengor. I will pray for you in this terrible situation, and so will my people."

"Thank you, brother." They clasped arms in the high handshake. Then Frengor gently prised the torch from his other hand. "My apologies. You did not give this to me—I took it."

A wan smile touched the Kindler's face. He closed the door.

Frengor was left with a hundred and thirteen priests, some petty cash, and a torch. But at least, thanks to the One's warning, they each had their travel clothes and a few supplies.

"To the docks!" he told them.

In an open piece of ground near the dock area where a house had been demolished, Frengor had them all sit in a large circle around him. He held the torch aloft. A ring of anxious faces glimmered in the flickering light. "Brothers, we've walked the roads, tired, thirsty, rain or shine, welcomed or reviled, for many a long day together. Every two weeks we've returned to the Domicile. But has that been 'home?'" He stared round at the intent faces. "I tell you, *No!* That Guard Lieutenant had the truth of it, though he didn't realise it. Our calling is to be travelling messengers of the Prince! To bring his truth, love and compassion to all we meet on the way. To where? Where are we going, Brothers?"

"*Home!*" came the chorus.

"Yes! We are going home. And we're not there yet. Where is our home?"

"With the One true God!"

"*Yes!* The place we called home here in Stillárre is now gone. *Does that matter?*"

"*No!*"

"Brothers, we are now adrift upon the mercies of God. But that's the safest place to be! We'll keep going, keep travelling, keep trusting in him who is the source of all we have and are. Now—" He let his eyes roam over them. Their faces were more reassured, more hopeful. Praise the Prince. "Let's get down to some practical arrangements."

They set up a new schedule of circuits, and agreed on times and places to meet. First they would target their brothers still out on the roads, to break the news. Some of the younger priests wanted to reassure their families in view of the inevitable rumours, and were given time to do so. Frengor kept the discussion quick and to the point. Before the first citizens began coming in to work from the docks, the travelling priests had dispersed to follow their calling.

Frengor led a group of twelve heading east for Darthane. Despite the brave face he'd worn for the sake of his brothers, his heart was heavy. Shambor's counter-stroke was brilliant. They could still travel and preach—so the poor, their main audience, would see little difference. Shambor knew that the priests would never prey on those they sought to serve. They would never ask for money. But how would they live in the months to come? The poor could not support them. And the wealthy Lightist donors who had freely subsidised them over the years... how many of those would continue to do so now? Expelling them from the Domicile had sent a powerful message to those donors. The Travelling Order was out of favour. Support them at your peril.

Many of the brothers, of course, had families they could look to for help, and he rejoiced in that. He himself had no one—except his nephew, Kindler Mâron in Sûrilane, and he wasn't about to start sponging on him. Besides, there was another problem. He was now a marked man. Shambor had a personal grudge against him. The threats made to Kindler Varlion proved that. They'd had little effect on the brothers as a whole; they'd just made his, Frengor's, job more difficult. Therefore he'd gratefully declined the many offers of hospitality and financial help from his brother priests. He could not bring Shambor's wrath down upon their families.

He sighed as he handed over one of the precious *demeril* coins from their petty cash to the ferryman. The boat ploughed slowly across the River Carreck towards the Darthane highway on the eastern shore.

Yes, now he must practise what he'd preached. He himself was adrift upon the mercies of God.

Chapter 14: *The Ambon of Sûrilane*

SHIVÁN SANK GRATEFULLY DOWN to join the others on the almost level patch of mountain grass. They'd left Thammeron early that morning for Carnem, the next Galeronden settlement to the east. The path was a gruelling switchback, and at the sight of this tailor-made resting place, no one had asked for permission. But in any case, Shîr needed frequent breaks. His wound had been treated, but he could not be allowed to overextend himself. Hastilen and Lantor, their dour Galeronden guides, squatted down philosophically to wait.

Shiván glanced around. Their numbers were growing. They'd escaped Billérasson accompanied by forty of the lowland refugees. Now their group—company?—merry men?—had risen to over sixty as others tagged on, keen to hit back at the bad guys. The Elder of Thammeron had sent them off first while the rest of his settlement stood poised to flee if the Grûzhack decided to expand eastward.

When Shîrin had caught his breath he turned to Shiván. "So. Tonight—Carnem. Tomorrow—Linnegon. Next day—Rommenardem. Where do we stop, Hero?"

That was a good question. He was still debating it with Lannie, 'Neesh, Gil, Perrely and Fira—the 'Council', as they were already being called, Lord help them.

He was conscious of the refugees' eyes on him. 'Don't know' was not an option.

"We carry on doing the job the Prince has given us, Shîr. One step at a time. For now we're heading to Rommenardem. He'll show us what comes next."

"When do we go down-country and fight?" a young fellow with smouldering eyes asked.

"When the One says we're ready. Not a moment sooner, not a moment later."

"What do we need to be ready? We're ready now!"

"No we're not!" an older man shot back. "Don't be stupid. We can't take on Shambor's army with only sixty."

"Look at what the Restorers did in Stillárre with only eight!"

"Shiván killed *one* man!" Fira rapped out. "Before we can do anything against a whole army, *you* need to be trained."

The argument became widespread. Shiván looked at Perrely. She gave the sad smile that seemed to be their trademark these days. "Our followers need an answer," she said. "You didn't mention the Ambon of Sûrilane."

'Neesh, Lannie and Gil happened to be nearby. He motioned them closer. They leaned together to hear one another against the heated uproar in the background.

"I didn't mention the Ambon," Shiván said, "because it would only show how little we know. The thing's been lost for centuries. Hundreds have searched and drawn a blank. Now we arrive, and *we're* 'sposed to find it? We haven't the foggiest clue where to start. Yet both Frengor and Destor tell us that's the one thing we've got to have to fulfil prophecy and prove we're real!"

They were silent. It wasn't the first time they'd ground to a halt discussing Mission Impossible — Finding the Ambon.

"Frengor also said we'd need it to 'summon' people to join us," Lannie mused. "To raise an army. I wonder what he meant? How would an ambon raise an army? It's just a one-armed cross with a circle. Do *you* have any idea?" She looked at Perrely. In the background Fira was going hammer and tongs with the young hothead, and everyone was enjoying the duel.

"I've read a few books about the Dûrian Founders. I know they either made the Ambon, or were the first to use it. It was their battle standard. They would hold it aloft during the fighting, and people believed it gave them victory."

"Right. But that's once they already *had* their army. Was there anything about using the Ambon to summon people, to *form* an army?"

Perrely thought for a moment, staring out over the tumbled forests and ravines below. "I remember reading about when they were in the market square of a town. They raised the Ambon, and it emitted a sudden flash of light. Soon afterwards many people came running to where they were. I don't know if that— What's the matter?" She stared from one face to the other.

A sudden flash of light. Shiván looked at Lannie, 'Neesh and Gil. Each had the same stunned expression. The hair on the nape of his neck prickled.

"I guess you all have the same thought as I do," he said slowly. "We've each seen that flash of light, haven't we?"

"In the Round Church of Leston," 'Neesh said, her eyes as round as the church.

Gil blinked. "The Irish cross above the altar! I thought it was just a trick of the light."

"It happened when I accepted Father Martin's challenge," Lannie said softly.

"Me too!" said 'Neesh.

Gil nodded, frowning.

"The same here," Shiván added. "Wow."

"Will someone tell me what's happening?" Perrely asked plaintively. They'd dropped back into English.

"Before we arrived in Dûrion," Shiván told her, "each of us separately visited a particular Hearth in Inglan—"

"And that's exactly what it was!" Lannie exclaimed. "Remember when we went into the Berûvis Hearth? It looked just like the Round Church of Leston."

Shiván translated for Perrely. She nodded, interest dawning on her face. Probably remembering how he and Alanya had suddenly stood stock-still after entering the Hearth. "On the wall above the altar of this Inglish Hearth was… not an ambon, but what we call a 'cross'—the symbol of our faith. Well, we each spoke to the, er, Kindler of the Hearth about the big problem on our mind at the time, and he gave each of us a different challenge—something hard that we had to face up to. We each accepted the challenge—and when we did, that cross above the altar gave a flash of light. Just like you said the Ambon did with the Founders."

"And very soon after that we were all in Dûrion," 'Neesh added softly.

Perrely looked at them, awed and slightly puzzled. Shiván suddenly realised there was silence all around. The heated debate had stopped. Everyone was hanging on their words.

"That's amazing," Perrely said. "But what does it have to do with the Ambon of Sûrilane?"

"We can't be sure," Gil said. "But it's an amazing coincidence."

"*No!*" Lannie exclaimed. They all stared at her. Her face was flushed and her eyes bright. "No coincidence! It has *everything* to do with the Ambon of Sûrilane. Because that 'cross' in the Church at Leston *was* the Ambon of Sûrilane!"

"*What!*" Three voices in unison.

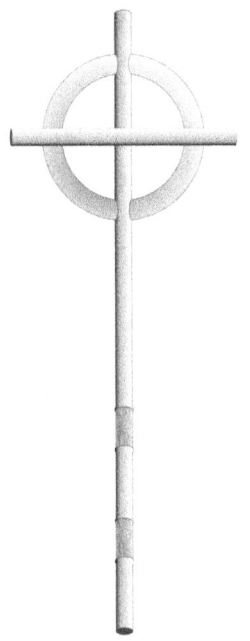

*The 'Round Cross'
of Leston*

"Picture it!" Lannie continued. "An Irish cross, yes? That means it had a vertical and a horizontal bar like a normal cross, with a circle round the intersection. Am I right?"

"Yes," from the other three. "Except the vertical bar was too long," Gil added critically.

"Right! Which makes it more like an ambon. In any case, what was an Irish cross doing in an Oxfordshire village church? I wondered about that at the time. But here's the clincher: *Do you remember anything strange about the horizontal cross-bar?"*

The others stared at her silently. Shiván shrugged. Gil shook his head.

"It passed *over* the circle and the vertical bar! I remember noticing that and thinking, how peculiar. Because in a cross, you'd expect the two bars to be joined *flush* with each other—and in an Irish cross, the circle would be flush too. But here the cir-

cle and the vertical bar were joined, and the horizontal bar was laid over the top. *Why?* Because *it wasn't part of the rest!* Maybe it wasn't even attached. Maybe it was just a bracket to hold it in place. *And what do you get if you take the horizontal bar away from an Irish cross?"* She stared at them triumphantly.

"An ambon." Shiván's voice was hushed.

By now the Dûrians were clamouring for a translation. Shiván did the best he could. Total silence descended over the group.

Gil was looking shaken. "Also, the vertical bar had two handles. Towards the bottom."

"Yes!" 'Neesh exclaimed. Her face was glowing. "Sleeves of leather sort of *inlaid* into the long rod. As if people had carried it in processions."

Shiván translated, and there were excited murmurs. Perrely's purple eyes were bright. "Normal ambons are not often carried, so they don't have

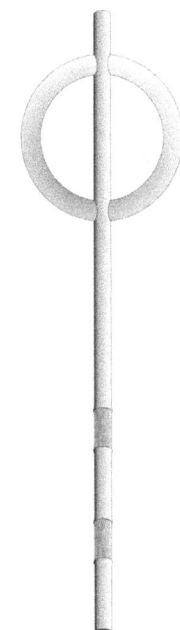

*The Ambon
of Sûrilane*

those leather handholds. *Only* the Ambon of Sûrilane had those handholds, because it was constantly carried—at the head of the army!"

"One more thing!" Lannie rapped out. "Perrely, from your books, can you tell us what the Ambon of Sûrilane was made of, and what colours were used?"

"Oh, every school child knows that," Fira intervened. "It was made of iron, but the rod was overlaid with gold, and the circle with silver."

Lannie looked at the others; they nodded. The vertical bar had shone gold, the circle silver. Shiván heaved a deep sigh of amazement. There was no doubt left.

"It seems," he said, hearing the quiver in his own voice, "that we've found the Ambon of Sûrilane."

* * *

An excited babble broke out. Danîsha sat shaking her head, tears in her eyes. When God had a hand in things, everything tied together in such an amazing way. Right from the beginning, it had been there. Their arrival in Dûrion was not a random, inexplicable event. They had been summoned by the Ambon of Sûrilane. As in the Bible, God had used a physical object to fulfil his purposes—like Moses' staff, Samson's hair, the hem of Jesus' garment. The Ambon—that precious, long-lost symbol of the Dûrian faith—*hadn't* been lost! It had been waiting on Earth, in the church at Leston, for *them*.

Danîsha came out of her reverie to hear Câr speaking.

"Just one problem. The Ambon's under *your* sky. We need it back under *ours*."

"Oh, but I think that's bound to happen!" she exclaimed.

"Why?" That was Gil, the academic.

"Because, don't you see, the Ambon of Sûrilane has *summoned* us to Dûrion. That's what we were talking about earlier. Perrely was telling us that when the Founders held up the Ambon in the town square, it gave a flash of light and *people came running*. Well, the Ambon flashed for each of us, and we sort of 'came running' to Dûrion! If the Ambon summoned us here, it's bound to... well, to *follow* us, isn't it? So we can use it as the Founders did?" She looked round anxiously. She sometimes found it hard to make others understand things that were quite obvious to *her*.

"That isn't logical." Oh dear.

"Maybe not," Lannie said. "But it ties in with something else Frengor told us: which was that the Bishop of Dûrion—the real Bishop, not Shambor—had prayed a special prayer that God would send us. I think it's not so much that the Ambon summoned us, but that God did—using the Ambon in a way we don't understand. And if he uses the Ambon in that way—to summon people to his cause—and if it's prophesied that we'll have the Ambon and use it like that—then I agree with 'Neesh that he's bound to cause the Ambon to reappear somewhere in Dûrion where we'll find it. After all, we know the Ambon was able to get *us* here—so why not itself?"

Bless her. That's what she'd meant, but Lannie put it so much better.

"Well, there you go, Doc." Shiván patted Gil on the shoulder. "We better believe the Ambon will find its own way to Dûrion, 'cos we sure as heck don't know any interplanetary courier service that can deliver it!" He grinned and turned to the Dûrians. "If Danîsha and Alanya are right, where is the Ambon most likely to reappear?"

"In Sûrilane!" came the unanimous response.

"There's the answer to your question, Shîr. When we reach Rommenardem, some of us will go and have a look in Sûrilane. We'll see what the One shows us there."

* * *

The two Galeronden had risen to their feet. The group took the hint and set off again for Carnem. Danîsha had been glad of the rest, and her sore muscles protested at being put to work again. But the path was wider and gentler here, so they continued chatting as they went. The four Restorers—and Perrely, of course—were grouped together in the middle. Jomel was further back, chattering away with Shîr and Câr again.

Gil was very quiet as they walked along. Danîsha glanced at him. He wore an abstracted frown, and she wondered if he was still puzzling over the Ambon of Sûrilane. He soon confirmed her diagnosis. In the midst of a light-hearted discussion about Galeronden food he suddenly said,

"So your God can move people to a different planet with a flash of light?"

There was a moment's silence.

"Our God can bring the dead to life," Danîsha replied.

"Compared to which, just moving us to a different planet must have been kid's stuff." That was Shivvie, of course.

Gil blinked. He looked from one to the other with a strange, intent expression. "Do you really believe that? That Christ was brought to life again after dying?"

"Absolutely." Shiván was serious for once. Danîsha and the others all nodded.

"Also Prince Orrénne," Lannie added.

"What are you saying about the Prince?" Perrely wanted to know. Shiván translated. "The Prince's body was re-formed after being destroyed in the fire," she said. "I suppose you could call that coming to life again."

"I don't understand how Christianity and Lightism can be the same religion when they developed on different planets, with different holy men — who died different deaths."

"But that's the wonder of it, Gil!" Danîsha exclaimed. "I also found it hard to understand at first. The amazing thing is that on Earth we have Jesus, who was crucified and rose from the dead; and here on this planet they have Prince Orrénne, who was burnt — and *also* rose from the dead. On the surface the stories are quite different; but underneath they're exactly the same!"

Gil looked at her doubtfully.

"Think of the probability of that happening, Doc," Shiván put in. "Two planets, two 'holy men', as you call them. Different names, different details. But both died, both came alive again. Both said anyone who trusted in them would find peace with God and everlasting life. What are the chances of two such similar 'stories' being hatched independently on different planets?"

"Mmmm." Gil thought for a moment. "But there are self-sacrifice stories in many cultures. It's not so surprising."

"Including atonement by God himself? Where he actually dies to take away the burden of people's wrongdoing, so they don't have to do anything to be completely at peace with him — and with themselves? I think that's pretty rare, Doc."

Gil walked on, head bowed. Then he looked up with haunted eyes. "So... Jesus and Orrénne. How did they take away the burden of wrongdoing?"

Danîsha's heart went out to him. "Are you still blaming yourself, Gil, for all those deaths at Carreck Manor?"

"And later. There are things I've done that I can… never forget."

"But those things weren't your fault, Gil," Lannie said softly, holding his arm. "You were being forced to do them against your will."

"Nevertheless… The blood is on my hands, and I have to live with that." He looked down at them, his face a mask of pain.

Danîsha sighed and shook her head. "It was your hands that committed those acts. How dreadful that must make you feel. Oh, I could wring that Mindbender's neck — except that, of course, he's dead now. What unspeakable wickedness, to burden you with his guilt!"

"But Gil," Shiván said, "we believe that Jesus — Prince Orrénne — has taken on himself everything you've done. It's as if he himself did those things. And he's paid for it with his life. Now he's offering you new, clean hands for your old blood-stained ones."

There was a hush all round. Gil stood staring at the ground.

After a while he looked up. His face was strangely vulnerable, quite unlike the self-assured Dr. Denbigh they were used to. "This is all very mystical and unscientific. It's hard for me to accept. How would I know it's real?"

"Oh, you'll know!" Danîsha exclaimed. "Your life will be completely new."

"You'll know the same way you know this mountain is real," Shivvie commented as they started walking again. "By experience. The only way you know physical things are real, is because you've had experience of your five senses, and you know they tell the truth. It's the same with God. Once you start actually trusting him, you discover you can trust him. Then you know it's real. Trust is like a sixth sense. It explains everything the other five can't — especially the why's, for which science has no answer."

After a moment's silence Gil muttered, "I need to think about it."

"Of course. Take your time."

They walked on. Shiván told Perrely in an undertone what had happened. *If only Gil would take that one necessary step*, Danîsha thought. *Open himself to God. Accept the gift that was freely offered.*

Then they would at last be united as the Restorers God meant them to be.

* * *

Jomel was relieved when they finally made it to Carnem. This endless walking up and down mountain paths wasn't her scene. At least the twins with their banter and light-hearted approach to life had made it bearable. They, too, she was sure, felt out of place among the dour Galeronden and the brooding refugees. As for Perrely, well, something had obviously gone wrong between her and Shiván; she wasn't much fun to be with these days.

The arrival of such a large group made quite an impression. There were a few refugees in the settlement, and during the daymeal they were full of questions about the Restorers. To Shîrin and Cârin, of course, this was like fireclay on a pair of firesticks. Jomel had to laugh as they kept the refugees open-mouthed with exaggerated versions of how Shiván had single-handedly killed the Mindbender of Stillárre—how she, Jomel, had been saved from the hands of a ravening mob—how Danîsha's bellaril had frozen a Guard company in full charge—and how Shiván had brought the Grûzhack down on Shambor's soldiers.

The last story hadn't gone down so well; there were doubtful mutters about all the trouble the Grûzhack were now causing. But as they chatted to the refugees who had come with the Restorers, quite a few began talking about joining them.

Halfway through the meal Gelmion stood up and left. He had a faraway look, and Jomel wondered what he was thinking. Shrugging, she turned back to her tasty platter of roast venison, *cay*-roots and green pulses. At least she could enjoy Galeronden meat, not like the twins, who were picking half-heartedly at some bean mush.

Finally, as the war chatter simmered down and she began to hope she could get the twins to herself again, Gelmion returned. What a difference! Talk died away as everyone stared. A broad smile covered his face. He walked directly over to where Shiván, Perrely and Alanya and Danîsha were sitting.

"You were right!" he declared. "I've spoken with the Prince! With Jîzis. The burden's been taken away. Clean hands!" He thrust them out to them.

There was an immediate outburst of congratulations and rejoicing. Shiván leapt up and embraced Gelmion, and so did Danîsha— and, of course, Alanya. Even the twins and Fira hurried over to clap him on the back. Perrely was laughing happily. The Galeronden leaders and the refugees came to shake his hand. They clustered round as Gelmion continued talking to the other Restorers in Inglish.

Jomel watched in disbelief. This was *Gelmion?*

The Elder of Carnem gathered everyone to celebrate the Remembrance of Flame, as the Lightists did every evening. They sang around the glowing embers of the fire, their hands and eyes lifted upward, remembering the Prince who had burned for them — and rejoicing with their new brother who had entered his light.

Jomel felt more out in the cold than she had for a long time. Was this what she needed, too? To have a personal 'meeting' with this unseen Prince? She *had* met with him, in her temple cell. She believed he'd spoken to her. But it seemed so long ago now. She didn't have the daily, ongoing 'friendship' with him that the Restorers and Perrely spoke about. Had her burden been taken away? She'd been rescued from becoming a human sacrifice; but that was different...

So now Gelmion was a true Lightist, and she wasn't. That couldn't be right! He'd been corrupted by his mindbending — she'd seen that already happening when he'd raped her in Stillárre. Could he have changed so radically, and so quickly? She found that hard to believe.

While the others rejoiced, Jomel sat wrestling with her confusion.

Chapter 15: *The Kindler of Sûrilane*

SUFFRAGAN BISHOP SHAMBOR's fixed smile felt engraved on his face. Blackwood cutlery rattled against porcelain bowls in the blue and gold of the Cathedral's smaller banqueting hall. These 'little diplomatic suppers' were the bane of his existence. Play acting! Every diplomat round this table knew that real power in the Dûrai nations had passed to the Cult of Gadesh. He himself as Mindruler had taken over the government of Dûrion from Bishop Harlon. In Marûvin and Pandiar, Mindrulers were the powers behind the puppet kings, their mindbent subordinates. Only Thrinar retained a semblance of independence, and that would soon change.

But the Strongholder, Chief Initiate of the Cult of Gadesh, Ruler of Mindrulers and Lord of Selmion, wished to let the farce run a little longer. Shambor therefore had to play the gracious host to these relics of an outmoded diplomatic corps. He feigned interest in what Second Marûvian Envoy Nessîn was starting to say while reaching out to take a reddish-orange *miléss* from the fruit bowl.

"*GARION.*"

Shambor froze with his hand still stretched out. *The Strongholder!* He'd been dreading this moment. But he quickly recovered and picked up the fruit.

"Afraid of your own food, your Serenity?"

Shambor scowled at the Thrinari ambassador. His mocking tone and insistence on the inferior title fell just short of an insult. Thrinar had never acknowledged his assumption of power in Dûrion. That would change!

"*Forget the Thrinari ambassador, Gari. You have me to deal with.*"

"*Apologies, Strongholder.*"

"*If they mock you, can you blame them?*"

"*No, your Supremacy.*"

He felt a hand on his arm. Ambassador Brinjond's sharp green eyes under his heavy brows were filled with simulated concern. "Serenity, your guests are speaking to you. Is it not courtesy in Dûrion to respond?"

He glanced round and saw the Second Marûvian Envoy sitting with raised eyebrows.

"I beg pardon, Nessîn. You were saying...?"

"I merely made the humble query, exalted ruler, whether any progress has been made—"

"Shambor, I will have your full attention. If necessary you will leave your guests. What they think of you does not concern me."

"Yes, Strongholder."

"—and whether you approve of this action?"

"Nessîn, all of you, please forgive me. A, ah, problem of extreme delicacy has just arisen, and I need to attend to it. I shall return as soon as possible. Please continue to enjoy your meal."

Brinjond leant back in his chair, a broad smile on his ugly, warty face. "It is a higher authority that calls, I see. Very well. We shall enjoy your hospitality without you."

Shambor fumed as he stalked out of the banqueting hall. That little story would do the diplomatic rounds in less than no time. The ruler who was at the beck and call of a 'higher authority'. Dûrion's prestige, which he'd striven so hard to build up, was now being eroded by—

"Aaaah!" A bolt of exquisite pain struck him and he fell to the floor. Two startled servants came running and helped him to his feet. With a curse he sent them packing. The diplomats would have heard that as well.

"May I remind you that it was the Strongholder—*my predecessor—who brought you to power in Dûrion? Are you ashamed to acknowledge that?"*

"No, your Supremacy. It's just that—"

The young Strongholder's mind-voice rose. *"'It's just that' nothing! You were a nobody, the oppressed son of a bigoted Lightist priest, searching for meaning in the Cult of Gadesh. My predecessor rescued you when you burnt your own home to the ground, and trained you here in Selmion. We made you what you are, Garion. And right now I am* your *higher authority, and you* are *at my beck and call. Is that clear?"*

"Yes, Strongholder." Shambor sank on to a chair in a deserted meeting room. There was no point in private thought. His autonomy had been invaded. That hadn't happened since—

"Since before you were a Mindbender, Gari. You no longer deserve autonomy. You have been criminally arrogant. I offer to make you my Second, and what do you do? You send your troops up to the very walls of a Grûzhack fort! Is this what you think my patronage entitles you to? The

right to strut your importance before the Grûzhack, of all people? Are
you insane? Or did it slip your mind that the Grûzhack are our sole
source of teméyn? On which all mindbending depends?"

There was a pause. Shambor sat with his head in his hands.

"WELL?"

"Strongholder, it was never my intention – "

"Of course! It was an accident, I fully understand. You just happened to
have troops up there, and by pure chance they wandered too close to Fort
Desheyn – even though that is clearly marked on both your maps and mine.
Any other excuses?"

"No, Supremacy."

"Good. And what, may I ask, do you plan to do about the loss of teméyn
that we here in Selmion, as well as our brethren in Marûvin and Pandiar,
will suffer when our last caravans for the winter fail to arrive? I assume
you are aware that all teméyn caravans to our nations have been stopped,
thanks to your strange notions of diplomacy?"

"I have – some surplus available. I will send it to you immediately, to
distribute as you see fit." He could not suppress his chagrin at having
to part with the drug. There was a grim smile in the Strongholder's
response.

"Very well. Then I will restore your autonomy. But you will only retain
it, Gari, if you sort this mess out that you have created." He paused, allowing the threat to hang in the air.

"Now tell me. You have been sending troops to Dhembis. Can I assume
that this is not for any idiotic reprisal attempt?"

"No, Strongholder. They are there merely as a precaution."

"Well, you'd better make sure that they don't go on any unauthorised
excursions. Meanwhile I am sending an embassy on behalf of all our mind-
ruled nations to the Grûzhack Grandmasters in Kharzil. You may supply
an envoy to abase himself before them."

"I will do so, Strongholder. I will also send a large indemnity in gold."

"I'm glad you still have some glimmerings of common sense. Oh, and
Gari – "

"Yes, your Supremacy?"

"That position as my Second. I'm afraid it's gone to someone else."

"I – understand, Strongholder."

"To Mindruler Nagôr of Marûvin."

Shambor swallowed. His pet aversion, as the Strongholder well
knew. "Yes, Strongholder."

With a contemptuous flick of his mental whip—which drew another cry of pain—the Ruler of Mindrulers was gone.

For a long while Shambor sat still in the darkened room. He could forget his half-formed plans to send another force up into the mountains after the so-called Restorers. They only had nuisance value now. His top priority was to make peace with the Grûzhack—whatever it took. The Strongholder had appreciated his prompt offer to pay an indemnity. He would follow that up with other offers—even cede a few Galeronden villages. Anything to avoid an all-out war. If he showed a sacrificial willingness to make amends and won a quick peace settlement, something might yet be salvaged from this disaster.

He might show up in a good light alongside Nagôr's well-known arrogance.

He might even regain his nomination as the Strongholder's Second.

He stood and straightened his robes to return to the diplomats' petty sniping. They mocked his subservience to a higher authority, but dreaded the day when they themselves would be subject to it. Then there would be no sniping.

* * *

Fira was pleased to find herself crossing a broad upland meadow as the Restorers' group approached the settlement of Rommenardem. A perfect place for the weapons training she was eager to start. They had picked up another eighteen refugees in Carnem and Linnegon, and she was confident that quite a few more would be added here. Rommenardem, she'd been told, was a large settlement given over to refugees, like Billérasson. She felt a thrill of anticipation. With a hundred recruits they would have a full Dûrian cohort. It would be like the Rebellion again. She would be a Lieutenant in more than name.

The path led into the forest and past many lamplit lodges until they reached the dining circle—which to her surprise was covered by a broad awning of some heavy material suspended from the branches above. The centre was open to allow the smoke to escape. The refugees' leader came forward to greet their large party. With him, to everyone's surprise, was Nist.

After the general greetings the large lady sat down with them on one of the logs around the cooking fires. She explained how Shambor's assault force had taken her by surprise in Jarmenis, with the loss of many of her network—including her brother Lishet. There were murmurs of sympathy. Everyone had warmed to the man's simple friendliness. Nist was silent for a moment, before declaring in her deep booming voice that the Usurper wouldn't get rid of her so easily. She had escaped from Jarmenis with several others, and was now based in the village of Fanderane, doing the same job of escorting refugees to and from the Galeronden area. She added that she would return to the lowlands the next day.

"Where is Fanderane?" Shiván asked.

"A few *aldoret* south-west of Sûrilane," Nist replied. Fira frowned. She could see what was coming.

"Could you take us there?"

Amazement spread over Nist's face. "What, the whole lot of you?"

"No, Shiván!" Fira exclaimed. "We need training—*including* you Restorers! We now have almost eighty recruits—and more are likely to join here. You all need weapons training! We can't face Shambor's army as we are."

"What we need is to find the Ambon of Sûrilane!" Perrely retorted. "Our campaign can't even begin until we have that."

There was a rumbling chuckle from Nist. "Still planning to rescue Dûrion, are you? Well, there's a few more of you now than last time. I think you might actually last a couple of days."

The refugees were listening as they spooned up the stew the cooks had provided. There was an outcry, and Nist was soon raising her hands in mock surrender, a broad smile on her face. Fira motioned Shiván to one side. Perrely followed.

"Shiván, we have to train!" Fira said, pouring as much urgency as she could into her voice. "What use will the Ambon of Sûrilane be if it gathers us a huge army that can't fight? Here we have the best opportunity we could hope for. An isolated location where we're not likely to be found; a large meadow nearby; plenty of wood and materials for practice weapons—"

"What are we relying on, Fira?" Perrely said. "Our training, or the One's power?"

Fira snorted. "That's very spiritual, I'm sure, but the One Creator God gave us hands, arms and legs to *use*, not to sit back and let him do everything."

Her Ladyship's glare was anything but spiritual. "Right! Let's be practical, then. Up here it may start snowing tomorrow, and not stop till Flowering. So much for the training *and* our mission — we'd be stuck here for the whole winter. *Or*, Shambor may send more troops up after us. Let's go down-country, find the Ambon, and *then* look for somewhere to do your training. If the Ambon brings us new recruits, they'll also need training. There are plenty of forests in Dûrion with secluded areas."

Fira's mouth opened for a hot retort, but Nist got in before her. She'd left the recruits to their glory-mongering.

"Hold it!" she boomed, her grin still in place. "Sorry to disturb your argument, but it's pointless. I can't take more than six tomorrow."

"Why's that?" Shiván asked.

"I'm still building up a network in this area," Nist said with slightly strained patience. "I don't have many places you can stay at short notice. In any case, I'd never take a whole cohort down at once. Even with plenty of notice I would take no more than twelve, who could pass as a family group."

"I think that settles it, ladies," Shiván declared with a grin. "Six of us go with Nist to Sûrilane, the rest stay here. That will include you, Fira. You can start your training without us."

"You *must* learn how to use the Blade, Shiván! There's a lot more to swordsmanship than waving it about in the air!"

"Fine. I'll wait for one of Perrely's lowland forests."

Fira snorted. The Restorers' casual attitude towards training was starting to annoy her.

In the end it was agreed that the Restorers along with Perrely and Jomel would accompany Nist the next day. Fira insisted on Jomel going. She wasn't having that loose-living cultist distracting the twins, *or* the refugees. Perrely was her cousin. She could look after her.

* * *

So this was the famous Hearth of Sûrilane. Lannie stood with Gil and the others, staring at the historic building on the opposite side of the market square. It was an older style of architecture, she felt, than the hearths they'd seen in Berûvis and Stillárre, and had a strangely English look about it. The great round edifice was of grey stone—not painted white, as in other towns—and at the top, surrounding the green-tiled dome, was a narrow parapet. The tall windows and grand front door were set in pointed arches, unlike the round arches elsewhere. The overall look was of a keep, or central tower, in one of England's mediaeval castles.

The whole town of Sûrilane, in fact, had a mediaeval look. Partly the grey stone everywhere, partly the cobbled streets.

They'd arrived after dark last night—they (the four foreigners), plus Perrely, Jomel, Nist and the three escorts who'd been with her in Rommenardem. The journey down from Rommenardem had not been difficult, just slow. All morning, till well after the midmeal, had been spent navigating the pathless routes to Fanderane Wood. From there to Sûrilane had been easy—though Nist had taken no chances. They had at all times been well surrounded by Dûrians to disguise their shiláy.

In Sûrilane itself Nist had hurried them to a large townhouse. A young man with startling orange hair, a square, tanned face and a permanent half-smile had opened the door. His eyes widened at the sight of the large group.

"Sandon!" Nist boomed after the shiláy-pause. "Here's your first assignment. Can you and your mother take in six people for a couple of days?"

The young man's grin had spread to his whole face. "Of course! Delighted." They had all warmed to Sandon. He was economical with words, but lavish with helpfulness. His mother, it turned out, was an invalid, and his father had died many years ago. His two elder brothers and his sister had married and moved out, leaving three bedrooms unoccupied. Sandon was a silversmith's apprentice. The family wasn't exactly wealthy, but it wasn't poor either.

So here they were, with Sandon and two friends, gazing through a gentle drizzle at their objective, the Hearth of Sûrilane. Lannie felt a shiver of anticipation. Had the Ambon preceded them—would they find it waiting? Perhaps the Kindler had found it and hidden it from the authorities. Its appearance certainly wasn't common knowledge, or the town would have been buzzing with it.

"Okay folks, let's go!" Shivvie said, and they moved out from under the merchant's awning where they'd been sheltering. Lannie pulled her robe tighter. It was distinctly chilly—though not as cold as the mountains. She wasn't sad to have left *that* behind.

They crossed the square in a tight group, foreigners surrounded by Dûrians. Sandon led them past the main Hearth entrance to a side door, where he plucked the recessed rod. A mellow chime sounded within. After a short delay the door opened. A tall gangly man with thick pursed lips peered out short-sightedly.

"Dhôret, greetings," Sandon said after the pause. "Visitors for the Kindler."

"Kindler Mâron's away in Darthane," the man replied in a deep, slow voice. "He'll be back this evening. Can I help?"

Sandon looked at Shiván. "Assistant Dhôret. Knows a lot about the Hearth."

"Yeah, okay, let's have a chat with him."

Dhôret ushered them into the Hearth. As at Berûvis, Lannie was struck by the uncanny likeness to the Round Church of Leston. This was much bigger—but the basic layout was the same. A thick blue covering on the floor, warmed by golden light from the tinted glass of the windows. Plastered walls, painted white. Rows of chairs in a three-quarter-circle facing the alcove at the front, where a bare altar of carved stone stood on a low dais. Above it, a plain white wall. And that was where the likeness ended. On the wall was a two-pronged hook, and below it a cylindrical socket—but no ambon.

They all paused in the space before the altar, where Sandon made brief introductions.

Lannie pointed at the empty wall. "You don't have a substitute ambon?" she asked Dhôret.

He gave a weary smile. "There is no substitute for the Ambon of Sûrilane. That wall has been empty for centuries."

"So, the Ambon has not, er, been found?" 'Neesh asked hopefully.

The smile became both weary and condescending. "No, indeed. As a foreigner, you would not be aware of this. But from your questions I assume you realise that this was a special ambon, the battle standard of our Founders." He gestured to the chairs, and they sat while he positioned himself facing them and launched into a well-rehearsed lecture. "The Ambon disappeared two hundred and forty-one years ago—in the year one hundred and twenty-two after the founding of the Dûrian Theocracy. This was almost thirty years after the last of the Founders had died. ..."

"What was his name?" Shivvie asked.

Dhôret paused, slightly taken aback. "Ah, that was Jemmet dos Simion."

Shiván nodded. "James Turner. Did he live at Carreck Manor?"

"Why, yes, in the last years of his life. You are well-informed."

"Yeah, we'd, er, worked that out. But please, carry on."

With a doubtful glance the Assistant continued. "When people heard the Ambon was gone, there was a great outcry. It was the symbol of our nationhood. The Hearth itself was turned inside out and there was no sign of it. The entire town and countryside were scoured, but in vain. Then people thought that enemies of Dûrion must have stolen it. Searches were made all over the country, and even in neighbouring lands. Some minor wars resulted. (You must understand that Dûrion was more powerful then.) But the Ambon was never recovered."

He sighed and shook his head. "In the centuries since, many more searches have been made. Every so often someone gets a bright idea they imagine has never been thought of before — though of course, it usually has. Even nowadays we've had ardent believers coming here and wanting to hunt under the dome or in the crypt — which were among the first places searched."

"So, no chance of us looking around and finding it, then?" Shivvie said with a grin.

"None whatsoever," Dhôret replied seriously.

Gil blinked and asked him, "What do *you* think?"

The Assistant shook his head. "I have no idea. Some are convinced the Grûzhack must have it. They are the only nation in the area that the Founders didn't conquer. Their land is an impregnable fortress in the Tallissôr Mountains. None of the expeditions that were sent up there returned. Even today, as you know, there is only one kind of commerce with Barazhân, and outsiders are never permitted to enter." He grimaced. "They keep themselves to themselves, and praise the Light, they are not warlike. I cannot see the Grûzhack sending an expedition down to Sûrilane to steal the Ambon! What need would they have of it? No, we simply do not know how the Ambon disappeared, or where it is now. It is a mystery that the One Creator God will reveal to us in his own good time."

Ah, but we do know where it is, Lannie felt like saying. *We just wish we could fetch it and succeed where so many others have failed!*

"Do you mind if we stay here a bit?" Shiván asked.

"Not at all," Dhôret said, smiling wryly as he stood up. "All I ask is that you don't start pulling things apart. I can assure you the Ambon is not in this building." With a farewell nod he went out through a side door. Lannie caught a glimpse of what looked like an office beyond.

"So, now what?" 'Neesh said. "We've come all this way, and the Ambon's not here. Was Frengor wrong, do you think? Maybe we're not meant to have it…"

"No, Frengor was right," Shiván declared confidently. "Destor said the same, remember."

"There's a prophecy about the Restorers that most people think refers to the Ambon," Perrely added. "It says, *They will lift high the Rod of Truth to summon the faithful; they will raise it above the altar of darkness, and release my captive people.* Armanet and Dôrion, the leaders of the Rebellion, maintained that the *Rod of Truth* was only figurative—they had to, because they didn't have the Ambon. But then, the Rebellion failed."

"Not to worry, 'Neesh." Shivvie laid a hand on her shoulder. "We will have the Ambon. It'll turn up—somehow. Maybe we'll have to wait a bit. But it will follow us to Dûrion. Remember what Lannie said: If it could send us, it can certainly send itself."

"All the same," Gil murmured, "it might be good to have a contingency plan. Not that we believe the Ambon *won't* come, but in case there's a long delay. Would we go back to Rommenardem?"

"I guess we'd have to. But that won't happen, Doc."

"Maybe not. But it's always as well to have a backup plan." Lannie looked at him fondly. Gil's wider experience of life was just what they needed.

Shiván shrugged. "Okay. Then that's the backup."

"Can we have a look around the town, now?" Jomel asked. But Sandon cut across her question with another. He was looking at Shiván with raised eyebrows and a quizzical smile. "Ambon. Prophecy. You the Restorers, then?"

Shivvie frowned. "*Sssst!*" he whispered, finger on his lips. "Secret. Don't tell a soul."

Sandon laughed. "Believe it when I see the Ambon."

Lannie sighed as they stood to leave. That about summed it up.

* * *

The next day was Anderil. The rain had stopped, and a pale wintry sun was shining. They set off early for the Hearth, surrounded once more by Sandon and his friends. Danîsha was so glad to be attending a proper service again. She'd missed regular weekly worship in the haphazard life they'd been living in Dûrion.

Though they arrived well before the hearthtime was due to begin, the circular auditorium was already half full. Sandon found them seats a couple of rows back from the front. As time went by more people streamed in, till the ancient Hearth was packed. Danîsha was delighted. The Kindler must be a dynamic preacher, to pull in such crowds.

Quiet settled over the sanctuary as the musicians filed in to the chairs on the left of the alcove. They began the Call to Song, and the congregation stood and joined in enthusiastically. She was revelling in the rich harmony of hundreds of voices, when there was a sudden, decidedly unspiritual exclamation from Alanya, standing next to her.

Startled, she looked at Lannie and saw she was staring with wide eyes to the right. Following her gaze, Danîsha saw a man in a white robe standing at the Kindler's lectern. There was something familiar about him.

Lannie turned to her, her face frozen in shock. "Do you see who I see?" she said, just loud enough to be heard above the singing.

"You mean the Kindler? He looks familiar, but I don't—"

Then he glanced towards them, and his expression of surprise was quickly followed by a delighted smile. Danîsha saw who it was. Her knees gave, and she sat down suddenly on the chair.

"Father Martin!" she gasped.

———————————

Chapter 16: *Blaise, Bess and Bellaril*

IT WAS DIFFERENT THIS TIME. The child looked about him, bewildered. They were standing at the edge of a wide meadow, and in it many strangely-dressed men were fighting each other with long knives. He clung terrified to Nanny. Faranu, his mentor, had brought them here. He was standing beside them, watching the fighting and holding a small knife.

Suddenly Faranu gripped his wrist and sliced one of his fingers. He screamed—but Nanny didn't pull him away. Instead she held him out towards Faranu, making it easier! "There, there, it has to be done," she kept saying—and "*Hsst*, my pet"—as if to comfort him. Faranu kept cutting and jabbing him. His mouth was open in a continuous scream while the fighters in the meadow kept clashing their long knives together. He struggled to get out of Nanny's arms, but she held him tight. The knife wounds hurt so much, but Nanny *helping* Faranu hurt even more. First Olôra, now Nanny. There was no one who loved him, not a single one.

Nanny wrestled him round so Faranu could cut his other arm. The pain and the fighting went on and on and on.

After what seemed like forever he felt himself fading away from the agony. The last thing he heard was Faranu saying, "… a ninety percent success rate".

It meant nothing. Nothing meant anything any more.

* * *

Shambor regarded the scout standing at rigid attention before him through slitted eyes. Beside him on the recliner sat Senior Legate Derlion, his florid face anxious, absently fingering his pursed lips. Multicoloured light from the stained-glass window lit up the silver-and-blue appointments of the Bishop's receiving room in Darthane Cathedral. Secretary Estaron stood working as usual at his writing table beside the ornately carved blackwood entry door.

"So Grûzhack numbers have increased in Galeron and Billéras-son?" Shambor queried the scout.

"Yes, Lord Marshal, sir." The man stared at a point somewhere above Shambor's left shoulder.

"By how much?"

"Lord Marshal, sir. Sixty new arrivals in Galeron, which had forty-eight. Forty-two new arrivals in Billérasson, which had thirty-six."

"Bringing the totals to...?"

"Lord Marshal, sir. One hundred and eight in Galeron, and seventy-eight in Billérasson."

"More than doubled." Shambor drummed his fingers on the arm of the recliner. "They like multiples of six, these Grûzhack," he murmured absently. "And you said they'd brought equipment with them. What kind?"

"Lord Marshal, sir. Eighteen two-wheeled carts carrying long metal tubes. Eight have been placed around the perimeter of Billérasson, and ten around Galeron."

"Some of their magical weapons, no doubt," Derlion muttered.

"Wood and metal are not magic, Derlion!" Shambor spoke sharply. "Maybe they include other things we don't yet understand — but they are real physical objects, which we can learn about and overcome. You tell your men that. In any case, we want to avoid a war at all costs. An embassy is even now on its way to Barazhân to sue for peace."

He turned again to the rigid scout. "And our garrisons in Thammeron, Carnem and Linnegon. Have they been established without trouble?"

"Yes, Lord Marshal, sir. But the local inhabitants have left."

Shambor's eyebrows rose. "Left? *All* of them? Where have they gone?"

"Lord Marshal, sir. As our troops approached Thammeron along the old teméyn route, the inhabitants fled east to Carnem. As they approached Carnem, the inhabitants fled east to Linnegon. As they approached Linnegon — "

"Yes, thank you, scout, I get the picture. So the entire Galeronden population is now crammed into Rommenardem and Dillerem. A just reward for harbouring enemies of the state all these years."

"Lord Marshal, sir. We understand from one or two captives that many have also fled to hidden refuges in the vicinity of each village."

"I'm glad to hear it. They'll suffer more hardship there. What about our own troops — have supplies been organised from Dhembis?"

"Yes, Lord Marshal, sir."

"Good. You may go." The scout snapped off a smart hand-to-chest salute, holding his arm there as he backed carefully to the door, then swivelled round and left.

Shambor turned to the Legate. "Your men have acquitted themselves well, Derlion. But I don't like this Grûzhack build-up. Now that you've laid the groundwork, I'll send a detachment of the Bishop's Guard to strengthen each garrison."

"Thank you, Lord Marshal."

"Let's hope the embassy succeeds in its mission and these precautions become unnecessary." He stood, and Legate Derlion scrambled to his feet as well.

"Keep me posted of any new developments as they occur."

"I will, Lord Marshal."

Shambor nodded, and the Legate repeated the scout's exit performance.

On his own, Shambor sat down again. His heavyset face was creased in thought. He passed a hand over his mouth. He'd done the right thing to put garrisons in the nearest villages. At least he couldn't lose any more territory without a *de facto* declaration of war.

He'd also sent Lord Narlet with the Strongholder's embassy to Barazhân—a first-class groveller, carrying with him a sizeable chunk of the Dûrian treasury as indemnity. That had to succeed.

His thoughts turned to the minor irritation of those would-be Restorers. They'd left the Galeronden area, that he knew. He couldn't move against them yet, since the Guards were useless against their instruments and all his regular troops were being deployed to avert the Grûzhack menace. As soon as that was over, their turn would come. Meanwhile… he had his eyes and ears.

* * *

In the Sûrilane Hearth, Shiván and Gil recognised Father Martin just after Danîsha and Alanya. Shiván's crisp "Yikes!" turned heads and earned an unusual glare from Sandon.

The rest of the hearthtime went by in a blur. Danîsha wished she could have appreciated the sermon and the moving celebration of the Remembrance of Flame that followed. But all she could think of was the amazing fact that Father Martin was *here*, in Dûrion! Was he really the Kindler? Or… Did the Dûrian Hearths have visiting speakers? Had he dropped in for the day from Earth?! *Stop it, now you're talking nonsense.*

Her mind boggled at all the questions his presence here raised. Was he from Earth? Or was he a Dûrian? Was this his home, rather than the Oxfordshire village of Leston? He did have a slightly narrow face and an olive complexion that might make him a Dûrian. Had he somehow been sent to fetch them? By whom? How? No, that couldn't be right. He wasn't a casual visitor in England, he was the Vicar of Leston. But if he was also the Kindler of Sûrilane... how could he be both at the same time? Did he jump to and fro between the worlds? Could he somehow 'use' the Ambon of Sûrilane at will? But then, how could he spend half his time in Leston and the other half in Sûrilane? People in both places would quickly notice and start asking questions...

Her head began to ache.

Eventually the hearthtime ended. People started mingling and greeting one another, and Sandon quickly stood to herd them to the exit. Shiván, however, had other ideas. Side-stepping the arm Sandon stuck out to stop him, he made a beeline for Father Martin. Danîsha and the others followed. With a desperate shrug the orange-haired man motioned to his friends and tagged along after them.

The Kindler—if that's what he was—was at the front of the Hearth, chatting in perfect Dûrian to a well-dressed couple with an aristocratic air. He gave the four of them a broad smile, and turned back to his parishioners. They waited impatiently. Watching him, she was reminded of what had first struck her about this young man, and that was his remarkable gift of devoting one hundred percent of his attention to whoever he was speaking to. The aristocrats were relating a tale of woe about a wayward daughter called Merilay. No visitors from Earth could distract him from their troubles.

"Shiván, we must go!" Sandon hissed from behind.

"We've got to speak to the Kindler," Shiván said. "We know him from— elsewhere."

"Stand back then. Not polite, so close."

They moved out of earshot, earning a relieved glance from the aristocratic lady. Sandon and his friends surrounded them again.

"*Is* that the Kindler?" Danîsha asked, just to make sure.

"Yes," he said with the quizzical grin. "Kindler Mâron."

Mâron — Martin. She shook her head. Which was the original? Eventually Father Martin — that was the only way she could think of him — bade farewell to the noble couple, and turned to them. "My friends!" he exclaimed, the broad smile back on his face. He gave them all the high handshake. "Come into the Kindler's Room where we can talk." He looked enquiringly at the Dûrians.

"Ah, Perrely and Jomel are with us," Shiván said. "Sandon, would you and your mates mind waiting?"

Sandon for once looked uncomfortable. "My mother —" he said, and stopped. Remorse struck Danîsha. They'd completely forgotten the cheerful, bedridden old lady they'd been introduced to the previous night. Sandon's anxiety to leave had not entirely been on their behalf.

"Oh!" Shiván looked the way she felt. "Fa— er, Kindler, our friend has a sick mother. He needs to get back to her."

"Of course." Father Martin knew Sandon, and told him that he and his friends needn't wait. He'd see to it that his guests were safely escorted home when the time came. Relief dawned on Sandon's face, and with brief farewells he and his companions headed out of the Hearth.

The Kindler then led them through the side door where Assistant Dhôret had gone yesterday. Inside was a spacious office-cum-sitting room. When all had entered he closed the door. "Welcome to Dûrion!" he declared in English, and embraced the four of them in turn.

Perrely and Jomel wore expressions of shock. He turned to them. "Yes, I speak their language. I'm a Dûrian, but I've lived under their sky. Since you are with them I trust you with that knowledge — but it should not go any further."

"So you're the Kindler of Sûrilane *and* the Vicar of Leston!" Danîsha burst out. "How is that possible?"

He pulled up a couple of extra chairs and motioned for them all to sit. "Well, it's a long story. A *very* long story, going right back to the Founders of Dûrion."

"James Turner," Shiván said.

His eyes widened. "How did you know?"

"Just a guess. But tell us the story."

"I will. But first, you've discovered *my* double life — let me just confirm yours! I assume you *are* the Restorers of the Way, whom

145

everyone has been talking about? The foreigners who turned Stillárre upside down, and who are being proclaimed everywhere by the travelling priests?"

"Oh, so Frengor is doing that? He said he would."

"I'll take that as a yes."

"What are you talking about?" Perrely asked. Shiván translated as best he could. Perrely shook her head in amazement. Jomel looked baffled and a little bored.

"Anyway, for now," Father Martin continued in Dûrian, "let me just say that by the One's power I am Kindler of both Sûrilane and of Leston under your sky. There has been a link between our two skies for many centuries. While I am here, no time passes there; and vice versa. I'll go to bed one night in Sûrilane, and wake up next morning in Leston. I'll spend a day, a week or a month in Leston, then one morning I'll wake up back here in Sûrilane. And it'll be the very next day after I had left. Don't ask me how this happens — it's the One who does it by his sovereign power. But you know this already — *you* woke up here one morning, didn't you? And have any of you found yourselves back on Earth since then?"

Lannie turned at once to Shiván. "That's what happened to you, isn't it?" The others were nodding. Shivvie had told them his strange experience when they were still up in the mountains. It seemed like a year ago.

"Yes," he said. "I had a few days back home. It's great to know I'm not the only one! And you're right, Kindler. No time had passed. Then one evening I fell asleep, and woke up in Dûrion. Again, no time lost."

Danîsha shook her head. She'd found it hard to accept Shiván's insistence that his experience was real, putting it down instead to a vivid dream. But here was Father Martin saying the same had happened to him — not once, but many times; and she'd met him personally at the Round Church in Leston. That wasn't a dream!

"Fact is stranger than fiction," Martin murmured.

"What about the Ambon of Sûrilane?" Gil asked. "We worked out that it must have been part of the Irish cross above the altar in Leston. Were we right?"

"Quite right. That was observant of you."

"It was Lannie who noticed it."

"And Perrely who told us the Ambon used to flash when the Founders raised it to summon people," Lannie added. "It flashed when each of us accepted your challenge." Father Martin smiled and nodded.

"So were you, like, a recruiting officer?" Shiván asked. "Were you looking for Restorers to send to Dûrion?"

"Not quite. But I have been praying every week for several years with the Bishop of Dûrion—the old Bishop, Bishop Harlon— specifically that the true Restorers would be revealed. This was after it became obvious that the leaders of the Rebellion were not the Restorers. He knew of my double life, the other half of which was spent under the sky the Founders had come from. We prayed that if it was the Prince's plan once again to summon our deliverers from that sky, he would bring them across my path. I was not specifically looking for people. I didn't single you out. Many came to share their troubles with me in my pastoral rôle at Leston, and I sought to challenge each of them as I challenged you. Quite a few responded positively. But you were the only ones the Ambon lit up for."

"But now the Ambon is back in Leston, and we're here," Gil commented with a frown. "We've been told that according to prophecy the Restorers are supposed to have the Ambon. How are we meant to get it here?"

"You don't get it here," Father Martin said gently. "The One Creator God has called you. He will get it here when you need it."

"And how do we know when that is?"

"You don't. It's called patience. You have to wait." Gil subsided under the quiet rebuke.

"Is it just the six of you who have come looking for the Ambon?" the Kindler asked.

"Yes," Shiván told him. "There are others in our group, but we left them up in the mountains with the Galeronden."

Father Martin nodded. "So that's where you've been since Stillárre. A wise choice. But for now, why don't you stay with me for a few days? I have rooms to spare in the Kindler's house."

"That would be great," Shiván said. Danîsha heartily agreed. It would be wonderful to spend time with this godly man—and to have someone new to speak English with.

"That's settled, then. I'll send a message to young Sandon. But first, let's go to my house." He went to the door and held it open for them.

* * *

The Kindler's house was a spacious residence not far from the Hearth. Like most Dûrian town houses, it was three storeys high and stretched a good way back from the street. To Lannie's surprise the entrance hall led into a little square of garden with a pond, open to the sky. Covered porticoes on either side led to the rest of the house beyond. "This is our pretence at magnificence," Father Martin murmured with a grin.

He led them into a reclining room with a tall, wide window looking out on to the garden. There Lannie — and all the Restorers — had another shock. An attractive woman with long chestnut hair and a warm smile rose from one of the recliners to greet them.

"I'd like you to meet my wife, Shindorel."

"You're *married?*" Shivvie blurted out in English — expressing the surprise on all their faces.

Father Martin threw back his head and laughed. "Did I seem such an ascetic in England?" His wife looked from one to the other with a doubtful smile.

"You gave a good imitation of a man married to his calling," Gil muttered ruefully.

The Kindler switched back to Dûrian. "My dear, they are amazed to find I have such a beautiful wife." Shindorel joined in the laughter, giving him a fond but quizzical glance. Then Father Martin — or Kindler Mâron, as Lannie supposed they must call him now — made the formal introductions. Lannie was interested to see the extra warmth with which Shindorel welcomed Jomel. Her shiláy must have revealed her cultist background, because nobody had mentioned it.

Later as they drank chass they learnt that Mâron and Shindorel had been married for four years now, but had no children. The Kindler explained that Shindorel knew all about his dual life at Leston; but she had never been there. "If we'd asked the One, he might have allowed an occasional visit. This has happened with previous Kindlers of Sûrilane. But we felt it best to keep the two lives completely separate."

Lannie frowned. "So this thing of being both Kindler of Sûrilane and Vicar of Leston—others have done it before you?"

"Oh, yes. Shiván hit the nail on the head when he mentioned one of the Dûrian Founders, Jemmet dos Simion—James Turner, son of Simeon Turner. It all began with him... But I'd need to go back a bit." He took a sip of chass.

Shindorel looked at the two Dûrian women. "I think my husband will soon be talking in Inglish with your foreign friends. Would you like to help me prepare the midmeal? I'm sure we'll be told all about it later." Perrely and Jomel smiled and followed her out of the reclining room.

"My wife is strong on tact," Martin commented in English, "and she also reads my mind. Anyway, I should explain that when their campaigns were ended, the Founders gave their battle standard to the new Hearth of Sûrilane, to serve as a symbol of our faith. You must understand that until then there had been no buildings for Lightist worship. The pastors of the Lightist flock were the travelling priests—who did not want meeting places that might be mistaken for cultist temples. It was the Founders who encouraged Dûrian Lightists to build Hearths—like English churches, but in the shape of an ambon, rather than a cross. The Sûrilane Hearth was the first to be put up—long before the Cathedral in Darthane.

"So that's how the Ambon came here. After peace was established the Founders were busy for many years setting up the new government, and so on. Then they died, and were mourned. But, of course, that's not really what happened." He paused for another sip of chass.

"Don't tell us. The Ambon flashed and they returned to Earth." Gil looked fascinated despite his offhand tone. Shiván gave a delighted laugh.

Martin—Mâron—smiled. "Exactly. The records of the time carefully gloss over the fact that their bodies were never found. Then we get to the bit you don't know. Your friend James Turner had married a Dûrian woman, Aleria. By the One's gift, she came with him to England. There he discovered that his father had just died, and he was now Squire of Leston. He became Sir James, with his mysterious foreign wife, Lady Aleria—a wealthy and influential couple.

"In memory of Dûrion, they decided to build a new church in the village—on the pattern of a Dûrian Hearth. That was how the

'Round Church' came into being. It took quite a few years to finish—as churches did in the sixteen hundreds. But one day, not long after it had been consecrated for worship, something rather amazing happened. A strange emblem appeared on the end wall. No guesses what it was! James summoned the other Founders. They were overwhelmed to see their Ambon again. They placed a horizontal cross-bar over it, so that the overall impression was of an Irish cross. Meanwhile in Dûrion, of course, the great Ambon of Sûrilane had disappeared."

"Amazing." Lannie shook her head, amazed at how God had worked over the centuries. 'Neesh had tears in her eyes.

"But how did this thing start of one person being both Vicar of Leston and Kindler of Sûrilane?" Lannie asked.

"The dual pastorate. Well, to cut a long story short, it began with James and Aleria's adopted son. Aleria found that he and she could go to Dûrion from time to time, thanks to the Ambon. Thus the boy began a double life. He showed an aptitude for pastoral ministry, and was trained both by the Kindler of Sûrilane and the Vicar of Leston. Eventually he was appointed to succeed them both! In that way he became the first of eleven generations who have held a dual pastorate in both Sûrilane and Leston. They've come from either world, and they've had a variety of backgrounds.

"Sometimes, of course, the pastor has found no successor—or one who turned out to be unworthy, and was never sent to the other world. But every time God has provided a replacement."

"Incredible." Shivvie was wide-eyed. "But how did they manage to keep it secret for all these years?"

"You've been back in England. Did you tell them about Dûrion?"

"Um, no. I see what you mean."

Shindorel put her head round the door. "The midmeal is ready."

"Right! Time for a break." Mâron stood and the others followed him to the dining room.

* * *

The next morning Mâron was at home, and they spent more time sharing together. A cold rain was falling outside, and Lannie was grateful for the fire Mâron had built in the reclining room. Also for the hot bath she'd enjoyed the previous night. She was soaking in the comfort of this home after so many weeks of living rough.

Mâron listened with deep interest as they described all that had happened to them in Dûrion. His occasional perceptive questions seemed to draw out the full depth of their experiences, and his empathy was a healing balm. He told them he saw the true Bishop, Bishop Harlon, every Freyneril, and the old man would be eager for every morsel of news about the Restorers who had come in answer to his prayers.

"Something his Radiance will be extremely interested in, is your *nestilar*—your instruments. These are described in our Book, and the fact that you have them destroys the argument of those who claim they have no connection with the Restorers! From what you've told me, the bellaril, sword and bess have proved their value already. What about you, Gelmion? Do you have an instrument?"

He shook his head. "No. I must be one of the exceptions."

Lannie stared at him in surprise. "Gil! Have you forgotten your *blaise?* The two-handed glass you found at Carreck Manor? Don't tell me you've lost it. I saw it in the pocket of your robe, up in Galeron."

Gil blinked. "No, I still have it."

"Ah! Have you used it, Gelmion?" Mâron asked.

"Yes, but it's only a magnifying glass."

"Are you sure, Gil?" Lannie prodded him. He seemed reluctant, for some reason. "Why don't you fetch it, and try it out again?"

He shrugged. "Okay. What magical stuff do you expect it to do, though?"

"I don't know. But glass lenses help people see better. If the bess enables me to hear things at a distance, maybe the blaise will enable you to *see* things at a distance."

"That is how the Book's prophecy has normally been understood," Mâron put in.

Gil's eyebrows rose. "Then it would have been a telescope, surely."

"Oh, Gil, for goodness' sake!" Lannie exclaimed, exasperated. "Just give it another try."

With a doubtful shrug Gil went upstairs to his third floor bedroom to fetch the blaise. While he was gone, Mâron asked Danîsha to play a popular Dûrian worship song, 'Through Fire Arise'. The rich tones of the bellaril filled the house. When she'd finished the Kindler sighed with pleasure. "That was magnificent. There's no doubt *this* is a special instrument. And you are a special player. If you weren't both urgently needed for other purposes, I'd do all in my power to enrol you among the Hearth's musicians." Dear old 'Neesh flushed with pleasure.

Gil returned with the blaise. He sat down and handed it to Lannie. It was a convex glass lens shaped as a four-inch square with the corners cut off. The metal frame had two wooden handles attached on opposite sides. She held it up and looked through it at the fire. All she saw was a blurred image. She examined her tunic-clad knee, moving the glass up and down before freezing in one position. "I can see every fibre in the fabric," she murmured.

"Well, there you are," Gil said. "Just a magnifying glass. Can't think why I've kept it with me all this time. Precious little use it's been."

"Maybe it was a reminder, Gil, of happier times at the Manor," 'Neesh suggested.

His lips quirked. "Could be."

"Wait!" Lannie exclaimed. She handed the blaise back to Gil. "Now. Hold it by *both* handles and look through."

Eyebrows raised, Gil took the blaise by both handles and looked through it at the fire. After a few moments he shrugged. "Nothing. Just blurry flames. What's your idea?"

Lannie frowned. "It's just that— When I first listened to the bess, all I heard was the normal sea-noise you get from a shell. Then one day I held it to my ear with both hands—and I heard 'Neesh speaking, miles away. Now I always use it with both hands. I thought maybe your blaise would work the same way."

"Ah, well. Good thinking. Pity it didn't work out."

She continued to stare at the blaise in frustration. It *had* to have some useful function.

"Is there anything else you do, Lannie, to make the bess work?" Mâron asked.

"No. I just hold it to my ear with both hands, and think of— *That's it!*" She turned to Gil, her heart beating faster. "You need to *think* of the person or place you want to see. Try again, Gil! This time, concentrate on someone or somewhere you know."

With a martyred sigh Gil looked through the glass with both hands again. A moment or two passed and he was about to put it down, when he suddenly stiffened. Shivvie exclaimed, "Look!" He was pointing at the fire. The hair on the nape of Lannie's neck rose as she saw an image slowly forming against the flames. It was a face! A narrow face, with a sharp nose, framed by straight black hair. It was scowling, and the lips were moving in words they couldn't hear.

"It's Fira!" several voices cried at once.

Gil's eyes were wide.

"It works!" Lannie exclaimed joyfully. "You're showing us Fira, up in Rommenardem!"

"That's who I was thinking of," he admitted.

There was a babble of excited comment. Perrely and Jomel were staring open-mouthed. Shiván's crisp *"Wow!"* brought Shindorel hurrying in. She stared in amazement. "Is that… teevee?" she asked her husband. He smiled. "No, my love, but it's the closest we'll get in Dûrion."

"You can't see Fira very well, because of the flames," Danîsha commented.

"Can you move the blaise a little, Gil?" Lannie said.

He shifted position slightly. Now the picture appeared against a shadowed stretch of wall beside the fireplace. It was much clearer, forming a circle about two feet across. Fira turned, and the image swivelled around to remain focused on her face. From the slight movements of her head you could see she was walking.

"Hey, Gil, can you zoom out?" Shivvie wanted to know.

"You people don't want much, do you?" Gil muttered, frowning in concentration. "Next you'll be asking for a remote control."

For a while they continued to watch a close-up of Fira's rather grim expression—then, suddenly, they had a bird's eye view of a wooded valley and a meadow. The Dûrians gasped.

"Whoops, too far," Gil grunted. Closer views followed in jerky succession, until they appeared to be hovering six feet or so above Fira. Now they could see Shîrin and Cârin at her side and the rest of the recruits following. They were walking across the meadow towards the forest and the settlement proper. The view Gil had given them was from the front, looking back the way they'd come. The recruits were carrying wooden sticks that after a while they realised were imitation swords.

"Fira's getting her training done at last," Shiván said. "She doesn't seem too happy about it, though."

"What are all those things beside the forest?" Perrely asked. Strange shapes had appeared to the left against the trees. With some difficulty Gil zoomed in on them.

"Shelters!" Perrely exclaimed. All Lannie could see was a lot of wooden structures that looked like half-roofs with one large sloping side covered in greenery.

"They're lean-to's," Shivvie said wonderingly. "Now why would they have put all those up?"

"Maybe we should ask Fira," Lannie said. She fumbled for her bess, and held it with both hands to her ear. Suddenly the thud of feet, outdoor noises, and distant voices filled the room. There were exclamations of surprise from the others. She took the bess away from her ear, and the sounds continued. She put it down, and they abruptly stopped. She grasped it again, and the sound-effects returned. They had a rather echoey, hollow sound, but were clear. Gil had returned the view to Fira and her merry band.

"... nonsense, Cârin!" Fira was saying, looking over her shoulder. "Only trying to help, Lieutenant," came the muffled response. There was an exclamation from Jomel at the sound of his voice.

"How—are—you—doing that?" Shiván asked in hushed tones. "We've never heard the other side of a conversation when you've been talking with the bess."

"I'm not doing anything! I don't know how this is happening."

"Whatever it is, it's rather wonderful," Mâron remarked. "Perhaps all your instruments are working together."

"You mean, the bellaril, too?" 'Neesh said.

"Well, it can't be the Blade, because I haven't got it with me," Shiván remarked. "Try taking your bellaril out of the room, 'Neesh."

As Danîsha walked toward the door, the sounds began to fade. "That's it!" Shivvie exclaimed. She came back, and the noises rose to their former level.

"Isn't that wonderful!" she exclaimed. "We're so few, and so weak, yet we've been given this special ability against the enemy's strength!"

Kindler Mâron nodded. "Now you're equipped with the full power of your instruments, thanks to Gelmion's blaise."

"I wonder if we can use each other's instruments?" Shiván said musingly. "I don't see any reason why not. They were given for all of us—"

"Look!" Perrely interrupted him, pointing at the image. Fira and the recruits had stopped, and were staring into the sky. "...Shiván! Is that you?" Fira's voice echoed hollowly from the bellaril.

"They've been hearing us!" Shivvie exclaimed. "Hey, Firey, we can see you! Can you see us?"

Fira's eyes widened. "Shiván, are you using the bess? How can you see us?"

"With Gelmion's blaise. He's found out how to use it. We're in Sûrilane, in the Kindler's house. How is everything up there in Rommenardem?"

Fira's face fell into harsh lines. "Not good, Shiván. There are hundreds of Galeronden here. Shambor has taken over Thammeron, Carnem and Linnegon. All the inhabitants have fled here. There are too many mouths to feed. The Elder has said we must leave as soon as Nist can find enough escorts. That will be before the end of this week."

There was silence in the room as everyone took in Fira's grim message. "That's why they've built shelters," Perrely murmured.

"Have you found the Ambon?" Fira wanted to know. By now Shîrin and Cârin had crowded in close. For once their cheerful faces wore no smiles.

"Not yet, Fira. We know it will come to us. We have to wait for it."

"*We* can't wait, Shiván. Everyone is on short rations already. We're taking food out of the mouths of people who desperately need it."

"All right," Shiván said slowly. "Come down-country as soon as you can. I don't know where you'll stay, but maybe Nist can work something out."

"Fira," the Kindler said. "I'm Mâron, Kindler of Sûrilane. I will work with Nist to find safe places for you to stay."

Relief appeared on her face. "Thank you, sir. That will be a great help."

"*Ney li omalend* — Light enfold you, Firey," Shiván said, "and everyone with you." Lannie and the others echoed the midday greeting.

With a sigh Gil laid the blaise down and the picture faded.

155

Chapter 17: *Sudden summons*

THEY WOULD ENTER LAST, Gwargif thought sadly as he led the battle company of Clan Dirkhas into the Great Gathering. So be it — though he was the one who had found the Warriors of Light. But Company Dirkhas had been held back by the marshals while all the others passed through the narrow defile into the natural arena where the Clans met for great occasions. Somewhere in the pack on the surrounding hills, Hishray and his little ones would be watching, huddled together against the bitter wind. On a rocky outcrop at the centre, *Bankhez* and the Clan Fathers waited. Facing them, every battle company of the Ten Clans would be arrayed. It was an event that had not happened in his lifetime, nor that of his father's father. The *Hrarkhoneyl* — the Great Legion — was being mustered. Here, today, a Commander would be chosen who would lead them into battle in the distant south.

The warriors of Company Dirkhas trotted behind Gwargif through the defile — a hundred hands of sleek, grey-white fighters, shoulder muscles rippling, teeth bared, all uttering the low, rumbling snarl of clan pride. Gwargif held his head high. He might be the youngest warrior leader, he might be relegated to last place, but there would be no hang-dog entry for Clan Dirkhas.

As each battle company entered, a roar of barks and howls arose from their clan. Some were led by scarred veterans who had fought off countless marauding wolves and Dark Dorbians in the lean years. Their names were household words. When they came in, the roar of acclaim arose from all over the arena. One of these would no doubt be chosen as *Hrarkhez*, the Commander of the Great Legion.

Gwargif approached the end of the defile. That was strange — the marshals were lined up, blocking their route to the back of the assembly. Then he emerged into the grey daylight. He stumbled at the vast roar that broke on his ears. A frantic glance showed every head in the arena raised in full-throated acclamation. He took the only path open to him, and Company Dirkhas lined up proudly at the forefront of the battle array.

Bankhez raised his hand in a beckoning gesture. In a daze, Gwargif trotted forward, hesitated, then at a further gesture he leapt up to the high rock and sat beside the head of the Clan Fathers. A deep hush spread over the assembly.

The grey-whiskered leader gave Gwargif a *whuff* of welcome, then let the silence draw out as he surveyed the Great Gathering. At last he raised his head and bayed in a deep voice that echoed across the hills,

"*Hail, Hrarkhez!*"

"*Hail, Hrarkhez!*" the people responded.

It was the proudest moment of Gwargif's life.

* * *

The discussion in Father Martin's reclining room had finally come to an end, and Gil settled beside Lannie on one of the recliners while the others straggled out. Lannie gave Gil a careful look-over. There was shadow under his eyes, but he seemed more relaxed. "You found using the blaise quite tiring, didn't you?"

He nodded. "Lot of heavy concentration."

"Well, you're still recovering, so you mustn't overdo it. We'll have to watch that."

His famous half-smile appeared. "Yes, Ma'am."

"But it was rather amazing, wasn't it, how the blaise, bess and bellaril all worked together? Who'd have guessed we could enjoy the benefits of Skype here in Dûrion?"

He shook his head. "Who indeed? Until a couple of hours ago I had no idea that glass had any use except to magnify text."

"Yes. God did a pretty good job of putting things in place."

Gil's face filled with that new earnestness that she loved. "I know. A couple of months ago I would have found that suggestion ridiculous. But now that I understand, just a little, what a great God he is, and how much he loves his people and hates injustice – it all makes sense. Our rôle, I mean, as Restorers of the Way, and the instruments he's given us to make that possible."

She tightened her hand around his. "Great! God's getting through to you. You've picked up a lot in a short time."

Gil shrugged and smiled gently. "What I have picked up is how little I know! All of you are way ahead of me. But I want to learn. You must teach me."

Lannie's heart glowed. Quite a transformation! "We will, Gil – of course we will. But even apart from what God's done for you, you have a lot of insight and experience of life. I'm sure God wants to use that. For instance... Realistically, what do you think our chances of success are? We're so few. Can we really overthrow Shambor?"

Gil blinked and stared unseeing at the glowing coals in the fireplace. After a pause he said, "Well, this is from a human point of view, of course. God may have different plans. But looking at it rationally, everything will depend on the Ambon and the Dorbians. If the Ambon is returned to us, and if it's as effective in summoning supporters as we're led to believe, then we'll have the numbers. But we'll also need trained fighters — and that's where 'Neesh's Dorbian Legion will be crucial. We'll have to build our numbers while heading for Carreck Manor to rendezvous with the Dorbians.

"Once we have them to spearhead our attack... Then, certainly, I believe victory will be possible — especially since many of Shambor's forces will be down south dealing with the Grûzhack."

He looked at her with grave sincerity in his intelligent face; and though it felt disloyal, Lannie couldn't help thinking how much better Gil would do as Overguardian instead of young, happy-go-lucky Shivvie.

* * *

After the midmeal Kindler Mâron said he was going to the Hearth, and Perrely asked to accompany him. Now that there was no future with Shiván, her only refuge was in prayer. Before joining the Restorers she had spent long hours alone in the Berûvis Hearth, rejoicing in the Prince's presence. She needed him more than ever now; and there was a sense of rightness about it. He had recalled her to her rôle as 'Lady of Prayer'.

Inside the Hearth, the Kindler left her with a friendly pat on the shoulder and went to his office. She found a seat farthest from the door next to the curving wall. The large auditorium would have been gloomy if it weren't for the rich ochre light from the windows. For a while she sat watching the raindrops running down the glass in their intricate, ever-repeating patterns. She found it hard to pray. Her thoughts kept turning to Shiván and all that had passed between them.

With an effort of will she looked at the altar and focused her mind on the Prince. On his love for her. On the hideous death he'd suffered in her place, on an altar just like that. Butchered alive and his body burnt by stages before his eyes. Then that glorious moment twelve hours later, when eyewitnesses saw the smouldering embers brighten and catch light again. As the fire grew and intensified, in the midst of it they saw a body slowly re-forming. The head and chest appeared, suspended in the flames; then the arms and legs; and finally the feet and hands, with the fingers stretched out.

The blaze filled the temple, enveloping the entire altar and reaching even to the lofty ceiling. The dazzled eyes of the watchers could dimly make out, standing on the altar in the heart of the flame, the radiant figure of a man. His head and arms were lifted up to heaven, his body shining as though made of pure light. Through the roar of the fire he'd cried out in a voice like thunder, "*Father, let Your Light break through!*"

And his Light *had* broken through. To tens of thousands over the centuries—and also, at last, to her. He had demolished every barrier, every unwillingness, every excuse she'd put up. His love had won her heart. Whatever happened about Shiván, she was Orrénne's, first, last and forever. The tears fell as his tenderness surrounded and comforted her.

After a long while her eyes moved from the altar to the empty wall above. She was so used to focusing on the ambon when she prayed. She'd had one above her bed at home. Every Hearth in the land had an ambon—except this one. According to the Restorers, it was gracing the wall of a Hearth in Inglan. But they needed it here.

In the intimacy of his presence, she asked the Prince about it. "You've called us to restore your Way," she said. "You've told us that we'll *hold high the Rod of Truth*. But we can't hold it, because we don't have it! What must we do?"

You know what to do.

She knew it was his voice, and that he was talking about her personally. But it didn't make sense. "How do I know what to do, my Prince? The Ambon is not even under our sky."

You know more about the Ambon than anyone in your group.

That was true. In the past she'd devoured every book she could find about the Founders, their campaigns, and their great battle emblem. A small flutter of excitement stirred in her heart. Was the One telling her that something she'd read contained the answer? It was her recollection of the Ambon flashing that had enabled the Restorers to identify it with the emblem they'd seen in Inglan…

She began running over everything she knew about the Ambon. It had been crafted in its final form here in Sûrilane. (Some said it had originally come from under the Founders' sky, but that was disputed.) The basic substance was iron, overlaid with gold for the rod and silver for the circle. It had two leather grips in the lower part of the rod. When raised aloft it summoned the faithful to the One's cause. The Founders had carried it to battle in all their campaigns, and the troops believed it gave them victory. When the last battle had been won, they had brought the Ambon to the newly-built Hearth of Sûrilane. Here they'd held a special hearthtime in which they committed the Ambon to the Kindler's keeping—

That was it!

It had been in the keeping of the Founders. They had committed it to the Kindler of Sûrilane and his successors. Now it was needed by the Restorers—but it was still in the Kindler's keeping. He had to pass it on to them.

Yes, my child. She felt a warm smile in her Father's affirmation. "Thank you!" she exclaimed as she leapt to her feet and hurried to tell Kindler Mâron.

* * *

The next morning the sun had broken through again, to Danîsha's relief. After the dawnmeal they all went to the Hearth. Mâron's wife Shindorel came along as well, since she was in on the secret; but the Kindler had given his assistant Dhôret the day off.

As they entered, Danîsha's eyes went immediately to the front wall. It glowed with golden light from the recessed windows on either side of the alcove; a wide expanse broken only by the double hook and socket for the missing Ambon.

The Restorers went and knelt together before the altar. Perrely came with them at Shivân's suggestion, since this private hearthtime had been her insight. Shindorel sat with Jomel in the front row of chairs. Mâron stood facing them all on the other side of the altar in his white Kindler's robe. He held the Book in his hands.

"Friends," he said with a smile, "there is no mention of an occasion like this in the Hearth's Book of Ceremonies. But we're not dealing with men's traditions. We're dealing with the One Creator God. Therefore let's speak and respond in reverence to him, as his Light reveals."

Mâron prayed, thanking the Prince for what he'd shown Perrely, and asking him to direct the transaction they were about to
make before him. Danîsha echoed the prayer in her heart, staring
up at the empty wall. Dear God, place your seal on our calling. Let
the Ambon appear.

The Kindler then read the passage from the Book containing the
One's promise that his Restorers would *lift high the Rod of Truth to
summon the faithful*. He laid the Book down on the altar and paused
while his gaze rested on each of the five before him.

"Shiván," he said, "You came to see me in Leston on a question
of leadership. The One called you here to Dûrion as Overguardian,
servant-leader of the Restorers of his Way.

"Alanya, you saw me in Leston on a question of listening. The
One has called you to Dûrion as a Restorer of his Way, to listen and
discern.

"Gelmion, you saw me in Leston on a question of truth. The One
has called you to Dûrion as a Restorer of his Way, to reveal the
truth.

"Danîsha, you saw me in Leston on a question of mission. The One
has called you to Dûrion as a Restorer of his Way, to spread his message.

"Perrely, the Prince gave you a vision of these Restorers, and
called you to support and pray for them."

He smiled, joy in his eyes. "Long ago, as the One has reminded
Perrely, the Founders of the Dûrian Theocracy committed their
great Ambon into the keeping of the Kindlers of this Hearth. I, by
his gift, am its keeper today. Now, in his name, I commit the Ambon of Sûrilane to you." He paused, looking at them intently. "Do
you accept it?"

There was a ragged chorus of *Yes* and *We do's*.

"Then I declare that from this moment the Ambon is in your
keeping, to use as the One directs." He raised a hand in blessing.
"May it strengthen and encourage you. May it summon all who
are needed to achieve his purposes. May it confound all who oppose you in restoring his Way."

There was a deep silence in the Hearth. The Kindler stood in an
attitude of prayer, his eyes closed. Danîsha stared up at the empty
wall. A sideways glance showed that the others were doing the
same. The wall stared back, bare as ever.

Mâron said quietly, "Let's continue in prayer." He came and knelt beside them.

For a long time they knelt there in silence, alternately praying and looking up at the wall. Nothing happened.

Finally Danîsha heaved herself awkwardly to her feet. "I'm sorry, my old knees need a rest." She walked stiffly to a chair beside Jomel. The others rose from the altar and came to join them.

"Don't lose heart," Mâron said. "I believe we've done what was needed. Now we must just wait for God." Danîsha sighed. So much of her life had been spent waiting. But he was right. She composed herself to exercise a little more patience. It wasn't easy. Beside her Jomel was shifting in her chair and fidgeting, obviously bored to the bone. Gil heaved deep sighs periodically, and Lannie's fingers kept tapping.

They endured maybe another fifteen minutes, then Shiván stood and gave a mighty stretch. "Aaaah! I vote we come back this afternoon."

They all got up, relief and disappointment mingled on their faces. The wall was still empty.

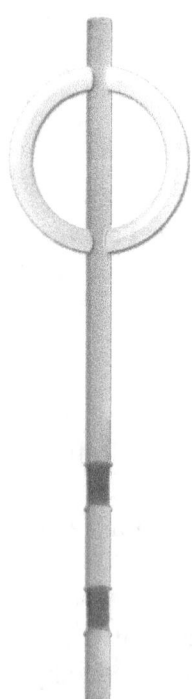

"Keep trusting!" Mâron urged them. "Just because the Ambon hasn't appeared immediately, doesn't mean it won't happen. It's now in your keeping. The One will bring it to you."

They made their way in silence to the side door. Mâron unlocked it and held it open for them. Danîsha was the last to go through. She glanced back at the empty wall, and stopped in her tracks.

"Oh! Oh my!"

The Kindler turned to look. "Dear Prince!" he exclaimed, as Lannie uttered a long, drawn-out "O-o-oh." There were gasps from the others.

The wall was empty no longer. The hook and socket now held a great gold and silver ambon, which sparkled in the sunlight streaming through the side windows of the alcove. Its glow seemed to fill the Hearth. It drew every eye and thrilled every heart. It was as if the old building had come alive again, its soul restored.

They stood in silence, drinking in the sheer beauty of the ancient emblem of the Prince. Shivers ran down Danîsha's spine.

"No wonder people mourned when it was lost," Lannie murmured. Her eyes were wide. Shiván's face was alive with joy.

"I can't believe I'm seeing this," Perrely whispered. Tears were running down her cheeks.

Mâron's eyes were not dry, either. "It's come home at last." He heaved a shuddering sigh. "Well, if we had any doubts, that's taken care of them. The Ambon of Sûrilane, missing for centuries, has returned into your keeping. Bishop Harlon will be overjoyed when I tell him."

"Now it all starts," Shiván said in a hushed voice. "What should we do? Take it with us?"

Mâron sighed. "Much as I'd love to leave it there, we can't. It would be disastrous if word got out before you were ready to use it. Would one of you like to take it down?"

They looked at one another. After a moment Shiván said, "Lannie. You worked out that the Ambon was part of the Round Cross at Leston, and that it had summoned us here. This honour belongs to you."

For the first time Danîsha saw Lannie blush. She gave Shiván a little bow, then turned and walked to the wall. She stood for a moment, staring at the golden rod and silver circle. Then she reached up and grasped the two leather handgrips on the lower part of the rod. She pushed upwards, to dislodge it from the hook and socket. After a moment of struggle it came free. She turned towards them, a delighted smile on her face, the Ambon lifted high. She looked like the standard bearer of a great army, holding its glorious emblem aloft. Perrely cried, "*Alanya – No!*" But she was too late.

A brilliant flash of light dazzled their eyes, and a trumpet call – high, sweet, and incredibly compelling – quivered in the air around them. An overriding urgency seized each one to be where the Ambon was. In a moment they'd all surrounded Lannie.

They stared at one another with horrified eyes.

"That's done it," Shiván muttered.

Chapter 18: *Bishop's Guard*

SHAMBOR SAT HUNCHED over his blackwood desk. What he was about to do was risky. But it was also bold — and the bold stroke often succeeded. The news from Thammeron today was devastating. So was the ominous silence from Lord Narlet, his representative on the Strongholder's joint embassy to the Grûzhack. There was no echo from Narlet's mind. Shambor knew he was dead. So, probably, were the rest of the embassy. If the Strongholder were to put that together with someone *else's* version of events at Thammeron, he could draw only one conclusion. With catastrophic results for the Mindruler of Dûrion.

No. He had to hear his, Shambor's, version first. *Not* that the newly-arrived garrison at Thammeron had been full of ogre-stories and in a highly nervous state. *Not* that their archers had opened fire on a harmless Grûzhack scouting party. Praise Gadesh, the Grûzhack themselves would never tell the Strongholder that. They responded with deeds, not words. The deathly silence from the joint embassy was their reply. That the Strongholder would have heard. There was no time to lose. Shambor had to take the liberty of speaking before being spoken to.

Though only his mind would speak, Shambor took a deep breath. *"Strongholder."*

There was an extended silence during which Shambor fought to keep his thoughts calm. Finally —

"Garion. Did I summon you?"

"No, Strongholder."

"Then why am I hearing your voice?"

"I apologise for the intrusion, your Supremacy. But I have information that may be relevant to the, ah, situation of our embassy in Barazhân."

"Oh. You mean you can tell me why they're all dead?"

"I believe so, your Supremacy. A couple of days ago the Grûzhack made an unprovoked attack on our village of Thammeron. We fought them off, but yesterday they came in greater numbers and overran both Thammeron and Carnem." (That much was true.) *"Now they've murdered our embassy. I fear, Strongholder, that they have abandoned their age-long policy of isolation."*

He held his breath. He knew that this fear had long been on the Strongholder's mind. Let the Grûzhack with their superior armaments start expanding, and the results would be catastrophic for all the Dûrai nations. By playing judiciously on that fear now, he hoped to divert the Strongholder's attention from the exact cause of the embassy's demise.

"I see. And now you are reaping the reward of your own incompetence!"

Shambor smothered a sudden flash of fear. Had he heard the true facts about Thammeron? But the Strongholder's next words showed that he was referring to the original incident when Shambor's troops had blundered up to Fort Desheyn.

"So. The Grûzhack are punishing you for a minor invasion of their territory by seizing Dûrian villages and murdering our embassy." His youthful mind-voice took on a reflective tone. *"This is an overreaction – and a major break with their traditions. Will it stop at a few villages? We can't be sure. If they launch their full strength against Dûrion, you'll go down like wheat before the scythe. No one can withstand their fireweapons. They operate from a distance – you can't get close enough to use mindpower. They'll sweep through your towns and villages like a raging tide."*

Shambor would have preferred a less graphic description. But it set the stage for his next move.

"My thoughts exactly, Supremacy. And will they stop at Dûrion? Once they gain a taste for power in the wider world, might they not press on into Pandiar, Marûvin, and even – Gadesh forbid – Selmion? I feel we need to stop them in their tracks right here, before they advance further into Dûrion."

"Well, of course you do, Gari. It's your neck that's at risk."

"But not only mine, as I'm sure you'll agree, Strongholder. Right now the teméyn trade is at a standstill. The Grûzhack depend on that to sustain their luxurious way of life. If by a concerted effort of all the Dûrai nations we can prevent them from breaking out of their mountain stronghold, then sooner or later their need will outweigh their aggression. But as you have said, Supremacy, Dûrion cannot do this alone. We need the support of the wider mind-realm."

There was a long pause during which Shambor worked on keeping his pulse-rate steady.

At last the Strongholder spoke. *"Very well, Garion."* A small sigh escaped Shambor's lips. *"I will help you, not for your own sake, because you're not worth it. But for the sake of all the Dûrai nations and our continued control of the teméyn trade. I will send you a weapon."* Shambor's heart sank. A single weapon? *"This is no ordinary weapon, Gari. It is a new device that has been developed over a number of years. It has just completed its field trials. And it so happens that it will be particularly effective against the Grûzhack. You can be sure I would not otherwise choose you to be the first to use it."*

"I am deeply grateful, Strongholder. May I ask — ah — what kind of weapon it is?"

"It is a Gorelenyu."

Shambor's eyes widened. The ultimate mind-weapon to subdue their enemies — one that had been dreamed of, talked about, argued over for years in the mindbending community. Now it actually existed? And the Strongholder was offering *him* the use of it? This was more than he'd hoped for — far better than the legions of Selmian cavalry he'd had in mind.

"I thank you, your Supremacy. With such a weapon I will surely halt the Grûzhack advance."

"Yes, even you should be able to manage that."

* * *

Kindler Mâron was the first of the little group clustered around the Ambon to recover. As Shiván and the others stood frozen, the clear, compelling trumpet call still ringing in their ears, he exclaimed, "You've raised the Ambon, Alanya, and it's summoned the followers of the Light! Others will be coming. Quick — take it to the Kindler's Room!" He put a hand on her shoulder and gently pushed her in that direction. She came to life and ran round the altar, clutching the Ambon against her chest. Mâron ran ahead and opened the door. She had barely wangled the tall emblem into the side office when the front door of the Hearth burst open. Three people came charging in — a young man with wild red hair who looked like an apprentice, gripping a hammer; a housewife with hands still coated in flour; and an older man in a threadbare robe. They ran down the aisle and stopped before the altar, looking bewildered. Their eyes fastened on the group under the empty wall.

"What was that sound?" "Did *you* call us?" "What happened?"

"You also! What did you hear?" Shiván shot back.

"I heard... well, it was like a trumpet calling, and I— had to come!" the young man exclaimed.

"I felt that the One needed me *at once*, so I dropped everything and ran..." The housewife glanced ruefully at her floury hands. She frowned, perplexed. "I don't know how I even knew where to go, but I just did!"

The older man nodded, still catching his breath.

"This sound that you heard—was it in your mind, or out loud?" Gil asked, blinking.

The three shared puzzled glances. "I'm not sure," the redhead said slowly. "But now you say that, I think it must have been in my head—'cos no one else noticed anything. I'm a mason's apprentice; my master is working on that house just opposite on the market square, and what he'll say about me dashing off like that..."

Mâron and Alanya had rejoined the group. "Farron, Lôray, Stembor, welcome. I'm glad you could come," the Kindler said, smiling and giving them each the high handshake. "Don't worry, Farron, I'll have a word with Master Nalleron." He turned to the Restorers. "These faithful members of my flock have come for the special hearthtime."

Before he could explain, there was a sound of running footsteps on the short flight of stairs outside the Hearth door, and two workmen burst in, their hands and tunics smeared with dirt.

"Hollet, Fennior, you've come as well. My friends, the One has summoned you. Don't worry about your clothes, or how you look. The important thing is that you are here. Take a seat—" he motioned to the front row of chairs. "The special hearthtime will begin soon."

The five new arrivals looked doubtful; but he was their Kindler. They went and sat, chattering volubly among themselves.

"Mâron, what's your idea?" Shiván murmured. He was grateful someone in the group *had* an idea.

"I saw in the Hearth's Book of Ceremonies in the Kindler's Room that today is officially a day of Harvest Sharing. Few Hearths still observe it—it's a relic of our cultist past, the festival of the harvest god; but it'll give us a reason for this gathering. You lot had better sit as well." He ushered them from behind the altar and took his place at the Kindler's lectern.

As Shiván and the others took their seats, more people came hurrying in. Mâron repeated his statement, but before he could finish yet more arrived—and now it became a flood, with people streaming into the Hearth both singly and in small groups. Shiván saw that they came from all walks of life—labourers, housewives, clerks, merchants, gentry; but there were no children or old people. In the row behind them a well-dressed family group was talking about their interrupted journey. Assistant Kindler Dhôret came to the front, looking dazed. Mâron directed him to a chair beside the lectern.

When the Hearth was almost full the Kindler raised his hands, and a tense silence settled over the gathering.

"Friends, welcome to the One's Hearth. You have come today at *his* calling. I didn't summon you. But we all suddenly felt a great need to be here, so we dropped everything and came. Many of you are faithful Hearth-goers, but some I know are followers of the Travelling Order, and I see a number of travelling priests." He smiled and nodded at a large group in purple robes. "We welcome you with all our hearts! This is a day when our differences fall away, because *each of us has heard the One's call.* You would not be here otherwise."

He paused, looking down for a moment. People were still entering the Hearth, though the flood was slowing down. Shiván saw a well-built man with a military bearing come striding in. He looked vaguely familiar. He stood near the door. All the seats were taken now.

"Today," Kindler Mâron resumed, "is the day of Harvest Sharing in the Book of Ceremonies. If anyone asks me why we were all gathered here on a working day, that is what I shall tell them—and I would advise you to do the same. In a few moments we will indeed celebrate the One's abundant provision—for *all* our needs.

"However—" He paused again, letting his gaze wander over the packed auditorium. "You know and I know that we each received a special summons to be here today. Something we haven't felt before. Maybe you're a little uncomfortable about that. You acted strangely, dropping everything and rushing here. You are wondering if you are quite 'normal'. If so, take comfort from those around you!" His hand swept across the crowd. "It can't be that *everyone* here is acting strangely. No. God has called us. And he has called us for a purpose.

"Exactly why that should have happened today, we do not know. We will celebrate the harvest hearthtime together. Then we will leave and resume our normal business. *But—we will not forget what happened today.* My friends—" he leaned forward, his face intense. "Let me repeat, *God has called you here for a purpose.* He has heard the prayers of his people in this land. He is answering them. I believe great events are on the move, and what you have experienced today is just the beginning. We cannot talk about it now. You know why.

"But do not write this off as an odd experience that you can go home and forget about. Regard it instead as a wake-up call! An important preparation for greater things to follow. And when you hear that summons again—as you surely will—do exactly as you did today. Obey it. Go where you are urged to go, and do whatever you are asked to do. And you will be part of what God is doing in this land."

"Now let us thank the One Creator God for his abundant provision—for our own needs, and those of our nation."

Everyone stood as he raised his hands in prayer. Shiván thought he'd done pretty well for a spur-of-the-moment job. Not everyone would be satisfied, of course; and the few who were steeped in the Ambon's history and the prophecies of the Restorers would already have put two and two together. But people like that could be trusted not to babble about it.

Mâron led them in a simple hearthtime of prayers and well-known songs, which the large crowd sang unaccompanied. Shiván began to wonder uneasily about the future. News of these strange goings-on in Sûrilane would spread like wildfire. How would the authorities react? Would they accept Mâron's explanation? Hundreds of people suddenly dropping everything and rushing to the Hearth—to celebrate some half-forgotten festival? It sounded thin. Dangerously thin. He chewed his lip.

The hearthtime ended. Some hurried out, returning to their abandoned jobs. But most people stayed, and Mâron and Assistant Kindler Dhôret became the centres of two clamouring circles of questioners. Shiván wondered what Dhôret was finding to say. The poor fish looked distinctly harassed.

Then a hand fell on his shoulder, and he turned to face a sea of purple robes. At its centre was a deeply lined face like a walnut, with a broad smile lighting up every crinkle.

"*Frengor!*"

"I knew I'd find you in the middle of this, young Shiván!"

They embraced, and Frengor turned to greet the others. Shiván was delighted. He'd been wondering where they'd meet up with him again — the last place he'd have imagined was here in the Sûri-lane Hearth! He must have been in the area and responded to the Ambon's call. Watching Frengor, Shiván frowned. Was he imagining it, or had the head of the Travelling Order grown thinner? His robes, and those of the other priests, had a dishevelled, slept-in look about them. What had they been up to?

He had no time to ask, because just then the well-built man with the military bearing whom he'd seen entering the Hearth came up and saluted.

Shiván stared at him. The face was familiar. Where had he seen him before?

The man smiled. "Captain Garset don Tembor at your service. We once met at the Westgate of Stillárre. Then again in the Guard-house."

"Captain Garset! Of course. It's thanks to you we weren't skewered by the Bishop's Guard that time."

He bowed. "And it's thanks to you that my officers and I are not still rotting in the Stillárre Guardhouse." His green eyes subjected Shiván to an intense gaze as they stood facing each other at the front of the Hearth. "My judgment at that time seems to have been confirmed. Only the true Restorers of the Way could have acted as you did; and only the Restorers of the Way could have recovered the lost Ambon of Sûrilane. Because that trumpet call *was* the Ambon, wasn't it?"

Shiván instinctively glanced around. His friends were laughing at something with Frengor. No one else was near. "It was. You don't miss much."

Garset nodded. "You, then, are the Overguardian. May I know your name, sir?"

"Of course! We didn't have time for names before. I'm Shiván dom Bernet. I must introduce you to the oth—"

Garset wiped the words from his lips by going down on one knee. Shiván gaped at the man. He bowed his head. Then he stood and saluted, hand to chest.

"I have waited long for this day, sir. I offer you my allegiance, and that of my Company, as the true Lord Marshal of the army of

Dûrion. I forswear our former allegiance to the Bishop Suffragan. We are yours to command, sir."

"Your Company?" Shiván said stupidly. Frengor and the others were staring at the little scene being enacted before them.

"Yes, sir. We are known as the 'Pure Company'. All four hundred and twelve of us are followers of the Light. I am here on my own now. The others will arrive in two days' time. Then we are at your disposal."

* * *

Shambor dom Beldet quivered as he sat at his blackwood desk, his eyes glazed. *The Ambon of Sûrilane — found!* By those would-be Restorers! According to his informant, it had been under their sky all these centuries. And now it was back in the Sûrilane Hearth! Real! Undamaged! It had just fulfilled its legendary function of summoning Lightists to the One's cause.

Panic and despair threatened to overwhelm his mind as it wrestled with this momentous development. All his background and upbringing screamed at him that this placed the four foreigners in a different category: no longer upstarts, pretenders, opportunists... They had the long-lost Ambon of Sûrilane: they were the true Restorers of the Way.

All of Dûrion would rally to the Ambon. Thousands would rise up against him. His forces, already stretched thin by the Grûzhack incursions, would be overwhelmed. The Restorers would sweep into Darthane at the head of a vast army of the faithful, and cast him from the Cathedral...

No! What nonsense was he imagining? Those were the fancies of childhood, implanted in him by bigoted, narrow-minded parents. These foreigners were just playing on the credulity of ordinary people. They knew the Lightist prophecy required them to have the Ambon, so they'd produced one to order.

Of course, there was still the sudden influx of people into the Sûrilane Hearth to be explained...

Shambor's eyes narrowed and he wiped a hand over his mouth. All right. Even if this *were* the real Ambon, and it *had* summoned those people, this was just another piece of Lightist magic on a par with the *nestilar*, the instruments: the sword, the bellaril, the shell and Gelmion's glass. They had temporary effects in specific types of situation—not like the powerful, long-term effects of mindbending. He had already learned how to sidestep the magic of the *nestilar*: he would do the same with the Ambon.

And when you came down to it, what advantage had the Ambon's summons brought the Restorers? One Lightist company—a mere four hundred soldiers. That was all. Against his many thousands. The common people who'd responded—the housewives, masons, merchants, minor gentry—what good would they be in a pitched battle with superior forces? None whatsoever! And he had a secret weapon these pathetic Lightists knew nothing of.

Shambor sat up straighter. Logic always overcame superstition. He knew how to handle this now. The only question that remained was whether to nip it in the bud right away, or let it grow, and then pluck the larger fruit.

He studied the ornate ceiling.

After a while a grim smile spread over his heavy features. *Let them grow. Until the Strongholder's Gorelenyu gets here. Even the Ambon will be no match for that.*

* * *

It was evening in the Kindler's house. Jomel tapped her fingers idly on the window ledge of the craft room on the first floor. The light of the two moons cast crossed shadows of her on the felt floor covering. To her right stood a small loom with spindles of brightly-coloured thread from the *hilminay* plant. To her left was a small carpenter's workbench. She was alone, which was not what she wanted, but she couldn't have stood any more of the endless discussion about the day's events that was still dragging on in the reclining room.

Yes, the reappearance of the Ambon of Sûrilane had been amazing, and so had Frengor and Garset's arrival; but did they have to go on and on about it, squeezing out every last drop of meaning? And the endless speculations about what would happen next, what to do, how the authorities would react. They were meeting with Garset and Frengor tomorrow to discuss those things—a meeting to which she was mercifully not invited. Couldn't they leave it till then?

There was a sudden gush of water from the smallroom down the passage. For a moment her mood lifted as she remembered what had happened a few days ago. Shiván had been the first of the foreigners to use the smallroom. There'd been the splash of water accompanied by a loud yell. Shiván had appeared with his clothing soaked. He'd been told about the flushing wheel, but the silly man hadn't taken his tunic off before sitting on the bench! Nor had he positioned himself properly. When he turned the wheel the jet of cleansing water had spattered all over him. What a backward sky they must come from.

She looked into the passage to see who would come out of the smallroom now. She was hoping to catch Perrely, but instead it was Gelmion. He gave her a tired glance, then smiled warmly. Well, that was a welcome change.

"You didn't make Shiván's mistake," she said, eyeing his dry tunic.

"No. Getting soaked in the smallroom is not my idea of fun. Nor is sitting about discussing things that may never happen. Looks as though you feel the same."

"Oh, I get so tired of all this seriousness."

He nodded. "I couldn't agree more. What's this room here?"

"The craft room."

He came in and glanced around. "So! This is where the Kindler and his wife relax. Weaving and carpentry. Each to his own, I suppose." Again he gave her his warm smile.

Jomel frowned slightly. Why was she getting such preferential treatment? But her brow cleared as she realised this was just the opportunity she'd been waiting for.

She glanced up at Gelmion, putting on her wistful look. "You know, ever since you used the blaise to see Fira up in the mountains, I've been wanting to ask you something…" She looked down, marking coy circles on the floor with her toes.

Gelmion's smile broadened. "And what's that?"

She hesitated a little longer, then let it come out in a rush: "Could you show me my parents in Stillárre?"

"Oh." His face clouded. "I don't know, Jomel. You see, I have to picture the person I'm wanting to focus on. And I've never seen your parents. But then—" The smile came again. "I know the area where they live. I could give it a try."

"Really?" She moved closer. "Would you?

He reached into his pocket. "Let's see what the blaise can do."

They sat on the floor facing the darkest corner of the room. Gelmion held both handles of the glass and stared into it, his features tight with concentration as he focused the light from the window on the wall. Jomel gasped as a dark image appeared. There were slightly less-dark objects moving in it, and after a moment she recognised it as a familiar Stillárre street in the moonlight, with a couple of people walking along and a horse and cart coming towards them, all moving in eerie silence.

"Why can't we —? Oh, of course. Alanya's not here."

"Nor Danîsha. All three instruments are necessary for everyone to hear. If it was just Alanya with the bess, only she or whoever was holding the bess would hear."

"We must do it with them. I want to be able to hear my parents, and talk to them."

"One thing at a time. Let's see if we can find your parents first. They live in the Gildane Hills outside the Berûvis Gate, don't they?"

"Yes."

Gelmion manoeuvred the blaise, and fragmentary scenes flashed across the wall. Then with a surge of joy she recognised the familiar moonlit hills of home. They were viewing them from a strange angle, as if she and Gelmion were suspended in the air.

"Guide me from here."

She pointed out the particular hillside. Gelmion zoomed in, making her feel queasy. She directed him till they were facing the house, with its broad, white-pillared façade. "Why are there no lights?" Jomel exclaimed. "There ought to be lights in most of the rooms at this time of the evening. Can you go inside?"

"I think so. Let's try…"

He moved toward the front door, as if walking up the gravelled drive. He reached the highly-polished blackwood door, then suddenly they were inside.

Jomel exclaimed in distress. The familiar entrance hall, with its expensive green marble floor, was shrouded in darkness — not a single lamp lit. They started moving through the house. Everywhere the window hangings stood open, bathing each room in the eerie glow of moonlight. Jomel shivered, biting her lip. At least they could see, though the drapes should have been closed by now… The dining room, the serving room, the reclining room. All dim, all empty. The kitchen, the cloakroom, the baths. Daddy's study, the inner courtyard with its ornamental pond. All the same.

"What's *happened*?" Jomel exclaimed. "Are they ill? Upstairs — the bedrooms!"

The bedrooms, too, were empty. But the lids of two of the clothes chests were standing open, the contents jumbled. In her parents' room the bedclothes were lying half on the floor.

"Where are the servants? Why hasn't someone tidied up?"

The top floor, housing the servants' quarters, was also unoccupied.

A cold fist closed over Jomel's heart. "Gelmion, something terrible has happened! Even if my family had gone away, they would never have left the house like this. In any case, the servants would still have been there. Why have *they* left?"

"Hmm. Rather a mystery. Let's try some other places where your family might be. Your father's work? Any relatives they might be visiting?"

Jomel guided him to all the places she could think of — even to Perrely's deserted home near Berûvis. There was no sign of her family anywhere. She began to weep silently.

"I wonder — could they have run into trouble with the authorities?" Gil said.

"No! *Why*? They've never done anything wrong. Daddy's an honest merchant, and Mum… Mum's so respectable it hurts!"

"Respectable people sometimes do un-respectable things for their children."

"Nonsense, *they've* never — Oh."

"Yes. Like lending their sinélle carriages so a beloved daughter can escape the Bishop's patrols."

She stared at him, aghast. "That time when you went into mindlock in the Forest of Janulane — and we travelled to Dhembis in my parents' carriages…? You think the Bishop has arrested them for *that*?"

"He's arrested people on less provocation."

Jomel sat clasping and unclasping her hands while Gelmion shifted scene to the Stillárre Guardhouse. Her heart was in her mouth as he checked in all the prisoners' cells. He needed no guidance there.

Her family was not in the Guardhouse. She heaved a sigh of relief.

"There's one other place we could look…" Gelmion said meditatively.

"Where's that?"

"In the Domicile of the Travelling Order."

"The Domicile of— What on earth would they be doing *there?*"

Gil blinked. "I don't know, the thought just came to me."

"That's ridiculous! They're not Lightists—they despise the Travelling Order. Why would they visit the Domicile?"

"No idea. But let's check anyway."

She stared at him, baffled, as he manoeuvred the blaise to the imposing portico of the Domicile. He moved inside. The entrance hall was well illuminated by light trees—and Jomel saw with a shock that several grey-cloaked Bishop's Guards were standing there, casually talking together.

"Guards! What are they doing in the Domicile?"

Gelmion didn't answer. He shifted scene to the cavernous, dimly-lit crypt. It had been divided—quite recently, by the look of the brickwork—into two rows of tiny rooms with a corridor down the middle. Gelmion moved down the corridor to the third door on the right. He went inside, and Jomel stopped breathing.

There was her family. Dear Daddy with his sticky-out ears, sitting on the floor with one hand manacled to the wall. Mum, looking like Jomel had never seen her—hair unkempt, dress filthy, slumped against a pillar. She, too, was manacled. Her sister, little Dûlay, was clinging to her mother. Her three brothers, Mel, Jinnet and Harron, sat huddled against their father with tear-streaked cheeks.

But it was the look of utter hopelessness on her parents' faces that brought a shuddering breath into her lungs and a cry of anguish to her lips.

"*Quiet!*" Gelmion's command was like a slap. "We don't want the others here in the craft room." Jomel looked at a face that was now all too familiar. The mindbent face of a Bishop's Guard.

"You knew…" she whispered.

"Of course."

"But how can you still be mindbent? Dhelgor's dead—Shiván killed him. All the Guardsmen froze."

"But *I* didn't. How do you think I revived so quickly? It wasn't because of the Lightists' prayers."

"Then how—?"

"I was no longer a slave of Dhelgor's. I answered directly to the Mindruler himself — to Shambor. I still do. He took me over shortly before Dhelgor died — to keep an eye on him."

"Gadesh help us!"

He chuckled unpleasantly. "Not much chance of that. But you're a Lightist now, aren't you? If only the One were real! Oh, I've felt the attraction of those Lightist myths — and I think I've played the part convincingly, don't you?"

Horror flooded her. He was mindbent by Shambor. That meant Shambor knew everything! All about the Ambon... the plans they'd made that morning... even where they were right now, in the Kindler's house!

She leapt up — but Gelmion was ready for her. He lunged and grabbed her arm, yanking her to the floor. He sprawled on top of her, pinning her down. His face filled her vision, a familiar, urgent desire disfiguring it.

"Now you will make love to me. And you'll never breathe a word of this to the others. If you do, it'll be your family that suffers. *Do you understand?*"

She nodded, tears welling in her eyes.

It was over. Her freedom — and all the hopes of the Restorers.

Chapter 19: *Strategy*

THEY GATHERED IN THE KINDLER'S STUDY on the top floor of the house: the four Restorers, Mâron, Perrely, Frengor and Garset. Shiván's glance kept returning to Frengor. The old man looked like a fish out of water in Mâron's green tunic and fur jacket. A bitter rain was pouring down outside, and Shindorel had taken one look at the drenched priest and insisted he change immediately.

What immediately struck Shiván and the others was the way she and Mâron addressed Frengor: as 'Uncle'. The Head of the Travelling Order turned out to be the uncle of the Sûrilane Kindler — though they belonged to two different branches of Lightism. With a twinkle in his eye Frengor had said there was a long story behind that, but they wouldn't air their differences right now. Mâron had just smiled.

They also learned that Frengor and his companions had been sleeping rough in the Denwood. Frengor explained that they had been evicted from the Stillárre Domicile. With a rueful grin he added that this was one of the few houses they now dared visit. They were marked men, out of favour with the authorities, and anyone they associated with would fall pretty low in the Bishop's estimate. But since his nephew and niece were already sheltering the Restorers, he reckoned they couldn't fall any lower.

Shiván tried to express his sorrow that they'd brought this on them. Frengor brushed it aside. "Not because of *you*, young Shiván. Because of the terrible state of this country — which you've come to put right!"

"But Garset, my old friend," Frengor continued, "finding you here yesterday was quite a surprise. I thought your legion had been transferred to Dhembis?"

"It has," Garset replied, a faint smile at the corner of his lips. He was sitting relaxed in an armchair opposite Frengor.

"Then, ah, pardon the question, but why aren't you with them?"

"Because I deserted." The smile grew broader.

Frengor's eyebrows shot up. "You *deserted?*"

"Officially. You see, I'm also a marked man, Frengor. The Bishop's Guard are after me for eliminating a few of their members to allow the Restorers into Stillárre. But my commanding officer, though not a practising Lightist, is a good man. He has a low opinion of the Guard, and did not want me to fall into their hands. So he devised a plan whereby I would 'desert' en route to Dhembis. Then he would send a whole Company to search for me — assuring the Guard he was doing all he could."

There was a twinkle in his green eyes as he continued. "But what he won't tell the Guard, is that the search party is my own Company! They've already been hunting all over this area without finding me. Tomorrow, though, I'll find *them* here in Sûrilane. This has all been arranged. After that I was supposed to return to the legion with them as a common soldier — and in due course, when the episode was forgotten, I would have resumed my rank as Captain.

"*However—*" he heaved a sigh and smiled. "As you know, the second part of the plan now falls away. I can't say I'm sorry. And my Company, I know, will be as relieved as I am to pledge their allegiance to the true Restorers. You have been a constant topic of conversation since the events in Stillárre. We are tired of being called in to assist the Bishop's Guard with their dirty work. Now at last we can offer our support to those worthy of it." He bowed his head toward them.

"Let's hope we *are* worthy," Shiván said. He was still trying to adjust to the idea of commanding a company of professional soldiers.

"You are the One's Restorers. You fulfil the prophecies and hold the Ambon. That is all the worthiness we need."

"Well. You've given us a massive gift, and we need to decide how to use it. That's why we're all here." He looked round at the others. "A couple of days ago we were a small bunch of ordinary people with about sixty untrained followers up in the mountains. Tomorrow, Garset tells us, we'll have over four hundred real, live soldiers at our command. That sort of changes things. What do you guys think? What should we do? We threw a lot of ideas around yesterday. Today, with Garset and Frengor's input, we need to make some quick decisions. Mâron's already fielded questions about yesterday's to-do from the Town Elder — and there'll be more to come. The sooner we leave Sûrilane the better."

There was a silence. Gil was gazing upwards, fingers steepled, the academic considering a problem. Lannie was looking at Gil. 'Neesh was looking worried.

Gil was the first to speak. Turning to Garset he said, "We have no funds, of course. Will you and your men be prepared to serve without pay?"

"That won't be a problem. In the army we do not receive a regular stipend. Food, shelter, clothing and equipment are provided. We're given spending money when we go on leave. Otherwise there is a large payment on completion of service. My men will not expect anything in the short term."

"And in the long term?"

"We expect to see the Dûrian theocracy restored, and funds once more available through normal channels."

Gil nodded, his eyebrows raised in appreciation. "Good to see such confidence. But what about food, clothing, and so on? We're in no position to find provisions for four hundred soldiers."

Garset was unfazed. "My company has been given funds to cover a lengthy search for me. They left nine days ago with fully-stocked supply wagons, and can continue replenishing them for about three weeks. After that—we're in the One's hands."

'Neesh's face cleared. "Thank goodness!" she exclaimed. "I'd been so worried about food. Isn't it wonderful how this has worked out? If we'd met you at any other time, you wouldn't have had that money!"

"No indeed, my Lady." Garset smiled at her.

"Okay, but what do we *do* now?" Lannie demanded. "We have around four hundred and ninety soldiers, including the recruits in Rommenardem. That's a flea against a warhorse compared to Shambor's army. Sorry, Garset."

"No offence, Lady. You're quite right. We cannot hope to engage Shambor's legions with a single Company."

"What would you advise, then?"

Garset paused, looking down at his hands. Then he glanced round the room, his eyes resting briefly on each person. "It's not my place to advise the Restorers of the Way," he said slowly. "But since you've asked, I will respond. I've studied the campaigns of our Dûrian Founders. They spent several years gathering an army strong enough to challenge the Tyrant of the day. After defeating him, they went on to build an even greater army with which they ousted the despots in all the surrounding nations.

"Defeating Shambor may be our immediate goal; but it will only be the beginning. Even more powerful than Shambor is the Strongholder of Selmion, who rules the Cult of Gadesh—which in turn controls the governments in almost all the Dûrai nations. If Shambor is removed, we will face the wrath of the Strongholder, and find ourselves at war with Selmion, Pandiar, Marûvin—and perhaps Thrinar. We therefore need a well-trained and experienced fighting force. This will not happen overnight. My advice is: Haste may win a battle—but patience wins a war."

Shiván glanced round the group. Several wore thoughtful expressions—it was no small thing they were embarking on. Perrely's face, though, was alive with interest. A fellow enthusiast for the Founders. But Lannie was unimpressed.

"The Founders took *several years* to gather an army? So you suggest we just sit around waiting for people to join us? Scuttle from one hiding place to another, picking up a company here, a troop there, and hoping Shambor doesn't lift his boot and stamp on us before we're ready?"

Garset's eyebrows rose. Gil cut in before he could answer. "I think the Captain has given a sensible response, but without full knowledge of the facts. He doesn't yet know about the Dorbians."

"Dorbians?" Garset's eyebrows had risen further.

It took a while to explain to him about Gwargif, the difference between the Dark Dorbian scavengers and the Light Dorbians, and the promised Dorbian Legion. But Garset finally got it, eyebrows still raised.

"So— Five thousand of these Dorbian warriors will be arriving at any moment near Carreck Manor? To fight for you against Shambor?"

"That's right," Shiván said.

"This is great news. Then our first destination— but pardon me. That's your decision."

"You were going to say our first destination should be Carreck Manor? Exactly the bright idea we had. En route we can raise the Ambon of Sûrilane, gathering an army as we go. That's what the Founders did, wasn't it?"

Garset shook his head. "Not at first, no. Only after they'd captured their second town. In the beginning they had to build up their forces much more quietly. Yes, even in hiding, with due respect,

181

Lady Alanya." He hurried on before she could fire off a retort. "I agree that we should go to Carreck Manor, taking the Ambon with us. But it should not be used until after the Dorbians have joined us. In fact not until – with their help – we have captured our first town. Then we will be a force to be reckoned with. People will *want* to join us. Shambor will be afraid of us. The town garrison and other near-by troops may defect, providing seasoned soldiers and the beginnings of a real army.

"If we raise the Ambon before then, what will we have? You saw the crowd in the Hearth yesterday. Good, honest Lightists – but traders, workmen, housewives, gentry. Hardly a soldier among them. What kind of army would they make? A field of hay to be mown down by Shambor's scythes."

He stared round at them. There was silence as they took in the grim picture he'd painted. "An army needs *training*," he added with quiet emphasis. He sounds like Fira, Shiván thought. "And the best place for training is the barracks of a defended town."

"But – That doesn't leave much of a rôle for the Ambon," 'Neesh said, frowning. "We've gone through a lot of struggle and prayer to find it, because we were told it was essential to our calling. Now you're making it sound like an optional extra. Something we can use if we like, but only after we've succeeded by our own efforts." She was shaking her head. "That doesn't sound right."

"'Neesh has a point," Shiván said. "That prophecy – what was it, Perrely?"

"*They will lift high the Rod of Truth to summon the faithful; they will raise it above the altar of darkness, and release my captive people.* It's utterance fifty-nine of the third discourse in *The Return of the Prince*." Her eyes rested sadly on his. He swallowed and looked away.

"Well, that, er, sounds rather central. Pretty much at the heart of our calling. Mâron, you were the Keeper of the Ambon before us. What do you think?"

He smiled. "You know the Ambon is at the heart of your calling. It brought you here. And we've seen how it 'summons the faithful'. That's no optional extra. But exactly how or when it should happen is another matter. Captain Garset also has a point."

He was saying both Yes and No. Okay. Shiván turned to the fur-wrapped figure in the armchair. "Uncle Frengor. What do you say?"

Frengor waved a hand dismissively. "Oh, I say the same as Mâ-ron. There's no division between Hearth and Order here."

"So we should follow Garset's plan?"

"Not necessarily," Frengor said. Mâron nodded in agreement. "You must follow the Light! *All* of you." The sharp brown eyes in the crinkled face moved around the circle. "This is your decision to make. It's a difficult one. Don't listen to your own voices, but to the voice of Truth."

"Right." Shiván sighed. "Okay. You've heard what Garset thinks and what I think. Any ideas on which is the voice of Truth?"

"I agree with *you*," Lannie said at once. "We should raise the Ambon. Why else were we given it?"

Shiván nodded. There was a silence. Then Gil spoke, his eyes unfocused, thinking aloud. "That's an important question. Why were we given it? I seem to remember from previous discussions that the Founders were the ones who had the Ambon made, here in Dûrion. Am I right, Perrely? Garset?"

"Yes," said Garset.

"Well, some say it may have come from your sky," Perrely added. "But most believe it was first constructed here in Sûrilane."

"Right. But did the Founders make it at the very beginning of their campaign, or later?"

Garset frowned. "Later. After they captured Sûrilane."

"Oh, so Sûrilane was that second town they captured, which you mentioned earlier?"

"Yes."

"And did they start using it immediately after that?"

"Yes."

"In other words, the Founders began using the Ambon as soon as they had it. They didn't keep it in reserve earlier on because they felt it was wiser to wait. They didn't *have* it then. Once they did, they knew it was given for a purpose, so they used it. It seems to me that this is exactly what Shiván is suggesting."

Shiván felt like cheering the good old Doc, but kept his face straight.

Garset was shaking his head. "A clever argument, my Lord, but here's the refutation: Yes, the Founders used the Ambon as soon as they had it. And what was the result? Does anyone know what happened after the Founders left Sûrilane?"

"I do," Perrely said in a small voice.

"What?"

"The Slaughter of Gend."

"Exactly." Garset looked round the circle, his face grim. "For those who don't know, it was the most tragic event in the Founders' history. They raised the Ambon in every hamlet and town after leaving Sûrilane. Thousands flocked to them. Then at the village of Gend near Janulane they were brought to bay by the Tyrant's army. Over five thousand were massacred in that battle — untrained craftsmen, housewives, farmers and shepherds summoned by the Ambon." He paused, his intense green eyes probing theirs. "The Founders learnt a lesson from that. I suggest we do, too."

"What lesson did they learn, Captain?" Gil asked him gently, his fingers steepled. Shiván frowned. He knew that tone of voice from sessions with the Doc at university. *Somehow* Dr. Denbigh was about to reveal a flaw in the officer's argument. Though he couldn't imagine what. To him it seemed watertight. No one would want a repeat of that terrible slaughter.

Garset's eyebrows rose. "Not to use the Ambon prematurely, of course."

"I see. So how did they later use the Ambon *non*-prematurely?"

"As I said before. When they were safe in a captured town and had facilities to train their new recruits."

"Oh, so *training* is the main issue?"

Garset hesitated, sensing a trap. Then he nodded. "Yes, that's one way of looking at it."

"Then, is it fair to say that if the Founders had been able to *train* those five thousand recruits before reaching Gend — the slaughter might not have taken place? Or might not have been so massive?"

"There was no way they could have trained them en route to Gend. They hadn't the time nor the facilities."

"That doesn't answer my question."

Garset looked sideways at Gil. "I think you're trying to trip me with words, m'lord. But yes, one cannot argue with that. If the recruits had been trained, there might not have been a slaughter."

"You've mentioned a town barracks as the best place for training. One can understand that viewpoint from someone with your background. But is that the only place where training can take place?"

"Perhaps not."

"No, it wouldn't seem so. At this very moment our colleague Fira en Tarrel, a former Lieutenant in the Rebel army, is training recruits at the Galeronden settlement of Rommenardem. There's no barracks there. She's been using an open field and home-made wooden practice weapons. Progress might not be as rapid as in a barracks with strict discipline and proper equipment; but the basic skills can surely be taught anywhere. Or wouldn't you agree?"

Garset sighed. "I agree, my Lord."

"Then to return to the matter under discussion, what is to stop us from raising the Ambon en route to Carreck Manor, as Shiván suggested, but planning our journey via forests and other secluded areas, where the new recruits can be trained?"

"Gil, that's a great idea!" Lannie exclaimed. "There are several forests between here and Carreck Manor where a large group could remain hidden for a week or more."

Garset was sceptical. "Almost five hundred? Camping? In *forests?*"

"Oh come on, Captain," Lannie retorted. "You've lived too sheltered a life. We've been camping in forests since we arrived in Dûrion."

"With respect, my Lady, until now you've been a fairly small group. Setting up camp for five hundred people in a forest is a different matter altogether. There would not be enough room to pitch tents, no roads for the supply wagons, probably an inadequate water supply, no open space for massed training exercises — "

"Alright, alright, not forests then. Beside secluded villages. Whatever."

"And if the Ambon draws large numbers? How can we remain hidden? How will we feed them all? My Company's resources are not inexhaustible."

"Those are legitimate concerns," Gil said gravely, his eyes blinking as he thought about it. "But we mustn't forget the spiritual aspect. As Mâron and Frengor have reminded us, we must be led by the Light. Sitting here in this comfortable room, we can't foresee all the different circumstances that may arise. We may plan a route, only to find that the Light leads in quite a different direction. We need to follow that leading. We need to look to God as to when and where we raise the Ambon. Clearly not in the immediate vicinity of Darthane. But if he leads us to raise it further afield, and adds many new recruits to our numbers, then we must trust him to provide for them and to hide them from the eyes of the enemy."

His earnest gaze passed from one Restorer to another. "As you've taught me, and as I'm beginning to discover, we serve a great and powerful God. *He* has given us the Ambon. *He* will protect us as we use it. We can't hold back because we're afraid something may go wrong. That's not trusting him, is it? We must go ahead in faith, as well as common sense."

Wow, Shiván thought in the hush that followed. Gil has learnt so much so quickly! There was a general chorus of agreement.

The two pastors held their peace. Garset smiled and shook his head, but said nothing. Shiván decided to leave it at that.

_____

Chapter 20: *The Pure Company sets out*

THE CHILD FELT PANIC RISING in him as the closed wagon began picking up speed. The regular thudding of the sinélle's feet, the swaying motion... soon they would crash! That's what he did to wagons. That's how this all started. That's how he'd long ago made his loving Ammi and Baaba die. Now *he* would die the same way! He struggled against Nurse's strong arms. A high, keening wail rose from his lips... and the sinélle went mad. They screamed in terror, the wagon jerked violently forward and careered headlong, lurching this way and that. There were shouts from the driver and the horsemen alongside. Nurse screamed as the boxes on the high racks came crashing down. One struck the child's leg, and his wails became cries of pain.

Soon after that the wagon began slowing down, then shuddered to a stop. Nurse was whimpering—he'd never heard her do that before. There was blood coming from her head, and a broken box on the seat beside them. The door was pulled roughly open, and his mentor Faranu peered inside. He looked afraid! The child could hardly believe it.

"Are you alright?" Faranu said, in a funny, gasping kind of way.

"I'm hurt!" Nurse said. Her face was very white. "*He's* alright." Though he wasn't—his leg was sore. He began crying again.

"What happened?" Faranu demanded.

"The brat started screaming."

Faranu's sharp eyes turned to him. "Be quiet! Why did you scream?"

He cowered against Nurse, bereft of speech, waiting for the blow. It came.

"*Stupid* boy! You nearly killed yourself and Nurse, and you've ruined two of our sinélle!"

Faranu stood staring at him for a moment, anger in his dark eyes. Then he turned to Nurse. "He can't continue in the carriage. He'll have to ride with me. Go and get yourself seen to."

Some time later the child found himself seated behind Faranu on his horse. He was strapped to the saddle so he couldn't fall off. They began riding. The wagon was in front of them. Nurse was in it, a bloodstained cloth round her head. There were other grey-cloaked men riding beside them. Behind was the supply cart and the servants, piled high because they were going a long way.

The horse began speeding up. He didn't mind. This was nice. The green countryside flowed by. He was leaning against Faranu's back and holding on tight. He felt almost happy, because his mentor had helped him.

* * *

Garset's 'Pure Company' arrived in Sûrilane the next day. He took the Restorers' group to meet them after the midmeal. They were camped in a couple of fields outside the town, some distance from the nearest house.

The entire camp erupted in cheers as Shiván and his companions entered. At Garset's signal silence fell, and they all went down on one knee. Then they rose, saluted, and began singing. Perrely leant forward and whispered from behind Shiván that this was the Song of Allegiance—which she'd last heard sung to the former rebel leader Armanet in Berûvis. There was a glint of tears in her eyes. Lannie and Danîsha stood on either side of Shiván, looking bemused and somewhat overwhelmed. Gil, beside Lannie, had a faint smile on his face.

When the rousing chorus ended, Shiván managed a few words of welcome to the Restorers' cause. Then, as he was now the only one who could do so, he reinstated Garset as Captain. That met with prolonged cheers—including those of red-headed Tarlion, the acting Captain, now restored as Garset's Second.

The Restorers returned that evening to the Kindler's house. After the daymeal, with Lannie's permission, Shiván used the bess to contact Fira—confirming what he'd suspected: that the instruments were not restricted to the person who'd found them. Fira told him that she and her band were preparing to travel down from Rommenardem with Nist the next day. There were safe refuges in Fanderane Wood where they would stay until Garset's company could meet them.

Mâron returned late that evening from his weekly visit with Bishop Harlon in Darthane Cathedral. He told them how the old man had wept for joy at the news that the Restorers had truly come, and that the Ambon of Sûrilane had reappeared. His lonely years of trust and prayer were at last bearing fruit.

Danîsha, in particular, valued the quiet day that followed, while Fira's group made their journey down from the mountains. The peacefulness of the Kindler's home was balm to her soul. She wanted to soak in as much as she could, to store up for the unsettled times ahead. They heard that evening that Fira's group were huddled in rustic forest shelters, unable to light fires for fear of attracting attention. She was glad to be where she was.

After that came Anderil, the One's day, and a final hearthtime in the ancient building on the market square. To her delight Mâron asked her to join the musicians with her bellaril. They had all responded to the Ambon, and could be trusted to keep her foreignness secret. She didn't know all the songs, but managed to harmonise. The music had a rich fullness to it, and compliments flowed freely afterwards.

Back at Mâron's house, everyone made their own preparations for departure. Mâron brought the Ambon from where it had been concealed in the Kindler's Room. Amazingly, there had only been a few cursory questions from the Bishop's Guard about the stampede through Sûrilane and the unscheduled hearthtime that followed. It was apparently written off as a minor case of religious hysteria.

Before dawn the next day, after a brief time of prayer, they said their farewells to Mâron and Shindorel. It was an emotional moment. 'Father Martin', as they still thought of him, had been instrumental in bringing them to this point. They embraced, and he murmured a few words of encouragement to each.

Then they made their way to a prearranged spot in a dark alleyway off the market square. Shiván and Gil carried the Ambon horizontally in the strong fabric bag Shindorel had made for it. They hadn't waited long when there was a tramp of feet, and a detachment of thirty soldiers appeared in the square led by Tarlion, Garset's Second. No one else was about. They hurried out and were soon surrounded by green capes. Tarlion gave them a salute and a broad grin, then they marched off to rejoin the main company just outside the town.

With Shiván's agreement Garset left Sûrilane by a roundabout route, avoiding the main highways. By the second hour of the

Dûrian day — approaching eight thirty, Shiván reckoned — they were following a small country road that meandered through fields to the village of Fanderane. It was an overcast day, but no rain yet.

Shiván couldn't help a surge of pride as he looked back from the crest of a hill. The Pure Company on the move was an impressive sight. The three infantry cohorts marched two abreast on the narrow road, their green capes swinging. Behind them trotted the cavalry squadron, a hundred riders with capes of light blue. Bringing up the rear were the four supply wagons, one for each hundred-man unit. With them were scouts, cooks, blacksmiths, farriers, and the other essential personnel of an army on the move. The column stretched six hundred metres — half an *aldor*. Every person a committed Lightist. All pledged to fight for the Restorers. Shiván marvelled. Only God could have done this.

The Company reached Fanderane around mid-morning. By discreet use of the blaise and bess they contacted Fira, and before long she and the twins, with ninety-one mountain refugees, straggled on to the road ahead of them. The Restorers, Perrely and Jomel hurried to join them. They caught a glimpse of Nist and a couple of her escorts at the edge of the nearby woodland. The large lady waved, then disappeared.

"So that's your tame army?" Fira said, with a jerk of the head at Garset's Company. She left them in no doubt what she thought of those she'd fought in the Rebellion. Lannie smothered a grin at the undercurrent of sour grapes. The Lieutenant had been looking forward to being the boss lady, had she? Garset's advent must have been a severe disappointment.

The Restorers and Fira's group moved on along the Lestack road. After a short break the Company followed. Then by agreement they paused while the Company overtook them, allowing Garset to lead. He planned a wide circle westward before heading north towards Berûvis and Carreck Manor. They would avoid all major roads, and the two groups — Fira's and Garset's — would remain separate, at least for this first part of the journey. Garset did not want to have to explain, if they met a patrol, why he was travelling with a dishevelled bunch of non-military personnel.

Fira sniffed. "Give my men a little more training and proper weapons, and they'll thrash an equal number of those spoiled infantry brats any day." They themselves would have no explanation for their large numbers and their rebel shiláy if questioned. "Let the army boys have their excuses. We'll trust God," Fira declared. In fact if there were any trouble Garset would intervene, and they'd all have to trust God for the outcome.

The day's march was uneventful, however. They bypassed Lestack, and by early evening had crossed the Sûrilane–Chale road just west of Cristane. One of Garset's scouts guided the Company to a dry cave system on the edge of the Bishop's Downs. Fira's group followed half an hour later, slipping quietly through the shadows.

After a hot vegetable stew prepared by the Company cooks, everyone began settling for the night. It was very dark, the stars blotted out by a heavy overcast. The soldiers were muttering about rain tomorrow. Lannie, Danîsha, Perrely and Jomel were in a semi-private side cave, where they pulled on extra layers of the warm clothing Shindorel had found for them. They lay down on the hard ground. 'Neesh heaved a martyred sigh as she shifted about trying to get comfortable. We've all been spoiled in the Kindler's house, Lannie thought.

Her mind turned to Gil. It was such a joy that he was now also a Lightist—or a Christian. Yet she sensed a barrier in him that she couldn't penetrate. He said and did all the right things, but there was something missing. She could only put it down to emotional damage resulting from the much longer period of mindbending he'd had to endure.

But here they were. The Ambon of Sûrilane was on the move. After they'd found the Dorbian legion, let Shambor beware. They'd be a force to be reckoned with. She shivered—whether from anxiety or anticipation, she couldn't tell.

* * *

Gil tossed and turned in the cave he was sharing with eleven other men. He couldn't get to sleep. His eyes followed the flickering light of the watch fire as it played over the rugged stone ceiling. He was thankful Shambor had granted him a degree of autonomy, so his overpowering presence wasn't here now to read his mind. He'd learnt always to display to the Mindruler his genuine desire to co-operate, which was the only way he could make a life for himself on this benighted planet. Yet... some spark of the old Gil deep within still hated the way he was living now.

The ironic thing was that his friends had *almost* succeeded in releasing him from the mindbending. When he'd gone into mindlock, it had been genuine. His teméyn supply had run out, and Shambor had lost contact with him. If it hadn't been for Lishet, Nist's half-wit brother, and his magic cordial, he would truly have escaped. The cordial, of course, was laced with teméyn — that was how Shambor had kept tabs on Nist's activities. Lishet had given him a good supply of the cordial when he'd left Galeron. It had seen Gil through all the way to Sûrilane — with Lannie actually encouraging him to take it, because it seemed to do him good! His gradual 'recovery' from the mindlock had been carefully staged. He was glad *that* charade was over now.

What he'd said to Jomel was true. He'd felt the attraction of his companions' earnest Lightist faith. What they'd said up in the mountains about finding freedom from the burden of the atrocities he'd committed — from the blood on his hands — had moved him deeply. That hadn't been faked. Shambor had realised this, and allowed him to react spontaneously. It was a diabolically clever move. It had prepared the way as nothing else could for his 'conversion' — which certainly *had* been faked. There Shambor's own inside knowledge of Lightism had come into play. He knew exactly what emotions to display, and how to express them in words.

He'd hated deceiving his naïve English companions — especially Lannie. But it was necessary for the rôle the Mindruler had for him in his wider plans. And that was the ultimate reality in this world. Not the wishful thinking of Lightists or Christians. If he'd believed for a moment that freedom from the burden of blood on his hands was really possible... But of course it wasn't. Only fools and religious mystics could believe that. Dream about a loving God long enough, and you could convince yourself all the pain you'd inflicted didn't matter any more.

No, the world was a much harsher place than that. It was a place where actions had consequences that couldn't be escaped. *But* — if you aligned yourself with the right people, they could be turned to your advantage. Even if that meant being the bad guy a little longer.

Here in Dûrion he'd learnt that there were realities beyond the physical. Actions taken purely in the mind that had real, physical effects — like mindbending. And other powers that he'd seen displayed during his time as a Guardsman. This was no mystical pie in the sky when you die. This was here and now, down to earth, and very practical.

One day his friends would discover this. In the short term he might seem to be betraying them, but in the long term he was working in their best interests. To bring them to the realisation that here in Dûrion the Realm of the Mind was the ultimate Truth. That they could never overcome so powerful a practitioner as Shambor – or, looming like a colossus beyond him, the Strongholder. That the best anyone could do was to work *with* such powers, and reap the benefits of co-operation.

He found himself heaving a shuddering sigh. Maintaining your own identity under the pressure of such overwhelming mental power was a never-ending struggle. There was no let-up – apart from fleeting moments like this. It was like surfing a tidal wave. One slip, and you'd be pounded in a maelstrom beyond imagination.

Yet, there were benefits. Not always ones that his Lightist friends with their narrow morality would approve of. But things that eased the strain of living. Like Jomel. What was she, when all was said and done? A temple prostitute. A whore who'd long ago abandoned any morals a Lightist would recognise. Look how shamelessly she'd flaunted herself at the twins. No, he felt no compunction about using Jomel for sex. His love was reserved for Lannie – his lust for Jomel. She had no other part to play in this Lightist circus; she might as well serve his needs.

* * *

"Gelmion."

"Mindruler."

"You've done well."

"Thank you."

"They're walking nicely into the trap. And your masterly performance the other day persuading them to use the Ambon means there'll be plenty of hay for our scythes, as the worthy Captain put it. He's no fool, that man. It's a satisfying irony that you convinced them to do precisely what he most feared."

"Yes, Mindruler. Your prompting helped."

"Of course, but you are justifying the limited autonomy I've allowed you. Spontaneous speech is always more convincing than a Mindbender's simulation. There's greater autonomy to come, Gelmion. Keep your eyes

on that. You have the potential to reach great heights in the Realm of the Mind."

"I look forward to that, your Dominance."

"So you should. Now, to allay Garset's fears when they first raise the Ambon – in Dharmack, I think you said, on the other side of the Downs?"

"Yes, Mindruler, that was the plan."

"Right. Tell them you've discovered in the blaise that I'm transferring every available soldier to Dhembis for use against the Grûzhack. If they want to see for themselves, just look along the highways and you'll find plenty of troops heading that way. Arrange a time tomorrow with Alanya to check my office in the Cathedral with the blaise and bess. Alert me, and I'll be having a conversation with someone about the Grûzhack situation. I'll say I'm only withholding the Darthane garrison itself. That should persuade the Captain it's safe to gather recruits with the Ambon."

"Very good, your Dominance."

"Yes, it is, isn't it? Then, when their rabble has grown to a full field of hay, we'll lure them to the right spot and mow them down. There's a saying in your mind that I like – killing many birds with one stone. We'll kill enough birds to discredit the Restorers permanently."

Gil felt a heaviness settle over him. A deluge of fresh blood on his hands. "Yes, Mindruler."

"Oh, and about Jomel. Enjoy. You've earned her."

"Thank you, Mindruler. Ah, I meant to ask – Can her parents' situation be improved? I'd like to keep her co-operating as long as possible."

"It will be done by tomorrow night."

"Thank you, Dominance. And – my friends. Forgive me for asking, but… do you still plan to spare them?"

"Oh yes, Gelmion. They'll be spared, never fear. They are reserved for better things."

Chapter 21: *Ambon and mystery weapon*

GWARGIF'S MOMENT OF GLORY had come. The Great Legion, the *Hrarkhoneyl*, was assembled before *Bankhez* and the Clan Fathers. They were ready to set off on the long run south. The integration of the ten clan contingents was complete. The chain of command had been established, ruffled hackles soothed. The training had been done, farewells said. The young recruits who would defend the clans in their absence had been chosen. These, led by a sprinkling of disappointed veterans, formed the first rank of the watching pack in the great arena.

The Chief *Varlaze* — the High Priest — had led the people's prayers to the Shining One, as they committed the Great Legion to his care and leading. A deep hush now rested over the gathering. Into it *Bankhez'* voice broke in a roar that echoed across the barren hills:

"Who are these arrayed before us?"

"The *Hrarkhoneyl!"* the pack thundered.

"Where are they going?"

"To the South."

"Why?"

"To break the darkness!"

"Whom will they serve?"

"The Warriors of Light!"

"Do we release them?"

"We release them!"

"Then GO!"

At the explosive command Gwargif leapt down the track leading out of the arena. Behind him he knew the warrior companies would be peeling off one by one in a sinuous grey-white stream of pent-up physical power. He heard his own voice, echoed by thousands of others, baying the great battle-cry of the people. He glanced up, to the left, to the topmost ridge of the surrounding hills. Somewhere among the densely packed bodies Hishray and his little ones would be calling their farewells.

Farewell, my beloved. I will come back — or wait for you in the Shining Place.

* * *

The Restorers' Company approached Dharmack in the late afternoon. It was a picturesque little village of thatched cottages beside
the River Mirith, which came tumbling from the northern slopes of
the Bishop's Downs. Shiván felt his pulse quickening. This would be
the first time the Ambon would be deliberately raised to summon
Lightists to the Restorers' cause.

The plan had nearly been shelved, though. That morning Garset
had again voiced his objections to raising the Ambon this close to
Darthane — and Fira had agreed with him. Dharmack was on a small
backwater of a road, buried deep in the countryside. Garset himself
admitted that troops seldom passed this way. Yet he and Firey had
stuck to their guns, swinging 'Neesh and Perrely to their side.

Then at their noon stop, Gil and Lannie — who were the opposi-
tion party, with himself doing an impartial Speaker-of-the-House —
had got themselves a major breakthrough. They'd used the blaise
and bess to spy on Shambor in Darthane — wonderful things, those
instruments! — and had caught him in the very act of discussing
troop movements with one of his lackeys. It seemed he was sending
everything he had to Dhembis, to use against the Grûzhack.

Gil and Lannie had gestured violently for the rest of them to
come. 'Neesh had brought the bellaril to do its broadcast act. Garset
and Fira stood blinking in disbelief when they saw the picture flickering against a broad tree trunk and heard the sounds emanating
from it. But they both clearly heard the last part of the conversation,
when his Bishophood declared that the only troops he would *not* be
sending to Dhembis were those of the Darthane garrison itself.

That had swung it for Garset. Fira kept shaking her head: "I
wouldn't trust anything that snake says." Gil had panned the blaise
over the major highways, revealing one legion after another all
tramping towards Dhembis. Fira still wasn't convinced, but in the
end she shrugged her shoulders and the decision was made.

Here they were, then, about to raise the Ambon for real for the
first time in this undistinguished little Dûrian village.

It didn't look too promising at first. As they drew nearer, the
place seemed deserted. Then Perrely pointed to a distant hillside
that glowed a deep purple in the afternoon light. "They're out gathering the late *hilminay* crop," she said. Figures could be seen cutting

and binding the Dûrian textile plant. The Company marched through the village. Children, older folk, and housewives appeared in doorways, silently watching them pass. Shiván guessed the army wasn't too popular since the Rebellion. They halted in a meadow beside the river, not far from the hillside where the people were working. A few of the harvesters paused to stare down at them.

Garset called the Company together into a tight-packed assembly around the wagons, where the Restorers and Fira's group were standing.

"Soldiers of the Way," he declared, "this is what we've been waiting for for many years. Now the Overguardian will raise the Ambon of Sûrilane. When its call comes, you'll want to be right up close to it. But you're already as close as you can get. So stay where you are, and no one will be hurt in the crush."

Shiván and Gil had laid the Ambon's carry-bag on the ground. Now Shiván squatted down and undid the fastenings. He carefully lifted the shining emblem out, and climbed the steps of one of the wagons, where he could be seen. A hush of awe fell over the assembled soldiers. The Ambon looked so beautiful, and so out of place in these rustic surroundings. Yet the worn leather handgrips on the golden shaft bore witness to the fact that—unlike them—it had seen many such events before.

"Right." Shiván gripped the leather and prepared to raise the Ambon aloft.

"Shouldn't we pray first?" 'Neesh prompted from the foot of the steps.

"Of course." Why hadn't that occurred to him?

He handed the Ambon to 'Neesh, and raised his arms in the Dûrian gesture of prayer. A forest of arms rose in response. Shiván prayed, asking God to start drawing in the folk he wanted to serve alongside them in restoring his Way in Dûrion. It was a rather halting prayer. Maybe from having to raise his voice unnaturally. Maybe because he needed to spend more time alone with God.

He looked out over the sea of expectant faces. Then he took the Ambon from 'Neesh, grasped the handholds, and with a determined movement thrust it skywards.

There was a moment of silence. Then a dazzling shaft of light burst from the tip of the Ambon, and at the same instant that high, incredibly pure trumpet call rang out, electrifying all who heard it.

Shiván shuddered at the impact. He found himself gripping the Ambon with all his strength, his knuckles white.

There was a universal surge towards him. Garset cried *"Hold!"* The upturned faces registered shock, wonder, joy, delight. There was a rising murmur of awestruck comment.

He looked toward the purple hillside. The villagers were stampeding down it. A few remained behind. Maybe some were old folk and children, who had not been called. On the other side, people were streaming out of the village itself.

The first group of panting, wide-eyed country folk reached the outskirts of the assembly. The soldiers parted to let them through. Housewives, young lads, girls and husky working men jostled up to the wagon steps, some still grasping their harvesting implements. Their eyes were riveted on the Ambon. Shiván's heart went out to them. These were the people God had added to their cause.

"Welcome, friends! The One Creator God has called you here today. You're full of questions, I'm sure, but let's wait till everyone has arrived."

When the last stragglers had come in, Shiván reckoned about three hundred and fifty villagers were staring up at him and the shining emblem. The crowd had swollen to fill the meadow, with Garset's company lining the perimeter. He and 'Neesh, Alanya, and Gelmion were now standing in the open end of a wagon.

He welcomed the newcomers again, and told them that the ambon he held was the long-lost Ambon of Sûrilane. There were gasps and mutters. "Did you hear a trumpet call?" he asked. They nodded. "And you *had* to come, didn't you?" A rumble of agreement. "That was the Ambon, summoning you to the One's service. That's how you can be sure I'm telling the truth. *We* didn't call you. *God* did."

He went on to declare that the four standing in the wagon were the true Restorers, and that they needed the support of every follower of the Light to restore the One's Way in Dûrion. *This* was the service they were being called to today. He introduced Garset, who told them how he had responded just like them to the Ambon's call, and now his whole Company had abandoned their allegiance to Bishop Shambor and were sworn to the service of the Restorers. There were some ragged cheers.

Shiván called up one of the refugees from Fira's group. He described how his family had fled from Shambor's persecution to the mountains, but now he and others like him—there were cries of support from Fira's group—had joined the Restorers to put an end to the Usurper's oppression. The villagers cheered again. Their shock was giving way to acceptance, even excitement at what God was doing.

"So now, my friends," Shiván concluded, "you have a choice. God has called you in a miraculous way. You can choose to obey his call, or ignore it. You can choose the hard way—to come with us and fight the powers of darkness that rule this land—or you can choose the easy way, and stay comfortably at home. I don't believe anyone who has heard the Ambon today is *unable* to join us. In that case, God would not have called them. Look around you! There are no old folk or cripples or children gathered here at the Ambon. Every one of you is able to join us if you choose. *So make your decision!* We'll be leaving in one hour." He gestured to the others, and they climbed down the steps of the wagon. Now it was in God's hands.

Garset hastily mounted the steps and shouted for attention in the hubbub that had broken out. He told the villagers that those who wished to join them should bring a blanket, warm clothes, any knife or implement they could use in battle, and enough food and water to see them through the next day. After that, God would provide. Some dubious muttering followed. Well, they needed to face up to that. Garset hadn't mentioned the biggest problem—shelter. For the meantime they could double-up in the tents. But if similar numbers responded at every village... They'd cross that bridge when they came to it.

The hour passed. Close on three hundred villagers returned, bags, sacks or tied blankets over their shoulders, many carrying staves, some with wicked-looking knives tucked in their belts. There were as many women as men. Their faces reflected almost every emotion: excitement, anxiety, determination, exaltation, uncertainty. About half the village seemed to be leaving. Friends and relatives crowded round, many weeping, some pleading.

Shiván felt a lump rise in his throat. How many would return to Dharmack? How many bereaved relatives might one day blame *him* for the loss of a loved son, daughter, father or sister? A heavy weight of responsibility settled on his shoulders as the enlarged company took to the road.

* * *

"Your Wisdom, is this *wise?*"

"Ongaret, you are funny sometimes." Frengor's eyes twinkled in his cheerful, deeply-lined face. There was a ripple of laughter from the other priests. The small group of purple-robed figures was making its way up Cathedral Hill in Darthane. Above them towered the great white building that was the heart of Dûrion's government and — once — its faith.

"But — If you are recognised *here* ..."

"My dear man, Shambor thinks I'm a spent force. He's thrown me out of the Domicile, branded me a dangerous subversive, and cut off my sources of income. If he found out I was here, he'd probably invite me to a meal just to gloat over me."

"He might also chop off the Order's head, so the rest of the body will die."

Frengor stopped under a tree on the broad avenue. The priests clustered round. "Listen. There are very few ways now in which we can actively support the Restorers. The least I can do is to sound out some of my old contacts here in Darthane, and learn what I can about Shambor's plans. Some of the people I know are quite high up — and not too happy about the state of the country. They won't give me away.

"I'm uneasy about what happened in Sûrilane," he continued in a low voice. "The stampede of people to the Hearth ought to have attracted more attention. It's been passed over much too easily. I have an uncomfortable feeling that that snake Shambor knows more than we suspect. I'd like to find out how much, and what he's plan-ning to do about it." He paused while a family group passed by.

"Then there's the Restorers' plan to raise the Ambon en route to Carreck Manor — against Captain Garset's advice. I'm not sure that decision was led by the Light. A large group travelling with an army company is bound to be noticed. If Shambor hears about them and takes counter-measures, I want to know what they are, so we can send a warning."

He turned to Ongaret. "Does that explain why I need to take this risk, brother?"

The thin, solemn priest nodded, his eyes sombre. "I understand. But I don't like it."

Frengor clapped him on the shoulder. "Sometimes liking and doing are different things. But come! Let's move on. I want to see if I can find my old friend Estaron—Shambor's secretary."

* * *

The flames were roaring up into the sky, and there was nothing he could do. He wailed in anguish, up there on the hill, watching his mother die. Great, dry sobs racked his young body. He had done this. He had killed her, in a childish fit of anger. He'd wanted to display his power, to show her he was somebody, not just the rebellious son of a Lightist Kindler. But his power had failed! He couldn't save her. When he needed it most, his power had failed—

Shambor woke up. Sweat was pouring down his face, and he could feel himself trembling. With an oath he heaved himself out of bed. Fortunately tonight he was alone. He hated it when a female was there to witness his weakness. He hated the weakness. Why did that terrible nightmare keep coming back—and more often these days? It had happened decades ago. He was long over it, had made a great success of his life, was now the most powerful man in Dûrion.

He had to prove his power. He had to keep on proving it. He had to show Mama— *Stop that!* He prowled through the darkened rooms of his suite till he came to the private store, known only to himself and Estaron, his secretary. He unlocked it and fumbled in the cages till he'd caught a small, grey rodent. It bit him, and he cursed again. He'd show it who was master…

Afterwards he disposed of the remains in a wooden waste box in the storeroom. There was a medley of squeals, squawks and hisses as the other occupants caught the whiff of blood. Estaron would clear it away later.

He washed himself, cleaned the wound in his finger, and climbed back into bed. His breathing slowed. There. He'd dispelled the aching void of failure.

* * *

"Your Radiance."

Shambor gave an exclamation of annoyance as he looked up from his blackwood desk. "Estaron, I thought I said I was not to be disturbed?"

The secretary's long, solemn face remained impassive. It was a strong face with a youthful complexion, surrounded by carefully-combed black hair. He was a young man who struck people as wiser than his years. His deep-set, pale blue eyes were watchful, experienced, reserved.

"My apologies. You asked to be informed as soon as the *Gorelenyu* arrived."

"It's here?" There was a sudden eagerness in the Bishop's tone.

"Yes, your Radiance."

"Then bring the Keepers to me at once—and Legate Derlion!"

Estaron bowed. The commands had been anticipated. He went to the blackwood door and ushered in the Legate, together with three men wearing dark grey robes. After the introductions he retired to his sloping writing table in the corner and busied himself with correspondence. He followed the conversation with half an ear.

Shambor began by explaining to the three grey-robed Selmians that he wanted his Senior Legate present in case there were any aspects of the special weapon's deployment that the regular army needed to be aware of. The Selmians assured him there were not. Derlion stayed anyway. Shambor began asking detailed questions about the *Gorelenyu*. Estaron spoke Selmian fluently and knew perfectly well what *Gorelenyu* meant, but he hadn't heard it used in a military context.

"What is its range?"

"Devastation greatest within radius of five *aldoret*," the leader of the grey-robes replied in his lilting Selmian accent. "Impact severe within twelve *aldoret*. Effects light to medium within thirty *aldoret*."

"Thirty— *aldoret*," Shambor repeated in a hushed voice. "A day's walk." There was a grunt from Derlion. Estaron's own eyebrows had risen. From Darthane this devilish instrument could be used against an enemy as far away as Sûrilane!

"What *kind* of weapon is it?" Derlion wanted to know.

"That is not concern for you," the chief grey-robe said coldly.

"But if it's going to travel with the army, there are questions of transport, maintenance, and so on—"

"We have own transport and supplies."

Derlion subsided.

"It's been fully tested?" Shambor asked.

The spokesman inclined his head. "Final field test was five days ago."

"How effective was it?"

"Army of one thousand condemned prisoners decimated. One hundred two-and-thirty survived, twenty died soon after."

"Nine hundred killed! By this one... device?"

The grey-robe shook his head. "Not killed. Incapacitated. Killing done by own army."

"I see. Well— That's all right. How long does the incapacity last?"

"As long as weapon is in use. Even after, recovery is slow."

"Good, good." Estaron's lips quirked. Small movements of the Bishop's shoulders showed that he was rubbing his hands under the table. As eager as a sinélle for a snack. "Derlion, be sure to spread the word among the troops about this wonder-weapon. No need to fear the ogres any more." He turned back to the grey-robe. "How long can it be used at one time?"

"Half hour."

Shambor's heavy features clouded. "Half an hour? That's not long for a battle."

"No battle with *Gorelenyu* last long." Estaron could hear the grim smile in the man's voice. "But can extend time with breaks. Use for half hour, rest for quarter. Up to three hours. Then longer break needed. Over-use reduces effect."

"Can you continue like that for several days?"

For the first time there was no instant reply. The spokesman hesitated, looked at his companions. Subtle changes of expression flickered over their faces, and Estaron's suspicions were confirmed. They were Mindbenders. After a rapid mental discussion the spokesman turned to Shambor.

"Has not been tried. But is possible. Longer breaks necessary. And not at night."

"Yes, yes, that's fine. I want you to start at once."

There was silence round the Bishop's blackwood desk. Estaron's pen hung frozen above the paper.

Derlion cleared his throat. "With respect, your Radiance, the Grûzhack are more than thirty *aldoret*—"

"I know that, Derlion."

The chief grey-robe spoke. "Weapon cannot be precisely targeted, Dominance. If you use here in Darthane, many innocent people will suffer."

"Can you lower the intensity without reducing the thirty-*aldoret* range?"

Again there was hurried mindspeech between the grey-robes.

"Can try. But cannot guarantee results. This has not been tested."

"I'm willing to take the risk."

"Would recommend location outside Darthane."

"That can be arranged. Somewhere not far, to the north-west. Distack, near the Larwood, would do. See to an escort, would you, Derlion?"

Derlion rose, saluted, and left. Once he was out of the room Shambor and his guests continued their conversation by mindspeech.

In the silence Estaron frowned at the paper before him. Continuous use for several days, in the obscure little village of Distack? What was Shambor up to?

Chapter 22: *Trap baited*

'THE RESTORERS' ARMY'—that's what people were calling it now. Lannie shook her head as she stared out over the sea of tents and makeshift lean-tos. The fields around the village of Larris were overflowing with them. Poor Garset was haggard with the strain of organising everything from food to latrine buckets.

Over five thousand people! After the first three hundred responded to the Ambon in Dharmack, the trickle had become a flood. News of the reappearance of Dûrion's ancient emblem had run ahead of them. In village after village people had flocked to join them as they'd made their way north over the past few days. Hardbitten veterans like Tarlion and Fira had shaken their heads. Nobody could have foreseen such a response so soon after the failed Rebellion. But the new recruits all said the same thing: the travelling priests had prepared them. *The true Restorers will have the Ambon of Sûrilane*, they'd said. *When you hear its call, follow!* Bless Frengor. His support meant more than they'd realised.

News of 'the Restorers' Army' had spread far and wide. Garset, of course, was convinced the Bishop must be planning a counterattack—no matter how often she and Gil checked and found Shambor's full attention on the Grûzhack. Blacksmiths had been drafted in from all around to make weapons, and Garset and Fira were organising a rigorous training schedule for the new recruits. The two of them kept up a constant drizzle of complaint that it would take more than a few days to turn farmers into soldiers.

Those self-righteous military types! Lannie felt a sense of relief, sitting up here on this small hill with its crown of trees. The Ambon's success and the thousands of new recruits ought to have created a buoyant, upbeat atmosphere in the camp. But it hadn't. There was a heaviness in the air. Faces were long. Arguments kept breaking out. Tensions were high between the soldiers and the recruits, between the army and the villagers, between the Restorers and the officers. All of them—even cheerful Shivvie—were getting irritated with Garset. He showed them great deference as Restorers, yet treated them as amateurs. In practice they were under his command, rather than vice versa.

She stared out over the tents, the village, and the looming mass of the Two Peaks behind it. In a day or so — when Garset said they were ready — they would cross those hills and head for Carreck Manor. It couldn't be soon enough for her.

* * *

"But that will leave Berûvis undefended!"

The Town Elder's pudgy face was distorted by a crease in the white tunic Gil had spread on the ground for the blaise's image, but they could see his anxious expression. The three of them — Gil, Lannie and 'Neesh — were sitting in the little grove of trees on the hill, using the instruments to spy on the military garrisons in nearby towns. Garset needed reassurance that no troops were being sent in their direction. 'Neesh sighed. The tensions in the camp were getting her down. It was good they'd caught this conversation in Berûvis between the Town Elder and the Legate.

"Undefended against *what*, Elder?" The interview was taking place at the garrison, and the thickset, choleric Legate was barely controlling his impatience. "What enemy is currently threatening Berûvis? My legion has only remained here for the sake of appearances since the Rebellion ended. There is now a very real threat from the Grûzhack, and Lord Marshal Shambor has ordered us to Dhembis."

"But what about this 'Restorers' Army' we've been hearing about? Ten thousand strong, they say…"

"Rumour!" the Legate spat out. "Don't believe a word of it. If there were any truth in the story, we'd have heard about it from Darthane."

"Some folk from Larris reported they'd actually seen them round the village — thousands of tents, filling the countryside!"

"Yes, yes, and we've also heard they're in Tamberane, and Demárre, and Sesten, and even Shilmis! We cannot spend our time checking out rumours while there's a war on in the south.

"Look," he continued in a more conciliatory tone, "I'll leave you a company, if that will make you feel happier. They can follow in a week. By then I'll wager this 'army' will have vanished into thin air."

"But if they *haven't* vanished, what use will a single company be — "

The Legate stood. "One company," he repeated firmly. "And now, Elder, if you don't mind, I have a lot to do before our departure tomorrow."

The Elder rose reluctantly to his feet, and the picture faded as Gil put the blaise down. "No danger from Berûvis, then," he murmured. He yawned and stretched.

Danîsha watched him sympathetically. Dear Gil. He was constantly checking the surrounding area with the blaise, for Garset's sake — though the mental effort of focusing the instrument obviously took it out of him. He was looking quite drawn these days.

Gil glanced down through the trees, and gave an exclamation. "There's Shiván! I need to speak to him. Be back soon." He hurried off.

Lannie heaved a sigh and settled against a tree trunk.

"Tired?" Danîsha said.

"Who isn't these days?"

"It's all this waiting around. It isn't good. We need something to *do.*"

"Like what? Apart from getting the heck out of here."

Danîsha's eyes strayed to the blaise, which Gil had left lying on the tunic. "I have an idea."

* * *

Shiván was feeling depressed. Since arriving in Larris he'd found it hard to think straight, let alone pray. People were demanding his attention all day long with questions, requests, suggestions, complaints. And it was always Garset who had the solutions. He was on his way to talk to him now... about what, again? Protests from the local farmers whose hedges had been damaged...? No, they'd sorted that out last night. *How could he have forgotten?* His brain was so foggy. Oh yes, now it was a whole section of the camp that had been without food this morning. Some supply wagons hadn't shown up, and the Lieutenant responsible hadn't listened to their complaint.

"Hey, Shiván!" He looked round. Gil was hurrying after him. He waited for him to catch up.

"How's it going?" Gil said. "On your way to see the Big Boss?"

Shiván scowled. "That about describes it. Gotta beg him to overrule that Lieutenant in charge of food supplies. He's not doing his job properly."

Gil grunted sympathetically. "Right. And of course you'll be told, very politely, that the chain of command is an essential element of military organisation, and he can't override a subordinate's decision without undermining the entire basis of efficient leadership."

"Hah! You've taken the words out of his mouth."

"Why do you put up with it, Shيván? *You're* our leader, not Garset. You're the Overguardian, for the One's sake!"

Shيván shrugged wearily. "What good will it do to pick a fight with Garset? He's the best officer we've got, his men are our crack troops, and they eat out of his hand. We need him more than he needs us."

"That's true. But I think you could assert yourself more. We're all behind you, you know that. For instance, this plan of crossing the Two Peaks — that was Garset's idea, wasn't it?"

"Yeah. Now we're so many, he wants to keep off the beaten track."

"Well actually, there's no need for that. Lannie, 'Neesh and I have just overheard a conversation in Berûvis. The garrison is leaving for Dhembis tomorrow. Only one company will remain behind."

Shيván's sluggish brain couldn't see where this was going. "So?"

"So, from here we can easily go round to the north, between the Two Peaks and Berûvis. It'll avoid the difficult terrain, be a lot easier on the recruits, and take us through more villages where we can raise the Ambon. If they do hear about us in Berûvis, they're not going to stop us with a single company. And from there we can get to the Manor through Carreck Forest."

"I see." Shيván's brow creased. This was forcing him to think. "And in the forest… we couldn't be so easily attacked."

"That's right. But getting *to* the forest through the densely populated area west of Berûvis has always been our main problem. Following Garset's route we'd end up closer to Histen, where there's still a full garrison. Now that we know there'll only be one company in Berûvis, it makes sense to go that way."

It did make sense, the way Gil put it. "Come with me. Say all that stuff to Garset."

But Gil shook his head. "No, Shيván. *You're* the Overguardian. This is where you exercise your God-given rôle."

He sighed. "Okay. Go over it once again."

* * *

The Mindruler of Dûrion was rubbing his hands as he walked down the Cathedral corridor to his private suite. He was pleased with the way the Restorers and their rabble were being out-manoeuvred. The necessary troops were already assembling, well away from normal locations like town barracks. Gelmion was turning out one of his finest weapons. That staged conversation between the Town Elder and Legate in Berûvis had worked perfectly — followed by the well-timed suggestion to Shiván. Now they were headed in the right direction.

To top it off the *Gorelenyu* was in operation, and having exactly the desired effect. They were doing a good job of lowering the intensity while maintaining the range. That had been a brainwave of his.

So, the hard nut would be cracked. First the sharp tap to weaken it: that would happen soon. Then the shattering blow to smash it to pieces. That was already being prepared.

Shambor entered the suite and went to his private storeroom. This called for a celebration. Nothing that could bite, though. He opened a cage and took out a frog. That's all his enemies were — helpless frogs in his mighty hands…

* * *

Lieutenant Fira stared at Garset in disbelief. "*North* of the Two Peaks? But that will take us far too close to Berûvis!"

The Captain sighed, and shifted on the camp chair in his HQ tent. "Nevertheless, that is what the Overguardian commands."

"What was he thinking? *Why?*"

A touch of frost entered Garset's weary voice. "Lieutenant, I don't know what your military discipline was like in the Rebellion, but in the Dûrian army we do not question our superiors' orders."

Fira's eyes hardened and she straightened her back as she stood before the small trestle table. "That may be so, sir, but *this* needs questioning. Forgive me for asking, but did the Overguardian give any reason for this change of plan?"

Garset sighed again. There was no way he could handle these former rebels as he did his own troops. Their discipline was slack, they questioned everything, and their special relationship with the Restorers prevented any corrective measures. Nevertheless he valued Fira as an efficient officer; she had trained her mountain recruits well in the short time available. Then his slow thought pro-

cesses threw up another consideration: Perhaps Fira's special relationship with the Restorers could be of value here? He relaxed his
posture, leaning back a little in the camp chair.

"The Overguardian's explanation was a little incoherent, but I
gathered he felt avoiding the Two Peaks would be easier on the
recruits, and—"

Forgetting military protocol the Lieutenant burst out, "He wants
to pamper the *recruits*?"

Her reaction was all Garset had hoped. "That's what he said. He
also mentioned something about there being more opportunities to
raise the Ambon in the villages around Berûvis..."

"Raise the *Ambon*? Around *Berûvis*? Is the man mad? Besides, we
already have more than enough untrained farmers in this army!"

"I can't fault you there, Lieutenant. I expressed the same misgiv-
ings, but the Overguardian swept them aside."

Fira's eyes flashed. "I'll sweep *him* aside!" She half-turned, then
remembered protocol. "If you'll excuse me, sir...?"

Garset smiled. "You are excused, Lieutenant."

* * *

Fira stormed through the camp. Shiván had gone too far this time.
Denying her and Garset time to train these raw recruits was bad
enough; but to head recklessly close to Berûvis simply to avoid a little hill-climbing—and to start summoning *more* recruits, Prince forbid!—that bordered on the insane.

She eventually ran the Overguardian down sitting beside the
stream that flowed through the camp. He was staring vaguely at the
looming hills of the Two Peaks.

She was too overwrought to ease into the subject gently. Besides,
the strange mental confusion that seemed to hang over this God-
forsaken camp made it urgent that she have her say immediately
before it got muddled in her mind. Stopping slightly behind the
Overguardian she barked out, "What under Malane do you think
you're doing, Shiván?"

His body jerked in shock and he leapt up. Seeing Fira, anger suf-
fused his face. "What are you doing, creeping up like that and
knocking ten years off my life?"

"Trying to talk some sense into you! Garset just told me you ordered him to take the northern route near Berûvis, instead of cross-

ing the Two Peaks as we planned—with some flimsy excuse about going easy on the recruits and raising the Ambon in more villages. Are you crazy, Shiván? Our existing recruits are more than we can manage, and you're wanting to get *more*? And you want to save them physical exercise, when that's exactly what most of them *need*?"

Shiván's face fell and the fight suddenly seemed to drain out of him. "Not you too," he muttered. "Garset said the same." He sat down again, turning his back on her. Fira sat down beside him.

"But Shiván, don't you see how crazy it is? We need to *avoid* Berûvis and *avoid* raising the Ambon again. We have more than enough recruits. Just tell Garset it was a mistake and go back to the original plan."

There was a silence as Shiván continued to stare across the river. Suddenly he seemed to remember something. He turned to her, a little life returning to his face. "But we don't need to avoid Berûvis! That's the point. Gelmion and the others overheard a conversation using the instruments, in which people were saying that the Berûvis garrison would be going to Dhembis, and only a single company would be left behind! So there's no danger, you see? Gelmion said we could easily overcome one company. And… and it would be quicker… what did Gelmion say? Oh yes, we'd get to Carreck Manor more quickly that way so we can meet up with the… whatsits… the Dorbians."

Fira frowned. "That's all very well, Shiván, but—… it's always better to be on the safe side. We can't be completely sure that what Gelmion and the others overheard will happen. Plans change in the army—like ours right now. We should still go over the Two Peaks and avoid Berûvis."

A mutinous expression crossed Shiván's face and he turned away.

"Shiván, don't be stubborn about this! Do what you know is right—what both your military advisors are telling you! You keep saying Gelmion told you this, and Gelmion said that—Gelmion's not the Overguardian, *you* are!"

Shiván rounded on her, fury in his face. "Yes, I *am* the Overguardian," he shouted. "And I've *made* my decision! Just for once accept that, and… and leave me alone!"

Shocked at the unaccustomed outburst, Fira stared at him for a long moment. Then with lips compressed she stood and left.

* * *

Danîsha picked up the blaise. "Gil always finds this so tiring," she said. "Why don't *we* use it, and give him a break?"

Lannie frowned. "I don't know. *Can* we use someone else's instrument?"

"Shiván used your bess to speak to Fira back in Sûrilane."

"Oh, yes—I'd forgotten that. Okay, but... Gil's very possessive about the blaise. Won't let me even touch the thing."

Danîsha's mind was not working at its quickest this morning. All she knew was that she wanted to do this. "Well, why don't we just try? If it doesn't work, he needn't know. If it does— then we can help him."

Lannie's interest was aroused in spite of her lethargy. "Alright. You try. I'll use the bess." She lifted it to her ear.

Danîsha held the blaise by both handles, looking through it at the tunic. All she saw was a white blur. She remembered what Lannie had told Gil about concentrating on the person you wanted to see. She thought of Jomel. The girl had been unnaturally subdued of late. Not even having the twins around had cheered her up. She seemed to have withdrawn into herself, spending most of her time moping in the tent—

—and there she was right now! She and Lannie both stifled a gasp as the figure of Jomel appeared on the tunic. She was sitting on her bedding, staring sightlessly at a sloping wall of canvas. Tears streaked her cheeks. What was wrong with the girl? She and Lannie exchanged a bemused glance. Something was eating away at her, and Danîsha wished she could get to the bottom of it. She'd talked to her, but only had monosyllabic replies. Shîrin and Cârin had shrugged their shoulders—they hardly saw her these days, Câr said.

Lannie touched her arm and jerked her thumb impatiently backward. Enough of Jomel—let's get out of there. Reluctantly Danîsha dragged her thoughts away from Jomel's misery. The picture faded.

"Well, you've shown we can do it!"

Danîsha nodded. She heaved a sigh. Even that short episode with the blaise had left her feeling dizzy.

"I'll have a go now." Lannie picked up the instrument. She looked at it for a moment, then grasped both handles firmly and pointed it at the tunic. "Let's see what friend Shambor is up to. You use the bess. It's not nearly so tiring."

Danîsha's eyes widened. "Lannie, are you sure? Gil's the expert with the blaise. We don't want to give ourselves away, or anything…"

"Nonsense. We just have to keep quiet, that's all. We all saw Shambor when Gil found him in the blaise, that time he was talking about sending all his troops to Dhembis: so we have an idea of what he looks like. And I've personally seen Darthane Cathedral. We'll find that, then look around inside. We may not find the Bishop, but let's have a go. You never know, we may learn something useful."

Her face was taut with effort as she learned to manipulate the blaise. Danîsha watched anxiously, holding Lannie's turquoise shell to her ear. Beside the white tunic lay the bellaril. A succession of scenes flitted across the tunic—jerkily at first, shifting in and out of focus, and making Danîsha feel sick; but gradually becoming clearer and smoother.

They saw massive yellowstone walls, the towering Cathedral, various rooms and corridors. At last they found an intricately carved blackwood door that looked significant. They passed through it into an ornate reception room decorated in blue and silver. Recliners were dotted about, and a circular stained glass window was reflected in the highly-polished surface of a wide desk beneath it. The room was empty. But from somewhere nearby, echoing woodily from the bellaril, came the sound of a man's voice.

They glanced at each other. Lannie followed the voice through a door off the reception room, through a palatial dining chamber, down a corridor with glimpses into other reclining rooms and a massive bedroom. Then a smaller passage past various storerooms. The voice had stopped, but Lannie followed the direction it had been coming from.

They entered a small room with a large window. It was bare except for a table and a bench in the centre. At the end nearest them was a wooden box containing various implements—knives, pliers, tweezers, and others Danîsha didn't recognise. But dominating the room was a large figure sitting at the table. From the high-quality blue robe with intricate silver embroidery she guessed this must be Shambor. He was bending forward, doing something to a small object on the wooden surface.

Then Danîsha saw what it was. A frog. He was pulling the legs off a frog!

Her tired brain lurched backwards in time. She'd caught him at it before—that lout Gary Sarnford on a church outing, sitting at a recreation ground table dismembering a helpless creature. She hated *any* mistreatment of animals—but deliberate, vicious cruelty…

"Gary! Stop that at once!"

By force of habit she spoke in Dûrian. The effect was electric. The figure at the table leapt up, dropping the frog. His face had turned a blotchy grey. "Mama—?" he gasped, then broke off when he saw no one there. He looked frantically around, his eyes bulging. Gradually his breathing slowed. Then his face crumpled and he sank back on to the bench. He leant on the table, burying his head in his hands. His shoulders shook with heavy sobs.

Lannie turned to Danîsha, her eyes round. The picture faded. *"Gary?"* she echoed in a hushed voice.

"I— don't know what came over me," Danîsha stammered. "I once found Gary Sarnford—you know, that teenage bully who used to come to our church—I don't know why he bothered, he's left now— I found him doing the same, so I …" She trailed off.

"Well, Shambor seemed to answer to that name," Lannie muttered, thunderstruck. "And did I hear him calling you *Mama…?*"

They stared at each other.

Chapter 23: *Bishop in crisis*

THERE WAS THE SOUND of approaching footsteps, and Gil appeared in the glade. Lannie took one look at him and exclaimed, "What's the matter?" His face was drawn and his eyes shadowed with pain.

"Sudden headache," he grunted. He looked around, and saw the blaise lying next to the tunic where she had dropped it. He bent and snatched it up, wincing at the rapid movement. He stared at them both suspiciously for a long moment. Then he slipped it in the pocket of his robe. "Have to lie down," he muttered. He turned and left.

Lannie let out her breath slowly.

"The less said about using his blaise, the better," she murmured. 'Neesh nodded.

* * *

The Mindruler stared dazed at the remains of the frog. Had he really heard Mama's voice? That had never happened before. Yet all his old fears and feelings had come rushing to the surface. He'd defied the One Creator God! He'd given himself to the service of darkness. God would not be mocked: what he had sown, he would reap. He would suffer the terrible wrath of the Maker of All Skies...

As if in answer to his thoughts, there came the sound of hurrying feet approaching his sanctum. A knock on the door. "Your Radiance!"

Estaron knew better than to interrupt him here. Some disaster must already have occurred. He threw the door open. "What is it?" He could hear the quiver in his own voice.

The secretary's sombre eyes were wider than usual. "Your Radiance, the Grûzhack have taken Dhembis."

It didn't penetrate at first. "What do you mean?"

"They've— They've captured Dhembis. With their fire-weapons. They control the town and all the area south to the mountains."

"*What!*"

"Yes, Your Radiance. They broke into the town an hour before noon. We've only just heard."

The magnitude of the disaster shocked Shambor into a semblance of normality. He began striding down the corridor to his office, Estaron trotting behind. A gap in his consciousness told him that the Mindbender of Dhembis was dead. "What happened to Jastor?"

"He and his subordinates were combining their mental energies, as you commanded, in an attempt to halt the Grûzhack. They were killed when one of the fire-missiles hit the Guardhouse."

Shambor grunted as the sickening realisation hit him. Jastor and his lieutenants had died in a vain attempt to project their mental energies a few aldoret. The *Gorelenyu* had a range of thirty aldoret. If he'd sent the Strongholder's weapon direct to Dhembis as intended, this would not have happened. He shuddered to think what his master would say.

Once seated at his blackwood desk he began issuing crisp orders. Legate Derlion was to lead every available army unit south to place Dhembis under siege. No, not *those* ones. The Stillárre legions would soon be on their way to Dhembis as well, and so would two of his Mindbenders in Darthane, together with their Bishop's Guard contingents. They were to surround the town at a safe distance. Yes, he knew the Grûzhack had occupied the villages, but they couldn't fill every last foot of land between the town and the mountains…

He mindspoke the Keepers of the *Gorelenyu*. They were to cease present operations and make for the highway at once.

Only when his forces throughout the country were jumping to his commands did he allow himself to think again.

A black depression settled over him. Everything had been going so well—and now these two blows in quick succession. Maybe Mama had been trying to warn him from the afterlife. *Stop that at once!* she'd said. Perhaps she hadn't only been referring to the frog. She might have continued, *That's not how you'll succeed. Not by power, Gari, nor by strength, but by the One's Light.* Her favourite text echoed from the distant past as if it had been yesterday.

But how could he stop what he was doing? As Mindruler of Dûrion he was as trapped in the Cult of Gadesh as the newest devotee…

Suddenly, unbidden, a memory from earliest childhood came to him. An innocent yearning to be good. To do what was right. To love God, and to serve him with all his heart. Tears stung his eyes. Sorrow as sharp as a physical pain forced a groan from his lips.

How had it all gone so wrong?

His mind ranged over his childhood and the years that had followed. Nothing he did had pleased his parents. All they wanted was blind obedience to Lightist dogma. He'd met the Selmian boy Barlesh at school and been initiated into the Cult of Gadesh—and suddenly he'd been valued for who *he* was. He'd received real powers and made his own decisions on how to use them instead of being jerked around by others like a puppet on a string.

Yes, and what had that led to? Pride and overconfidence. The fire and Mama's death.

But what could he have done differently after that? He had to escape, or forever be hated by his father and the entire Lightist community. As it was, the Gadeshites had spirited him away to Selmion, and everyone thought he'd died in the fire with Mama.

Then came his training, where his potential was further developed and he was initiated as a Mindbender. He owed his present life to the Cult in Selmion, who had altered his appearance and set up a new Dûrian identity for him as Shambor dom Beldet. They had arranged his legal apprenticeship in Janulane, made sure he was elected Town Elder, and thus brought him to the attention of the Bishop. So he became Bishop Suffragan, and then Mindruler of Dûrion.

And yet, if he could relive his life, which would he choose? To be Mindruler, with all the attendant fears and struggles to retain power; or that child, who only wanted to do good?

The truth was, he'd been driven into his present path by those who most wanted him to follow a different Way.

Anger gradually replaced sorrow. It focused on the one person in recent years who had repeatedly let him down. His wrath grew as it churned over accumulated grievances. Finally he could contain it no longer. He stormed out of his office down marble corridors and through gracious anterooms, brushing people aside, until he reached Harlon's apartment.

He unlocked the door and burst in, to find the Bishop in the midst of his weekly barây game with Mâron, the Kindler of Sûrilane. Well, he had no time for that sneaking traitor. His business was with Harlon.

"Do you remember the town of Dhembis?" he demanded. The old man had his hand poised over the circular board, a cavalry-piece between his fingers. He and Mâron stared up at him, eyebrows raised.

"Of course I do, Shambor." Harlon carefully placed the piece on the board and leant back, hands folded in his lap. "Take a seat."

Ignoring the offer, Shambor stood over the two men, legs apart, arms folded. "Tell me, in your time, what country did it belong to?"

A shadow crossed the Bishop's face. "To Dûrion, as you know. You're not saying—"

"*Yes, I* am *saying!* The ancient town of Dhembis is now part of the Grûzhack Magistry—thanks to you!"

There was pain on both men's faces. "I am deeply sorry to hear that," Harlon murmured.

"Sorry! That's wonderful. It's a little late to be *sorry*, isn't it? *You* prayed for those so-called 'Restorers'—*you* supported them behind my back—*you* said you were glad they had come, even when I told you they'd brought the Grûzhack down on us. But now you're 'sorry' we've lost Dhembis!"

"I am sorry whenever my people suffer—whether from foreign tyranny, or the tyranny of their own government."

Shambor felt the blood suffuse his face. "How dare you accuse me of tyranny! I have brought in the most liberal government Dûrion has ever known. People are no longer bound by the strictures of your religion! They are free to worship who or what they will. I have fostered the sciences—scholars come from far and wide to study at our university. I have promoted trade with surrounding nations—we're stronger economically than ever before. Dûrians have never had it so good!"

"Materially, perhaps. Spiritually they have lost their way."

Harlon's clear grey eyes stared into his own. He faltered, faced again with the uncompromising pronouncements of his Lightist past. "That's just— empty dogma!"

"Labelling an uncomfortable statement as 'dogma' doesn't stop it from being true."

Panic surged up in him. This conversation was not going as planned. "You've never appreciated all I've done for this country! You measure everything against the letter of Lightist law. You reject achievements that benefit everyone, because of some obscure utterance in the Lightist Book. You see no value in a person's ideas if he isn't a 'true believer'! You've impeded me all along, you've never supported me—*never!* If you'd given me *any* encouragement—"

He broke off. A silence followed as he struggled to master his emotions. Harlon continued to survey him with those calm grey eyes.

Finally the Bishop asked in a conversational tone, "Have you stayed in touch with that Selmian friend of yours — Barlesh?"

"Of course not!" he snapped — then realised his mistake. He turned and blundered out of the apartment, his vision blurred by tears.

* * *

"What was that last part about?" Mâron asked.

Harlon sank back on the recliner. He heaved a deep sigh. Mâron came over and laid a hand on his shoulder. The old man looked up at him, his face haunted.

"Shambor was right," he said. "It *is* my fault. All these years — " He drew a shuddering breath. "All these years."

* * *

Estaron's lips twisted with distaste as he brushed the dismembered limbs of the frog into the wooden waste box. Around him in Shambor's secret chamber the other animals squeaked, whined, chattered and hissed. The smell was disgusting — it always was after one of the Bishop's little torture episodes, when the chamber's occupants voided their bowels in fear. This was the part of his job that Estaron hated above all else.

Yet what could he do? He would leave tomorrow if he could — take up some menial post as a legal assistant far from Darthane — but Shambor wanted his services, and Shambor got what he wanted. Estaron shuddered to think what would happen to his parents in Astenar if he defied the Bishop. There was no need to speculate: Shambor had told him exactly what would happen.

Of course, his parents were delighted that he'd secured this prestigious post with the Bishop of Dûrion. They regarded it as a One-sent preparation for the greater task that lay ahead. The task that would devolve upon all of them once the impossible happened and they resumed their true position in society. Sadly, the impossible often took some time to happen, so that task might well devolve upon him alone after their passing. All the more reason for him to appreciate the excellent preparation he was now receiving...

Well, he hadn't disillusioned them. Better they think he was gaining valuable experience handling affairs of state than the ugly truth: that he was a mere hand-holder and hey-you to a deranged megalomaniac — more often washing away animal faeces and smuggling in prostitutes than learning the intricacies of diplomacy.

He put the waste box on the floor and leant with both hands on the metal table, head bowed. *Dear Prince, set me free of this madhouse.*

* * *

Shambor was riding in the Bishop's Park, to the south-east of Darthane. It was his only recreation while in the city. The trees were losing their leaves, and his horse trotted lightly over a red-gold carpet. In the distance a small group of Bishop's Guards kept watch.

He had just come out of the wood and was looking across Darthane Water at the reflection of the city walls in the smooth surface of the lake, when the blow fell.

"Well, Gari. So now you've managed to lose a major Dûrian town to the Grûzhack?"

Shambor jerked in the saddle and the horse reared. He just managed to retain his seat. *"Supremacy! I, ah — The attack was completely unexpected. The Grûzhack came down the old teméyn road from Thammeron during the night, hauling their distance weapons with them. There was no indication beforehand that they had any intention of advancing into the lowlands."*

"And where was my Gorelenyu *when they attacked Dhembis?"*

"It was en route, Supremacy. Sadly it had not yet reached the town."

A bolt of pain made Shambor leap and cry out. His horse shied, and he barely won the balancing act.

"How is that possible?" the Strongholder's mind-voice rapped out. *"You've had the* Gorelenyu *for four days — and you have excellent highways in Dûrion. It could easily have reached Dhembis by now."*

Shambor dismounted and handed the reins to one of the Guards, who had ridden up. He found a seat on a stone and stared sightlessly at the peaceful lakeside scene. This was it: time to risk everything on the truth. *"Yes, your Supremacy, you're right. However, without any forewarning about the Grûzhack, I felt I needed first to deal with these so-called Restorers who have been disturbing the countryside."*

He gasped at another explosion of pain. *"You dare to regard a few rabble-rousers as more important than the Grûzhack and our teméyn supply?"*

"With respect, Supremacy, ten days ago I would have agreed with you. Then there was that incident in Sûrilane."

"Stop wasting my time, Gari! That was an outbreak of religious hysteria."

"In fact, Sir, I have since discovered that it was more than that. The ancient Ambon of Sûrilane has been found – and these 'Restorers' have it."

There was a sudden silence. Shambor waited with bated breath.

The mind-voice when it came again had lost some of its asperity.

"You're telling me the ambon those rabble-rousers have been showing off in villages is not a fake? That it's the real Ambon of Sûrilane, which has been missing for centuries? How can you be sure of that?"

"I have no doubt about it, Supremacy. It fits all the historical descriptions, including the ability to summon Lightists when lifted up. That is what caused the stampede to the Sûrilane Hearth ten days ago; and that's why these would-be Restorers now have over five thousand followers."

"How did they *find this Ambon when thousands have searched over the centuries and failed?"*

"They claim to be from a different sky, Supremacy. They say the Ambon has been under their sky all this time, but now it has returned at their call. Whatever the truth about that, there is no doubt they are convincing the common people, who are joining them by the hundreds every day."

There was another silence. *"Hmmm. Yes. Well, it appears they could be more of a problem than I thought."* Shambor heaved an inner sigh of relief. *"So you want to use the* Gorelenyu *to deal with them first?"*

"With your permission, Supremacy."

"It will have to be rapid and overwhelming, so the Gorelenyu *can return as soon as possible to its intended function against the Grûzhack."*

"All the preparations have been made, Sir. With the Gorelenyu *this threat will be eliminated in a matter of days."*

"And how do you intend to accomplish that?"

Shambor outlined his plan.

* * *

A few days later Frengor met with Estaron at a small inn near the Galmanest Gate. His priests were scattered about in twos and threes, watching for the Bishop's Guard or their spies. Contacting the Bishop's secretary had been the difficult part, but a mutual friend had acted as go-between.

Frengor had known Estaron for a number of years, and was impressed with him. He was in many ways quite an extraordinary young man. Despite working for Shambor, he had remained faithful to the One. He was highly intelligent and displayed a self-possession and natural authority that was at odds with his lowly position. Frengor had first known Estaron as a brilliant young law student at Darthane University, where he'd had glittering prospects — only to see them swept away by an unprecedented run of ill fortune. In his second year, after inexplicably failing his assessment by senior scholars, he'd been summarily 'cancelled' — thus ending his university career.

Then out of the blue Shambor had entered the picture, offering Estaron a top-level position as his personal secretary. Frengor had been saddened, but not surprised, when Estaron accepted. He strongly suspected that Shambor had engineered Estaron's failure so that he could pluck the brilliant young lawyer for his own use. It had come as a great relief to learn later that Estaron had not been mindbent. Frengor found a grim irony in the Mindruler's tacit recognition that an uncontrolled mind produced better results.

Since then Frengor and Estaron had met occasionally when he was in Darthane. The secretary could not do so often; the fact that he had risked seeing him now was an indication that there were important matters to discuss.

Now the young man rested his folded hands on the table and fixed him with his solemn gaze. "Why did you want to see me?"

Frengor's lips quirked. "Because I wanted to find out how you were."

"And?"

"Okay, I won't pretend there wasn't another reason. I need information. Don't worry — it's for myself only. Twelve days ago rather a strange event took place in Sûrilane. Did you hear about that?"

Estaron nodded. "I thought you might be involved. It was the Restorers, wasn't it? Shambor knows all about them."

"*All* about them? I suspected he must know *something*. That stampede to the Sûrilane Hearth was passed over far too easily. What does he know — and what is he doing about it?"

Estaron steepled his fingers and looked towards the ceiling. They had been talking softly, but now he dropped his voice further. "He knows the Ambon of Sûrilane has been found." Frengor reared back in shock. "He knows the Restorers are with a renegade army unit called the 'Pure Company', led by a Captain Garset. He knows they were headed north towards Larris — "

Suddenly he stopped. His eyes widened. "*That* was why!" he exclaimed.

"Why what?" Frengor asked faintly. He was still trying to assimilate the extent of their enemy's knowledge. This was a disaster.

"Why he sent that weapon to Distack, south of the Larwood."

"*What* weapon?"

"It was a weapon the Strongholder sent. It was meant to be used against the Grûzhack. By the way, did you know Dhembis has been captured?"

"Dear Prince!" It was one shock on top of another today. Frengor's heart went out to all his friends in the town.

"Yes. The army was helpless against their fire-machines."

"But—this weapon. Are you saying Shambor was using it against the Restorers instead of the Grûzhack?"

"I've just realised that's what he must have been doing. I couldn't understand why he'd sent it off to an obscure place like Distack."

"But what kind of weapon is it? The Restorers were going to Larris. That's a long way from Distack. I don't see how it could do them any damage from there."

"I couldn't make out exactly what it was, but its Keepers spoke of a thirty-aldoret range."

"Thirty aldoret!"

"Yes. They called it a *Gorelenyu* in Selmian. Rather a fanciful name for a military weapon, but—"

Frengor felt the blood drain from his face. "Prince have mercy on us," he whispered.

A frown of concern appeared on Estaron's face. "You know about this weapon? Why is it so terrible? You look as though you've seen a wraith."

"Perhaps I have," Frengor said, his voice unsteady. "Perhaps I've seen the wraith of the most vicious, most depraved abuse of the human mind come to life. The Selmians have been working on this... this abomination for decades. Now you tell me that right here in Dûrion—"

He leapt to his feet. "I must go!" Lowering his voice as Estaron also rose he added, "The Restorers must be warned."

"Wait!" The young man caught Frengor's arm as he was about to hurry off. "The *Gorelenyu* is not staying in Distack. Shambor has ordered it west on the highway the day after tomorrow."

"To Janulane?"

"Yes. En route to Dhembis, I assume."

"That's the first good news I've heard. Thank you, my friend. Only the One Creator God knows the value of what you've told us today!"

Clapping Estaron on the shoulder, he left to round up his priests. They would go to Gend, on the Janulane highway. The *Gorelenyu* was bound to pass through there. They would follow, and find out where this abomination was headed.

Chapter 24: *Hook, line and...*

"LADY OF PRAYER!"

The trooper was clearly startled to find Perrely serving him his soup. She managed a wan smile.

"You should not be doing this. *We* should be serving *you!*"

"Why? Just because someone prays, doesn't mean they can't be useful."

"Yes — but, I mean, you're on the Council — "

Cries of protest arose from the long line behind the trooper. "Get on!" "What's the hold-up?" A thin drizzle was falling, and those not under cover were getting wet.

"Enjoy your soup. Make way for the next person now."

Shaking his head, the trooper moved off.

As the woman behind him came forward, Perrely's eyes flickered over the broad field full of smoking fires, serving tables under awnings, and shuffling lines of people waiting to be fed. Beyond in the gathering dusk rows of tents had sprouted like a late crop of mushrooms. Somehow Garset had managed to provide both food and shelter for their growing numbers. Well, not Garset, but the Prince — and many local landowners.

Since leaving Larris yesterday another five hundred had joined as they'd raised the Ambon in villages en route. Garset had pursed his lips about that, and Fira had a face like thunder. Perrely didn't understand why; she felt they ought to have been glad, but her own heart was heavy. The mechanical action of ladling soup helped her to think — as well as giving her something useful to do. The 'Council' met seldom now; it was Garset and his officers who made all the day-to-day decisions. She and Shiván hardly ever spoke, though she knew he wanted to. But she daren't encourage him. That was an ache that throbbed within her all the time.

Then there was Jomel. Something had happened to her cousin that she wouldn't talk about. Perrely was deeply worried about her. All her natural gaiety had dried up. Even the twins could hardly get a rise out of her. Her face was drawn, her eyes often red-rimmed. When they were on the move, she walked alone. In camp, she spent all her time in the tent. Surprisingly, apart from herself it was Gelmion who seemed most concerned about Jomel. He'd been in several times to talk to her, but came out shaking his head sadly.

Now, as they drew nearer to Berûvis, another pain was rising to the surface. This was home. She'd known these fields, and the nearby village of Demárre, since childhood. That day when she'd abruptly been separated from her family and joined the Restorers seemed a lifetime ago—though it was actually less than two months. But now the longing grew stronger each day to find out what had happened to them, how they were—just to *speak* to them all again. Father, Mums, her brothers Larion and Barlet… Did they escape, that day when the Bishop's Guards descended on their home? If not… Father was a wealthy and influential man. His armoury helped to equip Shambor's troops. He and his family would surely have been re-leased once the Guards had failed to trap the Restorers in their home. Surely…?

She had resisted the idea of asking Gelmion to use the blaise, knowing how much in demand it was to keep a lookout for enemy troops. Garset had not been happy about the change of route Shiván had insisted on, and suspected a trap round every corner. The scouts he sent out reported nothing, and Gelmion saw nothing but the single company in the Berûvis barracks—yet he still had to keep scanning the surrounding countryside.

Now, though, she could no longer deny her own need to call on his help. When the last bowl had been filled, she helped herself and hurried through the drizzle to the sheltered table where the Restor-ers had been served their meal. Shiván and Danîsha had already left, but Gelmion and Alanya were lingering over a cup of chass, chatting together in Inglish.

"Perrely!" Alanya exclaimed. "Have you been dishing up again? You do punish yourself!"

"It's something to do," she shrugged.

"I could find better things—but I salute your unselfishness."

"Thank you. Actually… There was something a little selfish that I wanted to ask you both."

Gelmion's eyebrows rose. "Perrely being selfish? Unheard of. But fire away."

She frowned. "Fire …?"

Alanya laughed. "Gil, you idiot! He's joking, Perrely. It's just an English expression that means, continue."

"Well, it would mean using the blaise again, and I'm really sorry to be asking this, but—"

"Your family!" Alanya exclaimed. "They live near here, don't they? We should have thought of that. Gil, why don't we have a look right now?"

"Of course." He reached into the pocket of his robe and pulled out the blaise. He turned to Perrely. "In fact, I hadn't forgotten—I was going to suggest it, but you got in first. You'll have to guide me. It's getting dark, and I've never seen your home."

"That's alright—I know every foot of land around here." Relief flooded her.

"I'll fetch 'Neesh and the bellaril." Alanya hurried off. Perrely looked after her gratefully. She should have known these kind people would understand.

The eating area was deserted now. Gelmion came and sat next to Perrely. He focused the blaise on the table in front of them. She saw their camp, as if from above, the embers of the cooking fires still glowing brightly. "Now I'm going to move north-west," Gil murmured. "Guide me."

"Follow the road to Demárre." Gil did so, the narrow country track showing dimly in the failing light. A cluster of cottages beside a gleam of flowing water appeared. "There it is, next to the River Berûn. Now carry on westward..."

Excitement mounted in her as they found the turn-off to Ganneck, passed between the lighted cottages, and continued up the hill towards her house. Oh, dear Prince, please let them be there!

Alanya arrived back with Danîsha, carrying the bellaril. She laid it on the table and sat next to them. "Have you found it?" she asked.

"Just a little further."

Alanya took out the bess and held it to her ear. At once they heard the soft rustle of the rain in the grass, and the occasional creak of a branch. They came to the crest of the last rise—

And there was darkness where the lights of Sesten Manor should have shone.

"Oh!" Perrely's hands flew to her face. It couldn't be!

"Oh, no," Alanya groaned. "Gil, go closer."

They passed through an overgrown garden to the weed-encrusted gravel before the front entrance. The carved wooden door was hanging half off its hinges. Perrely started breathing rapidly, her eyes on the broken door. "Oh no, oh dear Prince no, no, no…" Danîsha put an arm round her shoulders. Gelmion moved the blaise inside the house. The place had been ransacked. The light trees were gone, the hangings ripped from the walls, every stick of furniture either broken or missing. Dust and debris littered the floor. This had happened long ago. Perrely buried her head against Danîsha's chest.

She heard Gelmion murmur, "It's what's left of Perrely's home." She looked up. Shiván had come. His eyes locked on hers, and there was such a depth of sorrow in them that every fibre of her being ached to throw herself into his arms.

With a monumental effort she pulled herself together. "Can we — look elsewhere?" she asked Gil shakily. "Around the area — in the cottages — my father was well-loved, maybe they've gone to stay with friends…"

Gil nodded, and they looked in all the homes Perrely could think of where her family might have taken refuge. There was no sign of them.

"Can we look on the roads — maybe they're travelling…" she pleaded.

"That would be easier in the morning, when there's more light," Gelmion told her gently.

Danîsha went with her to their tent, murmuring words of encouragement. They would search again the next day. Perhaps her family were staying further afield, with relatives, or business contacts of her father's? Perrely appreciated her loving concern — though the comfort she longed for was Shiván's.

She was up early the next morning after a sleepless night. She tried to pray, but all her words ended in a single plea to find her family. Finally she felt a measure of comfort. The Prince knew. He, too, had lost all who were dear to him. He understood the pain in her heart, and he would never leave her.

The Restorers joined her in the eating area while the dawnmeal was still being prepared. Shiván stood beside her, and his arm brushed against hers. She wanted to clutch his hand, but instead fixed her eyes on the image Gelmion was projecting on the table.

He found the Manor again. It looked even more desolate in the early morning light. Many of the green roof tiles were missing, the fountain and pond in the courtyard were dry and the garden was overgrown. He began scanning the surrounding area, moving outward from the house. He checked the fields, the woods, the country lanes. Not many people were about, but they saw a few labourers on the roads, and some ragged beggars sitting under a hedge near the village of Ganneck. Perrely shook her head. They'd never had beggars in the area before. Father had always helped them, if he felt they were worthy, or moved them on. Gelmion continued to the other side of the village, then returned, passing over the beggars again. There was something familiar about them.

"Gelmion!" Perrely exclaimed. "Go back to those beggars."

He did so. As he zoomed up close, the faces of the four figures huddled under the hedge resolved themselves into a ghastly parody of her family. The cadaverous face of the man wearing the tattered remains of a once-fashionable tunic might have been her father, twenty years from now. The haggard woman leaning against him resembled her childhood memory of Grandma, her mother's mother... The younger man hugging his thin legs might be Larion... And the emaciated boy with the huge eyes... was Barlet.

It *was* her family. She screamed.

The beggars leapt up, staring all around them. Their rags were pitiful to behold.

"Father! Mums! Is that really you? This is Perrely!" She was shivering violently, but Shiván's arm was holding her tight.

"Perrely? Where are you?" Her heart clenched at the quavery voice that came from her father's lips. So unlike the strong baritone she remembered.

"I'm— You can't see me, but I can see you. Don't worry about where I am. This is a miracle the Prince is doing. Just tell me what's happened to you! Why are you out on the roads, wearing rags like beggars?"

"Perrely, how wonderful to hear you!" Mums' voice was a croak, but her eyes shone as she looked vaguely upward. She was wearing that lilac gown she'd loved so much—now torn and frayed, held together with string. Once a solid, statuesque woman, she was painfully thin. Perrely felt hot tears trickling down her cheek.

"If you can see us, you know what's happened to us, Perrely," Father said. His lined face was solemn, but there was a smouldering fire in his eye. "We've been beggared. All our lands and possessions confiscated. Turned out into the roads. One of Shambor's footlickers has been appointed to the Barony of Sesten. He can't even be bothered to live here—has a grand house in Darthane, and sends a pack of bully-boys to collect his rents. And our own people have been warned, on pain of beggary themselves, not to feed or aid us in any way. We've only survived this long thanks to a few who have dared to defy that edict."

"But— What about your friends in Berûvis? The other merchants? You were always highly regarded—won't they help you?"

"No. They don't want to know us. We went to Nemeron's house, just across the valley. His butler slammed the door in our faces. As for Berûvis, we're not allowed into the town. They keep us within the Barony."

"Perrely, is that you?" young Barlet piped up. "I lost all my toys, but I made this—look!" He held up a square contraption of sticks tied together with string. A round *shey* nut was attached on either side. "It's a sinélle racer!" It wobbled unevenly as he pulled it along the ground. Perrely felt her heart would break.

"But what about you?" her mother asked. "Where are you? Are you still with those foreigners?"

"Yes, Mums, I'm with the Restorers. We're not far away—" She turned to Shiván in mute appeal. He nodded. "We're going to come for you. Stay right where you are, and don't be frightened—we have quite a big army..."

Shiván leaned towards her and whispered in her ear. "But I'll be near the front," she continued. "We'll find you. You'll be safe with us."

"The Restorers' army?" Father's face had come alive. "Then the rumours are true. Praise the One!"

"Yes—we're more than five thousand. Just wait—you can't miss us!"

Gelmion put the blaise down and the picture faded. Alanya took the bess from her ear. "The lines are forming for the dawnmeal," Gelmion said. He looked at Shiván. "If we're going to make a detour, you'd better tell Garset."

Shiván nodded. He let go of Perrely, and set off towards Garset's tent. Her hand went to her shoulder where his had been. The warmth of his touch lingered.

Later, as they marched down the track towards Demárre, Shiván told her that Garset had not been pleased with this further change in plan. It meant delaying on a dangerous road too close to Berûvis. But he'd given way in the end. He had scouts out, checking for any sign of the enemy, and cavalry patrolling alongside the foot soldiers. The army stretched back over three aldoret on the narrow country roads, leaving them dangerously exposed.

"Thank you for doing this," she murmured, wishing she could squeeze his hand.

"What hurts you, hurts me." He looked at her with such intensity that she had to blink back the tears.

It was nearly midday when they reached the final stretch of the road to Sesten. South lay the brooding heights of the Two Peaks, thick forests mantling their foothills. To the north Gan Hill rose up with its scattered woodland and fields. Near the top she could make out the empty shell of her home. The road to Sesten ran directly west at the foot of the hill. She was walking with the Restorers, Garset and other officers in the vanguard of the army. Gelmion was constantly checking in the blaise. "Turn off here," he said, when they reached a small country lane that wound up the hill between tall hedges.

"We can't all go up there, it's too narrow," Garset muttered. "I'll wait for the rest to catch up." They had to pause every half hour to keep the column compact. "Tarlion!" His second hurried forward. "Escort the Restorers up this lane with one cohort. Return as soon as you can." Tarlion saluted. Garset turned to Shiván. "It would be good to have a link. Might I ask if Lady Alanya could stay here, so she can contact you with her bess if anything arises?"

Shiván looked at Alanya, who shrugged and nodded.

"I'll stay too," Danîsha said. "My legs could do with a rest."

They set off up the lane. After several twists and turns they rounded a bend and there, at the end of a long straight stretch, sat the bedraggled family group at the roadside. Perrely ran the whole way to meet them. She joyfully embraced Father and Mums, Larion and Barlet, and all were weeping at the reunion.

It was then that Shambor struck.

Chapter 25: *Trap sprung*

SOLDIERS BURST THROUGH the high hedges on either side of the family group. Before Shiván's horrified eyes two burly troopers seized Perrely and began dragging her up the hill north of the road. Terrified screams broke out in front of him as the other troopers slaughtered her family where they stood. Ganneret, Nelláy, Larion and Barlet tumbled to the ground like puppets with their strings cut. The troopers leapt over their bodies and formed up in the narrow lane, weapons at the ready, as Tarlion yelled to his men to charge. It all happened in seconds.

He looked back up the hill and saw Perrely struggling in the hands of her captors. Sweeping the Blade out of its sheath he leapt toward her. The soldiers on the road fell back—but at the same moment a broad line of grey-cloaked horsemen broke out of the trees further up the hill and came thundering down. Bishop's Guards! He jumped through the trampled gap in the hedge after Perrely, though he could see that they would cut him off. Dimly he heard someone shouting his name. Then strong arms gripped him and he crashed to the ground.

"God's Light, Overguardian," Tarlion panted as he yanked him to his feet, "you can't take on a whole company of Guards!"

"But Perrely—"

"She's lost, man! We can't lose you, too." The officer dragged him back to the cohort, who were fending off the infantry in the lane. The clash of metal and cries of battle filled the air. "We have to get back to the army. *Retreat!* Your sword, Overguardian—raise your sword!"

In a daze Shiván flourished the Blade. The enemy infantrymen paused, then came on again. The charging Guardsmen shuddered to a halt fifty yards from the hedge. Several horses went down. "*Retreat!*" Tarlion yelled. His cohort began giving way, back towards the turnoff where they'd left Garset.

The infantry pressed hard after them, their numbers seeming to swell every minute—but they were confined by the narrow lane. Shiván found himself exchanging sword thrusts with a grim-faced veteran. His old fear of causing injury, going back to that long-distant episode at school, briefly raised its head. He faltered, narrowly avoiding a side-sweep at his legs. Self-preservation reasserted itself and he feinted with the Blade, drawing aside his opponent's guard, and delivered a kick that sent him crashing to the ground. A swift thrust with the razor-sharp instrument finished it. Now he knew how to fight. The Dûrians were better swordsmen, but they couldn't handle his martial arts.

Mechanically he continued attacking and defending. Soldiers on both sides fell and were trampled. Somehow he managed to survive. Nearby Gelmion was showing unexpected skill with the sword. Vaguely he was aware that the Guardsmen were riding parallel to the hedge, aiming to cut them off. His mind was numb, but inside a deep pain was spreading. Perrely captured. Her family, whom she'd just found, murdered in cold blood. Oh, dear Lord. *Why?*

* * *

"Holy Flame," Garset muttered. This was just the sort of trap he'd feared. "*Hurry!* Don't let the Guards cut them off, Fennior!" The Lieutenant waved, and urged his cavalry squadron to a gallop up the lane. They'd been summoned from their patrolling duties along the column. Already the Bishop's Guards were breaking through the hedge ahead of Tarlion's cohort.

Suddenly a glorious, stirring music rose above the sounds of battle. Lady Danîsha's bellaril! How could it be so loud? He didn't know, but gladness filled him. It would encourage the troops.

A moment later his eyes widened. It was doing more than that. The leading Guardsmen had frozen halfway through the hedge. There was chaos behind them as new arrivals cannoned into those already at a standstill. Fennior's riders began attacking, then stopped. To have continued would have been cold-blooded murder. The Guards sat unresisting on their horses, none raising a hand to defend himself. He turned and looked at Lady Danîsha, shaking his head in amazement. The Restorers had told stories of this, but he'd thought they were exaggerating. Now he knew better.

Further up the lane, though, the pursuing infantrymen continued to attack, unaffected by the music. Fennior let their own foot soldiers through, his riders replacing the hard-pressed rearguard. They had the advantage of greater height, and the warhorses using their hooves. The first ranks of Tarlion's cohort had almost —

There was a cry behind him. *"Attack from the south!"* He whirled round. Dûrian cavalry in their light blue capes were streaming across the fields on the other side. *Where had they sprung from?* The whole area had been thoroughly scouted and scanned with the blaise... He ordered his troops into defensive positions on the road. There was no hedge as a natural barrier to the south. His eyes ranged east over the long column. They were badly exposed – with only one cohort of his own veterans widely spaced among the new recruits. However the enemy cavalry were charging the head of the column... Then his heart sank. Infantry were emerging from the southern woods, a couple of aldoret away.

He ordered his last experienced cohort back down the column to strengthen the recruits. Here at the front he'd have to rely on Tarlion's battered veterans, Fennior's cavalry squadron and Fira's mountain recruits. Praise the One for the bellaril! That would keep the Guards out of action. The Restorers had explained that it only affected mindbent troops. Pity the southern horsemen were regular cavalry.

Tarlion and his men came panting up. Garset was relieved to see the Lords Gelmion and Shiván – but Lady Perrely was missing. Tarlion gave him a hurried report. He shook his head in disbelief. There was nothing they could do. The Overguardian looked dazed. He laid a sympathetic hand on the young man's shoulder, then called Fira over to him.

"Lieutenant, I place the Restorers in your care. Guard them!"

"Sir!" She gave a cold-eyed salute, and began snapping out orders to her refugees. They quickly surrounded Lady Danîsha as she played the bellaril. After a brief argument the other three Restorers remained in the centre of the defensive ring. Garset nodded approvingly. Once again the rebel lieutenant was displaying her cool efficiency, though her eyes shot bolts of flame at the Overguardian.

Garset sent Tarlion's men to face their pursuers in the north, then deployed Fennior's riders to meet the oncoming cavalry.

There was a clash of weapons as the southern force surged into their lines. There must have been two companies at least – eight hundred riders – spread out along the column. On the other side Tarlion had his hands full with the infantry, whose numbers were also increasing as more came down from the northern hill. They couldn't survive such an onslaught!

At that moment cries broke out from the front of the column, where the Restorers were. Garset turned, and saw blue-caped cavalry galloping along the road from the west. There was only a thin line of defenders between them and Fira's refugees—he'd concentrated his troops north and south. Shouting for reinforcements, he struggled through the mêlée towards them.

Before he could reach the Restorers' group the cavalry punched through. He saw Shiván, wildly brandishing the Blade of Darthane, and Fira and those rebel twins using their weapons with skill—

Then the music of the bellaril stopped abruptly. Garset's heart was in his mouth. Was this the end of the Restorers—of Dûrion's struggle for freedom? He had a brief glimpse of Lady Danîsha being hauled up in front of a rider, her instrument still dangling around her neck.

He and the men he'd brought arrived in time to see the cavalry detachment galloping back the way they'd come. Many of the refugees lay unmoving, and so did at least ten of the enemy. They hadn't given up their Restorer lightly. Lieutenant Fira was moving among them, rallying those who could could still wield a weapon. Garset blamed himself bitterly for not leaving more experienced troops here.

The other Restorers were bloody, but alive. He breathed a prayer of thanks. Then Tarlion's voice came to him. "*Captain! The Guards!*"

He swung round to the north. Dear Prince—the bellaril was silenced, and the Guard company had come to life! They were streaming down the lane towards them.

"Garset!" Shiván was clutching his arm. The young man was pale, blood staining the arm of his tunic. "Apart from those Guardsmen, there'll be quite a few Lightists among the soldiers attacking us, won't there?"

"Yes, but—"

"*The Ambon!* Where is it, Gil?"

The tall foreigner frowned. He was breathing heavily, but seemed unharmed. "I left it with you."

"No you didn't." Lady Alanya looked up from the wound she'd been examining on her forearm. "You dropped it in a ditch." She hurried to the side of the road and came back with a long, muddy bag. "Really, Gil!" Her eyes shot fire.

"*Raise it*, Lannie!" The red-haired woman bent and fumbled with the straps on the bag.

"This could turn the tide!" Garset exclaimed, new hope dawning. "And Overguardian—your sword! Lord Gelmion, the blaise. We need every power at our disposal." He ordered his men to strengthen the bodyguard round the Restorers. The guardsmen came thundering down the hill.

When Lady Alanya raised the Ambon, all chaos broke loose. The high clarion call rang out above the noise of battle. Garset scrambled on an unmanned horse to get a better view. He watched, awestruck, as hundreds of enemy troops lowered their weapons and surged towards the Restorers. Their former comrades tried to stop them, and furious skirmishes broke out on both sides of the road within a wide radius. The guardsmen were caught up in the general fray. Gradually the newcomers linked up with their former foes, and soon the attackers were being pushed back. *Light be praised,* Garset murmured.

But further down the column it was a different story. The infantry he'd seen emerging from the southern forests had reached their line, and it was already broken in places. There was no time to lose.

"Back! Back down the line!" he roared, pointing his sword. Tarlion, Fennior and his other officers relayed the command. The whole swollen front section of the column began moving back the way they'd come, spilling out into the fields and fighting off the remaining enemy troops.

Their progress was agonisingly slow. From his vantage point on horseback he groaned as he saw their line to the east shattered into small fragments. These were the raw Ambon recruits, untrained farmers and traders, fighting for their lives. Others were fleeing and being mercilessly cut down. It was a massacre.

At frequent intervals the Ambon gave out its summons. As they drew nearer, increasing numbers of the enemy infantry broke away and joined them. By the time they finally approached the scene of devastation, the enemy was suffering heavy losses. Trumpets sounded the retreat, and both north and south the Bishop's forces withdrew. The Guards made a last attempt to reach the Restorers' group around the Ambon, but were beaten off. The survivors galloped back up the hill.

Garset called a halt. There was no point giving chase. He sat on the horse, his eyes ranging over the mounds of bodies scattered far and wide across the fields. There must be at least three thousand dead and wounded. Tears pricked his eyes. It was just what he had most feared—a tragic repeat of the disaster the Dûrian Founders had suffered at the Slaughter of Gend. Of the two hundred veterans from his own Pure Company guarding the column, only a handful had survived. Among the dead lay loyal comrades he had known for years.

They had won. But at what a cost.

* * *

The rest of that day was the hardest time Shiván had ever known. He was exhausted from the battle, the wound in his arm was throbbing, his heart was aching from the multiple losses of Perrely, Danîsha and thousands of recruits; and the poisonous glances Fira kept throwing at him didn't help. He stumbled along as the army made its slow way to Hemmeris. The commander there was a personal friend of Garset's; the garrison would almost certainly defect to the Restorers. And right now they desperately needed a place where the wounded could be treated. Hemmeris was a small town that had a Care House, but not a Guardhouse. It fitted the bill.

They'd spent over three hours on the heartbreaking task of sorting the wounded from the dead in the mounds of fallen bodies. Pathetic cries for help filled the air. A dying man calling over and over for his wife. Another raging at God and all who tried to help him. A woman with a horrific face wound whimpering that she couldn't see. They'd loaded the worst cases on the four wagons—whose contents of food and supplies had been dumped at the wayside. But there wasn't nearly enough room for all. Hundreds were still crying out in distress, supported by comrades or carried on makeshift litters. Those near death had been left behind. It was a scene from hell indelibly seared into his mind.

The Bishop's Guard had twice launched a lightning strike on the front of the column, where Gil and Lannie were taking turns to keep the Ambon aloft. They would have broken through if it weren't for the nearly fifteen hundred Lightist troops who had defected. That was the one bright spot in the day's disastrous events.

With every fibre of his being he'd longed to order their cavalry to pursue the Guards and find Perrely and Danîsha; but he knew that wasn't possible. They were encumbered now with over a thousand wounded, and every defender was needed.

The army reached Hemmeris after dark, hungry and footsore. The garrison had been mobilised, but when the commander learnt that this was the Restorers' army, led by Captain Garset don Tembor, they were welcomed in. The news spread like wildfire, homes opened, and people thronged around them asking eager questions. There were impromptu celebrations in the street when it became known that Shambor had been defeated. They left a bitter taste in Shiván's mouth. Didn't these people understand? Today was a disaster, not a victory.

Tarlion was soon busy arranging billets for the wounded. The Care House was opened, assistants drafted in, and the worst cases from the wagons transferred there. On learning that the army hadn't eaten since dawn, housewives busied themselves in hundreds of homes, and every last soldier was soon sitting down to a hot meal, answering breathless questions, and doubtless giving exaggerated replies. Shiván sat silent at the Town Elder's table, leaving Lannie and Gil to satisfy their host's interest. For him, both present and future were bleak.

* * *

Gil was jerked from sleep by a peremptory voice in his mind.

"What do you have to say for yourself?"

"Mindruler, ..."

"Do you realise what your carelessness has cost me? The plan was running so well, I even had the Restorers within my grasp — then Alanya finds the Ambon. In a ditch! Was that the best you could manage? To drop it in a ditch, right there, where anyone might notice?"

Gil sat up on the bed. He'd been given a room to himself, a rare luxury.

"Your Dominance, I took the best opportunity I had. We were turning off into that narrow lane, which had no ditches. I thought no one was looking — Aaaaah!!"

A bolt of pure pain lashed through him.

"I'm reprimanding you, and you're arguing with me?"

"Apologies, M-Mindruler."

"Thanks to you I've lost not only the Restorers, but over fifteen hundred troops. In case you think you're indispensable," the voice continued silkily, *"let me disabuse you of that notion. You will most certainly be dispensed with if you fail to win people over tomorrow. Let me down again, and you'll regret it for the rest of your life — which will be long and painful."*

Gil let out a shuddering sigh as the presence faded from his mind. There was a knock on the door. The Town Elder's tousled head appeared.

"Are you all right, Lord Gelmion?"

"I'm fine, thank you."

"I thought I heard a cry."

"Just a nightmare."

"Oh! I quite understand." The man nodded sympathetically and closed the door.

Gil eased himself back down on the bed. His body ached all over. His whole life here in Dûrion was a nightmare.

* * *

In another home, Jomel had covered her head with a pillow to muffle her sobs. But she couldn't keep her body from shaking. Next to her on the bed, Fira heaved a deep sigh. Jomel tried to restrain herself. This had been a dreadful day, she'd been utterly terrified. Ghastly pictures still flashed across her mind. But worst of all was that Perrely had been captured. Last night she'd decided that come what may, she *had* to confide in her cousin what Gelmion was doing to her. She couldn't carry the burden alone. Tonight she'd been going to tell her. But tonight Perrely was gone. She had no one to share with, no one she could trust to keep it quiet.

At least Gelmion couldn't force himself on her here in the town. For that she was profoundly grateful. And if she feigned period pains tomorrow, she could beg some precious monthweed from her hostess. Her own supply was almost finished. Without it, the prospect of falling pregnant with Gelmion's child made her blood run cold. He would deny all responsibility, and her own lips would be sealed to protect her parents. What would the army Council do? All those righteous Lightists would hustle her off to a Care House at once, to prevent the scandal becoming known. And how could she survive at the mercy of strangers, eyeing her with disgust as a 'loose woman'?

That loomed over her as a terrible possibility even *with* the monthweed — which was known to fail every so often. She groaned, and pulled the pillow tighter over her head.

But her greatest fear was what would happen when Gelmion got tired of her — as he surely would. He was only using her for sexual release right now. But if Shambor crushed the Restorers, as he was bound to, then Gelmion would claim Alanya, and she, Jomel, would be discarded. Along with the rest of her family.

It was true that her family's situation had improved *now*, while Gelmion needed her. One day in the tent he'd shown them to her in the blaise, still prisoners, but better dressed, in a comfortable room, sitting down to a decent meal. They'd all looked *so* much happier. But she had no illusions. The moment Gelmion lost interest in her, she and her family would be out on the streets — like Perrely's poor parents. Or worse: he might complete his revenge for the wrongs she'd done him, by handing her over to the new Mindbender of Stillárre! Then she'd be back in the temple cell, awaiting slaughter as a human sacrifice.

So all she was doing now, was buying time. For what? She could see no way out. A fresh bout of sobs overtook her.

A memory took shape through the pain. She'd been here before, hadn't she? In an utterly hopeless place, where there was no way out. What had she done? She'd asked the One Creator God to rescue her. She'd asked, not because she had any right to, but because he had invited her to. *Ask, and you will receive.* He had heard her stumbling request in that condemned cell, and rescued her. Otherwise she would now be dead.

How could she have taken such an amazing act of love for granted? Less than a week later she'd been her old, careless self, relegating to the background of her life the unbelievable mercy of God.

Her sobs subsided. She climbed out of the bed and lay face down on the wooden floor, as she'd done before in the temple cell. She clasped her hands over her head.

"Great Creator," she whispered, "forgive me. I don't deserve to ask you anything. You have been so good to me. And I've lived as though that counted for nothing." She felt tears trickling down her cheek. "But God, you said — *Ask, and you will receive.* Would you — Can I ask you to rescue me again? If I can be any use to you. But you know the place I'm in now. I'm stuck, Creator God. I can't see any way out."

She lay still on the floor. Nothing happened. But warmth slowly seeped into her heart. She knew he was there. Awe and an overwhelming love filled her.

"Child," he seemed to say. "With me there is always a way out."

Chapter 26: *Challenge for leadership*

THE CHILD PULLED HIS ARM out of Nurse's tight grip, which was hurting him. "Just you be quiet, now!" she hissed. Then with a sigh she put her arm around him. "Don't worry about the noises. They'll soon stop."

He cowered against her solid, comfortable body, still tense and stiff. The carriage's blinds were all closed as it moved along slowly, often stopping for a while before jerking into motion again. All around were the sounds of people speaking a strange language — talking, shouting to one another, laughing, crying out, jostling the carriage when it stood still. There were bumps and thuds, the more distant sound of doors being opened and closed, the rumble of other wheels, the bellows of grûnet as they pulled their carts and the occasional yelp of a whipped sinélle. He shivered, and a whimper escaped his lips.

"It's a big town, see?" Nurse hurried to explain, squeezing him gently. "The town of Janulane. You're not used to that, 'cos we've always avoided towns. Even Darthane — we didn't go in, we waited for Faranu outside. But we'll soon be out of this one. And nothing can hurt you in the carriage. Faranu will keep you safe."

The child shivered again. He knew how Faranu kept him safe.

*   *   *

The next morning Shiván found himself on a hastily-erected platform in the town square, formally receiving the allegiance of the Hemmeris garrison and the defectors from Shambor's forces. About sixty more had arrived during the night, and others were still straggling in — soldiers who had slipped away during Shambor's retreat.

He went through the motions Garset kept murmuring in his ear, but his heart was not in it. Tears came to his eyes as the entire gathering sang the Song of Allegiance. When he'd first heard the Pure Company singing it back in Sûrilane, Perrely had clutched his arm in excitement and told him what it was. *Dear God, where is Perrely now? Is she being tortured? Lord, strengthen her… Be with her…* The pain never let up.

"Overguardian…?"

Garset was gripping his elbow. The show was over, and those up on the platform—the Town Elder, civic dignitaries, the garrison Commander, Gil and Lannie—were waiting for him to lead them off before the soldiers could be dismissed. With an effort he gathered himself together and walked across the planking and down the wooden stairs. The townsfolk—crowding every side street and building around the square—were cheering wildly, but he hardly heard them.

Back in the Town Elder's house, he made at once for his room. Not only his heart, but the wound in his arm was aching. It had been expertly treated last night—six stitches—but between the physical pain and the loss of Perrely he hadn't had much sleep. He needed to lie down.

He turned at the sound of someone striding rapidly after him.

"Shiván," Gil said, his eyes concerned. "I'm deeply sorry about Perrely. I can't begin to imagine what it must be like for you."

Shiván nodded, tears pricking his eyes. It was good of Gil to express sympathy; he wasn't a great one for talking about emotional matters.

"But, you know," Gil continued, "we do need to call a Council meeting as soon as possible. We must discuss where we go from here, what our future strategy will be ..."

Shiván groaned, and half turned away.

"No, Shiván, wait! We can't put this off. The Town Elder is already asking how long we're going stay. And I've heard mutterings among the officers about lack of leadership. It's not your fault, but they're saying it was Garset who won the battle and brought us to Hemmeris, and he's the one who's organising everything now. The Overguardian is no longer capable. That's what they're saying. You've got to prove them wrong! If that rumour spreads, it'll cause a huge drop in morale. We may lose many who've just joined us."

"The Council's no longer complete," he muttered. "Perrely and Danîsha are gone."

"I've thought about that. They can't be replaced, of course, but how about adding Tarlion, Garset's Second? Garset discusses everything with him. And, as we have so many defectors, we could include the most senior officer among them—Legate Brennor, I think."

Shiván sighed. "Okay. That sounds good. Will you organise it, Gil? Just tell me when I'm needed."

"Right." Gil gave a relieved smile, and hurried off. Shiván walked slowly to his room. Gil was right. He *had* to get over this, and become once more the leader God meant him to be. Even without Perrely…

An hour later he woke to the sound of someone knocking at the door. It was Gil.

"Everyone's gathered in the reclining room, Shiván. We're just waiting for you."

He dragged himself out of bed, wrestled a Dûrian fine-toothed comb through his hair, and followed Gil to the meeting.

The Town Elder's plush reclining room was decorated in matching shades of Dûrian bluish-green. The wall hangings had stylised tree and leaf motifs against a paler background. The recliners were of dark green leather on an emerald floor covering. In the centre of one wall was a blazing fire. It felt like gathering in a woodland glade for the Remembrance of Flame. He took the seat left vacant for him on the central recliner facing the fire. Gil sat with Lannie and Fira on his left; to his right were the army men, Garset, Tarlion and Brennor.

"Well, er, shall we start?" He looked around the group and tried a friendly grin. It felt like cracking a mask. "Garset—will you ask for the One's Light in this meeting?"

They all looked heavenward, palms upward on their laps, as Garset uttered a brief, soldierly prayer.

Shiván took a deep breath. Here's where he had to reassert his leadership. But before he could speak, Gil nipped in.

"I think we should say at the outset, how deeply we all sympathise with those who suffered painful losses in yesterday's battle. With you, our army colleagues"—he nodded towards the opposite side of the semicircle—"for the hundreds of your comrades who fell defending us. We owe you more than we can say. And also with you, Overguardian, on the loss of Perrely. We know this has been a grievous blow to you.

"In fact," he continued smoothly, overriding Shiván's second attempt to speak, "I think I can say for all of us, that we have been deeply concerned about the devastating effect this loss has had on you." He glanced around briefly. Several were nodding. His face as he turned back to Shiván was full of concern. "So much so, that it was I who prompted you to call this meeting. Now, that's not a criticism …" Shiván stared at Gil in amazement. Was this his way of helping to restore the Overguardian's authority? "We all know how much strain you've been under, and we deeply sympathise. However — Am I right, Lieutenant Tarlion, that your men have been saying the Overguardian is no longer competent?"

Red-haired Tarlion looked uncomfortable. He shifted in his seat and glanced at Garset before replying. "Well, yes, Lord Gelmion. I mentioned that to you in confidence — "

"Saying it here is no breach of confidence. This is something that vitally affects the future of our mission, which is exactly what we're discussing today. If the troops are beginning to doubt the Overguardian's ability to provide a decisive lead, there will be a loss of morale that could be disastrous. I'm sure our military colleagues would agree." He glanced at the officers and Fira. Fira nodded at once, her face stony. Garset inclined his head slightly, his eyes narrowed. Legate Brennor — a hard-bitten officer with a square face, greying hair, and a commanding eye — returned Gil's look without comment.

"Now, just a minute, Gil, what's all this about?" Shiván at last managed to say. "We met here to discuss future plans. Why am I suddenly on trial?"

"Yes, Gil, tell us." Lannie added, her brows drawn. "You've said nothing about this before."

"Shiván," Gil said, a wealth of sympathy in his voice, "you're not on trial. No one's *blaming* you. You've done the best you could, and now you've suffered a major blow which you're struggling to cope with. We understand, and feel for you. However — We're in a difficult situation right now in which strong leadership is required. Your actions, or lack of them, since the battle have shown that you're not in a position to provide this at the moment. And, even before the battle — " he raised his voice slightly to override Shiván's indignant protest " — even before the battle, you've made some unwise decisions, with costly results."

"Unwise decisions! Such as?"

"Well, for instance... I'm sorry to bring the painful subject up, but — stopping to rescue Perrely's family. That cost the lives of thousands."

"We couldn't have just passed them by!"

"Gil, that's a cheap shot!" Lannie exclaimed. Gil glanced at her, then turned back to Shiván. Was there a touch of annoyance in his eye?

"If we stopped to rescue every victim of Shambor's tyranny, we'd never get around to overthrowing him. As I'm sure Captain Garset would agree." Garset shrugged a shoulder and gave a half-nod. "But let's call that a commendable act of compassion, though it had disastrous consequences. What about your earlier decision when the army was in Larris? You ordered Captain Garset to take the northern route, closer to Berûvis. If you'd followed his wiser plan of crossing the Two Peaks, we'd have kept well away from Shambor's forces. And today we might still have an army of over five thousand."

Shiván gaped at Gil. He could hardly believe his ears. "But— It was *you* —!" he spluttered. "*You* told me it would be better to take the northern route. You said— you gave all sorts of reasons. I agreed, and spoke to Garset."

Gil's eyebrows were raised. "*I* told you? Really, Shiván. It's not like you to try and foist the blame on someone else. What reasons am I supposed to have given?"

"Well, you said —" Shiván desperately searched his brain, but his memory of that conversation was foggy. He'd felt sluggish and dull-witted throughout their time in Larris. One detail finally came to mind. "You said it would be too tough on the recruits to make that climb."

Tarlion laughed. Fira snorted. Garset smiled. Even Legate Brennor's lips quirked. "Too tough on the *recruits?*" Gil said incredulously. "Light above, man, they were in training! It would have done them good. You'll have to come up with something better than that."

"Gil," he said fiercely, "I *know* we had that conversation. I can't remember all the details, but I know we *had* it as well as I know I'm sitting here. I can't imagine why you're denying it, but *you* suggested it would be better to take the northern route. I agreed with you, and that's why I went to Garset. If it was an unwise decision, we were both unwise."

"Then why didn't I come with you to speak to Garset?"

"I asked you to. You refused. You said I needed to do it myself."

There was doubt in Lannie's eyes as she stared at him. There was doubt in all their eyes.

Gil leaned back on the recliner and surveyed Shiván pityingly. "Well, that's very convenient. No, Shiván, let's face it. There was another reason you wanted to pass closer to Berûvis, wasn't there? A reason to do with Perrely. That's where her home was, isn't it?

You wanted a route nearer Berûvis for personal reasons to do with the girl you love — not because it was good military strategy. Yet you're our leader. You should have put the safety of your troops above your own personal desires."

"Gil, that's a load of grûn shit, and you know it!"

"Then give me another reason why you made that decision. Not the recruits, please."

"Dammit, *you* had the reasons! I can't remember."

Gil sighed, and turned to the others. "Friends, you've all heard it. Shiván denies responsibility for the deaths we've just suffered, and blames me for what went wrong. At this point I feel it is my duty to challenge for leadership."

An electric silence followed. Shiván was stunned. This was a coup d'etat! Gil's denial of that conversation was a blatant lie. Yet only he, Shiván, knew it. And Gil had so cleverly destroyed his credibility, that he could never convince the others. In an instant his entire picture of Gil changed. This was not the work of a Restorer of the Way. This was deliberate, calculated sabotage. Who *was* Gil? Who was he working for? Horrifying vistas opened up.

*   *   *

He pulled his mind back to the present. A sense of outrage swept over him. Gil was a liar and a deceiver. For weeks he'd been acting the humble follower of the Light, the devoted colleague — but it had all been a hollow sham! His entry into the Light, up there in the mountains — a cynical pretence! Now he was trying to seize control for his own devious purposes — or someone else's. No way! He was *not* going to let Gil get away with this. His fists itched to punch that mock-humble face. But it wouldn't achieve anything. Gil had swayed people's minds with words. He'd have to hit back in the same way.

"I don't accept your challenge," he said, glaring at the man. "You've accused me of causing the deaths of thousands. What about *your* part in that? Who was it who argued like a lawyer with Garset back in Sûrilane, saying we should raise the Ambon en route? *That's* what really caused yesterday's disaster. With all those recruits, even if we'd gone over the Two Peaks, Shambor would have attacked somewhere else. That was an unwise decision we *all* made — including you."

A look of sadness crossed Gil's face. "There I agree. Garset, I owe you an apology. You were right. I deeply regret those unnecessary deaths."

Garset nodded.

Shiván stared at Gil. The slimy trickster, gaining sympathy now with a handsome apology.

"However," Gil continued, "the fact remains that a bad situation was made worse by the two decisions to pass closer to Berûvis, and to try and rescue Perrely's family. If we had crossed the Two Peaks, as Garset intended, we would have avoided open areas like the Sesten valley. As you say, Shiván, Shambor might have attacked anyway; but he would have found it harder. We might then still have had Perrely and Danîsha with us. The loss of the bellaril is a particularly heavy blow."

There were nods all round the circle. Shiván seethed with frustration. Everything he said was being turned against him! Dr. Denbigh had always been a skilful debater. But this wasn't an academic debate, and he wasn't going to give up.

"Okay. Big of you—you've admitted one mistake. But here's something else. *You* were meant to be checking ahead with the blaise the whole time. How come you missed seeing so many of Shambor's troops?"

"Now you're being unfair, Shiván!" Lannie retorted. "Gil spent *hours* every day staring into that glass, as you well know. He can't see through the branches of trees. He can only look into the woods at random—and there are a lot of woods around here! It's like looking for a needle in a haystack."

"Garset had scouts out the whole time, and they didn't spot anything either," Gil pointed out mildly.

"You were checking every day for a week!" Shiván declared hotly. "I can't believe you saw *no* sign of over three thousand troops being moved into position—or that you never once, even with random checks, saw traces of *that many* soldiers hiding in the forests near Sesten!"

"Oh, come off it, Shiván. You're clutching at straws." Lannie's voice was tired. A glance round the other faces showed that he'd lost them. A wave of humiliation washed over him. He'd been outgunned after all by this smarmy, lying politician.

"I'm challenging for leadership," Gil said quietly. "Will you now accept, Shiván?"

"No! I may have made mistakes, but you've been using lies and trickery today, Gil. Why didn't you discuss this with me beforehand? Why have you sprung it on us out of the blue? That's not straight. That's a sneaky, underhand trick. I don't know what you're up to, or who's paying you, but I'd trust your leadership less than a blind man's in the dark."

"What are you saying, Shiván?" Fira exclaimed. "That Gelmion is a *spy?*" She leant back on her recliner, her narrow, hawk-like face cold. "You made a foolish decision, invented a conversation with Gelmion to back it up, and then agreed to a disastrous delay under the influence of your love for Lady Perrely. You have forfeited your right to lead."

Shiván stared at her, shaking his head. It was pointless to argue.

"Shiván does not accept my challenge," Gil said. "That means the rest of you have to decide between us. If you are divided, the group must split—which would be a disaster in our present situation. If you are unanimous, then the loser must choose between accepting the new leader and remaining in the group; or leaving. Am I right?" He looked at the Dûrians. There were nods of agreement.

"Very well. Let's hear each person's decision."

"I accept Gelmion," Fira declared. There was a long silence.

Garset heaved a deep sigh. "I am sad that it has come to this. Despite Lord Gelmion's prominent rôle in the discussion about using the Ambon, it was clear that all the Restorers were inclined that way, and it was a joint decision. But in the other two matters…"

He looked directly at Shiván. "I don't know what happened between you and Lord Gelmion regarding the change of route. All I know is that you were the one who overruled my objections. The same goes for the decision to rescue Lady Perrely's family. Thousands might otherwise have lived. I respect you highly as a person, but… I've always felt you were rather young for such a rôle." He paused, sadness in his gaze. "I accept Lord Gelmion. But you are still a Restorer. I hope you'll remain with us." Shiván felt tears pricking his eyelids.

Gil looked at Tarlion. "I accept Lord Gelmion," he muttered.

There was another silence. Lannie was twisting her hands in her lap. Finally she turned to Shiván. There were tears in her eyes.

"Shivvie, I'm sorry," she whispered in English. "*Please* don't think I'm doing this just because I love Gil. You're a great guy, and I'm very fond of you, but ..." A sudden bitterness rose up in him, which must have shown in his face. She broke off and turned to the others. "I accept Gelmion," she said unsteadily in Dûrian.

Legate Brennor shook his head. "This is an appalling business," he said brusquely. "My troops have just sworn allegiance to Lord Shiván as Overguardian. Now I'm to tell them they have a *new* Overguardian? What will they think? Yet if I support Lord Shiván, I'll split the group." He turned hard eyes on Gil. "I'm not entirely sure of your motives in making this challenge. I hope they're as pure as you'd like us to think. But I have no choice. I accept Lord Gelmion."

Shiván gazed with unfocused eyes at the fire. That was it. He was out.

"Shiván." Gil's voice was quiet and sympathetic. The snake. "I'm sorry. I know this must be very hard for you, on top of everything else. But you need to tell us whether you can accept my leadership and stay on, or whether you'll... go elsewhere. I want you to know that I'd be very happy for you to stay, and to remain on the Council. I'd value your support—"

"Oh, cut the generous victor act," he snapped. "You know I'll stay. Where else can I go? I'll support the army—not you. I'll fight to overthrow Shambor. And when your lies find you out... I'll be there."

Gil sighed. "Very well. And now, I believe our hostess has laid on a daymeal for us."

Shiván remained in the recliner as the others filed out. They all avoided his eye, except Lannie. She gave him a tortured look, hesitated, started to say something, then left.

He felt more alone than at any time since arriving in Dûrion.

Chapter 27: *Unexpected captive*

NEWS OF THE 'VICTORY' over Shambor spread like wildfire. Scattered groups of Lightist soldiers kept straggling in, and soon after dawn-meal the next day over three hundred cavalry arrived from Histen. The newcomers took the oath of allegiance to Gelmion as Over-guardian. Lannie couldn't help a surge of pride as Gil stood before them, a striking figure in the green infantry cape Legate Brennor had found him, a sword strapped to his waist. Here was a leader the troops could look up to — unlike dear, casual Shivvie.

Her heart was still torn about Gil's takeover yesterday. She was furious with him for springing it on them unannounced, and had told him so. His reply — that people's immediate gut reactions brought out the truth in a situation like this — had made her even more indignant. How could he be so callous? He'd said that it was only after he'd seen Shiván's apathy about calling a Council meeting that he'd decided this couldn't wait any longer. Well, *that* made sense, she supposed. Since Perrely's capture Shivvie definitely hadn't been with it. Decisive action was needed, and he'd obviously been in no fit state to provide it.

Yet... The shock of Gil's challenge had roused Shiván from his lethargy. Couldn't they have done this outside the Council — told him that if he didn't shape up, Gil would have to take over? Before Garset had joined them, Shivvie had shown himself not a bad lead-er. With his talent for lateral thinking, he'd rescued them from many tight places. Charging the Bishop's Guard with the Blade at Carreck Manor. Getting them into Stillárre to rescue Gil — and out again. Decoying Shambor's soldiers to the Grûzhack fort. *That* had resulted in the Grûzhack War, which was keeping Shambor off their backs right now.

She wished so much that she could talk it all over with 'Neesh. She was a wise old mother hen, and Lannie missed her sorely. She shuddered at the thought of what Danîsha might be suffering at Shambor's hands even now. And Perrely.

Well, maybe Shivvie had been the One's leader for the small group they had been at the beginning. Now, with an army of thou-sands, a different leader was needed. Someone who could think strategically. Someone who could see the wide picture. Someone who could inspire the troops. A *strong* leader, who would go the way the One led him, never mind what Garset or Brennor might say. In short, Gil.

He was capable of lateral thinking, too. She thought of the daring plan that was taking shape in his mind, which he'd shared with her last night. That would put the cat among the pigeons when he raised it in Council later today. But she had no doubt he'd push it through. He'd have thought of every difficulty, and found a way round it. And he'd present it so well, that people's arguments would fall away. She felt deeply sorry for Shiván, but Gil was a *real* leader. They needed someone like that right now.

The Council gathered in the Town Elder's reclining room soon after midmeal. Shivvie came in last, his face grim. He grunted in response to the sympathetic greetings several gave him. At least he'd decided to stick it out on the Council. Lannie was glad of that, but she hoped he wasn't coming to make trouble.

After the opening prayer, Gil told the gathering that a new strategy was needed to deal with a new situation. "As we're all sadly aware," he said, "our recent battle with Shambor's forces was a victory only in name. We lost thousands, and so did the enemy. We have both retired to lick our wounds. But, thanks to the blaise and the bess, Alanya and I can give you the good news that Shambor does not intend any further action against us in the short term. Lannie, would you tell the Council what we overheard last night?"

The military types transferred their intent gazes to her. She shot Gil a fiery glance. Trust him to rope her in without warning! She cleared her throat. "Well, we found Shambor in conference with some of his senior advisors. He was ranting on about his failure to capture all of us Restorers, and to destroy our army at Berûvis, but he said that for the moment he can't do anything further. He suffered too many losses — both casualties and defections. He can't risk any more non-mindbent troops, and the Bishop's Guard are too thinly stretched. In any case, the war in the south is now demanding all his attention. Apparently Dhembis has been captured by the Grûzhack."

She waited for the exclamations of shock and horror to die down.

"Shambor said he could only come after the Restorers when the cavalry he's requested from Selmion arrive. He believes we've been sufficiently weakened—despite all those who've joined us—to eliminate us as a threat in the short term. He said, I quote: 'They'll think twice now about swaggering through the countryside with huge numbers of farmers and traders!' He assumes we'll lie low for a while and try to build up our strength with real soldiers—which will take time."

"Not as much as he thinks!" Tarlion exclaimed. "More than eight hundred and fifty have joined us since the battle."

"But we can't assume that it'll carry on like that," Fira retorted. "In the Rebellion we also had a lot of defections immediately after our victories. It didn't last."

There was an awkward silence as the army officers eyed their former enemy. Gil cut in smoothly.

"Right. But fortunately, there are other things in our favour. This morning we saw large numbers of troops heading south from Berûvis—along with two or three Guard companies. Shambor knows we're here in Hemmeris; but his forces were on the Stillárre road. I think that bears out what we overheard him saying: he has no time for us now. He's sending every available soldier south to try and recapture Dhembis. What's more, I had a good look in Stillárre itself. There were hundreds of troops heading out, but only a couple of companies in the barracks, and less than half the normal contingent in the Guardhouse.

"Therefore, I suggest that *now* is the time to hit Shambor hard—when he's least expecting it. I propose we capture Stillárre."

The uproar that broke out now totally eclipsed the shock over the fall of Dhembis. Lannie had to repress a smile. All four officers spoke at once, staring at Gil in outrage, until Legate Brennor's strident baritone drowned the others out.

"—quite out of the question! Stillárre is a walled city. It can hold out against thousands, even with a handful of defenders. A siege might last months, and we have no assault weapons! No catapults, siege ladders, battering rams. Just to build a sufficient stock of *those* would take weeks—assuming we had the necessary craftsmen..."

Gil held up a hand for silence. "I'm not suggesting we lay siege to Stillárre. As you rightly point out, Legate, we have neither the equipment nor the time for that. My idea is almost the opposite. That we take Stillárre by stealth—from within. Then let Shambor face the problems of besieging a walled city."

That effectively silenced the officers. Frowns appeared on every face. "How do you propose we do *that*, Gelmion?" Fira wanted to know.

"I suggest we act out a little play for Shambor's benefit. Once all his northern troops have passed Bornis on the Stillárre highway, you, Legate," — he nodded to Brennor — "will march out of Hemmeris at the head of those who have defected to us. In the centre of the column, closely guarded and with our hands loosely bound, will be the Restorers and their close associates — like you, Fira, and maybe you, Garset, with Tarlion and a few others. When you reach Bornis you'll join the highway to Stillárre. I believe that was your original destination, before Shambor diverted you to Berûvis?" The Legate nodded, his brows drawn tightly together.

"So you'll be reporting back for duty. Behind your column our remaining Ambon recruits and Fira's refugees will follow as ordinary travellers. If anyone challenges you, you will say you are reporting to Stillárre as ordered. If they ask about your prisoners, you will say that they are rebels whom you've taken into custody — which will be true. But you're hardly likely to be challenged: by then most of Shambor's troops will be ahead of us.

"Thus, when we reach Stillárre — we'll simply walk in. We'll make our way to the Guardhouse and neutralise the Bishop's Guard. Then we'll raise the Ambon. That will bring in the Lightists from the unmindbent garrison. The remaining troops will probably join us anyway — we'll deal with any who don't. Then we'll hold Stillárre — a walled city — which Shambor will not have the manpower to retake while he's involved in the Grûzhack War. We'll have time to consolidate our position in the west and north of the country, and to build a strong base from which to attack later. Among other things we'll make contact with the Dorbians when they arrive, and coordinate a war strategy with them. Any questions?"

A silence followed. Lannie could see the officers' expressions wavering between doubt and appreciation.

"Sounds a little elaborate to me," Brennor grunted. "Rather too many 'ifs'."

Gil shrugged and quoted a Dûrian proverb. " 'If you never sow for fear of weeds, you'll never reap'."

The Legate nodded, but his scowl didn't ease. He doesn't trust Gil, Lannie thought with a flash of annoyance. Maybe because Gil had challenged for leadership. She could imagine a dyed-in-the-wool military type like Brennor not appreciating that.

Garset's expression was more evaluating than antagonistic. "Shambor's bound to have scouts and spies out, watching our every movement. They will report our departure, and follow us along the way. Will they believe we've actually taken the Restorers captive?"

"Then we must make it convincing," Gil said crisply. "I would suggest we're hauled from our lodgings on the day of departure, bound, and led off with the army. That should convince any spies who are watching. We'd have to leave quickly, though, for fear of a riot in the town. The Restorers have become rather popular here."

"We might find Stillárre closed to us and a large force waiting."

Gil shrugged. " 'Might', Captain. Many things *might* happen, and no plan is foolproof. We can only rely on the best intelligence available to us. The evidence of the blaise and bess is that Shambor doesn't believe us capable of doing him any serious damage. He also needs every soldier he can lay hands on for the Grûzhack War. The last thing that would occur to him is that we'd march straight into Stillárre and take it over!" He glanced around the group. "Any other comments or objections?"

Fira spoke up. "I think this is a good plan. It has the element of surprise. And holding Stillárre would put us in a very powerful position. We found that in the Rebellion. Shambor was cut off from the whole of the north-west. He only drove us out by throwing everything he had at us." She looked at the army men. There were a couple of rueful nods. "But he can't do that now, because of the Grûzhack War."

"You're right." Brennor nodded slowly. "The plan is well thought out." The gaze he turned on Gil was sharp, but no longer antagonistic. "It still has too many uncertainties for my liking, but it's better than staying here or going into hiding."

"Good. We are agreed, then?"

"No."

Lannie's heart sank. Shiván was going to make trouble after all.

"I agree with Legate Brennor. The plan has too many uncertainties. But there's another alternative to staying on here or hiding. You all seem to have forgotten our original plan—to go to Carreck Manor and meet up with the Dorbians. They may be there already. Gil and Garset, you were both quite insistent on this in our early discussions. Why not do that first? Then we'd have five thousand powerful warriors to scare the living daylights out of Shambor's troops."

"I've checked Carreck Manor with the blaise," Gil said quietly. "There's no sign of the Dorbians."

"That doesn't mean they won't come."

Lannie's patience snapped. "Shivvie, for goodness' sake! Gil gives us a perfectly good plan, and you have to propose something different. Are you just trying to be obstructive?"

Before Shiván could reply, Garset intervened. "The Dorbians will be a great asset, I agree; and I did earlier feel we should wait for them. But the strength of Lord Gelmion's plan is the element of surprise. If we detour all the way to Carreck Manor and wait for the Dorbians, we will have lost that."

"Exactly," Brennor added, scowling at Shiván. "We need to strike now, when Shambor least expects it. Not bury ourselves out on the fringes while he receives reinforcements from Selmion."

Fira and Tarlion were also giving Shiván stony looks. As always, Gil had sold his idea well. Everyone now felt it was 'their' plan. Shivvie seemed to realise this. Bitterness touched his face, and he shrugged.

"Very well, then," Gil said. "Legate Brennor, Captain Garset, the three of us will meet later to work out the details." He looked round the group. "Not a word of this to anyone, please. We don't want rumours reaching the enemy.

"Now, about the food situation…"

Shiván stood and walked out of the room, his face set.

* * *

Back in his room, Shiván banged his fist on the window sill in frustration. The Town Elder's house faced on to the square. Below he could see troops mingling with the townsfolk. Many were out, despite the cold and the overcast sky. A cavalryman, smart in his light blue cape, was swaggering along with a girl at his side. She was looking up into his face with wide, admiring eyes. A group of infantrymen were laughing together beside the white Hearth building. All those soldiers, and the thousands of others scattered through the town, might soon be dead. It was as plain as daylight to him that Gil was leading them into another trap with this attack on Stillárre.

To march right up to Dûrion's second city! It was crazy. Yet everyone had been swayed by Gil's smooth tongue. No one had listened to him—Shiván. He'd proposed an alternative that could easily be combined with Gil's plan, while hopefully derailing whatever hidden agenda he was following. But all the others had heard was the sour grapes of a deposed leader.

If only Danîsha or Perrely were here! His heart lurched at the thought of Perrely. They would have believed him! Lannie was too besotted with Gil. But somehow, *someone* had to believe him. The situation was desperate. Thousands had died already because of their mistake in using the Ambon. Must thousands *more* die? Would this be the end of all they'd been sent to do in Dûrion?

No. He couldn't believe that.

He rummaged in his bag and took out the old, battered King James Bible. Shame came over him that he hadn't looked at it for over two weeks—not since leaving Sûrilane, in fact. He riffled through the Old Testament, and his fingers found the twenty-third psalm. Tears dimmed his eyes as he read the words that had comforted millions through the centuries:

The LORD is my shepherd; I shall not want.
He maketh me to lie down in green pastures: he leadeth me
    beside the still waters.
He restoreth my soul: he leadeth me in the paths of righteousness
    for his name's sake.
Yea, though I walk through the valley of the shadow of death,
    I will fear no evil:
    for thou art with me; thy rod and thy staff they comfort me.
Thou preparest a table before me in the presence of mine enemies:
    thou anointest my head with oil; my cup runneth over.
Surely goodness and mercy shall follow me all the days of my life:
    and I will dwell in the house of the LORD for ever.

David had lived through many desperate situations. Hounded by a hostile king, facing death daily, not knowing how he could possibly survive. Yet his simple trust in God shone through. *He* was with him; that was all that mattered.

He knelt beside his bed—an old habit from childhood. "Father," he prayed. "Lead us through the valley of death that lies before us now. Thank you that you're with us. Whatever plots Gil or his master may be hatching, bring them to nothing. Prepare a table before us in the presence of our enemies. We *know* we can trust your goodness and mercy. Show me what you want me to do."

He knelt, silent, as peace flowed into his heart.

Gil wasn't in charge. God was.

* * *

Perrely peered through the high window of the small, enclosed vehicle.

"We're in Herminar," she sighed as she slumped back on her seat. "Another three hours in this horrible coach."

"Oh, dear. Yes, the padding on these benches has almost worn through," Danîsha croaked, shifting uncomfortably. She was losing her voice after two nights on cold stone floors. "Why have we stopped?" she asked. Anything to keep the poor girl's mind off her pain.

"They're letting the grûnet drink from the village trough."

"I suppose the animals need refreshment." She coughed and cleared her throat. "They're painfully slow, aren't they? Not like those *sin-... sinay-...* what are they called? — the really fast ones."

"Sinélle. No. You can almost *walk* faster than a grûn."

Danîsha looked at Perrely's drawn face sympathetically. She herself had a dried gash on her forehead, left by a sharp buckle on the horse she'd been abducted with; and her right shoulder was still aching. It had been yanked almost out the socket when that cavalryman had hauled her bodily up in front of him. The bellaril had been on its strap around her neck, so that had come up too. She didn't know if it was still in one piece—they'd taken it away from her almost at once. She fingered Teynel's comb in her robe pocket. At least she still had that.

But her small losses bore no comparison with the agony Perrely was going through. Roughly snatched away from that joyful reunion with her family. Knocked unconscious—she had a large swelling on the back of her head, and a persistent headache—only to come round in the Berûvis Guardhouse, bereft of everyone she loved. Then the short-lived relief of finding that the two of them would be travelling together—wiped away by the terrible news that she, Danîsha, had had to give her. That her entire family had been brutally slaughtered. Almost worse was the lack of any details—Shiván had gasped out the bare fact just as the fighting began.

The poor girl had wept for hours yesterday as the coach trundled down the highway to Lômack. All Danîsha could do was to hold her till there were no more tears to cry. She knew the names of Perrely's brothers as though they were her own. She'd repeated them over and over: Father, Mums, Larion, Barlet. And Shiván. Danîsha knew it was *his* arms she needed now, not hers. Her heart bled for the girl. *So* much loss and pain in a single day.

They'd spent last night in the Lômack Guardhouse—praise the One, in a single cell. Perrely had curled up against Danîsha like a little girl and sobbed herself to sleep. Today they had a new escort of Guards and a different coachman, but the same uncomfortable vehicle with its high, narrow windows. Destination—Darthane.

What then? Hauled before Shambor? Danîsha almost hoped so. She'd give that monster a piece of her mind—if she hadn't lost her voice entirely.

* * *

Shambor sat at the blackwood desk in his receiving room, waiting with grim satisfaction as the captives were brought to him. He'd anticipated this moment for weeks. Far better, of course, if the other two Restorers could have been there as well—he cursed Gelmion's carelessness about the Ambon for the thousandth time. But these two would do to be going on with. He had the bellaril—which freed him to use mindbent troops against the Restorers. And he had Shiván's intended fiancée—a powerful lever should anything go wrong with the next stage of the operation.

The door chime sounded. He plucked the answering chime at the side of his desk. Secretary Estaron entered. "The prisoners, Your Radiance." Two Bishop's Guards came in, with the women between them.

The world changed.

The older woman opened her mouth to speak, but she barely got one hoarse syllable out before the Guardsman to her left snapped *"Silence!"*. She tried again, and he moved behind her and clapped a hand over her mouth. Shambor hardly noticed. His attention was riveted on the girl.

It was incredible. She was the living image of Yestel! The only woman he'd ever loved. He carefully felt her shiláy. Pain, overlying a clear, straightforward honesty and fair-mindedness. A strong mind, but open and trusting. All those cloying Lightist beliefs, but a deep capacity for love.

He stared at her, hardly able to take it in. She was perfect. The woman of his dreams, whom he'd never thought to meet again!

Doubt was clouding those beautiful purple eyes; and Estaron was frowning at him. He pulled himself together with an effort.

"Guardsmen, you may leave. Take the old lady away. Estaron, you can go, too. Send for some chass and cakes."

Once more the foreign woman tried to get a word in, but she was hustled out by the Guards. Estaron followed with raised eyebrows. Let him think what he liked.

He came round from behind the desk. "Come, my dear, take a seat. Oh—your hands are tied." He hurried over, taking a small knife from the pocket of his robe—one that he normally used on the animals. Standing behind her, he took hold of a slim arm, preparing to slice through the rope binding her hands. Her hiss of pain startled him, then he saw the bruises. He readjusted his grip, his heart going out to her. She'd been manhandled. He'd make sure *that* didn't happen again.

He cut the rope, and she stood rubbing her wrists. He put a hand gently on her shoulder and guided her to one of the recliners. He sat on another facing her. Multicoloured light from the great circular window lit up her face.

Suffering was written there, and perplexity. It was not a stunningly beautiful face, but there was a winsomeness about it that set his pulse racing. He had seen her often enough through Gelmion's eyes, of course; but images via someone else's brain were never the same. That sweet face, seen now as it really was, brought back poignant memories of his brief, happy period with Yestel. Until she'd seen his darker side, and turned away from him. No, he wouldn't think about that. With Perrely it would be—had to be—different.

"I'm very sorry you've been hurt," he told her. "I'll arrange for my personal physician to treat you. And I'm devastated that your family was killed." Her eyes filled with tears, and she turned away. He wanted to take her hand, but—not yet. "Believe me," he said, "I did not order that." Well, not specifically. He'd merely instructed that they be disposed of. Which was before he'd fully appreciated what Perrely was like. He gazed at her earnestly. "Those who committed this atrocity will suffer the same penalty."

Perrely shook her head. "That won't bring my family back."

Shambor's heart leapt. It was the first time he'd heard her speak. A clear, light contralto — so like Yestel. "No, my dear, you're right, it won't. I respect your compassion. They will be punished in lesser ways."

There was a chime at the door, and two servants in blue and silver livery brought in a tray with a silver beaker of chass, a matching pot of honey, delicate cups with attached saucers, small shallow bowls, blackwood cutlery, and a silver plate piled high with sweet pastries. Steam curled up from the chass beaker's mouth. One servant moved an occasional table between them. The other placed the tray on it and, at Shambor's nod, began pouring chass into the cups. The first offered Perrely a bowl, then the plate of pastries. The second held out a cup of chass with a dainty blackwood spoon, and the honey pot. Her face showed delight, quickly changing to suspicion.

Shambor smiled at her. As the servants left, he raised his cup in salute. "You are a remarkable woman, Lady Perrely. A very courageous one. Now that I've met you, I deeply regret the trouble you've been through. Your capture was a necessity of war, but I intend you no harm. The death of your family was an appalling mistake for which the perpetrators will pay. But now I want to make amends in whatever small ways I can. I'd like your stay in the Cathedral to be as pleasant as possible. If ever you need anything," he said earnestly, "or are in any way uncomfortable, please let me know, and it will be put right immediately."

She gave him a level look. "I'm your enemy. Why are you doing this?"

That directness. Just like Yestel. "Perhaps I'm not as evil as I'm made out to be," he murmured. "I respect my enemies. You are acting according to your beliefs, I according to mine. There's no cause to despise an honest opponent."

She took a sip of chass and lay on her elbow looking down at the cup in her hands. The pastry sat untouched in its bowl on the receptacle built into the recliner. When her eyes met his again, there was fire in them.

"Then why isn't Danîsha with us? Why are you favouring me, and not her? She's a Restorer of the Way — I'm just a helper."

For a moment Shambor was at a loss for words. It had been many years since anyone he was favouring had dared to contradict him. But with Perrely it brought no anger, only a painful surge of longing. It was so long since anyone had been honest with him. He needed that.

"I assure you Danîsha will not be mistreated. But, yes. You're right. I singled you out. Because I saw something in you — something I greatly admire. And I wanted to start making amends for the loss of your family."

She looked at him sceptically. "How can I believe you? When Alanya met you here in the Cathedral, you deceived her and then mindbent her. *That* showed no respect. How do I know you're not deceiving me now?"

In her mistrust she looked vulnerable and utterly desirable. He replied softly, "By the simple fact that I'm not mindbending you."

"How can I know that? Everything I think I'm experiencing might be placed in my mind by you — cutting my bonds, letting me lie in this recliner, treating me to chass and cakes…"

"That's true. There's no way I can prove otherwise. But listen. Everyone who is brought into the Realm of the Mind realises what's happened fairly quickly — even while they're still mindbent. Didn't Alanya tell you something like that?"

She nodded reluctantly.

"Then, if you *are* mindbent, you'll realise it in the next few days. Will you suspend judgment until then?"

Scorn touched those beautiful eyes. "You sound so kind and con-cerned — but I'm still your prisoner! If you really cared about me, you'd let me go. What good am I to you? I'm not a Restorer, and I'm not an army officer. Keeping me here won't help you in the least."

Oh, yes it will, he thought. But he didn't say so. He murmured, "I'm deeply sorry for the military necessity. But I want to reassure you in every way I can. I'd like to invite you to share the daymeal with me. That's not a command — you can refuse if you wish. Will you join me?"

For a long moment she stared at him suspiciously. Then her face relaxed. "I can't dine with the Bishop of Dûrion looking like this." She waved a hand at her torn, grubby shift and tangled hair.

Shambor's heart leapt. "I'll see you are moved to a new apart-ment with washing facilities, toiletries, and a complete wardrobe. And Danîsha, too," he added as an afterthought.

"Very well, Your Radiance. I assume Danîsha is included in your kind invitation?"

He masked his discomfiture. "Of course. With apologies for my discourtesy to her earlier."

"Then I'll suspend judgment."

A faint smile transformed her face. Shambor's heart was thudding as he escorted her to the door. She was everything he'd ever desired in a woman.

Chapter 28: *Journey into darkness*

"THE *GORELENYU* IS GOING NORTH to the Berûvis Gate," Ongaret declared flatly.

Frengor closed his eyes and shook his head. "May the Prince have mercy."

The small group of purple-robed priests followed at a distance behind the *Gorelenyu* and its escort of soldiers as they entered Berûvis Street from the Stillárre market square. Until this moment Frengor had hoped that they would leave the city by the Southgate, headed for Leváris and the Grûzhack War. That hope had now been dashed.

"Does that mean, Your Wisdom," a young novice asked, "that this— weapon— will be used against the Restorers?"

"I can see no other reason for it to go north, Berion."

They'd trailed the small carriage all the way from Gend to Stillárre. At first it had been pulled by sinélle, and they'd followed on foot, asking questions at inns till they knew it was headed for Stillárre. Once there, further questions had led them to the Guardhouse. They'd stayed nearby, keeping a constant watch, and today it had set off, escorted, praise the One, by a contingent of Guards on foot. That small mercy meant that they could keep up, and see where it went. But his heart was heavy.

"Other troops are going this way, too," Ongaret murmured. Frengor looked behind him. An infantry cohort was just leaving the square. Up ahead a large contingent of mounted Guards began filing into Berûvis Street, holding up the traffic. His heart sank further.

They followed the carriage and its escort along the northern highway for over four hours. The Guards marched fast; even novice Berion was weary by the time the vehicle branched off on to a side track.

"We'll continue beyond— then turn back," Frengor said, breathing heavily.

"All the military traffic is turning off too," Ongaret muttered. Frengor nodded wearily. The highway had grown increasingly congested with troops— mostly mounted Guardsmen. Now many were filing on to small roads leading off to the left and right.

They passed the carriage as it made its way slowly up towards the wooded crest of a ridge of hills east of the highway. The priests walked on. After a while they stopped and sat on a low cluster of rocks, looking back the way they'd come. Behind them rose the dark mass of the Hills of Géris. Facing them on the other side of the highway was the wooded ridge. It angled away from the road in an easterly direction. Together with the Géris foothills it formed a natural funnel for anyone travelling south, reaching its apex at a narrow gap through which the highway passed. The *Gorelenyu* would be located right beside that gap. Columns of Guards were winding up into both sets of hills.

Frengor nodded sombrely. "It's an ambush."

* * *

Although she was prepared for it, the dawn arrest came as a shock to Alanya. Soldiers banging on the Town Elder's door, indignant protests, the sound of heavy boots on the stairs as she hastily pulled on her travelling clothes. Then she, Gil and Shiván bundled out into the freezing cold, their bags snatched from them, hands bound behind their backs, marching off into the market square. The Town Elder shouting to his neighbours to rouse the town: *Mutiny! The Restorers are being arrested!* It was all according to the script worked out by Gil, Garset and Brennor, but it felt too real for comfort.

In the town square of Hemmeris the army was assembling. Fira, Shîr and Câr, Jomel, Garset, Tarlion, Fennior and several others joined them as 'prisoners'. Their hands were loosely bound behind them and they were surrounded by burly troopers from Brennor's legion, who winked and looked stern. They set off out of the town with the vanguard while the rest of the army was still forming up behind them. Clusters of angry townsfolk began to appear. There were ugly incidents as several groups of hotheads tried to break through the ranks to where they were, yelling for the Restorers to be freed. She could only hope no one was hurt. Fortunately they were soon out of the town, and gradually the cries of the townsfolk dwindled behind them.

It was a cold day. There was a bitter wind, and dark clouds covered the sky. Lannie shivered. She wished she could wrap her arms round her shoulders. She tried to distract herself by thinking of other things.

They'd left the town by the same road they'd come in on several days ago. So they must be heading north. She frowned. That couldn't be right... She turned to Gil, beside her.

"Why are we going north? I thought Stillárre was to the southwest.

He smiled at her. "It is. But the nearest ford across the River Carreck is at Shider. We'd need to use boats if we wanted to cross from Hemmeris—and there weren't nearly enough. We're up to almost three thousand five hundred now, did you know? That's with the second lot of cavalry who came in yesterday from Finien."

She smiled back. Gil was so proud to be really making something of this army. She glanced at Shivvie. He was walking on her other side, paying no attention to their conversation. His face had a faraway look. Maybe he was thinking of Perrely. Since yesterday he'd simmered down about the leadership issue, which was a relief.

After a two-hour march they reached the ford at Shider. It lay just downstream from where the River Sest flowed into the Carreck, and the enlarged river was wide and shallow. The walking had warmed Lannie, but taking her shoes and leggings off and putting her bare feet into the cold water soon changed that. There were groans as the army made double speed across the ford. On the other side the little village square was soon overflowing with soldiers sitting and pulling on their dry footwear with relief.

A few miles out of Shider it began to rain. Lightly at first, but rapidly turning into a downpour. Everyone plodded along doggedly with their heads down and shoulders hunched. Gil assured Lannie that they were now heading south-west towards the village of Bornis. They would camp there for the night. Having their hands bound while they marched was annoying; but Garset reminded them that they would join the highway before reaching Bornis. They might encounter other troops there—not to mention Shambor's spies. They had to look like prisoners.

As they trudged on, a heaviness settled over Lannie. It was as if the raindrops that spattered her cheeks brought whispers of discouragement. Why were they doing this? How could they have imagined they could just walk into Stillárre and take it over? Why was she even here, in Dûrion? She didn't belong here. She was a— What was she? A website designer! —back on Earth. Heavens above, her very identity was meaningless over here.

She wanted to stop, to turn back... but she couldn't. It was as if she was locked into a relentless treadmill of moving forward, one weary step after another. A glance around showed other faces, equally grim. Even the irrepressible twins. All talk had died away.

As darkness fell the army marched silently into Bornis.

* * *

Jomel sat toying with her food under the awning. The rain had stopped, and the soldiers were putting up tents in the damp fields beside the village. Gelmion had just passed by, laying a hand on her shoulder and murmuring that he'd like to see her in his tent later. That meant in the dead of night when no one would see. She shuddered at the thought of climbing out of her warm blankets, struggling into outdoor clothing, leaving as if to relieve herself—then finding her way through the cold night air to his tent. Where she'd have to pull everything off again to 'service' him. Yet if she didn't—

What would happen if she didn't come to him tonight? Pain seared her heart as she thought of how her family might suffer. But Gelmion was going to betray this 'Restorers' Army', wasn't he? That was as clear as a sunlit sky. And they—the true Restorers—were the only hope for Dûrion. If Shambor crushed them, with Gelmion's help, where would they all be? Under the iron heel of the Cult of Gadesh. She knew what it was to be enslaved to that deadly cult. She also knew that its leaders intended to make it the new religion of Dûrion. Then all hope would be lost.

A strange peacefulness had sustained her since that night in Hemmeris when the Creator God had said: *With me there is always a way out.* On the journey today she'd been tempted to fall back into despair. But those words had been like a shining beacon in the darkness. This God never lied. In Stillárre, against all likelihood, he'd told her he would rescue her. And he had. Now, despite her impossible dilemma, he'd told her there was a way out. That meant there was.

What if this was it? To stop doing as Gelmion demanded. To risk causing her family to suffer now, so that later, if the Restorers won, they might live in peace. Or—her heart clenched—to risk losing them altogether, if that would give the Way of the One, of the *real* God, a chance to be re-established.

She stared unseeing into the darkness beyond the awning. Everyone else had left. The stew on her plate had congealed. This was a moment of truth that would determine her own life and that of many others in the days to come. She had to choose between her family, and her God. Between their immediate wellbeing; and the long-term good of the whole country. It was no choice, really.

She lowered her head and clasped her hands. *Creator God,* she said silently in her mind. *I will go your way. I'll take your way out. Please look after my family.*

A joyful response echoed in her heart: *I will. Come with me!*

She looked up, and the night was different. There was a gap in the clouds through which the stars shone. Their pale light filled the shadowy landscape with God's goodness. His joy and his peace were all around her.

Come with me! Where, my Prince? It dawned on her that she'd called him that for the first time. So *this* was Prince Orrénne—that Person the Lightists so revered. Now she knew why. She couldn't see him, but she knew he was with her. He was more alive than anyone she'd ever known. Yet he'd sacrificed all that was dear to him—even his life—for her. Now there was some small thing she could do for him. Her heart overflowed with gratitude.

What can I do? she asked. *Just tell me.*

Go to Gelmion, the answer came. *Don't worry, I'll take care of you. He has something that belongs to me. I want you to give it to Shiván.*

For a while she sat in restful silence, trying to puzzle this out. Then light dawned. *Oh!* she gasped. *Of course. I'll do it.*

I'll be with you. All the way.

* * *

He was. His love warmed her as she made her way later that night to Gelmion's tent. Then, as she knelt beside the would-be Overguardian and touched his face, Gelmion jerked from sleep and reared back as if slapped.

"*Aarrgh!*" he snarled. "What's that Lightist stink?" His eyes focused on her with loathing. "Is that *you*, Jomel? What's happened to you?"

"I've met the Prince."

"Well, leave him behind when you come here." He rolled over and closed his eyes. "Go away," he mumbled.

Jomel waited, and soon his breathing became slow and regular. She reached for his outer coat, which was hanging as usual from a hook on the cross-pole of the tent. She felt about in the capacious pockets. His gloves... the blaise... some coins... Ah, there it was!

She slipped the slim Dûrian key into her own pocket and left the tent. Her heart was singing. It was the first thing she'd ever done for the Prince. His smile was a warm glow within her.

Again, he'd kept his word. She hadn't had to make love to Gelmion. The Prince had given her a way out.

* * *

The army left Bornis early the next morning. Everyone seemed driven by an urgent need to march south. Yet every step they took increased the darkness they travelled in. It was not the darkness of the black clouds above. It was a darkness within that corroded courage, sapped strength and ate away integrity. It questioned every principle, every good intention. It brought to mind every evil deed, every weak response or careless omission, and made that the norm. It blotted out purpose, reduced all of life to the meaningless suffering of this present moment.

Legate Brennor marched like his soldiers with growing horror, mindless of his goal, drawn irresistibly to the darkness that lay ahead. The escorts around the Restorers forgot their duty. The prisoners dropped the ropes loosely binding their wrists and walked on in despair. Garset knew that the end had come of all his hopes. Their plans had collapsed. Resistance was useless. Fira's thoughts had reached a dead end. She would die soon. She knew it. The twins were silent, their faces dark, their laughter silenced.

Lannie walked in a red mist of self-loathing that increased with every footfall. She was arrogant and self-opinionated, a miserable failure as a Restorer, hopeless as a fighter, good for nothing but to die in the agony that waited at the end of this God-forsaken highway.

All she wanted was to turn back — but she couldn't.

Chapter 29: *Child of Despair*

AS HE MARCHED, SHIVÁN found himself repeating softly over and over, *Yea, though I walk through the valley of the shadow of death, I will fear no evil: for* thou *art with me…* The assurance of God's protection didn't banish the darkness that threatened to overwhelm him; but it kept it at bay. It also gave him space to think.

At first he was only aware of a growing frustration. Here was an entire army marching in silence under a black sky to its doom. They all knew it! Yet they couldn't do a thing about it. He glanced at Lannie to his right and Garset on his left. Both their faces were inward-looking, set in long vertical lines of pain. Earlier he'd tried talking to them, pleading that the army should turn back. Lannie had ignored him. Garset had muttered, "It's no good." He himself could feel the fatal pull southward. They were like canoeists caught in a mighty current, being swept helplessly toward the waterfall.

He shivered and pulled his cloak closer around him. He couldn't just accept this! *Somebody* had to do *something!* Yet the minds of those in command were closed to him. How could he turn a whole army around on his own? *Father God, please show me what to do.*

Do what you can.

The words were only in his mind — but he knew that voice. *Thank you, Father. I will.*

Okay, what *could* he do? He could stop mindlessly marching south. He could leave the army, go it alone. But what would that achieve? He needed companions. In an army of over three thousand Lightists, there must surely be others who'd managed to resist the despair. Not many, from the faces all around him. But even a few would achieve more than he could alone. They couldn't fetch reinforcements, because there weren't any. But they could shadow the army, slipping through the empty fields to the east… Then when disaster struck, maybe — just maybe — they could form a rallying point for the survivors.

It was a desperate apology for a plan, but it was the best he could do. And that was all his Father was asking.

He slowed down. Infantrymen in their green capes marched past, their tread unvarying, misery etched on their faces. He began speaking to individual soldiers, selecting those with the least hopeless expressions. The few who responded uttered variants of Garset's "It's no good". It was heartbreaking work. Yet here and there a soldier would look him in the eye and agree to come with him. Half an hour later, and halfway down the column, he had gathered four companions. Each of them was speaking to others.

Someone tugged at his arm. He turned, and saw Jomel. She was wearing a warm green ankle-length coat. Her cheeks were red, her eyes sparkling, and to his utter amazement she was smiling.

"Shiván, I've been looking for a chance to speak to you," she said. "Come with me! I've got something for you."

Her optimism was so unexpected that, with a quick word to his friends, he followed her. They moved back down the line. No one commented that they were going the wrong way—all were too engrossed in their own misery. They reached the first supply wagon. Jomel pulled a Dûrian key from her pocket. As the wagon creaked along she bent and inserted it in the lock of an outside compartment that stretched the whole length of the vehicle. She opened it, and started rummaging among the contents as she walked along with the wagon. No one paid any attention. After a few minutes she moved aside and pointed. There, lying on top of the tent poles, guy ropes, mallets and peg bundles lay a long, mud-encrusted bag. Shiván's eyes widened and his jaw dropped.

It was the Ambon.

"Where— How did you find it?" he stuttered.

"It's a long story," she said, flashing that new, serene smile of hers. "Let's just say that I discovered where Gelmion had put it, and last night I took the key from him—without his knowledge. It's yours now."

"Why have you done this?" he asked.

"Because the Prince told me to."

He stared at her. "You've met the Prince?"

"Yes!"

Her joy was so obvious, there could be no doubt. His own heart lifted. "Praise the One!"

"Yes."

Her whole face was shining. The Prince was with her, here in this valley of the shadow of death. Joy washed over him. What an encouragement—from the last person he would have expected.

"That's tremendous! Absolutely wonderful! How—? No, there isn't time. But— You know about Gelmion?"

"I know he's mindbent by Shambor."

"What!" Shiván gaped at her. "By *Shambor*? Oh, dear Prince. I thought he might be mindbent—I even checked in his tent for teméyn; but I never guessed he'd been caught by the Big Man himself! That explains a lot. Especially—all this." He gestured at the army marching silently to its doom. "But now, even if we could prove it, the army wouldn't turn back... How did you find out?"

"I—knew Gelmion quite well. We talked together often. I've been in the Cult of Gadesh. I realised he was mindbent."

"I see." Shiván nodded absently. His mind had gone back to their present situation. "But now that we have the Ambon—"

"The Prince showed me that with him, there's always a way out."

Her quiet confidence thrilled him. "That's right! And thanks to you, he's provided it."

They lifted the precious emblem out of the compartment and wrestled it from its bag. The wagon trundled on and the soldiers kept marching. The golden rod and silver circle of the Ambon of Sûrilane gleamed against the mud on the road. No one spared it a glance. They stood up, and Jomel handed it to Shiván.

"Are you going to raise it?"

He nodded slowly. A passing infantryman brushed against him. He planted his feet firmly, and with a sudden movement thrust the Ambon skyward.

As from a great distance they heard a faint echo of the ringing trumpet call.

Shiván stared at Jomel in horror. She frowned back. "Is that it?" Of course. She'd never heard the real thing.

"No, it's not. Something's wrong." He thrust the Ambon higher. There was another distant echo.

The four troopers he'd spoken to came hurrying up, along with six others. "You raised the Ambon!" one exclaimed. His face fell as he glanced around. The army was continuing its mindless march south.

"Seems not even the Ambon can help us against... whatever's up ahead," Shiván muttered.

"But the Prince will still show us a way out," Jomel said with quiet confidence. "Maybe we can't use it now, but he hasn't given it to us for nothing."

The little group stood silent as the last of the four wagons groaned past. High against the clouds a single bird soared. Its desolate call faded slowly in the bitter air.

Shiván took a deep breath. "We'll stick to the original plan. But we'll take the Ambon with us."

Two of the troopers carried it horizontally in its bag as they all made their way through the stragglers trudging behind the wagons. In the process they persuaded two others to join them. Shiván shook his head. Twelve. Out of over three thousand. But there was no time to gather more. They all felt the disaster ahead growing steadily closer.

They dropped back behind the column, and found themselves among the refugees and Ambon recruits, who were following the army as ordinary travellers. Most of them, too, were locked into the darkness. But Shiván spoke to some he knew, and seven more joined them.

They slipped off the highway and began moving as fast as they could across the muddy fields, keeping parallel with the army. They followed paths wherever they could, but more often stumbled over rough ground. Mud quickly found its way through chinks in their boots and shoes. With squelching feet they struggled to move faster than the army, to reach a position alongside the vanguard so they could be there with the Ambon when the army met whatever was waiting for them. God had told Shiván to do what he could: this was it.

Only the Light carried them on through the growing despair.

* * *

By a miracle—and a narrow track running parallel to the high-way—they caught up with the front line of the army as it tramped past a road that turned off to the east. South of the road was a ridge of hills. Jomel knew that this was where the focal point of darkness lay. She felt despair like a heavy blanket threatening to enfold her. Her feet were clumsy lumps of hardened mud. Her arms and right shin were bruised from falls. They were hurrying toward an uncertain fate. The Ambon—the Prince's gift to Shiván, which he had enabled her to find—had somehow failed. She didn't understand why. But the Prince understood; and that was all that mattered. He was like a light shining around her in the darkness. All she had to do was to stay in that light.

As they crossed the eastward road, she heard Gromon, a refugee from Billérasson, telling Shiván that it led to the village of Rafe on the River Carreck. "Good escape route," he added. "Many boats. We could take them across to the 'Island'. Then the enemy can't follow." It was getting harder to talk—and to think. But she knew he was referring to the south-western section of the Two Peaks district, surrounded by four rivers. It was inaccessible from this side of the Carreck, except by boat. The man had the right idea—if they lived that long.

They reached a small knoll on the other side of the road. From here on the going would be even tougher. The track they'd been following headed up towards the ridge—but they needed to continue parallel to the highway. She sighed, a wave of exhaustion hitting her. She turned her thoughts to the Prince, and kept trudging along beside the hardened fighting men.

Shiván led them east of the knoll, so that they were briefly hidden from the highway. Suddenly he stopped. Six figures had appeared in front of him from nowhere. They wore dirt-smeared robes that might once have been purple, and carried staffs in their hands. They must have been coming round the knoll from the other side. The short one in front pulled off his hood.

"*Frengor!*" Shiván exclaimed. Jomel's heart leapt. She hurried forward.

"Shiván, Light be praised!" There he was, his wise, wrinkled face lit up. When she'd met him briefly in Sûrilane she'd thought him a weird old throwback to a previous century. Now he was like a beacon of light in the darkness.

The other five priests all crowded round Shiván, greeting him with obvious delight. Frengor turned to her, pausing for the shiláy moment. She felt his warmth, weariness, love, and depth of wisdom. His smile widened, and joy shone in his eyes. "Welcome, younger sister," he said softly. She nodded, suddenly unable to speak. The Prince was there, his hands on both their shoulders.

Frengor turned back to Shiván. "This is a meeting the One has made," he declared. "But we have little time. Come with us, and I can explain on the way."

Shiván beckoned to the men, and they followed the priests up the track towards the ridge. Jomel heaved a sigh of relief.

"Where are you taking us, Frengor?" Shiván asked.

"Exactly where you'd be going if you hadn't met us."

Shiván frowned. "You mean, to this — whatever it is — that's pulling us all towards it?"

"Yes." The track was getting steeper, and the old priest paused to negotiate a muddy patch of rock. Shiván held out a hand to Jomel. She smiled at him in gratitude. Above the rock Frengor stood leaning on his staff.

"This 'whatever-it-is', Shiván, is one of the most horrible abominations mindbending has produced. I believe the One has caused our paths to cross so that you can end it here and now — and maybe save many of your comrades' lives."

"Um… right. So what exactly *is* this abomination?"

Frengor sighed. In the dim light he suddenly looked older. The twinkle in his eye was gone. The wrinkles in his face had fallen into lines of sadness.

"It's a *Gorelenyu*. That's Selmian for a Child of Despair."

* * *

The grim name sent a chill down Jomel's spine. What followed was worse.

"For years the Mindbenders of Selmion — which as you know is the main stronghold of the Cult of Gadesh — have been trying to develop the ultimate mind weapon to subdue their enemies. They have now succeeded. What you have just seen happening to your army is the first use of that weapon in actual warfare. We feel it all around us right now, don't we? A great wave of despair threatening to sweep us away if we let it. Do you know what that despair is, Shiván?"

Shiván shook his head, his face solemn. There was silence as the men crowded forward to hear.

"That despair is the utter misery of an innocent child. His loneliness, deprived of love. His anguish, betrayed by everyone he trusts. His agony, subjected to the most barbaric tortures. His fear of more to come. His needless guilt, feeling this must be punishment for some terrible crime. His hopelessness of ever finding relief.

"This is a real child, Shiván. We've heard his cries and seen his torturers. They are just a little further along this ridge."

They continued up the track in silence, stunned by Frengor's words. They'd reached the trees near the crest, and were walking under snow-decked branches.

"How are they— making *us* feel his pain?" Shiván asked in a hushed voice.

"The Child is a natural mind-speaker. An extremely powerful one, though he's not aware of that. He's very young. Only five or six years old."

Jomel's stomach churned. That was the age of her little sister Dûlay.

"I imagine he's been prepared for several years now, using various techniques to enhance his power of projection. The Mindbenders themselves will be mentally amplifying his distress to give it greater range and intensity. That is what we last heard from our brothers in Selmion before they were silenced..."

There was a pause. Then Jomel asked, her voice unsteady, "If we feel his despair, don't the enemy feel it also? How can they still fight us?"

They'd reached the crest of the ridge, and came to a stop under the snowy trees. One of the men stooped to pull his shoe off and shake out a pebble. The two carrying the Ambon leaned the bag against a tree.

Frengor turned to her. "The Child will affect anyone who is moved by innocent suffering. All the troops assembled against you are mindbent. Most are Bishop's Guards. They are so given over to evil that the Child's pain leaves them untouched."

Several of the men made small noises of disgust. Jomel found sorrow welling up in her. She knew that mindset. She'd shared it once. And the Prince had paid for it in an agony of flame.

"My friends," Frengor said, "I think the One has brought you here for a purpose. Would you agree?"

"We'll put an end to this," Shiván said. There was a steely edge to his voice that Jomel hadn't heard before. His eyes were hard. He turned to the others. "We'll rescue that child. *Are you with me?*"

Nineteen voices chorused, "Yes!"

"All right, keep it down," Frengor said. "They're not far away. Follow me!"

He and his priests led them along a disused path that followed the tree-lined crest of the ridge. They began to hear high-pitched screams in the distance. At one point the path skirted a high shoulder of rock. Here Frengor stopped. He squatted down at the base of the rock, and motioned to the rest to gather round. Pain was reflected on every face. This close the pressure of the poor child's anguish was overwhelming. Somehow through ghastly images of Dûlay being tortured Jomel managed to hear what Frengor was saying.

"Ongaret and I will guide your fighters from here to the camp. We know a way to avoid the two Guards keeping watch at the back. They don't expect an attack from this direction. Jomel, you'd better stay here with the rest of the brothers. The Ambon, too." She breathed a sigh of relief. The Prince knew she was no fighter.

"The camp is on a flattish ledge in the hill slope," Frengor continued quietly. Sweat beaded his forehead. He wasn't immune to the child's suffering. "There are five tents, a fireplace—and the torture area. That's close to the fire. It has a table with straps for the Child, plus a smaller table with implements, jars and pots. There's a large barrel of water. The people in the camp are the Child, his nurse, three Mindbenders, a general servant, and eight Guards. Six of those are ranged around the front."

He turned to Shiván. "There are some things you should bear in mind. First, you mustn't alarm the child any more than you can help, or your rescue will be over before it starts. Also, whatever you do must happen all at once—you can't kill one Guard at a time. These are Mindbenders you're up against. The Guards will have been transferred to their control. Not only they, but Shambor and all his forces will know the instant you attack any of them. This needs to be a very quick operation." He sighed, and a faint smile touched the corners of his lips. "I'll leave you to work out the details."

"Thanks," Shiván muttered.

* * *

The army marched on. They passed the turnoff to Rafe, every step a growing agony. To their right rose the bleak heights of the Hills of Géris, to their left a ridge of hills that angled in towards them. The highway passed through a narrow gap where the two almost met.

Lannie's world had shrunk down to two things: a crushing weight of sorrow that squeezed the air from her lungs; and her feet. All her soul, every atom of her being, screamed at her to run back up the highway till her legs would carry her no further; but something up ahead—something beyond the uttermost limits of despair—was forcing her to lift one foot after the other, inexorably, relentlessly, onward.

She wasn't the only one. She glanced at Gil's tortured face on her right, Shiván's on her left... No! It was Cârin. Where had Shiván got to? It didn't matter. She had to keep walking till she fell into that gaping chasm of agony, where every last drop of pain would be wrung from her tortured mind.

She was dimly aware of trumpets sounding in the hills. Mounted Guardsmen came pouring down the Géris slopes — and more on the other side. They were being ambushed.

Good. It would soon be over.

*   *   *

The little group beside the rock sat frozen as the trumpets brayed below on the hillside. The ground trembled with the beat of horses' hooves.

Frengor's face was grim. "It's started. You'd better be quick. I doubt if your friends in the army will be able to defend themselves."

Shiván forced his battered mind into overdrive. "Right. Here's what we'll do. No time for anything fancy — and as Frengor says, we've got to be quick. When we get to where we can see the camp, you five — Gromon, Delmior, Hillet, Orlion, Galdet — stay with me. We'll take out the Mindbenders. The rest of you will create a diversion. We'll work that out when we get there. *Let's go!*"

They leapt to their feet. Frengor and Ongaret led them round the rock. Shiván turned and waved to Jomel, sitting hugging her knees among the priests. She gave him a tentative wave back, her eyes anxious.

They hurried along the ridge path until they came to a small gully running down the hillside. Frengor led them into it, motioning for silence. They moved precariously from one slippery rock to the next. All the time the child's screams and agonised wails grew louder. It became an almost physical struggle to concentrate on finding their footing.

Holding up a hand to halt them, Frengor climbed the gully wall and peered over the top. After a moment he beckoned, and they followed him up into a small open area among the trees. Through the branches they could see the camp below. There were five tents, as Frengor had described. Towards the middle was a clear area containing two fire pits. Metal fire irons straddled them both. Several pokers hung from one, their tips in the flames. A large woman in a dirty blue smock sat on a log nearby, the water butt just beyond her. On their side of the fires four people were standing round a table. Three wore grey robes, the fourth had a brown worker's tunic. They couldn't see what was on the table, but the high, childish screams that arose from it froze their blood.

"Look over there," Frengor whispered. They followed his pointing arm, and saw a Guardsman standing not far away at the edge of the shelf of land that held the camp. His back was toward them as he looked out over what must now be a battlefield. Between the child's screams they could hear distant shouts and the clash of metal. Further along the edge of the campground they could see a second Guard. He was sitting on a rock, also surveying the scene below. A third and fourth were over on the far side.

"Two others in the woods," Frengor breathed, "our side and the far side. Another two up on the ridge behind. But if you kill the Mindbenders..." He left the sentence hanging.

Shiván turned to two of the men behind him. Both had bows and quivers strapped to their backs. "Gindor and Shildet," he whispered, "Can you target the two nearest from here?" They peered through the branches. Both nodded. "The rest of you—apart from the five with me... I want you to creep round below those Guards. Don't know what the land's like, but try. Get as far as you can without attracting attention, then make a noise. You two—" he pointed at the bowmen "—that'll be your signal." They nodded. He looked at the others. "Go, and the One strengthen you."

The diversionary force disappeared back into the gully. They heard occasional noises—pebbles falling, twigs snapping—and held their breaths. Once the nearest Guard turned and stared into the trees; but he soon relaxed. Apparently the carnage below was more absorbing. Shiván cried silently for strength as the child's agonised screams threatened to break his mental defences.

The second Guard suddenly stiffened. He shouted to his comrade and pointed downward. Both drew their longswords. The third and fourth Guards came running, one pulling a bow from his back. There was a loud *twang* from beside Shiván and the Guard sprawled on the ground. The nearest Guard fell immediately afterwards. The other two ran back, yelling for their comrades. Then shouts broke out below, and they heard the clash of weapons. Shiván looked at

Frengor. The priest closed his eyes and shook his head. He hadn't known. There must be more Guards further down the hill.

Time for action. Shiván thrust aside his sudden fear at the thought of inflicting deliberate injury. Shouting to the bowmen to cover them and the other five to follow, he drew the Blade of Darthane and charged through the trees toward the child. The four torturers stood in a frozen tableau. He was fifty paces away when the large servant lumbered to the fire and turned to face them with a glowing poker in each hand. A distant *twang* sounded and he fell backward, an arrow in his chest. His screams joined those of the child as he writhed in the fire.

The three Mindbenders stood still and stared at their attackers.

Time slowed down.

A molten river of anguish poured over Shiván. One of his companions cried out and fell. He hardly heard. Agony beyond anything he'd known engulfed him. Unendurable pain fuelled his legs. Sprinting ever faster towards the Mindbenders, he raised the Blade and screamed defiance.

"In the name of the Prince!"

The Mindbenders kept up their stream of concentrated pain. It beat against Shiván, numbing his senses, wiping out all thought or planning. He hurtled towards them, carried forward by pure momentum, the Blade held high.

At the last moment the Mindbenders turned to flee. They were too late. The Blade of Darthane came flashing down on the nearest as Shiván cannoned into the group. The others were thrown aside. The table jerked, and the child screamed. Shiván collapsed to the ground, anguish searing his mind. Soon after that a whole pile of bodies seemed to collapse on top of him.

The screaming stopped, replaced by the child's heartrending wails. Shiván struggled out from under the bodies. He staggered to his feet and looked down. There were two of them, and they wore grey cloaks. Then his companions began clapping him on the back. They had followed his charge, and run the other two Mindbenders through. His own grey-cloaked victim was sprawled nearby, the Blade embedded in his neck. The nurse lay dead by the water butt. A stink of burning clothes and flesh rose from the fire. Two of his men were pulling the servant off it. Frengor and the two bowmen were running towards them.

The child lay wailing on the table, wiping out his horror at the deaths they'd caused. He went over to it, and had a shock. It was big for a six year-old. Lank strands of dark hair contrasted with a deathly white skin. It had a heavily-ridged face and wrongly-slanted eyelids. Where oriental eyes angled up from the bridge of the nose, these angled down. The eyes were screwed up in misery as it emitted high, keening wails. Its hands and legs were strapped to the table. There were wounds and burns all over the body.

Frengor and the two soldiers came panting up. The bowmen were full of apologies that they'd been thrown off their aim during the final wave of anguish. "Got the nurse by mistake, though," the one muttered. Shiván smiled and reassured them. He and Frengor turned to the child.

"Oh," Frengor murmured. "He's Grûzhack. I didn't know."

* * *

Silence settled on the devastated campsite. Six Guardsmen lay unmoving—some dead, others frozen in mindlock with their masters killed. There was no sign of the diversionary party.

"We can't rush off anyway," Frengor said. "That child is hurting, and if we snatch him up and run, he'll start screaming. We know what *that* does to us. We must treat his wounds and make him comfortable."

While the others removed the bodies, Frengor and Ongaret went to find bandages and warm water. Shiván undid the straps binding the ugly, wounded child, his heart strangely moved. Poor kid. What a raw deal he'd had. Snatched away from home and parents so young, to be systematically abused at the hands of foreigners. Anger flared in him. Those who'd done this had got what they deserved. But what about all the others in that cursed Cult of Gadesh? What other innocent children were suffering at their hands right now?

At that moment the child's eyes opened. Deep black wells of pain looked up at him. The anguished wails gave way to the sobs of a lost, hurting kid. Shiván took his wrist—the hand had six fingers instead of five, and all the fingernails were missing. He spoke to him softly in English. "Hey, listen. You don't know me. But I'm your friend. You're with me now. I won't let anyone do this to you again!"

Frengor handed him a clean cloth, and placed a bowl of warm water on the table. "I'm afraid he doesn't know Inglish, Shiván."

Shيván took the cloth and began gently cleaning the child's wounds. "Doesn't matter. This kid needs friends. I'm English, and I'm his friend." He continued cleaning and talking to the child softly, while Frengor bandaged his wounds and burns. The sobs continued, punctuated by cries of pain when they hurt him. When that happened everyone shuddered and waited for the shock to pass.

Gromon and his companions were keeping watch. He called to Shيván, "The others are coming!" A few moments later a ragged bunch of nine soldiers came scrambling over the edge of the shelf of land. A corner of Shيván's mind noted that three were missing.

"There's a squadron of Guards coming after us!" the first man cried. He ran panting up to Shيván, and reared back when he saw the Grûzhack child. "Prince's blood! Shيván, we have to leave."

"Let's go!" Shيván shouted. He lifted the child under the armpits and Frengor quickly wrapped a cloth and a small blanket round his naked body. The child cried out, making the newcomers gasp. Shيván eased him against his chest. The kid wrapped his arms round Shيván's shoulders and his legs round his waist. Shيván supported him on one arm, leaving his sword hand free to yank the Blade from the dead Guard's body. Talking quietly to the child in English, he set off at a trot. The kid continued to sob, but not enough to make them lose their footing.

Frengor and Ongaret led them up by an easier route to the ridge path, avoiding the gully. "Good thing we explored this all," Ongaret panted. Behind them they heard shouts from the camp.

They ran along the ridge path till they reached the rock where they'd left Jomel and the priests. No one was there. Then they appeared a little further along, where they'd been hiding. "You did it!" Jomel exclaimed, her face bright with relief. Shيván smiled and nodded, without breaking his stride. She fell in behind him, and he heard her gasp when she saw the child's face over his shoulder. Two of the priests were carrying the Ambon.

They heard shouts and the thud of feet behind them. The guards were gaining. They ran faster.

They reached the track that led down to the highway and the road to Rafe. For the first time Shيván saw the battle. It was not far away to the south. The Restorers' army was spread out across the narrow valley between their ridge and the Hills of Géris, doing battle with ranks of grey-cloaked guards. Their numbers had shrunk; but Light be praised, they were fighting back.

They began hurrying down the steep track. Shiván slipped and nearly fell. The child screamed. It was a like the stab of a sharp sword. There were cries from the others.

They reached the knoll at the bottom beside the Rafe road. Their pursuers were hot on their heels. Fighting broke out as they leapt up the rocky hillock.

"Raise the Ambon!" Shiván gasped. He drew the Blade. He, Jomel and the priests were in the centre, at the top of the knoll. Around them the faithful few were striking down at the Guardsmen below. More kept pouring down the hill. The child clung to him, uttering high keening wails. Jomel undid the straps on the bag the priests were holding, and pulled out the emblem. Gripping the handholds awkwardly, she held it shakily aloft.

A high, sweet trumpet call rang out in the bitter air.

The child was instantly silent. He turned against Shiván's chest and stared at the Prince's emblem gleaming against the dark sky. A sudden surge of joy burst over their hearts.

The Guardsmen cried out in anguish. Several clapped their hands over their ears. Others, distracted, fell to the defenders' swords. Those at the foot of the hill scattered off the track. Some higher up began running back the way they'd come.

To the south, the Restorers' army had turned and was streaming towards them.

Chapter 30: *Ambush*

"THE AMBON!" LANNIE EXCLAIMED, joy lighting her face.

Gil stood stock-still. His sword arm dropped. The Guardsman he'd been fighting lowered his weapon and waited. Gil looked round. Everywhere the embattled soldiers of the Restorers' army were running back toward the Rafe turnoff.

"Gil, come on!" Lannie cried, poised to follow Cârin and Garset.

An irate voice exploded in Gil's mind. *"YOU FOOL! First the* Gorelenyu *is stolen, now this. How did they get the Ambon?"*

"Mindruler, I don't—" He broke off. Fury flooded over him as he remembered who had been there when he stowed the emblem in the wagon. "That bitch Jomel!"

Lannie paused, a frown gathering on her face. *"What?* Come *on,* we'll be killed!" The crowd around them had already thinned out.

"You allowed that miserable, no-account girl to take the Ambon from you? And others to escape and steal the Gorelenyu*? You imbecile! You stupid, over-confident halfwit! Once this battle is over, so is your autonomy. Do you hear me? DO YOU UNDERSTAND?"*

Agony lanced through him and he cried out, clutching his head. Mistaking what had happened, Lannie lashed out inexpertly with her sword at the Guardsman facing Gil. The Guard easily parried the blow, and stood waiting for Gil's orders. A dozen or so other Guards were doing likewise. The rest were charging in pursuit of the Lightists.

Lannie's eyes widened, horror dawning on her face. She turned to flee, but Gil leapt after her. He grabbed her arm and swung her round.

"Oh no, you don't," he snarled. The Guardsmen had surrounded them.

Lannie stared at Gil. He'd become a stranger. His eyes were bloodshot, his face transformed into a mask of fury.

"You deceived us," she stated flatly. "You were never unmindbent, were you? You never met the Prince. You never loved me. It was all lies. And now you've betrayed us. You *bastard!*" She spat in his face.

Gil wiped the spittle off and slapped her. Her head snapped sideways, and she cried out. A burly Guardsman pinned her arms.

She stood glaring at Gil with a reddening cheek, her eyes smouldering.

"One day you'll belong to me, and I'll *break* you," he ground out.

"*Oh no, Gelmion. She'll belong to me, and I'll break her. Send her to me at once. You go and recapture the Ambon, or you'll discover what I'm like when I'm displeased.*"

With an oath Gil slapped her again. He jerked his head at the Guards and strode out of the circle. Four of them hustled Lannie away from the battle.

* * *

As she stumbled along, Lannie's mind was in a whirl. In a few brief moments all her thoughts about Gil had been turned upside down. Tears of mortification burnt her cheeks. What an idiot she'd been! Shivvie had discovered the truth in Hemmeris, and she hadn't believed him. She hadn't wanted to. Like a naïve teenager she'd allowed herself to be besotted by a smooth-talking rogue with a handsome face. The care she'd lavished on him while he was 'recovering' up in the mountains... Her joy at his so-called conversion... Her pride when he'd replaced Shiván as Overguardian... And it had all been a clever con-job. She felt utterly humiliated.

Well, that was over. What she'd thought was love had died. She'd never trust Gil Denbigh again. If there *was* any 'again' for her...

* * *

Shiván stared out over the battlefield from the knoll. After the child's burst of joy the Guards had regrouped and returned to the attack, but by then the first wave of soldiers summoned by the Ambon — some two hundred — had reached them.

Now the outlook wasn't so good. The furthermost troops were being cut down from behind as they tried to get to the Ambon. Many were fighting rearguard actions. The whole area was covered with small groups of opposing soldiers battling fiercely. But too many of theirs had been slaughtered before the child was rescued. Shambor had the advantage of numbers, and the grey tide was relentlessly pushing towards the knoll where he stood. The child still clung to him, glancing around with wide eyes. Praise the One, he wasn't emitting waves of despair. But that could change if the fighting came any closer.

It was a terrible decision to have to make. He stood wrestling with it on the rocky knoll, a bitter wind knifing through his coat, the child providing welcome warmth against his chest. Out there on the battlefield Garset and the Pure Company were fighting for their lives. So were Brennor's legion, and the others who'd joined them at Hemmeris. So were Fira, Shîrin and most of the refugees — though Cârin and a few others had reached them here on the knoll. Then there was the brave remnant of the Ambon recruits, who'd stuck with them after the disaster at Berûvis... How could they survive against the Bishop's Guard?

If he were to mount a charge with the Ambon, he might rally their troops, even turn the tide. But he couldn't risk the child. He'd tried handing him first to Jomel, then to Frengor, but had hastily taken him back each time when the kid cried out and reached for him. Even those brief waves of distress had caused their soldiers to falter.

He prayed desperately for wisdom. He could give the Ambon to someone else — Câr, maybe — who could lead a charge while he stayed behind with the child. But then they'd be unprotected. And he could not allow this hurting kid to fall into enemy hands again. Not to mention the folly of letting Shambor recapture his strongest weapon. The child and the Ambon were their best hopes for survival. It would also be folly to separate them and risk losing one or the other.

There was a forward surge by the enemy in the distance and a whole section of their troops seemed to vanish, overwhelmed like a sandcastle by the grey sea. That decided him. A heroic charge with the Ambon was unlikely to succeed. And as things stood now, they could still escape along the Rafe road.

No. At all costs he must save the Ambon and the child. If the Ambon moved, those responding to it would follow. At least some of those fighting out there might succeed in crossing the River Carreck; he could only hope Lannie, Garset and some of the others would be with them.

With a heavy heart he turned to Cârin, who had taken the Ambon over from Jomel.

"We must retreat to Rafe. Will you spread the word?"

Cârin looked at him. The sparkle was gone from his eye. "My brother's out there," he said softly.

"I know. I'm sorry."

Câr nodded, swallowed, and began shouting *"Retreat!"* in a ringing voice. Others took up the call as Shiván walked down from the knoll holding the child.

They reached the road and began hurrying eastward. Jomel and the priests walked with Shiván and the child, Frengor and his brothers praying audibly for the One's protection. Gromon — the Billérasson refugee who came from this area — had also joined them. Cavalrymen rode alongside. Shîrin had handed the Ambon to three tall troopers, who were taking turns keeping it aloft. Shiván could hear Câr's voice further back, organising a rearguard.

They had been travelling for about three quarters of an hour when the road began sloping downwards, and they saw ahead the broad expanse of the River Carreck. Shiván breathed a sigh of relief, and shifted the child slightly to ease his arms. The kid had fallen asleep, and uttered a small whimper without waking up. At the end of the road was a cluster of thatched cottages at the river's edge. The village of Rafe. Two piers extended out into the grey waters, forming a small harbour. No boats were visible, but Gromon assured Shiván they would be pulled up on shore in this rainy weather. On the opposite side of the river they could dimly make out another harbour — the village of Arneck on the 'Island'.

When they reached Rafe they found twelve white-hulled fishing boats on the gravelly beach. Hard-bitten men and women in rough clothing had come spilling out of their cottages at the call of the Ambon. Shiván thanked them for responding to the One's summons, and told them the best help they could give was the loan of their boats. Doubtful glances were directed at the child, but the villagers quickly made the boats ready.

"Leave now!" Shiván told them. "Shambor's troops are following us. There may be fighting, and we don't want any of you hurt. We'll have your boats sent back to you." There were cries of dismay as the villagers scattered to collect children and warm clothing. They were in for a miserable wait in the muddy fields.

The troops who'd been at the knoll kept streaming into the little village. Gromon took charge of the boats, bellowing for any who could sail to step forward. He soon had twelve volunteers, and began directing soldiers into the small craft. Some held as many as ten, others only five. Shiván's heart sank. At this rate it would take three trips just to ferry across the two hundred from the knoll. As if in answer, Gromon shouted to him: "There'll be more boats at Arneck! We'll bring them back."

Cârin came running up. The rearguard was in. "The army's coming, Shiván! But they're spread out, and the Bishop's Guard are breaking through. I don't think we can rescue any more. We must go! Garset's Second — Tarlion — is organising defences round the village. They'll hold them off as long as they can."

The clash of weapons sounded in the distance. On the rising land to the west Shiván saw a knot of soldiers engaging grey-cloaks as they slowly retreated toward the village.

"And Shîr…?"

Câr shook his head, a deep sorrow in his eyes. "He's out there. I can feel him. He's dying."

Shiván laid a hand on his friend's shoulder, feeling his pain.

Gromon was calling for them to board the last boat. The priests and Jomel were already aboard. Tears stung Shiván's eyes as he and Cârin crunched across the gravel towards them. Frengor and Ongaret had the Ambon. He had the child. They had to be saved. Even if it meant the deaths of many whom he'd come to love here in Dûrion.

* * *

They rowed across the river to Arneck, a smaller village which had only seven boats in its harbour. The inhabitants, who'd gathered to watch the fighting across the river, helped them ashore. One of them invited Shiván, Jomel and the child into his cottage, thinking they were a family. Shiván was glad to rest in a chair, still holding the sleeping child.

Gromon sent the fleet of nineteen boats back to Rafe. They returned two-thirds full — all that could be spared from the rearguard. Shîr was not among them. Gromon's face was grim as he told Shiván that Tarlion's last stand against twice the number of greycloaks had been all that enabled them to get away. "They won't have lasted long," he muttered. "But they stopped those Guards from getting the boats. We'll be safe for a while now."

Shiván nodded, not trusting himself to speak. They had escaped with about a hundred and fifty soldiers. Only God could bring victory out of such a defeat.

* * *

In Rafe, Gil stood on the empty gravel beach. Shambor was screaming in his head. Tarlion and his pathetic bunch were dead — but it
was too late. Shiván had escaped with the Ambon and the child.
They'd taken every boat — and the Guard officers assured him there
were no others along this stretch of the Carreck.

All his hopes had collapsed. Lannie taken from him. No ad-
vancement, even his limited autonomy revoked. He was a slave
once more in his own body.

"Back to the battle!" Gelmion snapped to the Guards around
him. "Shiván's escape will cost the lives of every last one of these
rebel filth."

Inside him, Gil watched in dull despair.

* * *

The Restorers' army fell apart at the renewed onslaught of Shambor's forces. They scattered in all directions, pursued by raging grey-
cloaks gone berserk. Thousands died.

Lieutenant Fennior shouted encouragement to the remnants of
the Pure Company. He'd been separated from Captain Garset and
Lieutenant Tarlion, and his group was hopelessly outnumbered.
They'd reached the knoll where the Ambon had been raised — but it
was long gone now. A horde of Guards had surrounded them. They
were making their last stand. One by one his men fell. He raised his
arm to lunge at the Guardsman facing him, and a longsword struck
deep through a gap in the bands of his armour. Fire exploded in his
chest, and he crashed down hard on a rock. He was surprised that
the fall caused no pain…

Then there was only Light.

Shîrin felt life slowly draining away from him as he lay in a discarded mound of bodies. He could dimly see one man's sandalled
foot, another's wounded shoulder, and — strangely — a tiny area of
clean green grass amid the trampled mud. How had that escaped?
But that's what the One was like, wasn't he? He always left a ray of
hope in the darkness. Like the fact that Câr had escaped. He could
feel him out there, somewhere, getting all teary. At least that self-
opinionated so-and-so wasn't putting on airs about being the better fighter. He'd tell him when he saw him that not everyone had

tried to save their own skin… He sighed, and the pure, green grass expanded to fill his vision.

Fira gasped as a lance rammed into her back. Her fingers lost their feeling, her sword fell from her hand. She pitched forward. She couldn't see. She couldn't move.

This was it. Her time under the sky was over. A strange numbness crept over her senses. Her last fleeting thought was, *I've fought for what I believed in. I've served my Prince.* She dimly heard the swish of a blade…

Then *he* was there, smiling. The numbness dissolved into joy.

Chapter 31: *Captives and fugitives*

"*GARI.*"

Bishop Shambor leapt where he sat, spilling sauce from his mid-meal on the tablecloth. He'd been dreading this interview with the Strongholder. He collected himself.

"*Yes, your Supremacy?*"

"*Why are the Keepers of my Gorelenyu dead?*"

Shambor swallowed convulsively. It was unavoidable that the Strongholder knew: the Keepers were part of his network, and he would immediately feel their absence in his mind.

The Mindruler infused as much calm into his mental reponse as he could manage. "*I deeply regret that, Supremacy. The Gorelenyu's position, though well guarded, was unexpectedly attacked using the Ambon of Sûrilane. The Keepers, sadly, were casualities. If you could send replacements...?*"

"*There are no replacements, Gari,*" the Strongholder said in a dangerously soft voice. "*This was an experimental programme, as you know. No one else has been trained to work with the Gorelenyu. You blame the Keepers' deaths on the Ambon of Sûrilane. That is not what I have heard. And why was the Ambon still in rebel hands? You assured me you would retrieve it.*"

"*I'm afraid my agent Gelmion —*"

"*Don't blame your shortcomings on others, Gari. You, and you alone, are to blame for this fiasco. Where exactly is my Gorelenyu now?*"

Shambor felt his defences crumble around him and closed his eyes against the inevitable.

The Strongholder's soft voice continued. "*You don't answer. But your memories tell me the Gorelenyu is now in the hands of your rebel 'Overguardian'. Am I reading you correctly, Gari?*"

"*Y-yes, your Supremacy.*"

The roar that followed sent him crashing from his chair to the floor.

"*HOW DARE YOU LOSE IT?*" A blast of exquisite pain convulsed Shambor.

"*HOW DARE YOU HAND YEARS OF EFFORT WITH THAT GRÛZHACK CHILD TO SOME FOREIGN UPSTART?*" The pain doubled and Shambor screamed.

"*AND THEN LIE TO ME, BLAMING IT ON THE AMBON?*" Agony exploded throughout the Mindruler's body.
"*YOU ARROGANT INCOMPETENT! YOU CARELESS, SELF-ABSORBED FOOL!*"

Shambor lay whimpering in a foetal position on the floor. He dimly heard the dining room door being closed and locked. That would be secretary Estaron, protecting him from the panic of ignorant servants.

Finally the tirade ended. He'd soiled himself, and every part of his body was shaking.

"*Get up!*"

Shambor wasn't sure he could, but disobedience wasn't an option. He staggered to his feet and collapsed into a chair.

"*Only because it would be too time-consuming and disruptive to take over the entire Dûrian network, I will allow you to retain your autonomy.*" A faint tendril of hope appeared in Shambor's mind. "*If you recover the* Gorelenyu *and if you use it for its proper purpose and drive the Grûzhack out of Dûrion, I may allow you to continue as Mindruler. To help with those endeavours I will even send you two cavalry legions, since you seem incapable of managing on your own.*

"*But I will be watching you, Gari. Every moment. That you can depend on.*"

*   *   *

Lannie sat staring at the e-mail. It was a brief message from Matt, her ex-fiancé, asking her to stop trying to contact him. It was over, he said. Time for them both to move on.

She was in her Birmingham flat. How she'd got there, she didn't know. They'd taken her from the battle in a rickety little carriage. She'd leant back against the thin padding of the bench, and must have passed out from sheer exhaustion. She'd woken up here.

So, was Dûrion over for her? She didn't know. Shivvie had had a similar experience, and he'd returned. At the moment she felt there wasn't much in it either way. Her heart was numb. Gil had betrayed her over there; and Matt had slammed the door on her over here. Her life was pretty much over in both places.

She levered herself up like an old woman from the neat little computer workstation and walked slowly through the sparsely-furnished living room to the kitchen. Her eyes hardly saw the expensive parquet flooring and cream throw rugs. She walked unseeing past the leather two-seat sofa and armchair, the indoor plants, the three matching prints on the wall. All arranged with care to give an impression of simple elegance. *Her* home, which she'd taken such pride as an artist in creating. It was meaningless now.

She made herself a cup of coffee in the kitchenette and perched on the bar stool to drink it. *Aaaah.* It was so long since she'd had coffee. The rich aroma filled the small room, the taste sparkled on her tongue. Maybe life was worth living just for the flavour of coffee.

When she'd savoured the last drop, she walked through to the bedroom and flopped down on the quilted satin duvet cover. Today was a Thursday. She was meant to be at work. That was unthinkable. If she was still here tomorrow, she'd try and pick up the threads of her shattered life. Not today.

Her Bible lay on the bedside table, illuminated by sunlight from the window. She picked it up. It was so long since she'd read it. She opened the brown, leather-bound book at random. She found herself looking at St. Paul's second letter to Timothy. Her eye ran down the first column of Chapter 1 and came to rest on verses six and seven.

... I remind you to fan into flame the gift of God, which is in you ...
For God did not give us a spirit of timidity, but a spirit of power, of love and of self-discipline.

Well, that seemed pretty irrelevant. It bore out the warnings she'd heard in sermons against treating the Bible as a magic talisman. Just opening it at random was *not* the way to hear God speaking to you. But she didn't have energy for proper Bible study right now.

She put the book down and lay back, her heart heavy. "Oh God, show me what to do," she whispered. A wave of weariness swept over her. A few minutes later she was asleep.

* * *

In their apartment in Darthane Cathedral, Perrely entered Danîsha's bedroom. The older woman lay propped up on pillows, a woolly granny-cap on her head. On a dresser beside her bed stood an array of bottles, tubs of powdered herbs, spoons, a water carafe and drinking glass.

"I see the physician's attended you," Perrely said. She sat on the edge of the bed, carefully smoothing the expensive fabric of her outfit.

"Yes," Danîsha whispered. Her voice was almost gone now. But her eyes were bright with interest. "How did the dinner go?"

The numbing mixture of fear and bewilderment that she'd felt during the meal rose up in Perrely again. "It was… strange. Very fancy — silver dinner service, blackwood cutlery, damask table linen, Marûvian wines…"

"And you. You look lovely, my dear." Perrely felt herself blushing at the older woman's sincere appreciation. She knew blue looked good on her, and hanging in the bedroom of the apartment she'd found this suit of twilight satin, with matching sleeved blouse and ankle-length culottes. It had been very slightly on the large side; but a word to the deferential guard at the door had brought a seamstress running to make the necessary alterations.

"Was Shambor annoyed that I didn't come?" Danîsha whispered.

"No." She heard the puzzlement in her own voice. "He asked a few polite questions, said he'd send the physician, but then he seemed to… forget about you. And you're a Restorer of the Way! He was so friendly to me. I couldn't work out why. I became afraid the dinner was a trick, that it was leading up to something bad. But then it ended, and he escorted me to the door and said goodnight! The thing I'm most afraid of is… Do you think he's mindbent me, Danîsha? I wouldn't know it — at first." An idea occurred to her. "Quick! Ask me what I think about Shambor. *Now.*"

Danîsha's eyebrows rose, but she obediently whispered, "What do you think about Shambor?"

"He's the most evil ruler Dûrion has ever had. There!" She sighed with relief. "At least I can still say it. What do you think, Danîsha? What was Shambor up to tonight?"

Danîsha sighed and shook her head. "You don't seem mindbent. What did you talk about?"

Perrely paused to gather her thoughts. Again she felt that strange mixture of alarm and uncertainty. "At first he seemed quite tense. He told me none of our friends have been killed or injured…"

"Oh, that's a relief!" Danîsha sighed, a smile wreathing her kindly face.

"In fact he said Alanya and Gelmion are on their way here to the Cathedral. I made him promise he wouldn't mindbend or torture them."

"And he agreed?"

"Yes."

"You think he'll keep that promise?" The older lady broke off to cough — talking wasn't helping her throat.

"I do. He seemed quite... sincere about it."

Danîsha frowned, increasing Perrely's own tension. She hurried on. "After that he asked me how we liked the apartment... whether we needed anything... apologised again that my family had been killed—" She swallowed the lump in her throat. "Then he talked a little about himself. Said he grew up in Yarbiless, where his father was a cloth merchant... But I didn't hear much. He kept looking at me so intently. He asked if I was alright..."

She broke off. Now it was Danîsha who was looking at her intently. "How did Shambor *behave*?" she whispered. "Did he touch you at all?"

Perrely blinked. "How did you know? Yes, he touched me quite often — that was one of the things I didn't like. He touched my shoulder as he showed me to the table, put his hand on mine when he asked if I was alright... My chair was next to his, instead of opposite, and he brushed against me several times when he was reaching for dishes."

Enlightenment had been dawning on Danîsha's wise old face. Her gaze sharp, she whispered intensely, "Right! Then I know what Shambor was after."

"What?" Perrely asked, bewildered.

"*You*, my dear!"

"What do you mean?" she exclaimed.

"He's attracted to you! He's romancing you." She paused to cough. "He hopes you'll respond to him as a woman to a man."

Perrely sat frozen. She opened her mouth, and shut it. Then her hands flew to her face. "No, that can't be — You must be wrong! He's old enough to be my father!"

"It happens, my dear," Danîsha whispered grimly. "I've seen it often enough under our sky." She broke off to cough again.

Perrely buried her face in her hands. "Dear Prince, what do I do *now*?" she cried.

* * *

Lannie dreamt she was in prison. A guard in a grey uniform was towering over her. He had Gil's face. "You'll do what *I* say, bitch!"

He slapped her. She jerked awake. It *was* Gil, and he *had* slapped her. He grabbed her arm and barked, "Out!" She almost fell from the carriage.

With a sinking heart she realised she was back in Dûrion. She must have slept through the whole journey. Had her Birmingham flat just been a dream? No. The taste of coffee lingered in her mouth.

Gil and two other Guardsmen were hustling her towards a forbidding building with high, bare walls that fronted on an urban street. A Guardhouse—but not the one in Stillárre. A few passers-by turned to stare, then hurried on. She looked up. The roof tiles caught the fading daylight. They were green. Not the red of Darthane.

They entered the building. Gil and his henchmen handed her over wordlessly to another pair of Guards in the utilitarian entrance hall. They left without a backward glance. A few minutes later she was in a narrow cell with a single bed. There was a stinking hole in the corner. Dim light filtered through the high, barred grille in the door.

Lannie sank down on the edge of the bed and buried her head in her hands. It felt like the end of everything. Of her hopes of happiness with Gil—and Matt. Of her career on Earth as a website designer. Of the mission she thought she'd had here in Dûrion.

"What now, Lord?" she murmured hopelessly.

There was a long silence. Then, as from a distance—

Fan into flame the gift of God which is in you.

The words echoed in her mind with a gentle ring of authority. That was the verse she'd read in the flat. Was God speaking to her? No, he didn't use verses picked out at random. It must be her mind playing tricks. Yet… What was to stop him speaking that way if he chose? He might not normally do so—but he was God.

Fan into flame the gift of God which is in you. What could that possibly mean in the situation she found herself in now? *What* gift of God?

Words came back to her from long ago. *Lannie, I believe you already have the gift of summing people up quite accurately… Are you willing to use that gift in a different way? Not just to label people as this or that type, but to find out what they're really like. Are you willing to listen to people? And to discover the truth about them?*

Father Martin had challenged her with those words in the Round Church at Leston. She'd accepted the challenge, wanting to mend her relationship with Matt. The Ambon had flashed. A few days later she'd found herself in Dûrion.

And here — at least since their escape from Stillárre — she'd forgotten all about it. Not only had she *not* tried to discover the real truth about Gil, but she'd deliberately closed her eyes to the telltale signs that were there. The way he'd avoided talking about his innermost feelings. The mechanical sound of the phrases he'd sometimes trotted out about spiritual things — prayer, faith, obedience — as though mimicking what someone else had said. His possessiveness about the blaise. *Of course* he'd had to make sure no one else used it, or they might have seen Shambor's troops assembling for the ambush! She and 'Neesh could have done so that time they'd 'borrowed' it in the camp at Larris.

Then she remembered Gil's drawn face when he came to fetch the blaise after that strange episode. They'd seen Shambor dismembering a frog, and almost collapsing of fright when he heard 'Neesh's disembodied voice telling him to stop. Soon afterwards Gil had arrived complaining of a sudden headache, and needing to lie down. That was very unlike him. Coincidence? Or had he been affected by his Mindbender's shock? Which made *Shambor* his Mindbender! That would explain a lot.

Lannie flopped back on the lumpy mattress. *So* much she could have understood if she'd tried; so much pain she could have spared them all. Her mind ranged over other clues she'd missed. There was the offhand way he'd sometimes responded when she'd shared a small difficulty she was having. As though he didn't care. She'd put that down to self-centredness, assuming it would change as the Light transformed him. At the same time, though, he'd shown almost excessive concern about other people, like Jomel. Spending time in her tent, trying to encourage her —

Lannie suddenly sat up, eyes wide, her mouth a horrified 'O'. A dozen little jigsaw pieces fell into place. Gil hadn't been 'encouraging' Jomel. Oh, no. Quite the opposite. He'd been — She couldn't bring herself to think the words.

She rocked herself to and fro on the bed, hugging her shoulders. Tears of rage, humiliation and pain wet her cheeks. *How could she have been so stupid, so totally blind!* It was glaringly obvious now. He hadn't cared for Jomel — not one bit. He'd just used her. No wonder the girl had been so miserable. But why hadn't she *said* anything? He must have had some hold over her. Probably her family. With Shambor as Gil's Mindbender, anything was possible. Disgust filled her.

After a while she heaved a shuddering sigh and lay back on the bed. Look how much truth she'd discovered with just a little careful thought. A little 'listening' to things that had and *hadn't* been said. *Fan into flame the gift of God which is in you.*

This was the gift she'd neglected.

A sudden determination filled her. God was calling her to continue fighting the evil cancer in this land. She didn't know how. There wasn't much prospect of victory; Shiván was their only slender hope, *if* he'd managed to escape... But she'd continue to fight using her brain and her faith and this gift God had given her—with or without hope. Her relationships with Gil and Matt might be over; but her mission in Dûrion wasn't.

* * *

Shiván and his remnant had a restless night in Arneck. The Grûzhack child, curled up against Shiván on a pile of sacks in their host's kitchen, kept waking up, screaming and trembling until Shiván managed to soothe him. His distress was broadcast on a wide waveband; Shiván had no doubt that when he woke, the whole village woke.

Unable to sleep, Shiván reached his lowest ebb. The magnitude of yesterday's disaster weighed him down. So many dead. So many friends he would never see again. Tarlion. The rest of that brave rearguard. Shîrin. And what about Lannie? Had she made it? And Fira, their rock-solid, reliable guide since Carreck Manor days? Garset? Fennior? The list went on and on, and Shiván felt himself slipping down the old, familiar slide into depression.

No! Now of all times he could not let that happen.

With slow, careful movements he disentangled himself from the Grûzhack child and tucked his robe around the boy. Their host's outdoor jacket was hanging from a hook on the kitchen door. He slipped it on, lifted the door latch, turning it to the open position, and let himself out of the cottage. There was a small *thud* as the door swung back into place. He froze for a moment, but there was no sound from the kid.

The clouds had been swept away and it was a rare, clear night, with both moons in the sky. He walked a short distance and sat on a low rock under a tree. He needed space to think and pray.

"No sleep for you, too, Overguardian?"

Shiván jumped. He had a flash of annoyance—then he realised who it was.

"Cârin! I didn't see you there."

The surviving twin came from the other side of the tree and sat down beside him. In the clear moonlight Shiván saw lines in his face that he hadn't seen before; and the irrepressible smile was gone. His heart went out to his friend.

"We'll come through this somehow, Câr. Together."

Cârin heaved a deep sigh and nodded. "He died peacefully, you know."

"You felt that?"

"Yes. It's funny. While Shîr was alive I never realised what a strong shiláy bond we had. But now... I knew what he was feeling, though we were several andoret apart." A faint smile touched his lips. "He was making a joke about me just before he died. I don't know what it was, but—"

His voice broke and he hunched over, his whole body shaking. Shiván put an arm around his shoulder. They sat there for a long moment until Câr's sobs eased.

"Sorry," he muttered as he straightened up.

"No need," Shiván said quietly.

They sat in silence together for a while. Then Shiván swallowed the lump in his throat and said what was in his heart. "You know, Câr, you and Shîr always cheered people up. It was great being with the two of you during hard times, because you always lightened our load."

"That's when we were together," Cârin muttered.

"I know. But I wondered... I know I can never replace Shîr. But we have the same kind of humour, you and I. I would be... deeply honoured if you would accept me as a second brother. Not to take Shîr's place. But to encourage each other—and to cheer others up, as you and Shîr always did."

Cârin stared at the ground for a long time, and Shiván began to fear his well-meant offer was inappropriate. Then Câr looked up, and Shiván's spirits rose at the smile on his face.

"Alright. But understand this, Lord Overguardian—I'll speak my mind plainly to you, as I did to Shîr! Think you can handle that?"

"I'd better, hadn't I?"

"Right. Then what are you doing out here, you slacker? You've got a child to look after!"

Smiling, they rose and clapped each other on the shoulder before returning together to the village.

* * *

Back in the cottage, Shiván eased in beside the Grûzhack child, who gave a hoarse little whimper and snuggled closer. Sleep didn't come quickly, and his thoughts turned to the plans he'd discussed with Frengor, Cârin and Jomel last evening.

If, as they all feared, Shambor's mounted Guards were coming after them, they couldn't hang around in Arneck—much as they wanted to, in case other survivors managed to cross the river. But if the Guards took the shortest route via Hemmeris, they would be here by mid-morning. It wouldn't be safe to rely on the child scattering them, as he had during the battle. Look at his distress now. One burst of unhappiness on his part when the Guards caught up with them, and they'd be discovered.

The impromptu council had decided, therefore, that all they could do for the moment was to keep moving, raising the Ambon frequently to attract other survivors. They would head up to the Two Peaks. If they were followed there, at least they'd have the advantage of higher ground. One thing they could not do, was to head for Carreck Manor to wait for the Dorbians. That had been Shiván's first impulse. But any route to the Manor would take them north—into the arms of the pursuing Guards. Besides—Shambor would have learnt about the Dorbians from Gil. His troops might already be lying in wait at the Manor. They could no longer rely on any help from Gwargif.

And what about the longer term? There were so few of them left. And would people still have faith in them, after two such disastrous defeats? But they would trust the One to increase their numbers through the Ambon. In any case, they would fight on against Shambor. They wouldn't give up. Just keep fighting on… Shiván's head drooped on the coarse sacking, and he slowly drifted off.

He woke early next morning, dizzy from lack of sleep. But they had to get moving. He asked Jomel for help cleaning the child and the bedding, which he'd soiled. The kid went to her reluctantly, but relaxed under her gentle care. As the eldest of five children, she knew what to do. The cottagers looked askance at the ugly foreign child who had so disturbed their night; but they found a small cast-off shift and coat for him to wear.

After a welcome breakfast of warm gruel, Shiván and Jomel left the cottage with the child. The first person Shiván saw was Cârin, stumbling bleary-eyed out one of the other cottages. "Hoy, wake up, you slacker!" Shiván called. "You look as tired as I feel!"

Jomel glanced at him with raised eyebrows; but Cãr turned a dark look on Shiván and shot back, "It's me that's wide awake, you washout. You're so dozy you're not looking where you're going!"

Shiván swerved at the last minute to avoid a cart. There was scattered laughter from villagers and soldiers. "Well, you two have cheered up!" Jomel exclaimed. He smiled at her.

Shiván gathered his hundred and fifty in the village square and asked Cârin to raise the Ambon. At the ringing trumpet call most of the village came running. Shiván explained that this was the Ambon of Sûrilane; it wasn't summoning them, but scattered survivors of the Restorers' army. If any came to the village, they should tell them that Shiván had left for Hemmerdan and the Two Peaks. He thanked them for their hospitality, and asked for their prayers. There was a chorus of warm responses; but many eyes were sad. It was obvious that this tattered remnant of a defeated army did not inspire confidence.

Two hours later they raised the Ambon in Garlane, nestling in the foothills of the Two Peaks. The snow-streaked head of Hemmerdan towered over them to the east. Once more many responded to the trumpet call. Shiván gave them the same explanation, asking only for their prayers. They stared at the weary soldiers and the strange foreign child in Shiván's arms. The child's eyes were riveted on the Ambon. Warmth flowed into Shiván's heart. They might be few, they might be defeated, but the One Creator God was with them. And there had been no sign yet of pursuing Guards.

A better-dressed member of the crowd stepped forward. He wore a fur-lined coat, fine leather boots and a warm cap. "You're going up to Hemmerdan? Where will you sleep?"

"In caves; or under whatever shelter we can find," Shiván told him. A shocked murmur arose from the villagers.

"You can't do that!" the man in the fur coat exclaimed. "It's too cold up there. Listen, I'm a cloth merchant. I'm on my way from Histen to Janulane—I was just passing through. That's my wagon over there." He pointed to a covered vehicle on the southern road out of the village. Two grûnet stood patiently on either side of the wagon's tongue. "It's full of outdoor fabric and furs. You could use it to make lean-tos. You're welcome to have the whole thing."

Shiván stared at the man. Joy welled up in him. "That's very good of you."

"It's the least I can do. When I heard that trumpet, I knew it was from God. So you must be from God, too. I don't see how you can defeat Shambor with so few—but God uses the weak to overthrow the mighty. If my little bit helps, I'll be well repaid."

"I believe you will, sir."

Standing beside Shiván Cârin snorted softly. "And will we get paid for *making* all those lean-tos?" he murmured. Shiván glanced at him. There was a half-smile on his new brother's face.

"What, you want to get paid for having a roof over your head?"

"Only when Shambor's dead and you're the top man in Dûrion. Then I'll send you a detailed bill."

Shiván laughed and clapped Câr on the shoulder.

A tall, gangly villager with a squint called out, "Do you have food?"

"Ah—no."

"Then we'll dig into our winter supplies—won't we, friends? That's the least we can do!" Voices rose in agreement and heads were nodding. "Fetch that wagon back into the village. We'll fill it even fuller!"

Shiván watched, marvelling, while the merchant brought back his wagon and the gangly man organised the food supplies that began to pile up in the village square. The cover was taken off the wagon, revealing bolts of heavy blue cloth lying three deep at the front, and stacks of furs at the back. The merchant produced boards to raise the sides, while the gangly man collected a mound of sacks. The soldiers gladly helped fill them with the grains, root vegetables, fruit, preserves, winter greens, nuts, chass beans and pulses that the villagers brought from their houses. A motley collection of milk jars and flasks also appeared, as well as cooking pots, fire irons and utensils.

"Enough!" Shiván called out. "You still have to feed your families through the winter!"

The flow dwindled to a stop, and the soldiers piled the sacks and equipment into the wagon. The merchant refitted the cover just as a fine rain began to fall. They set off on an easterly track up into the highlands, the whole village accompanying them. Gromon had taken charge of the grûnet, and was crying *"Hay-aay!"* to keep the heavy wagon moving. The villagers halted at the crest of the first rise and shouted their farewells. With them the merchant waved goodbye to his wagon. Shiván called out a few words of heartfelt thanks, then they pressed on. Shambor's Guardsmen might appear at any moment.

Frengor joined Shiván, Cârin and Jomel as they trudged up the track towards the bleak white hills. "The Ambon has more uses than summoning soldiers," he commented.

Shiván paused to take back the child, who had allowed Jomel to carry him for a while. Now he was reaching out to Shiván.

"Yes! I've been thinking about that. At first we imagined that if someone responded to the Ambon, it meant they should come with us and fight. We couldn't have been more wrong!" He heaved a deep sigh. "So many died at Berûvis."

"You cannot blame yourself for that."

"I suppose not. It still hurts, though. But what happened today was good. People helping in the best way they could. I wonder—" He stared at the hills through the faint curtain of rain. "What if that's how the Ambon is *supposed* to be used? Maybe we should be praying before we raise it. Asking the One to summon *only* those we need, not all and sundry. What do you think?"

Frengor's wrinkled face lit up. "I think that's a God-given insight, young Shiván! You can ask the One to supply your needs through the Ambon—*whatever* they may be. Today you needed food and shelter—the Ambon drew those who could provide it. Another day you may need prayer—trust the Ambon to bring those who will pray. And when you need more fighters—"

"—we'll ask the One to send us experienced troops!" Cârin finished. "That sounds wise, y'r Wisdom."

"But do you think it'll work, Frengor?" Shiván said. "Those old Dûrian Founders only seemed to raise the Ambon to bring in recruits."

"Exactly *how* the Founders used the Ambon is not recorded. But they had to learn by trial and error, too. Remember the Slaughter of Gend."

Shiván's mind went back to the chilling story Garset had told at Kindler Mâron's house in Sûrilane, of the five thousand untrained

Ambon recruits who had been massacred. He understood, now, exactly how that had come about.

"The Prince knows we need experienced soldiers, Shiván," Jomel said, her eyes bright. "If we ask him, I'm sure he'll send them." Frengor nodded, a smile lurking at the corners of his lips.

"You're right. So let's keep raising the Ambon, but we'll ask him to send only the people we need."

They trudged on. A couple of hours later, higher on the slopes of Hemmerdan, a little hamlet appeared ahead of them. Shiván called a halt. Below them to the south-east they could see the Janul Stream tumbling down toward the distant blur that was the town of Janulane. They decided to let this hamlet be a trial run of the new way of using the Ambon. Shiván, Jomel and Câr prayed with the priests, asking God to send only those they needed. The child looked from one to the other afterwards, his down-slanted eyes alive with interest.

They continued on to the little cluster of houses. Villagers peered out of their doors. Shiván explained who they were, then Cârin held the Ambon aloft. There were exclamations at the trumpet call, but for the first time no one came out to join them. Frengor said with a crooked smile that this was just what they'd asked for. Others must have heard the call instead. Now they had to wait and see.

They found a wooded, fairly flat area a couple of aldoret beyond the hamlet where they decided to camp. A small stream bubbled beside it. Some of the soldiers cut support poles, while others unpacked the wagon and began slicing the merchant's cloth to make waterproof lean-tos. Others collected firewood. Soon the savoury fragrance of vegetable stew began wafting over the camp. The child gave a whimper and reached out toward the cooking pots.

"All in good time, young 'un," Shiván murmured, stroking his head. The kid looked up at him. "*Gorana sidilai?*" he said in a hoarse little voice.

Shiván's eyes widened. "So you *can* talk!" He looked round at the others. "Anyone speak Grûzhack?"

Jomel laughed. "That's not Grûzhack! It's Selmian. He's saying, 'Are we going to eat?'"

"Of course! His Mindbenders were Selmian, so he learned their language. Tell him—"

There was a cry from the soldier on watch to the west. "*Troops approaching!*" Everyone scrambled for weapons—except Shiván and

Jomel, who hurriedly comforted the child. They ran from the fire into the woods, where the men were taking up defensive positions. Cârin was holding the Ambon. Gromon and a dozen others gathered round them, weapons drawn.

Then a voice called out from the westward path. "Shiván, are you there?"

It was Garset.

* * *

Hours earlier, Gwargif and the *Hrarkhoneyl* — the Great Legion — had reached the desolate uplands of Thargen. Only the Kennissôr Mountains now stood between them and their goal. For nearly three weeks they had run tirelessly, day in, day out, over hills and mountain passes, through forests and across streams, under iron grey skies and through veils of snow. They had stopped only to feed from late-ripening fruits and berries, and from the people's supply caches that dotted the route; and to sleep a few hours each night.

But at last they were within reach of their goal. Two days along the westward track would bring them to Bellarniar. A day to cross the Bellarniar Pass that led into Dûrion. Then to Carreck Manor, where the Warriors of Light would meet them.

Gwargif's thoughts returned to Hishray and his little ones as he led the grey tide that flowed along the track. How he missed them! To romp again with Hreldaz, Gishrin and Sykhar; to lie with Khelris curled up against his flank and little Barkhim between his paws. To nuzzle his beloved Hishray again …

The Great Legion swept through Dompesi, where the long-haired villagers ran screaming. This was the effect they always had; Gwargif hardly noticed. Up ahead were the snow-clad heights where more supply caches were hidden. Soon they'd stop for a meal.

Suddenly the whole legion skidded to a halt. They stood electrified, every nose pointing south-west. The trumpet call was distant, beyond hearing, yet utterly compelling. *They were summoned by the Warriors of Light, who were in urgent need.*

Without a word Gwargif leapt off the track to Carreck Manor, following the call that still echoed in his mind. This way was harder, the pass was higher, but that summons could not be ignored.

The grey tide flowed after him.

Chapter 32: *The real Shambor*

SO THIS WAS THE REAL SHAMBOR. Lannie took in the large, heavyset figure in the dark blue robe; the hunched, aggressive stance; the drawn brows above cold grey eyes. A formidable man; one you would not lightly oppose. When he had mindbent her so many months ago, she'd only seen the mental image he had planted in her mind of a benevolent, silver-haired scholar. The reality couldn't be more different. Yet in the blaise she'd observed this same man leaping in terror at the sound of Danîsha's voice. There was an inner weakness behind that strong façade. In the time left to her she intended to find out what it was.

Meanwhile she watched with interest as Shambor dealt with Gil. There was no love lost there. Without a word Shambor held out his hands, and Gil, wooden-faced, gave him the blaise and the bess. Lannie felt a pang as her beautiful shell disappeared into a pocket of Shambor's robe. The Mindruler turned away from Gil, who left with the two Guards who had accompanied them.

Lannie stood alone before Shambor in the ornate chamber with the oval stained glass window which she and Danîsha had seen in the blaise. She tensed as those hard grey eyes turned on her. Any minute now she might be mindbent for the second time.

"Take a seat." He indicated a nearby recliner. Surprised, she rather awkwardly arranged herself on the long chair. Shambor did likewise. They faced one another, propped up on an elbow in the Dûrian fashion. Lannie felt an absurd inclination to laugh. How would this look to an observer? The ruler of Dûrion, splendidly dressed, having a tête-à-tête with a wild-haired woman in a filthy, tattered shift, lying casually on his best blue-leather recliner.

"You will not be mindbent," Shambor announced without preamble, his cold eyes boring into hers. "Nor will you be tortured. Your army has been destroyed, your cause is lost. Shiván will be arriving soon. You will wait here until he does. Then I shall decide what to do with you. Meanwhile I have a few questions to ask."

Lannie blinked. This was a lenient side to Shambor that she hadn't expected. Her eyes narrowed. Or was there some hidden reason?

"And if I don't answer your questions?"

"It's up to you. If you co-operate, I can make your stay here comfortable. If not… let's just say you won't like it."

"Why not mindbend me? You'd get your answers a lot quicker."

"You're no longer worth mindbending."

"Nor worth torturing? Now, why would that be? I'm your enemy. I've put you to a lot of trouble. Are you telling me you don't have the slightest desire to make me suffer?"

Shambor's heavy lips compressed. "If it were up to me—" he growled, then caught himself. "Just consider yourself fortunate. Now, tell me. When did you find out that Gelmion was working for me?"

"At the last moment, during the battle. You both did a good job of hiding it."

"Why do you say 'both'? What did *I* have to do with it?"

"Oh come, Your Excellency, you must think me naïve. When Gelmion didn't follow—didn't even *hear*—the Ambon, an idiot would have realised his 'conversion' to Lightism was fake; and when the Guards who were supposed to be fighting him stood idle, do you think I didn't guess he was mindbent? From there it was a small step to work out that you must have been his Mindbender."

"And what was that small step?"

"A process of elimination. He was first mindbent by Dhelgor in Stillárre. But when Dhelgor was killed, Gelmion did not freeze like all Dhelgor's other slaves, though he pretended to. Now it turns out that he was still mindbent—by someone else. So another Mindbender must have taken him over *before* Dhelgor's death. I reckon the only one who would have done that was Dhelgor's superior. You."

Shambor nodded, his eyes narrowed. "Cleverly worked out. But rather too late, don't you think?"

"Too late to stop your cowardly plan of killing us all off when we couldn't defend ourselves." The image of Shambor dismembering the frog came to Lannie's mind.

Shambor's head jerked back as if slapped. "Cowardly! That plan resulted in the total defeat of your army. Hardly the achievement of a coward!"

Prudence warned Lannie to ease off. Yet she was obviously hitting a nerve. "*Only* a coward would be proud of such an achievement!" she spat. "Using a mind-weapon to deaden our wills, and *then* attacking. You might as well boast about killing a tethered animal."

The ruler of Dûrion froze. Then rage mounted in his face. He stood, towering over her. "You weren't a helpless animal—you were endangering all I've built up, and I destroyed you! I engineered your whole campaign through Gelmion, and you fell into one trap after the other, exactly as planned. You needed to be eradicated like vermin, and you have been. *That* is an achievement. *That* is real power."

Two Guards entered. "Go!" Shambor barked at her, pointing to the blackwood doors of the reception chamber.

Lannie stood as the Guards marched over to her. "I'm helpless, Your Highness," she taunted, holding her arms apart, open palms toward him. "I have no weapon. I can't fight back. Kill me. What a great achievement *that* will be!"

"*Get out!*" the Mindruler bellowed.

* * *

As Gil made his way out of the Cathedral to the small cubicle he shared with four men in the Guard barracks, his thoughts were desolate. His grand plan of making a life for himself in this miserable apology for a country had collapsed. Shambor had only one criterion by which he judged the usefulness of his autonomous subordinates: success. Fail—no matter how unavoidably—and that was it. Your autonomy was revoked and you were sent to your room like a child to 'wait until called for'.

That's what Shambor had said to him by mindspeech at their recent interview. A curt dismissal. Before then there had been periodic blasts of pain when his thoughts became too rebellious—underlining his loss of autonomy. Of course his present gloomy meditations would only delight the vindictive sod. As the thought escaped him, he tensed for a whiplash—but none came. Sometimes colloquial expressions slipped past— *aaaagh!* He stumbled and barely avoided a fall. Sometimes they didn't.

Yes. The biggest mistake—perhaps of his life—had been to assume co-operation would be rewarded. Only success was rewarded.

And he had failed.

* * *

Lannie sat on the floor of the bare cell the Guards had brought her to. It looked as though it had once been a storeroom. There were marks on the walls where shelves had been fixed. Now it was completely empty. Not even a bed. Shambor was right about one thing: he'd said she wouldn't like it, and she didn't. It was damp and chilly. She was huddled against the door, as far from the outer wall as she could manage. She hugged her shoulders and rubbed her arms to keep the circulation going.

She forced herself to review the recent interview with Shambor. The most suspicious thing was that he'd neither mindbent nor tortured her. That went against everything she knew about him. Why? His reply that she wasn't worth mindbending was rubbish. He would delight in making her his slave.

A faint warmth was seeping under the door from the passage outside. She shivered and huddled closer to it. What was that other thing he'd said that had caught her attention? Oh, yes! *"If it were up to me –"* That implied it wasn't up to him. But how could that be? He was the ruler of Dûrion, no one could tell him what to do.

Well, except maybe for that Selmian Mindbender Garset had once mentioned – the one who was even more powerful than Shambor. What had he called him? Oh yes, the 'Strongholder'. But Garset had only considered the Strongholder a danger to them *if Shambor were removed* – she remembered him saying that. Which implied that Shambor had full authority in his own country…

She puzzled over this, squeezed up against the wooden door. If that restriction hadn't come from the Strongholder, then Shambor had bound *himself* not to resort to mindbending or torture, going against his own nature. Why? Had he made someone a promise? Who? Certainly not Gil! Supporters he needed to appease? Hardly. Who else would want him to go easy on the Restorers?

Wait. There were probably two people here in the Cathedral who would want that: Shambor's other prisoners, Danîsha and Perrely! Could Shambor have given an undertaking to one of *them* that he wouldn't harm the other Restorers? But why would he do that? Danîsha he would hardly have listened to, and Perrely –

Ah. Perrely was young and attractive. That might induce Shambor to give in to her wishes. He was old enough to be her father – but that meant nothing. Poor girl. What a position to be in! If that was what had happened. On the other hand she couldn't altogether rule out the Strongholder. He might be keeping them unharmed for his own dark purposes. She shuddered.

Well. For one or the other reason Shambor felt himself bound not to harm her. That was a weakness. And what about the way she'd been able to wind him up so easily with the accusation of cowardice? If he hadn't been bound, he would have made her suffer much more for that. An obvious weakness there. He wanted to be considered strong and powerful. Calling him a coward undermined his self-image. There had been something childish about his vehement response. Just as in the earlier episode, when she and 'Neesh had seen him with the blaise dismembering a frog. 'Neesh had burst out, *"Stop that at once!"* and he'd leapt up like a naughty child caught in the act.

A disturbed personality. Probably some kind of early trauma …

She fell asleep wondering how she could capitalise on Shambor's weaknesses if ever the opportunity arose.

* * *

Shiván and Cârin had a bittersweet reunion with Garset. Shiván explained about the Child of Despair, and they shared news of the recent battle during the daymeal. Shiván could see that Câr shared his anguish as they heard of so many dead, including Fira and Fennior. Lannie had probably been captured; Garset had last seen her with Gil. Yet despite the grief, Shiván was overjoyed at Garset's arrival. Battle-worn and wounded though he and his men were, their mere presence was an encouragement. An air of quiet confidence settled over the camp. In response to the Ambon, God had restored Garset to them.

They continued talking after the meal, discussing the battle, their lost friends, and the present situation. The vertical lines on Garset's face had deepened, he walked with a limp, and his green eyes were weary — but they lit up on hearing that in answer to prayer the Ambon had summoned *his* group, but not the local villagers. That, he said, gave hope of rebuilding the army with experienced troops. But what they urgently needed now was somewhere to regroup, treat their wounded, and prepare once more for battle. With a pang Shiván realised that they'd never again have Fira's sharp, insightful comments on military strategy.

But Frengor and Jomel joined in and they discussed various possibilities for a temporary refuge, finally settling on the Larwood. It was a forest full of thick evergreen trees and undergrowth, hard to travel through—they would be as safe there as anywhere until they were ready to face Shambor in a final showdown before winter. Or until he found them with Gil's blaise…

Shiván wondered where Gil was now, and what reward he'd get from Shambor for his treachery.

Garset went on to tell them how he and his survivors had managed to reach the Two Peaks. They had become separated from Tarlion and Fennior's groups, and had escaped from the battle towards the south-east, hoping to double round and rejoin Shiván. "As soon as we heard the Ambon," Garset added, "we knew it must be you." But they'd been cut off by the Carreck Marshes. Eventually a group of fisherman, fleeing the fighting, had ferried them across the river to Bast; and from there they'd gone on to Arneck, where they heard news of Shiván. A few villages later they'd heard the Ambon—and here they were.

"And we're gladder to see you than a grûn to see its food trough!" Shiván said, quoting a Dûrian proverb.

"That goes both ways," Garset replied with a grin.

Cârin looked from the one to the other. "So who's the grûn and who's the trough?"

They chuckled.

* * *

During the next two days they slowly made their way along the southern slopes of the Two Peaks. There was still no sign of pursuit. Ahead of them across the Larris valley they could see the Larwood—a dense mass of grey branches and dark evergreens.

They raised the Ambon every time they took a rest break; but no more troops joined them. Shiván began to wonder whether the Ambon had lost its power, until they met a trader with a wagon. As they approached he called out, "Did you hear a trumpet call? Came from somewhere up there." He pointed behind them towards the towering peak of Lardan.

Cârin raised the Ambon. The compelling notes rang out, and everyone surged closer.

"Was that what you heard?" Shiván asked.

"Yes!" The man was overcome with excitement. "Then this wagonload belongs to you! God told me my food was for those who sounded that trumpet!"

As the supplies given in Garlane were already running out, they accepted gladly. They transferred the trader's goods to their wagon. He left promising to find them in the Larwood with more food in a couple of days.

Shiván shook his head, marvelling at God's provision.

Later, as they were crossing the Larris road to reach the Larwood, they saw troops approaching from the north. "To the forest!" Garset yelled; but Shiván shouted, "*Wait!*" and called to Cârin to raise the Ambon.

"Shiván, we have only half a company! That's at least two..."

The Ambon sounded.

The approaching troops broke into a run. Their own soldiers hurriedly drew swords and fitted arrows – then lowered them. The attackers showed no weapons. They came charging up to Cârin and the Ambon, clamouring to know whether this summons, which they'd first heard yesterday, was from the Restorers.

After explanations and declarations of loyalty, the newcomers accompanied Shiván, Garset and their remnant into the Larwood. They were two companies from Lômack, sent belatedly to the Grûzhack War under the command of Captains Hastor and Dolmet, both devout Lightists. Three supply wagons followed the companies. Shiván exchanged glances with Cârin. He was grinning. In a moment their numbers had more than quadrupled.

They spent all afternoon hacking a way for the wagons deep into the Larwood. Beside a small stream they found an area not quite so clogged with undergrowth. Garset and the other two Captains declared it the nearest they would get to a suitable campsite. Tents and lean-tos, cooking fires and awnings began to appear.

As Shiván stood holding the child and watching all the homely activity, he felt a weight roll off his mind. Here they would be safe – for a while. He looked down at the poor, ugly kid who'd suffered so much. His face was relaxed, the down-slanted eyes warm. He wondered whether this little fellow was silently broadcasting much of the optimism that pervaded the camp. Was that the first glimmering of a smile around his lips? He bounced him gently in his arms. "Hey, friend. Life's not so bad, is it?"

The lips widened into a broad grin. The kid's face was instantly transformed from a mask of sadness into a comical picture of surprised delight. Shiván burst out laughing, and bounced him again.

The child laughed back—an infectious, bubbling chuckle. All work stopped as soldiers and officers joined in the mirth. There was no doubt about it, this kid could broadcast happiness as well as despair.

Jomel came running up, a delighted grin on her face.

Shيván bounced the kid towards her. He crowed with delight. Shيván paused to change his grip. "*Dara!*" the child cried, in his hoarse little voice. "'More'!" Jomel interpreted the Selmian word. "He wants more!"

"Alright, then, *dara!*" Shيván kept bouncing him up and down, the kid laughing, while the hardened soldiers who'd gathered round mirrored his delight, clapping in time to the bounces.

Finally Shيván stopped to let the soldiers get back to work. "*Dara!*" the child demanded. When the men had left, grinning over their shoulders, Shيván bounced the kid to Jomel. His peal of laughter almost brought everyone back. Jomel bounced him for a while, then the child reached for Shيván.

Instead of taking him, Shيván placed a hand on his own chest. "Shi-*ván.*"

"*Dara!*"

He took the kid, bounced him, then held him out to Jomel, pausing halfway.

She took the hint. "Jo-mel." She put a hand on her chest.

The child looked from one to the other. Jomel took him, bounced him, and passed him back to Shيván, who repeated his name. They did the same several times, chorusing the names together. The child began to chime in with his own hoarse imitations, holding his open hands out toward their chests as he was passed to and fro.

"Shi-*ván!*" — "Shi-*bán!*"

"Jo-mel!" — "Jo-mil!"

Finally they stopped. Shيván put a hand on his chest and said "Shi-*ván.*"

"Shi-*bán.*"

He pointed to Jomel: "Jo-mel."

"Jo-mil."

He pressed his hand against the child's chest and waited, his eyebrows raised. The child stared back, then his grin broadened.

"Bra-*khól!*" he cried.

They all laughed. "Bra–*khól!*" Shiván and Jomel repeated, imitating the hissing *kh* sound. The kid chortled with delight, and they went into a new round of the game.

Praise the One. Their waif was no longer a nameless pawn in other people's games.

He was accepted for himself, and his name was Brakhól.

Chapter 33: *The Bishop and the smallroom*

GWARGIF LED THE GREAT LEGION across the Dûrian mountains. A hard journey; thirty-three warriors died, either collapsing from exhaustion or slipping off the icy paths and plunging to their deaths. But now at last they were coming down to the lowlands. The mining village of Istenar lay ahead.

Gwargif lifted his nose, and sniffed. He let out a full-throated bay, which the *Hrarkhoneyl* echoed, making the ground quiver. The grey tide poured through the village, while the occupants cowered in their houses.

To the south they smelt deep darkness confronting a small, bright light.

* * *

Lannie leant against the wooden door and asked God to let her out of this desolate storeroom. It was approaching evening on the second day that she'd been here. A Guard had brought her a bowl of greasy slop each day at around noon. Yesterday, thankfully, he'd also brought a lidded bucket—to prevent her stink from disturbing passers-by, he told her. At noon today he'd removed the bucket, and she'd been waiting with increasing anxiety for him to bring it back.

"Please, God, I really can't stay here," she murmured, running a hand over her matted hair. "You know how horrible it is—but apart from that, what can I do for *you* here? How can I use the gift you've given me?"

After what felt like an hour or two, she heard a couple of people coming along the passage outside, chatting together. When they reached the storeroom they stopped, still chatting. She heard the *thunk* of something being put on the floor. To her disappointment neither of them sounded like the Guard. They appeared to be kitchen servants.

"So old Gonny, he tells me to store this stuff. So I ask him, where? So he says, 'Use your head!' No room there, I tell him. 'Now, *that's* a fact!' he says, and cuffs me over the ear. Then he just walks off. Well, what am I supposed to do? You know what Herion's like. Won't let anyone near his store cupboards. And Gillay wants everything sort-

ed—flat pans here, skillets there, big pots, medium pots, little pots…
Well, I couldn't be bothered. So I'm just going to dump the stuff
here. This room hasn't been used for months. If they need these
things again—well, that's their problem!"

The two sniggered, and Lannie heard the nearer man fumbling
with a large bunch of keys. He obviously hadn't been told there was
a prisoner here! Lannie scrambled into the corner where she'd be
hidden by the opening door. She quickly pulled off her military
boots. She heard a key finally entering the lock and turning. She was
poised to try and escape, but before she could do anything a couple
of hairy arms rapidly shoved a wooden box into the room and shut
the door again. In the dim light from the small grille in the door she
could see objects of various shapes sticking out of the box.

The two men carried on chatting outside the room, taking their
time. Lannie hoped desperately that they wouldn't relock the door.
But finally Hairy-arms said, "Well, I suppose I'd better lock up and
get back before old Gonny asks what took me so long…" He started
fumbling with his keys again while rambling on to his friend.

Thinking frantically what to do, Lannie's eyes were drawn to a
narrow gap between the edge of the door and the frame. She scuttled over to the box and grabbed the first flat object she could find. It
was a thin wooden board with tapered edges. Some kind of scraper?
She pushed it gently between the door and frame, so that it blocked
the point where the bolt moved across into its socket. She was just in
time. Hairy-arms tried to turn the key, but the bolt stopped against
Lannie's board. He swore, and tried again. Then he pulled the key
out. With the speed of a sinélle Lannie removed her scraper, shot
back into the corner, and froze. Hairy-arms opened the door. He
came partway into the room—a large young man with a pudgy face,
green smock and black apron. His eyes were on the lock. He fiddled
with it, tried it from the inside, went out and closed the door again.
While he was re-inserting the key, Lannie nipped across and pushed
her scraper into the gap. Once again the door wouldn't lock.

"*Flisht!* Dunno what's wrong with this thing. Oh well, no great
loss if anyone nicks that junk. I'll tell Andor about the lock. He
might get round to it by Prince's Birth!" The two tramped off chuck-
ling.

As soon as their footsteps died away, Lannie breathed a prayer of
thanks and peered cautiously round the door. The corridor was emp-

ty. There was no time to lose—that Guard might reappear at any moment with the bucket. She slipped barefoot out of the storeroom.

Though the floors and walls of the corridor were of pale yellow marble, there were no ornaments. It stretched a long way in both directions, dotted with white doors like the one she'd come out of. The occasional window on her side let in some fading daylight. There were a number of passageways opening off it. She had no idea where to go, except that it had to include a toilet. She sprinted towards the nearest passage.

It was darker and less grand than the corridor, which suited her. There was a felt covering on the floor, and the walls were wood-panelled. She hurried down it, passing various doors to the left and right. She wanted to put plenty of distance between herself and the storeroom before she tried opening doors. On the other hand, her need was growing…

One passage led into another, and she lost all sense of direction. Now everything was strictly utilitarian, with bare stone and unpainted woodwork. She seemed to have reached a dormitory area for the domestic servants. It was deserted—they were all at work. She was looking urgently for a communal smallroom, but not finding anything.

As she turned a corner into yet another dim passage, she heard voices behind her. Then she saw that the passage ended in a red painted door. She stopped, looking forward and back. The voices were drawing nearer; and she was almost bursting.

She had to risk the door. She ran to it, found a key sticking out of the lock. She turned it, and stumbled into a small kitchen. Now, if she could just find…

A tall old man in a blue satin house-robe was coming through a doorway. He gave a startled exclamation and dropped a cup. "Who are you?"

"Who are *you*?"

"Bishop Harlon. You must be—"

"*Ney li silmend*—Light stay with you, Your Eminence. Where's your smallroom?"

* * *

When Lannie had relieved herself, she found the Bishop of Dûrion making chass in the kitchen. He turned a pair of clear grey twinkling eyes on her.

"It's not every day I have a young lady bursting in here to use the smallroom. This calls for a celebration."

"Your Lordship, I'm sorry, you shouldn't—"

"Oh, but I should. You don't realise how momentous this is. But first, can I say…" He turned from the little percolator, a smile tugging at the corners of his lips. "If you *have* to use a formal title, it should be 'Your Radiance'. But I'd be just as happy if you called me 'Harlon'. You do realise you've set me free?"

"I— what?"

"Yes. You unlocked that door—" He pointed to the red door she'd come in through. "And left the key in the lock. I've now retrieved it." He held up the slim, indented metal shaft. "The next servant who comes will think it was accidentally removed, and get another one. Meanwhile, when I'm ready, I can leave. You've achieved something I've been praying for for almost twenty years. You knew I was a prisoner?"

"Yes, I'd heard. But Your… Radiance, why are you telling me this? You know nothing about me! I might give you away—"

The old man's face lit up in a broad smile, making it live up to his title. "Ah, but you're wrong! I *do* know something about you. And I hardly think you'll give me away." He reached out and took both of her hands in his. "My dear, I may be mistaken, but I believe you're the answer to another prayer of mine. You're very foreign, you know. You have the shiláy of a stranger and a loner—and a follower of the Light. In fact you're a Restorer of the Way, aren't you?"

Lannie stared at the old man's face, full of joyful anticipation, and marvelled at God's planning. "Yes. I am," she said simply.

Tears brimmed over from the Bishop's eyes as he stood holding her hands. "Then you must be Alanya. Praise the One. Praise him. Praise the Prince," he murmured. Lannie felt her own eyes moisten as she thought how long this man had faithfully prayed and waited. She raised her arms up to his shoulders and embraced him.

"Just yesterday," the Bishop said, letting her go to wipe his eyes, "I was praying with your friend, Kindler Mâron. He's told me everything he knows, up to the time you left Sûrilane. But now that the Prince has brought you to my very kitchen, I want to hear it all from your own lips. Including what you're doing here in the Cathedral, looking for a smallroom! But have some chass first, then you can wash and change. You'll have to make do with some old clothes of mine, I'm afraid…"

Later they shared a simple daymeal of bean soup and bread. It was better than a restaurant dinner to Lannie. She was dressed in a brown tunic and grey shift which scuffed the floor when she walked, and her fresh-smelling hair was still damp. But she was clean! And fed.

After the meal they sat in the reclining room in front of a crackling fire, and Lannie answered Harlon's eager questions about every aspect of their time in Dûrion. He was appalled to hear that Gil had been mindbent by Shambor. She told him about the ambush, the destruction of their army, and her own capture; and went on to describe her interview with the Dûrian ruler. She was surprised to see pain in the old man's eyes when she told him about Shambor's reaction to her taunt of cowardice.

"He's a coward, Your Radiance. He needs to feel he's always in control."

"Yes. Yes, he does. I know him only too well." Harlon heaved a deep sigh. "Let me tell you a little about Shambor dom Beldet. His mind is not stable — and if you knew his background, you would hardly blame him …"

Lannie was prepared to dispute this, but she waited while the Bishop added more logs to the fire. When it was burning brightly he settled back on his recliner and began to speak, gazing into the middle distance. He spoke for quite some time. As she listened, Lannie's eyes widened in amazement. Harlon was not saying what she'd expected. His words put Shambor in a totally different light.

"I didn't suspect this myself until recently," the Bishop concluded. "Then a couple of weeks ago Shambor stormed in while Kindler Mâron was here. I set a little trap for him, and he fell right into it. That was when I knew for sure."

In the silence that followed, Lannie's mind went back to the episode of the frog. She told the old man about it. He shook his head, tears in his eyes, and described why he thought Shambor would have reacted as he did. Lannie nodded. It made sense now.

They prayed together, asking the One for wisdom. Then they prepared a makeshift bed for Lannie in the Bishop's small writing chamber with some cushions and warm clothes.

Lannie's last thought before dropping off was that Shambor needed to be confronted with both Harlon and Danîsha at the same time.

The only problem was how, and where.

And first she had to find Perrely and Danîsha.

Chapter 34: *The Little Fool*

"CAPTAIN, SIR." Cârinor, the former rebel soldier, gave a lazy salute.

Garset sighed and pushed from his mind the makeshift smithy he and the other two captains were setting up. Despite all they'd been through together, there remained an awkwardness in relating to the man who stood before him. He still wore the rebels' brown cape, and though technically a sergeant he did not command any of Garset's men. His exact rôle in the Company had not been defined — though he often went out with the scouts guarding the forest's perimeter.

But he was the designated Ambon-bearer and the Overguardian's close friend — he'd even heard Shiván calling him 'brother'. As such he deserved respect and inclusion where possible.

"What is it, Sergeant?"

"News from the scouts near Larris."

Garset frowned. Beckoning, he moved away from the bustle of activity around the temporary forge. "Tell me."

"An infantry company arrived in the village around noon. They've started patrolling the paths leading into the forest. The scouts and I saw them turning back a wagon: it was the one we met on the way here with food."

Garset's frown deepened. "That's bad news. He said he would send another wagonload, and we were counting on it..." He paused. "Please don't spread this about, Sergeant. If you hear any more, come directly to me."

"I will, sir." With another perfunctory salute he left.

Garset stood staring across the camp. Soldiers were still hacking away at undergrowth a day after they'd arrived, but space had now been cleared for most of the tents and lean-tos. Men and women off-duty were sitting chatting, cleaning their weapons, or playing the wargame barây with makeshift pieces and circular 'spider-webs' scratched on the ground. At the central hearth the cooks were hanging large pots on the fire irons for the daymeal. There was a remarkable spirit of confidence and goodwill.

That might change after the dawnmeal tomorrow, when people discovered there was no more food.

The situation was serious. They depended on being able to bring in food from Larris and other nearby villages. A thousand men could not live off what the forest provided this late in the year. But now Shambor had found them—either through his spies, or using Gelmion's blaise—and was cutting off their supplies. These troops at Larris would not be the only ones he'd sent. He would be guarding the southern, eastern and northern entry points as well. Shambor intended to starve them out—which would happen well before winter, when his own troops would have to return to barracks.

No, they'd be forced to leave the forest—and the minute they did, Shambor would pounce. Their meagre thousand would be no match for the numbers he would have saturating the area. And his troops guarding the entry routes would prevent others who had responded to the Ambon from joining them.

As Garset walked slowly back to the smithy, he wondered grimly whether they would be dismantling it tomorrow.

* * *

That night Garset had a strange dream. He and Shiván were camped on a hill with their thousand men. The hill was surrounded by Shambor's army, which covered the entire countryside as far as the eye could see. Nevertheless they were planning to try and break out. But Shiván rejected first one of their own units, then another. The bowmen were no good in a charge, they should remain behind. The cavalry horses needed resting… The Fourth Company's second infantry cohort were too nervous…

In vain he remonstrated with Shiván. "Overguardian, just look at Shambor's army! We have no hope of breaking out, but if we're going to try, we need every single soldier at our disposal!" The young man remained adamant.

Finally Garset lost patience. "You little fool!" he exclaimed. "You're going to throw these men's lives away needlessly! We might as well stay on this hill and die with dignity."

But Shiván would have none of it. After whittling down their attack force until only a couple of cohorts remained, he lifted the Ambon in one hand, holding the Grûzhack child in the other, and yelled "*Charge!*"

As the small force streamed down the hill, Shambor's vast army melted away. The massed ranks of bowmen, cavalry, infantry, lancers, and spearmen thinned to a few legions, a few companies, a few scattered individuals… then vanished. Shiván's men were shouting and dancing in triumph on an empty battlefield.

Garset led the rest of the men down to join them, shaking his head in wonder.

* * *

Garset woke in the pre-dawn dark, the dream still vivid in his mind. He found he couldn't sleep, and got up, putting on his outdoor jacket. He left his tent and threaded his way through the others to the embers of the cooking fires.

To his surprise, Shiván was already there. Garset joined him on one of the logs arranged round the fires.

"You're up early," Garset said. "I suppose what's-his-name — the child — is sleeping?"

"Yes, Brakhól's enjoying sweet dreams — I hope."

"I've just woken from a dream. About you."

" 'Zat so? What was I up to this time?"

Shiván laughed as Garset described the senseless elimination of the various units from the attack force. Garset himself was grinning as he went on to say how he'd lost his patience and called Shiván a little fool. But at that word, the grin suddenly vanished from the young man's face. Garset paused, surprised.

"*What* did you call me?"

Garset repeated it. Surely the foreigner couldn't have taken offence?

No. An intrigued smile was playing about Shiván's lips. "Tell me the rest of the dream."

Garset did so. Shiván's grin broadened. "Well, blow me down." He used the strangest expressions. "I've never believed much in prophetic dreams, Garset, but I think you've just had one."

"What do you mean?"

"Well, you called me — "

He paused as Cârin appeared in the dim glow around the cooking fires. "Mind if I join you?"

"Not at all. Take a log. Garset was telling me about a fascinating dream he's just had."

The rebel scout sat beside Shiván, leaning forward to focus on Garset. Garset repeated the dream a little stiffly for the new arrival. When he'd finished Cârin turned a disgusted scowl on Shiván. "Up to your old trick of upsetting everyone for nothing! You *knew* Shambor would run away if you came charging down, because your shiláy frightens him silly. But did you tell the good captain here? No!"

Garset's skin crawled at the familiarity of the sergeant's comments; but the Overguardian just laughed.

"Ah, but wait till you hear what I was about to say to Garset," he continued. "In your dream, Garset, you called me a 'little fool', right?" He repeated the Dûrian word Garset had used — *gîdion*. Garset nodded. "So I was a little fool who defeated a mighty army with only a couple of hundred soldiers. In our Book we have a story exactly like that. And guess what the hero's name was?"

"Little Fool?"

"Yes! Though it doesn't mean that in our language. It's just a name. *Gideon* was a leader of the followers of the Light under our sky. At that time — many hundreds of years ago — the, er… Who were the followers of God who came *before* the Lightists?"

"The Renegade Royalty of Selmion," Garset said at the same moment as the rebel scout replied, "The Chosen."

"Which of those were the ones who believed following the One was a matter of keeping his laws?"

"The Chosen," Garset told him. "Their history goes right back to the beginning — the Selmian royal house was descended from them. The Renegades rediscovered their heritage, but they laid equal emphasis on the One's mercy."

"Okay. Anyway, coming back to Gideon: He was one of the Chosen on our world, and at that time his people were being oppressed by foreigners who had a huge army. God told Gideon to attack them, but first he made him reduce his own army from over thirty thousand to just three hundred. That was so they couldn't take the credit for themselves when they won. And they *did* win! Just like in your dream, the huge army melted away. They fled from Gideon and began fighting among themselves. In the end they were driven out of the land."

"Prince's blood!" Cârin exclaimed.

Garset stared at Shiván. "That — is amazing," he said slowly. "So I dreamt a story that is actually in your Book — and I even called you by the name that is used there?"

"That's right."

While Cârin went to add more wood to the nearest fire, Garset stared out into the darkness of the surrounding forest, trying to take in what Shiván was saying.

When the rebel sergeant had built up the fire he came back to join them. "So, *Gîdion*," he said to Shiván. Garset shuddered. "What does this amazing story mean for us, right now?"

The Overguardian grinned. "Let's think about it. What would it take to totally destroy Shambor, Garset?"

Garset fingered his chin doubtfully. "Well. We'd need to trap him in Darthane and then capture the city. He hardly ever leaves it. But now we're wandering off into children's tales. City walls are not like an army that will just melt away."

"Ah!" Shiván exclaimed. "But that brings us to another story from our Book. About an earlier leader of our ancient Chosen people — a man called Joshua. He surrounded a city in obedience to the One, and the walls collapsed!"

Cârin frowned. "What, large, well-built walls like Darthane's?"

"Well, I can't say exactly what size the walls were. But they were preventing the Chosen from capturing the city, and God brought them down." There was excitement in the young man's eyes. Garset hoped his dream hadn't triggered off an impulsive line of action that would lead to disaster. On the other hand... the correspondence between his dream and that story in their Book was remarkable.

"The great thing about both these stories," Shiván continued, " — Joshua's and Gideon's — is that the victory was won without the attackers doing any fighting themselves: it was the One who defeated the enemy. All they had to do was to obey, then follow up afterwards."

Garset shook his head. "It would be a massive risk to take. The other captains will need a lot of convincing before they'll agree to attack Darthane itself. But we do need to bring the war to Shambor before winter."

"Right. Which is why we need the other part of Gideon's story."

"What was that?"

"How he asked the One to confirm to him that he should attack the huge enemy army."

"Ah!" Cârin exclaimed. "So he had doubts? I begin to like this man."

"Yes, he had doubts. So much so, that he laid down a condition for the One. He put a fleece of wool on the ground one evening. Then he said to God that if he wanted Gideon to attack the enemy, he should let the dew that night fall only on the fleece—not on the ground around it."

Garset blinked. "That's impossible. You're not telling us this actually happened?"

"Yes, it did! The next morning there was enough dew in the fleece to fill a bowl with water—but none on the ground. Yet Gideon *still* wasn't convinced! He asked God to do it again—only the other way round. The following morning there should be dew on the ground, but none on the fleece!"

"I really like this man," Cârin said.

Garset shook his head, stunned. "And you're going to tell me *this* happened as well?"

"Yep! Next morning the fleece was dry and the ground was wet. After that Gideon had run out of excuses, so he went ahead and prepared the attack. It was then that the One told him to reduce the size of his army."

A distant wail reached them in the morning stillness. They all winced. "I'll go and see to the kid," Shiván said. "Think about it!"

When Shiván returned a while later with a clean, smiling Brakhól trying to bounce on his arm, the camp was stirring, Sergeant Cârin had left, and Garset had done his thinking.

If Shiván had brought this idea up on his own, Garset would have dismissed it as the Overguardian's youthful enthusiasm. But it had arisen out of *his* dream, with its amazing parallel in the foreigners' Book. That he could not dismiss. He told Shiván, "I think we should share this with the Visionary first. If he's in favour, we should ask confirmation from the One, as your 'Little Fool' did. If the confirmation is given, we should lay the whole matter before Captains Dolmet and Hastor, seeking their agreement to march on Darthane."

"Sounds good to me!" Shiván said with a broad grin.

They found the purple-robed priests engaged in their morning prayers. Garset remembered that today was Anderil—the One's Day—and later Frengor would lead them all in worship and the Remembrance of Flame. Shiván caught the Visionary's eye, and he came over to join them. They went to his neatly arranged lean-to, where they told him all about it. Frengor was immediately taken with the story of Gideon, and the parallel with Garset's dream. He described several occasions when he and his priests had sought confirmation from God in ways similar to Gideon's fleece—though, as he said, none as outrageous.

"I see the One's Light in this, friends, but it means sending our troops into great danger. It will also be an irrevocable step. If we lose, it will be a much greater setback than the recent ambush. If we win... we may defeat Shambor, but we will be declaring war on the Strongholder. He controls almost all the surrounding lands, and will be a far more formidable foe than Shambor. We should certainly seek confirmation, as the 'Little Fool' in your Book did, Shiván."

There was a pause as they considered the enormity of what they would be undertaking. Then Frengor's face lit up in a smile.

"But if the One Creator God is with us, we have nothing to fear! What kind of confirmation did you have in mind, Garset? It clearly does not have to be the same as *Gîdion's* fleece of wool."

"Well," Garset said slowly, "I had in mind what we most need right now: *food*. A wagonload from that trader in Larris was turned back by Shambor's troops yesterday. We have no more after today's dawnmeal." Concerned frowns appeared on Frengor and Shiván's faces. "Why don't we simply ask the One to send us food today? Our scouts report that all the major tracks entering the forest are being patrolled. The likelihood of a wagon getting through is low. If God were to do *that*, against all the odds, I believe our colleagues—and the troops—would have the confidence to take this daring step."

"I'll go for that," Shiván said. "But—supposing we do get the food—how soon should we attack? Do we wait for more food the next day, and so on?" The child reached up to pull his hair, and he gently pried the little fingers loose.

Garset shook his head. "No. That would be like constantly pleading for a delay. If we are going to take this rash course of action, we need to do it quickly. Shambor will be expecting us to leave the forest eventually, but not at once."

"So we should attack immediately? Like, tomorrow?"

"Perhaps not tomorrow, but ..."

"I have a suggestion," Frengor said. "Why don't we ask God to show us how soon the attack should be launched, by the amount of food he sends? If he sends us enough for three days, we'll prepare to set out on the fourth day; if we receive food for two days, we'll prepare for the third day—and so on."

Garset smiled and shrugged. "We're praying some daring prayers. Why not?"

"Then let's ask the One right now," Frengor said.

They sat, palms upward on their laps, and each in turn asked the One Creator God to confirm that they should march on Darthane, by sending them enough food today for as many days as they should take to prepare for the attack.

Afterwards Garset could see that others felt God's peace, as he did. Brakhól looked from one to the other and gave his infectious chuckle. They all laughed.

Later at the dawnmeal, Garset announced that their food had run out, and Shambor was blockading the forest, preventing more supplies from coming in. He appealed to all to pray, but said nothing about attacking Darthane or their request for confirmation. A spirit of sober concern spread through the camp—but with the child projecting the peace of his immediate circle, there was neither panic nor despair.

Frengor summoned them all to worship after the meal. Over a thousand men and women gathered in concentric circles round the cooking fires, the crowd stretching back among the tents, while the small priest climbed up on an open wagon where all could see him. With his strong, carrying voice he led them in asking God to supply their needs, and they sang songs of trust and praise. Garset only wished Danîsha were there to accompany them on the bellaril.

Then came a rousing talk by the Visionary, encouraging them to have implicit trust in the God who had sent his own son to die so that they could live. They closed by celebrating that act of overwhelming love in the quiet adoration of the *Limmeris Narac*, the Remembrance of Flame. All came away encouraged, Garset felt. No matter what the outcome of their request for confirmation, this army was trusting God.

* * *

It happened in the late morning, when the cooks would have been preparing the midmeal. Sergeant Cârinor came running up to Garset with the news that a food wagon from Larris was on its way to them! Garset could hardly believe it. He called Shiván and Frengor, and with Cârin they hurried along the rough-hewn track. Before long they heard the bellowings of the grûnet. The heavily-laden wagon lumbered into view, creaking to a halt as it reached them. The carter confirmed that he'd been sent by Sharmeron, the trader who'd given them his food a couple of days ago. When they asked about the vehicle that had been turned back yesterday, he shrugged his shoulders.

"Dunno 'bout that. I seen troops on the roads, but there weren't none around when I came through."

They escorted the wagon into the camp, where there was wholesale rejoicing. Then Shiván summoned the other Captains, Dolmet and Hastor, to one of their own half-empty wagons. They had to squat on boxes and barrels, their heads brushing the canvas cover; but it was necessary to minimise the risk of Shambor finding them with the blaise and bess. Shiván had given the Grûzhack child to Jomel, after explaining to her what had happened. The girl's joy was communicating to Brakhól, and there were shouts of laughter around the camp.

They told Hastor and Dolmet the whole story. Hastor was a tall, sandy-haired man with keen eyes in a thin face. He immediately declared himself impressed by God's obvious hand in the situation. Dolmet, however, had a permanently dubious expression on his heavy features. It took much longer to convince him, and after half an hour's fruitless discussion Shiván fetched Frengor. The Visionary's obvious commitment to the plan had its effect.

The decision was finally made. They would do the impossible, and break through Shambor's cordon around the Larwood to attack Darthane itself. Tomorrow, since they had only received one day's food.

Chapter 35: *Victory and defeat*

SHAMBOR SAVOURED PERRELY'S FLUID MOVEMENTS as she mounted her horse. Hands clasping the grips on each of the animal's humps, a foot in the stirrup, then a smooth swing up and over into the saddle, the riding boots below her culottes sliding neatly into place. She set his heart pounding with a tentative smile as she took the reins from the stable boy. This outing to the Bishop's Park had been a good idea. It was cold, but dry; and the girl looked charming in the fur-lined riding coat he'd found her.

They set off at a brisk trot along the wide bridle path. On either side the trees stood bare on a fading carpet of golden leaves. In the distance a troop of grey-cloaked Guards shadowed them. It was un-avoidable—he could not allow the girl to escape—but the riders would come no nearer unless she left his side.

Perrely ignored them. Her eyes drank in the bleak beauty of trees, earth and sky. From time to time she lifted her head to sniff the clean autumn air.

"Enjoying it?" he asked.

"Yes, this is wonderful. Thank you." Again that tantalising half-smile.

"I'm glad."

They rode on in silence. Then she asked, "How is the war going?"

"Not too badly. We've been unable to dislodge the Grûzhack from Dhembis or Leváris, but they haven't advanced any further."

"Not that war. I meant the one against my friends."

"Oh." He shifted uncomfortably in the saddle and cleared his throat. "It hasn't gone too well for your friends." She shot him an anxious glance. "They are unhurt, but their army has mostly been destroyed."

"And Shiván?" The pleading in her eyes was like a knife in his heart.

"Shiván, as far as I know, is still leading them."

Joy blossomed in her face before she could mask it. "Are you… trying to defeat him?"

"Yes, I'm afraid so. He's the one attacking me, my lady."

She nodded and dropped her eyes.

They rode out of the trees into an open area of the park, where green lawns sloped down to the reed-fringed margin of Darthane Water. In Flowering and Summer there was a riot of colour here, but now the flowerbeds lay fallow and the ornamental shrubs were bare, though the trees still revelled in their autumn glory. Across the Water rose the high, yellowstone wall of Darthane. A faint echo of the city's activity drifted across the lake, emphasising the quiet remoteness of the park.

Shambor looked at Perrely as she rode alongside him. She was gazing across the Water, and again, as he had several times before, he sensed an underlying sadness in her shiláy. It was strangely at odds with her joy at hearing that Shiván had escaped—yet somehow, he knew, it was bound up with her feelings for the young foreigner. There was a barrier between them whose exact nature he couldn't fathom. Not without invading her mind, and that he could not bring himself to do.

But this sadness was the one thing that gave him hope. Maybe she found Shiván too young and callow. Maybe one day she would see past her empty Lightist ideals and respond to him, Shambor, as a successful, experienced man who would cherish her and lay the world before her...

Perrely turned to watch the lake as they followed the bridle path along its margin. A flock of green-and-gold *eyret* burst out of the reeds ahead of them with a great clatter of wings. The girl watched them dwindling towards the grey clouds and her shiláy darkened. It wasn't hard to guess her thoughts.

Shambor thrust aside the pain. He knew she would rather be with Shiván. In military terms this bond between Perrely and the Overguardian was crying out to be exploited. He was all too aware that Shiván was extremely resourceful: Shambor had underestimated him in the past, and would not do so again. Shiván now had both the Ambon and the *Gorelenyu*. His mind told him that against Shiván, Perrely was the most effective military weapon that could have fallen into his hands—after the *Gorelenyu*. Though he shuddered to think of it, an innocent young woman was the next best thing to an innocent child: and if tortured, the telepathic effect of her suffering would be almost as great as the Child's on those who loved her—including himself.

But that would be the very last resort. He still had his Guards and the Strongholder's newly-arrived cavalry legions. Only if they failed, and Shiván was threatening Darthane itself, would he be forced to make the agonising choice between love and survival. The very thought filled his heart with pain. He'd do anything rather than that. She was all he'd ever desired in a woman.

He gazed at Perrely's profile, lifted up to the sky. He longed to clasp her in his arms.

One day.

* * *

The Restorers' army left camp in the early hours and made their way cautiously through the thick, tangled forest. Cârin and the other scouts preceded them in a wide arc, checking for enemy troops. Bit by bit the reports trickled back to Shiván, Garset and the other two captains. The enemy was everywhere, west, east and south. In places they'd penetrated the forest, setting up 'listening posts' hidden among the thickets of undergrowth. Shiván's heart sank. It would truly be a Gideon-like achievement to break through the cordon Shambor had set up.

Garset called a halt to discuss strategy. Hastor and Dolmet favoured caution, carefully probing the cordon to find the weakest point. But Garset, to Shiván's surprise, agreed with him and Frengor that in keeping with his dream they should simply storm through to Distack, a village on the nearest country road that led to Darthane. They recalled the scouts, and when all were ready Cârin raised the Ambon. Its high, clarion call trumpeted defiance at the enemy. They set off at a trot in a long line along one of the few forest paths, Shiván in the vanguard with the Blade of Darthane gleaming in his hand. Towards the rear Jomel ran, with Brakhól strapped to her back chortling with excitement.

An enemy patrol of ten soldiers appeared briefly ahead of them — then scattered with cries of alarm. The Restorers' army didn't stop. A little further they met a hastily erected barricade of logs and bushes across the path. Cår thrust the Ambon skyward and Shiván raised the Blade. As the trumpet sounded the terrified soldiers manning the barricade fled. They leapt over it and thrust it aside.

Now they were getting closer to Distack. Soldiers appeared on either side of them, but became tangled in the thick undergrowth, and in places seemed to fighting one another. Cries and battle noises echoed through the forest.

Then, up ahead, they saw a full cohort of a hundred infantry blocking their path. Shiván was in the lead. For an instant the old fear descended on him—was he truly going to kill or maim people? He sent a desperate plea to the One who was his refuge and strength. *Remember the Blade*, came the reply. *Yes!* He whirled the Blade above his head. Enemy eyes widened and swept from side to side, seeing three attackers for every one approaching. They melted away and Shiván praised the One Creator God.

Moments later they broke out of the forest. To their left a couple of aldoret away was a small village—Distack. Immediately ahead of them were two squadrons of Bishop's Guards—two hundred menacing grey figures on horseback with drawn longswords. In the distance was the road, with more troops swarming on it. Shiván halted, and Garset raised a hand to bring the rest of their troops to a stop. With rapid hand movements he directed them to spread out left and right into a long line facing the Guards.

"We outnumber them, but they're mounted and their longswords are deadly," Garset warned. "It'll be a hard fight; we'll lose quite a few."

Shiván sent up another lightning prayer. Then he smiled at Garset as the Guards began to advance slowly towards them. "No, they'll melt away like Gîdion's enemies. You'll see." He turned and called, "Jomel! Bring Brakhól!"

From the rear Jomel hurried forward, panting, Brakhól in her arms. When the child saw Shiván a broad smile appeared on his face. "Shibán!" He stretched his arms out. "Bounce him to me!" Shiván told Jomel, handing his Blade to Garset.

Jomel repeated the game they'd played in camp, while the Guards came closer. They were now only a couple of hundred paces away, and gaining speed. The soldiers' eyes switched anxiously from the little tableau around Shiván to the Guards and back.

Brakhól gave a squeal of delight, and a wave of joy swept over the opposing troops. The Restorers' soldiers roared with renewed vigour and defiance, while the Guards' advance suddenly lost its impetus. Some of the horses stumbled, others careened into them, and there were cries of fear and pain. Shiván bounced Brakhól back to Jomel, and his infectious laughter triggered another wave of sheer happiness. The Guards' line stumbled to a halt, and some horses trotted off, their riders clasping their heads. As Brakhól continued broadcasting happiness, more and more Guards broke ranks, until all were in retreat.

Shiván grinned at Jomel. "Thank you!" She returned his smile, bouncing Brakhól in her arms. Shiván tousled the child's head, then nodded, and Jomel took him back to the rear.

"Câr! The Ambon! Let's go!" he shouted, and they trotted after the Guards towards the country road that would take them to Darthane.

On the road there was chaos. Infantry and cavalry were fighting one another and the fleeing Guards. Câr kept the Ambon raised, two other scouts alongside to relieve him when he tired. The stirring calls kept ringing out, and as they reached the road many of the unmindbent troops there joined them, while others fled the confusion.

Finally they slowed to a steady march. Shiván glanced up at the sun: it was not yet noon. It had taken five hours and no fighting at all to break through the Bishop's cordon. He turned to Garset and grinned. "Well, what do you say to Gîdion — your little fool — now?"

A rare smile touched the Captain's face. "You were right!"

Captains Hastor and Dolmet were beside them in the lead. "We did the impossible, thanks to your Book and the One!" Hastet declared.

Dolmet nodded, his grim face almost relaxed. "Wouldn't have believed it if I hadn't seen it myself."

"Praise to the One Creator God!" Frengor cried behind them, and the whole army took up the refrain.

As they approached Distack, the Ambon's calls still sounding, infantrymen from the garrison there came streaming out to meet them. Weapons were drawn but soon replaced as the new troops joined them, jostling to be close to the One's emblem. Shiván learned that only Lightist troops now remained in the village — the rest had fled.

"Join us for the midmeal!" one of them said. "We have plenty of food — just been resupplied!"

Shiván and Garset gratefully accepted. Soon close to fifteen hundred men and women were crowded in and around the village square, standing, sitting and sprawled on the ground, while at the barracks and in many private homes warm meals were prepared.

* * *

During the midmeal Shiván and the Captains discussed their next move. There were too many of them to stay overnight in Distack — besides which, if they delayed they'd only give Shambor time to regroup. Despite some head-shaking on Dolmet's part, they decided to "strike while the iron was hot", as Shiván put it. The Captains smiled at the novel expression.

Before long the Restorers' army was marching south-east along the country road towards Dûrion's capital city. Pale sunshine lit up the brown, harvested fields of the Plain of Darthane. In the south the yellow walls of the city towered up, fixed and immovable in the clear morning air. Cârin held the Ambon high in the vanguard, the circle gleaming with light as the clear, sweet trumpet tones rang out.

What a glorious sight they would have made, Shiván thought, if they'd equalled the ten thousand who marched behind the Ambon in the Founders' time! Their numbers had increased this morning, but they were still only a legion and a half — a laughable army compared to the thousands Shambor could bring against them.

Yet, as he walked in front with Cârin and the Captains Garset, Hastor and Dolmet, Shiván felt a deep peace within him. This march could not have been more different from their disastrous progress towards Stillárre. Now everyone shared the certainty that the One Creator God was leading them — fools though they might appear to others.

And somewhere in the centre of the column, Jomel was carrying Brakhól. The child who had caused their deep despair before, was now calming their hearts with his contentment. As Frengor had said, joy lighting every wrinkle in his face, the *Gorelenyu* — the Child of Despair — had become the Child of Hope, and had proved this morning just how effective he was in that rôle.

Scouts came cantering back from reconnoitring the way ahead. "Cavalry on the northern highway! At least two legions, with infantry in the rear."

So. They would have to fight their way on to the highway — the only feasible route to Darthane. Well, they'd expected that.

An hour later Garset raised his hand to call a halt. Half an aldor ahead — seven hundred yards — their country road reached the highway. On the highway itself a wall of horses stood blocking the way. No other traffic was to be seen. Only the snuffling and stamping of the animals and the occasional creak of armour disturbed the total stillness.

Garset turned to Shiván. "Right, Overguardian. This will be the real test of what the Blade of Darthane, the Ambon of Sûrilane and the Child of Hope can do together."

"And fifteen hundred soldiers of the Light," Shiván added. His smile belied the tension within him. This was the moment of truth.

With a ring of steel he drew the Blade.

* * *

Mindruler Shambor sat hunched over his dining table, focusing the blaise on the white cloth. Beside him Gelmion stood with the bess held to his ear, and the bellaril lay further down the table. The picture on the white fabric showed Shiván and those renegade Captains on the one side, and the Selmian cavalry on the other. From the bellaril came distant, woody voices. He'd given instructions to his subordinate Mindbenders that he was not to be disturbed for any reason.

If both Shambor's hands hadn't been holding the blaise, he would have been rubbing them together. The little fools! They were going to launch a direct attack. After the utter fluke of their breakout this morning—he still trembled with rage over that, and heads would roll—they thought the Blade, the Ambon and the Child could defeat his Selmian cavalry. The utter, over-confident imbeciles! The cavalry commanders had been warned about the Blade. Its effect would be temporary. As for the Ambon, a few infantrymen had already started responding to it, but their Captains—good, ambitious men who'd been promised high rewards—had dealt with them swiftly.

Then the Child. Those poor, deluded innocents, thinking it would have the reverse effect on his troops! What they'd failed to appreciate was that it was Bishop's Guards whom the Child had scattered during their breakout. *Mindbent* troops. The Child's effect on the *un*mindbent soldiers now facing them would be exactly the same as on their own troops.

It was a good thing the Selmian cavalry had arrived yesterday. Otherwise, with the vast majority of his unmindbent troops away fighting the Grûzhack and the few he'd kept here now scattered, he would be in the precarious position of again opposing the Child's positive broadcasts with mindbent Guards.

But as it was, the Child would not be positive for much longer. He would soon return to his proper function.

* * *

As Shiván swung the Blade up, Garset gave the signal to charge. With a roar the Restorers' army began streaming along the final straight towards the highway and the waiting cavalry. Cârin ran beside Shiván holding the Ambon aloft. The trumpet sound immediately changed to a continuous, rousing battle call.

Sparing a glance upward, Shiván saw that the ancient emblem was pulsing with light. "Restore the Way of the One!" the trumpet seemed to cry. Joy filled his heart, and righteous anger flamed within him. Evil had stained this beautiful land. The Way of peace, of truth, of justice had been perverted. Men who served the dark god had seized an authority to which they had no right. It was time to sweep them away! To make a straight path for the Prince of Peace. To break down every barrier to the waiting flood of his cleansing Light.

Such was the force of their attack that the massed ranks of cavalry gave way before them. They gained the highway, and began driving the milling horsemen south towards Darthane. Exultation filled Shiván's heart, sweeping away the last of his fears about causing physical harm. He and Garset and the other Captains were bringing down horses, driving their riders back, preventing the enemy from regrouping. Shiván used the Blade in combination with his martial arts as he'd learnt at the Battle of Berûvis; and it seemed that no one could stand against him. The vanguard of their army was filling the highway, pushing forward while the enemy troops were falling over themselves.

They continued for what seemed like an hour, driving the disorganised cavalry down the highway. Sweat stood out on Shiván's brow as he kicked, swiped, dodged, blocked. In the confusion he went from one encounter to another, leaving others to finish off what he'd begun, or leaping in to help a comrade. But he knew he'd killed at least three of the enemy, pulling one from his horse, stabbing another from below, running the third through when his mount fell. The righteous anger that filled him allowed no remorse.

Then there was a prolonged horn blast from among the Selmian cavalry. The horsemen in their dark tan tunics rallied. Somehow the milling confusion of riders and mounts resolved itself into a solid line again, and they began pushing back. Garset was shouting *"Retreat! Retreat!"* Shiván glanced around, and saw with a shock that cavalrymen were pressing in from the left and right, as well as ahead. It was a trap: they were being encircled! Cârin had passed the Ambon to a lieutenant from one of the other companies, and was guarding Shiván's back.

Jomel and the Child! If the circle were closed, they would be in danger. He could *not* allow Brakhól to be killed or recaptured. He struggled back through the retreating soldiers with Câr beside him, shouting encouragement, until he found Jomel. She was standing wide-eyed clutching Brakhól, surrounded by the remnant of Garset's Pure Company. They cheered when they saw Shiván.

There was blood on Jomel's cheek. "Are you all right?" he shouted.

"Yes, just a graze. Thank you for coming!"

Brakhól reached out for Shiván, joy on his ugly little face. But Shiván gently shook his head, and held the Blade ready to defend them.

The Ambon was making a different sound now — a more mournful, intermittent call. Shiván took it to be the Retreat. They kept moving north, and for a while it looked as if they might make it to a nearby hill. Then the Pure Company was fighting all around them, and Shiván saw the Selmian cavalry closing in at the rear. Cârin was fighting beside Garset, dodging the downward swipes of a cavalryman who was scowling with the effort of trying to make his blade connect with the agile Dûrian scout. A sudden upward thrust from Câr and the man slumped forward on his horse before slowly falling out of the saddle. But all the time the Selmian cavalry pressed inexorably inwards and more Dûrians fell.

Shiván glanced at Jomel. She looked terrified, and there was doubt on Brakhól's face. The underlying optimism that supported their army was wavering. Shiván gave the kid a wide grin, and was rewarded with a small spike of happiness.

The Pure Company was fighting valiantly, but the grim-faced Selmian riders were slowly cutting their way through the ring that surrounded Jomel and the child. One defender after another fell. Shiván and Cârin were brothers of the blade, defending each other and the two non-combatants in the centre. Shiván continued using his martial arts together with crude swordsmanship, kicking and head-butting as well as striking with the Blade. Praise the One, Brakhól's eyes were following Shiván's antics and he chuckled occasionally, as if this entertainment were being provided especially for his benefit.

Shiván leapt to help Câr when a cavalryman struck the sword from his hand. The Blade of Darthane flashed in a downward arc, and the enemy's lance was shattered. The Blade's return swing slashed the horse's ribs. The animal screamed and reared. Shiván's right hand seized the rider's flailing arm, and yanked down hard. The horseman catapulted out of the saddle. A swift thrust, and he was out of the picture. "Thanks," Câr muttered as he rapidly retrieved his sword.

There were cries of relief as a large contingent of spearmen pressed in from the south to join them. The Ambon bearer was with them, still holding the precious emblem aloft. The beleaguered Pure Company stood aside for the spearmen, whose longer weapons were more effective.

Somewhere behind him Shiván heard Garset shouting, "Break out to the north! To the north!"—but at that moment a cavalryman lunged directly towards Jomel and the Child, and Shiván lashed out with the Blade to fend him off. Then someone tripped him, and everything became confused. Brakhól screamed and darkness crashed over Shiván as he saw the Child snatched out of Jomel's arms and swept up on to the cavalryman's horse. Both armies faltered as Brakhól's terror pulsed out over the battlefield—but then the rider was gone, galloping through the enemy's ranks toward Darthane.

Shiván staggered to his feet, stunned. This could not have happened! Dimly beside him he was aware of Jomel sobbing. Then the jagged anguish of Brakhól's terror stabbed his heart. He'd failed the child. As well as Garset and all who had risked everything to fight with him today. In the end the great enemy army hadn't melted away. It had surged over them and snatched Brakhól—and with him most of their hope.

Gideon's victory had been followed by a little fool's defeat.

* * *

Cârin seized Shiván and dragged him out of danger and into a small group led by Garset, which included Jomel and the Ambon. The sacred emblem was trumpeting the Retreat more urgently now.

Their minds buffeted by Brakhól's pain, the small, close-knit group fought their way through Shambor's troops, northward toward the Herm Downs. Shiván saw soldiers falling all around him, protecting him and the Ambon, and his heart cried out in anguish to God.

* * *

Finally they found clear highway in front of them. Just ahead the land rose in small, knobbly hills towards Herminar.

"That cleft up there!" Garset shouted. Through the mist of despair Shiván saw the cleft he meant, through which the highway passed. It was bounded on both sides by cliffs and rough ground — not a place that could easily be encircled. He ran towards it, his breath coming in ragged gasps.

Suddenly Cârin cried out, "Stop! Listen! What's that noise?"

"No stopping!" Garset bellowed. "We need a safe —" Then he heard it. So did Shiván and the other survivors. A deep, resonant sound to the north, drawing slowly nearer. Like the distant baying of a vast pack of wolves.

"Shiván, what is it?" Jomel cried, huddling closer to him.

Garset came to a standstill. Their pursuers heard it too, and pulled their horses up, milling about uncertainly.

"*It's the Dorbians!*" Cârin shouted, leaping in the air and swirling his sword in a circle.

"Gwargif! He's come!" Shiván exclaimed, joy flushing the despair from his heart. "Garset, we must clear the highway! Let them through!"

With a few rapped-out commands Garset had them all running for a patch of woodland just off the road. Some of the Selmians came after them, but straggled to a halt as the wild, primitive baying grew louder and closer. Both attackers and defenders turned to stare north. Cârin thrust the Ambon skyward, and a challenging trumpet call rang out.

The cleft in the highway changed colour as a grey tide flowed through it.

"The Dorbian Legion!" Shiván yelled.

"The Dorbian Legion!" Garset and the Pure Company took it up as a battle cry.

The grey flood swept rapidly nearer. Wolf heads became visible, jaws wide, fangs gleaming, the deep baying of five thousand voices drowning out all other sounds. They spread out below the cleft, bearing down on the Selmian cavalry. At the centre Shiván thought he could see a familiar figure.

The feral scent of the Dorbians reached the Selmians' horses, and they reared up, neighing in terror. Riders had their hands full trying to control their mounts. Garset and his men charged back into the fray, Cârin with them, pulling horsemen down, driving them back, killing those who'd fallen. The air was full of the screams of horses and the cries of desperate men. Captain Hastor brought his remaining archers to bear, and a shower of deadly arrows fell among the seething mass of Selmian cavalry. Shiván stayed back with Jomel, holding high the Ambon.

Then suddenly the howls of the approaching Dorbians burst into a full-throated roar as they charged. The Selmian horses reared and plunged, screaming, fighting one another to escape. Riders were thrown, others clung helplessly to their mounts. The Dorbians leapt on the backs of the riders, bringing them down with their horses. Enemy soldiers cried out in terror as the grey, snarling forms of Gwargif's warriors fell upon them. Shambor's infantry broke ranks and fled. The Ambon's call changed to a stirring paean of victory that sang out over the noise of battle. In time to it the Restorers' army cried "*For the Light! For the Light!*" as they sent the Selmians fleeing back to Darthane.

Shiván met Gwargif for a brief moment. Jomel screamed as the great, grey-white wolf leapt towards them. Then they saw the smile on his dark, intelligent face. He paused beside Shiván.

"Father of Warriors, we have come!"

"Praise the One! You were just in time."

Gwargif gave a small bark that might have been a laugh. Then a grim, intent look settled over his features. "Now we kill darkness." He bounded off.

The Dorbians knew no mercy. The remaining horses had stampeded back towards Darthane, some with riders still clinging to them. The Dorbians pursued them. Shiván watched as they systematically destroyed Shambor's army. The Dorbians easily outran the horses, and all over the southern plain he could see grey shapes leaping on the riders' backs, or snapping at the mounts until they stumbled and fell. The escaping foot soldiers disappeared under heaving grey mounds.

Shiván remembered Gwargif's words long ago about 'smelling' Light, and his deep anger against all who darkened it. Today that anger was multiplied five thousandfold, and over two thousand agents of darkness died. Only a couple of dozen made it to the city gate.

The great army had melted away after all.

But they had taken Brakhól.

Chapter 36: *Deepening despair*

SHAMBOR SAT AT THE GREAT BLACKWOOD TABLE in his reception chamber, clenching his fists. Gelmion stood beside him, grinding his teeth. Secretary Estaron stood at his writing table beside the door, calmly continuing with his administrative duties.

"Two legions, Gelmion! Wiped out. The *Selmian cavalry*, by the seven portals!" The red-faced Bishop rounded on Gelmion, his eyes wild and heavy jowls quivering. "What am I going to say to the Strongholder?"

"I don't know, your Radiance." Inside the Guard uniform, Gil seethed with frustration. A punching-bag. That's all he was these days. Destined to stand forever beside this maniac mouthing soothing platitudes. That used to be Estaron's job, but that aloof so-and-so was excused now, and glanced at Gil from time to time with thinly-veiled amusement.

Returning his unfocussed gaze back to the opulent reception chamber, Shambor continued his rant. "Who could have expected the Dorbians to arrive *here*? They were expected at Carreck Manor. And to come in such numbers! The 'Dorbian Legion'. A legion is *one* thousand!" He banged a fist on the shiny blackwood table. "How was I supposed to deduce that one thousand at Carreck Manor would turn into five thousand here? And my subordinate in the north, Mindbender Hollet—he can't have missed five thousand Dorbians crossing his territory! Why did I hear nothing from him?"

You heard nothing, Gil thought, *because you gave instructions not to be disturbed on pain of physical mutilation.*

With a typical switch of emotions, Shambor turned to Gelmion again, smiling grimly. "But we recaptured the *Gorelenyu!* That was a well-executed manoeuvre. It will go some way towards appeasing the Strongholder, I'm sure. And those rebels won't do so well against the Child of Despair! Tomorrow I'll send my Guards legion against them—though they're my only defence here in Darthane (apart from the city red-cloaks, and they're useless). I've recalled two Guard legions from the Grûzhack War..." His voice trailed off.

Yes, Gil thought, *and next thing the Grûzhack will be seizing more Dûrian towns and you'll be in even deeper trouble with the Strongholder. How did I ever imagine I was joining the winning side?*

"The Child will go with the Guards," Shambor continued, "along with some of my Mindbenders to torture him: his pain won't affect mindbent troops. But my Mindbenders won't be as effective as the trained Selmian Keepers. Thanks to *you* losing the Ambon—" Shambor shot Gelmion a poisoned glance: pain lanced through him, making him gasp "—the only trained Keepers were killed last time. So we'll somehow have to make do."

Gil's inner thoughts turned to the Dorbians. *How would they—?*

Shambor anticipated his question with a muttered comment. "We'll see what effect the *Gorelenyu* has on the Dorbians."

* * *

"Gari."

There it was. Shambor swallowed convulsively. He'd sent Gelmion out while he waited for the inevitable. *"Yes, your Supremacy."*

"Now you've lost my cavalry." It was a bald statement of fact. *"Of the two thousand I sent, less than a hundred remain."*

"Yes, Supremacy, I deeply regret that, but they were up against—"

"I know what they were up against. Your lack of forethought."

"I— Yes, your Supremacy." You didn't argue with that mind-tone.

"In fact they were up against the monumental incompetence you've shown ever since you allowed your troops to blunder up to a Grûzhack fortress."

There was a pause. Shambor didn't dare break it. He sat staring down at his blackwood dining table, shivering slightly, his hands between his knees.

"If it did not involve taking over the whole Dûrian network at a moment's notice— and *the oversight of two wars—I would strip you of your position right now and send a replacement as Mindruler. But that* will *happen. Soon.*

"Your time is over, Gari. Do you understand?"

Shambor struggled to take in the enormity of what the Strongholder was saying. Not, stripped of his autonomy (which might later be restored); but stripped of his position—which would never be restored once someone else took over as Mindruler.

"DO YOU UNDERSTAND?"

He arched backward on his chair at the accompanying pain, and almost fell to the floor. "*Y–yes, Sup– premacy.*"

The Strongholder continued in his quiet voice, which struck more terror into Shambor's quivering soul than his shouting. "*Your rescue of the* Gorelenyu *shows a slight residue of good sense that might just enable you to defeat these upstart 'Restorers'. I will leave you to complete that one last task. When it is done I will send your replacement. Then you will join me in Orselm.*"

A slow horror began to spread over Shambor's mind.

"*Should you fail again, you will come to Selmion while your replacement deals with the Restorers. Here you will experience every day what your enemies felt when you lured them to the* Gorelenyu.*"* The horror deepened into abject despair. Shambor slumped forward over the blackwood table, bereft of the will even to sit upright. A pitiless vista of empty existence opened before him, devoid of all significance, stretching to the distant horizon. He would spend the rest of his days in a hopelessness so complete that he could barely comprehend it.

"*This is just a taste, Gari, of what will happen if you fail. If you succeed against the Restorers –*" Gari felt the darkness lessen, and his mind clutched desperately at the tiny ray of hope. "*– you will still come to Selmion, where you will perform whatever small tasks I may find for you. But whether you defeat these Restorers or not, your days as a Mindruler are over. Is that clear?*"

This time the Strongholder did not wait for a reply. His young, uncompromising strength and absolute control slowly faded from Shambor's mind, and with it the utter blackness that deprived him of the will to live — yet left him living.

He lay gasping on the blackwood table.

* * *

This was the third night Lannie had crept out of Bishop Harlon's apartment to search for 'Neesh and Perrely, and she still hadn't found them. The poor Bishop was becoming increasingly anxious about her. Two days ago there'd been a thorough search of Harlon's rooms: she'd only avoided capture by hiding in an under-floor cavity where the Bishop kept a few precious possessions he didn't want Shambor to find. For once she'd been grateful for her small size.

Tonight she was making a more extensive search of the top floor of the Cathedral, where Bishop Harlon's apartment was located.

Her heart thudded as she trotted silently up the passage. She was wearing a black robe over a dark brown shift, which she'd shortened. Below it she wore brown woollen stockings, without shoes. She was holding a small shuttered lantern the Bishop had found for her. From time to time she raised the shutter briefly, allowing a wavering beam to give her her bearings.

She passed her old storeroom-cell, and made her way further through the maze of passages, keeping careful track of her turns.

After a while she came to a bleak, walled-off section of cubicles that seemed deserted. She followed a servants' access way behind it and took a risk, opening the lantern shutter. There were back doors to the cubicles, and she peered through the small grilles. The lantern's flickering light revealed a ghastly array of implements whose purpose was only too clear: wheels and racks, chairs with protruding nails, pincers, mallets, wicked-looking objects that might be thumbscrews. Many of the wooden surfaces had dark stains on them, and there was an unpleasant smell. Torture chambers, in the Cathedral! She grimaced and moved on quickly.

But there were no more discoveries that night. In the early hours she made her way back to the Bishop's apartment. He was half-asleep in a recliner and jerked awake as he heard her entering.

"My dear, I'm so relieved to see you!"

She smiled wearily at the tousled old man in his blue satin houserobe. "I'm glad to be back."

He levered himself up out of the recliner. "Now, I expect you'd enjoy a cup of chass."

"You never said a truer word."

They went through to the kitchen to make the beverage. "It looks as if you didn't find your friends tonight," the Bishop said as he prepared the percolator.

"No, but I found something else." She described the torture cubicles. Harlon's eyes went round with horror, and he exclaimed repeatedly about the unspeakable evil of torture in the Cathedral, the High Hearth of the One Creator God.

They chatted together as they finished their chass before turning in to sleep.

* * *

Jomel sat on a small rise outside the makeshift camp, tears trickling down her cheeks. To the left and right low cliffs arose, the sides of the cleft in the Herm Downs that enclosed them. Ahead, to the south, the Bishop's Guards fought to break through the ranks of Dorbian warriors and Dûrian soldiers that held them at bay.

Mostly Dorbians. When they'd done a count last night they'd found that of the fifteen hundred Dûrian troops they'd set out with from Distack—was it only midday yesterday?—just over three hundred remained. Jomel shivered, as she always did when she thought of that terrible battle; especially the moment when the horsemen were pressing in, and one of them snatched Brakhól right out of her arms...

Since then there had been no time to rest. The Dorbians had rescued them, and they'd set up a makeshift camp in the cleft, where she'd passed a sleepless night mourning Brakhól and fearing what would happen now they'd lost their best defence. Shiván had announced a war council for this morning, but there'd been no time for that: new Guard companies on foot had attacked at the crack of dawn, and very soon afterwards an aching darkness had fallen on them—the darkness of an innocent child helplessly broadcasting his pain.

Nearby a grizzled Dûrian warrior sat on a rock, fidgeting restlessly with his sword. Jomel knew he would much rather be in the battle below than guarding her. Yet his eyes, too, were moist. What good person could fail to weep at the suffering that flooded their hearts? Especially if you knew the child being tortured. Even more so if you knew all he had already been through. She had cared for Brakhól ever since the Ambush, and had learnt to love the outgoing, cheerful spirit inside his ugly little body. Her heart ached for him now.

His terrible screams echoed in their minds despite the noise of battle. She clasped her hands to her eyes to try and shut out the dreadful picture of that small form strapped to a table somewhere behind the battlefield, grey-cloaked Mindbenders cutting and mutilating while they broadcast his agony, battering all hearts—except the heartless Guards—with an unrelenting anguish that drained them of strength and thought.

From the Dorbians' sluggish movements compared to yesterday she guessed that it affected even them, though maybe to a lesser extent. The clear trumpet calls of the Ambon, held aloft just inside the camp, seemed to be the only thing that kept the army fighting the total annihilation the Guards intended for them. Their original goal of attacking Darthane now seemed a distant dream.

Yet despite it all, Jomel was aware that the pain Brakhól was now broadcasting was not the all-encompassing, mind-numbing despair they'd experienced in the Ambush. It was a good deal less than that; and she offered up a quick prayer of thanks to the One.

* * *

Though pain enveloped his world, Brakhól's agony was for his lost friends. *Shibán! Jomil! Where are you? Why haven't you come? Why am I back with these bad men who are hurting me?* A knife sliced his finger and he screamed. *"Shibán!"* Why didn't he come? He came before. He took him away from the bad men. Shibán loved him. He looked after him. And Jomil. They would come for him again. They *must* come again. They would stop all this hurting.

Shibán! Jomil!

Chapter 37: *Captives connect*

GARSET SAT IN A TENT with the Overguardian, Visionary Frengor, the Dorbian Commander, and Captain Hastet. Garset regretted the death of Dolmet, captain of the other company who had joined them. Now they had this Dorbian with them—Gwargif, his outlandish name was. He and Hastet kept glancing uneasily at the creature. The great, grey... animal? person?—sat serenely upright like a dog on the floor of the tent, while Garset and the others squatted on a motley collection of stools and chairs. Their heads were at the same height. He was still trying to get his mind around the fact that this Dorbian was intelligent, spoke Dûrian, and was now their most important ally.

The purpose of the council of war, hastily summoned during one of the lulls in the fighting, was to discuss their current predicament. The lulls occurred every hour or so, presumably to give poor Brakhól a break. At first they'd taken advantage of them to attack without Brakhól's despair disabling them; but now they found they were too much in need of a break themselves. The constant gusts of pain wore people down, sapped their strength, and confused their thinking. Even now Garset was finding it hard to concentrate.

"I'm sorry, Gwargif," the Overguardian was saying. "Your warriors are doing most of the work. Our people are badly affected by the torture."

The Dorbian gave a little shake of his head. "Is Dorbi is fight. Is fight hard. But dark-pain hit Dorbi too." A low growl rumbled in his throat, making Garset start. "Is want to *kill* dark people, *stop* dark-pain... But no room for fight!"

Garset nodded. In their exhaustion after the battle with the Selmian cavalry they had camped in the cleft, the Dorbians ranged below and above them. It had seemed like a good idea at the time. But the Guards arrived the next morning and started torturing poor Brakhól, and in the following confusion they'd driven the Dorbians and Shiván's forces back into the cleft, blocking its southern opening and the road to Darthane. Now they were stuck in a bottleneck, with a long journey over difficult terrain to the east or west if they were to try and circle round the Guards.

Also, the Dorbians were not doing well fighting at close quarters. They needed open ground to run and leap at their enemies. Here the Guards' longswords kept them at bay and did steady, terrible damage. Ninety-four Dorbian warriors already lay buried behind the camp.

"We need to break out!" Hastor said. "If scouts could... could..." He groaned and clasped his head for a moment.

Garset knew how he felt. "Could show the way," he continued for him.

"Yes, then your warriors," Hastor nodded to Gwargif, "could follow, and—"

"We come behind dark people," Gwargif completed. "Yes, we can do. But is take time."

"And time is what we haven't got," Shiván said. "Food is running out. If we divide our forces we need separate supplies—which we can only get from Herminar at the moment."

"We also know," Frengor added, "that Shambor must already have summoned all the troops who were guarding the Larwood. They may arrive at any moment, and could attack us from, er, from—"

"From behind," Shiván concluded. "Dividing our forces may not be a good— *Aaaaagh!*"

They all cried out and Gwargif yelped as distant screams and new shafts agony pierced their tired minds.

"Council is over," the Overguardian said. "We'll try again tonight. Frengor, keep praying!"

"I will. Oh yes, I will."

They hurried back to their posts.

* * *

The next day, during another lull, Shiván stood with Garset and Cârin at the top of the western side of the cleft overlooking the battlefield. Câr was holding the Ambon upright, and its unimpeded influence washed over them and the army in healing waves.

Nevertheless, a despondent silence lay over the three of them. Shiván was only too aware that the interrupted war council had not reconvened the previous night; everyone was too worn out by having to share Brakhól's torture. No decisions had been made. From the crack of dawn this morning all anyone could think of was defending themselves against the unwearied Guards and the constant mental barrage of pain.

"How long can we carry on like this?" Shiván muttered.

Garset shrugged, and for once there was no cheerful response from Cârin.

They stood silent for a while longer. Then a crazy idea struck Shiván. "We need something to cheer us up. What about a song?"

Garset's eyebrows shot up, but Cârin cracked a weary grin. "Good idea, boss."

"Something really stirring. How about that great hymn, *God above all kings and powers*? Garset, you've got a good voice. Get us started!"

A faint smile touched Garset's face. "Thank you, Overguardian." Then he launched into the hymn in his strong baritone: "*God above all kings and powers…*"

Cârin and Shiván added their tenors, and soon nearby Dûrian soldiers were joining in. By the second verse everyone was singing, and suddenly, to Shiván's delight, they heard the clear trumpet tones of the Ambon playing the counterpoint. A wave of joy and relief swept across the whole army.

Then Brakhól's distant screams broke out again, and familiar shafts of despair disrupted the beauty of the song.

"*Keep singing!*" Shiván shouted as the Guards resumed their attack, and for a moment it seemed as if they could surge to victory on a wave of song. But then shouts, growls and snarls broke out, the song died, and they were back to bare survival.

* * *

Jomel had been praying, hoping to regain the peace the Prince had given her during the Ambush. This afternoon that wonderful hymn, accompanied by the Ambon, had reminded her of the absolute, overriding authority of the One Creator God; and peace had flowed gently into her heart.

Now, after the scanty evening meal, she saw Shiván sitting on his own and went over to join him. He gave her a weary smile and she said, "It's not going well, is it?"

He nodded.

"Will it help to talk?"

He looked at her, hesitated a moment, then said, "Thank you. Maybe it will." A short silence followed as he gathered his thoughts. "We haven't had a council meeting in two days. No one knows what to do. We keep fighting every day just to survive, with the faint hope of breaking out of this cleft and marching on Darthane. But that seems completely unrealistic now. We're all getting so—so—tired—from Brakhól's pain." Jomel's eyes filled with tears, and Shiván nodded. "Poor little guy." He took a shuddering breath, and silence fell again.

Jomel gently prompted him. "But that singing today was wonderful. Everyone felt good after that."

"Yeah," Shiván muttered. "But we can't sing *and* fight. Once we're back in battle it's just Brakhól's pain again. The Ambon helps, but not enough."

"The Ambon sounded wonderful with the song."

Shiván sighed. "Yes, it did. If only that could carry on the whole time we're fighting."

There was another moment of quiet. Then a startling thought came to Jomel. She looked at Shiván as he stared grimly into space. She opened her mouth and closed it again. Then, hesitantly, she spoke.

"Shiván?"

A weary "Yes?"

"What if we had other people to sing with the Ambon?"

"Other people...?" He turned and stared at her.

"Yes. Not fighters. A choir. People who can really sing."

"A choir with the *army*?"

Jomel dropped her head. "Sorry, it was just an idea. A stupid one, I know—"

"No, Jomel!" Shiván jumped up, his voice vibrating with excitement. She looked up at him and saw his eyes bright, his face alight. "That's a *fantastic* idea! In fact, I'm sure it's from the One. The choir and Ambon would cancel out Brakhól's despair, leaving the army free to fight! How many singers would we need? To get the volume high enough—"

"Shiván, wait, wait!" She was taken aback by his overwhelming reaction. "It was just a crazy idea! Where would we get a choir from?"

"But that's just the thing!" he said urgently. "Don't you remember, we discovered on the way to the Larwood that with prayer the Ambon will summon whoever we *need* at a particular time. When we needed soldiers, it brought us soldiers. When we needed food, it brought us food. So if we pray for *singers...*"

"It will bring us singers!" Jomel responded, smiling at the wide grin on his face.

* * *

It was the sixth evening of Lannie's search for Danîsha and Perrely. She was almost beginning to accept Bishop Harlon's urgent warnings that she should stop now. Almost. But not quite. They were here, somewhere. The Cathedral was an enormous place, with a rabbit-warren of passages and rooms on each of the top three floors. She *had* to keep looking.

She'd searched those upper floors thoroughly without finding any guarded doors. Some were locked, but there'd been nothing to suggest that those behind them were prisoners. She had to trust that God would show her clearly when she reached the right place.

Tonight she'd decided to go down to the second floor—the third up from ground level. This was the really posh part of the Cathedral, Harlon had told her, where Shambor had his reception chamber. She hadn't told him she was going there tonight: the poor man would have had a fit. Mind you, it was hardly likely that prisoners would be residing on the same floor as movers and shakers and foreign dignitaries; but she had to check.

She paused, as always, outside Harlon's apartment and silently asked the One to lead her to Danîsha and Perrely.

She flitted silently along passages she now knew well, and took two staircases down. Carefully she peered out into a wide passage with a thick blue and silver floor cover. Ornate matching hangings covered the walls completely. White lily-like flowers abounded in vases on the occasional tables. As on the floor above, a few lights were lit here and there for late night arrivals. Fortunately she was the only one of those.

To her left the passage ended in a pair of intricately carved blackwood doors. She remembered them from when she first arrived in the Cathedral—they led to the Bishop's reception chamber where he'd interviewed her, she'd taunted him, and he'd consigned her to her storeroom prison. No, she wasn't anxious for another tête-à-tête with Shambor just yet.

To her right, a long way off, there was a T-junction. On both sides of the passage there were white doors with silver edging at widely-spaced intervals; but none of them had guards outside. She turned right and padded noiselessly down the deep pile, carefully trying doors. If the lever went down a certain distance she knew the door was unlocked and stopped before it could click open. All of these were unlocked.

She reached the T-junction and glanced back up the main passage. No, she wasn't going any closer to that blackwood door. She decided to try one of the side passages. She slipped into the right branch of the T, which was just as luxuriously appointed, then suddenly gasped and darted back into the main passage. *Careless!* Halfway along a Guard was sitting outside one of the doors. *Did he see me?*

Lannie peered cautiously around the corner. *Thank the One!* The man's head was drooping towards his knees. She re-entered the passage, her heart beating furiously. *Is this it? Have I found one of them?* A guarded door—just what she'd been looking for. That couldn't be coincidence. Either 'Neesh or Perrely, or both, must be behind that door. If her earlier guess was right, that Shambor was attracted to Perrely and she'd made him promise not to harm the other Restorers, then it made sense that she'd be given a room in this posh part of the Cathedral.

"Thank you, Father," she breathed. "Now what do I do?"

She peeped round the corner again. The Guard's head was still drooping. It was too good an opportunity to miss.

She slipped into the passage and walked slowly, carefully, towards the Guard, ready to freeze if he stirred. But he didn't. It seemed the longest walk of her life. Finally she was standing beside the dozing man, trying to control her breathing.

At this point, in books and movies, she ought to have seen a large bunch of keys dangling from his belt. No such luck. She tiptoed round him. Nothing on the other side. His eyes were closed, his knees drawn up to his chest, his hands clasped around them. He couldn't be fully asleep, or he'd have keeled over. A little more relaxation, and he'd jerk awake. Her heart was racing. She had to act quickly.

There was no way she could pick his pocket. She looked at the fancy white door, with its silver-lined decorations. She reached out and gently tried the door handle. It only moved a little way before silently stopping. Locked.

Lord, please help me. She stared at the door and the Guard. There must be *some* way she could get in. A back passage, like the one she'd used behind the torture chambers? That would take too long to find. Then her left hand felt something in the pocket of her robe. The key to Harlon's apartment. It was a very long shot, but she was out of options. She inserted it carefully into the door lock and tried to turn it. It wouldn't move. She shifted it a little and tried again. The lock opened with a loud click.

She froze. The Guard stirred, grunted, and tightened his grip on his knees. His eyes remained closed, and soon his head began to droop again. Lannie slowly let out her breath. She opened the door and slipped through. Then carefully re-locked it. No click this time. *Praise the One!* She glanced at the key: it must be a master, opening all doors.

Finally she looked around inside the apartment. A light tree had several lamps burning on its upturned branches. In the soft white light she saw a plush reclining room beyond the entrance passage. A suite, no less! Perrely was doing well. *If* she was here...

She walked through the reclining room, and found a dining area leading off it on one side. Beyond that was a neat little kitchen, bathroom and smallroom. Returning to the central room, she looked at the two doors on the other side. They had to be bedrooms.

She put down the lantern, took a deep breath, and opened one of the doors. The clear glow of the light tree lit up the room beyond. It was a nicely-appointed bedroom in matching shades of blue. A smallish person was huddled under the coverings on the far side of the wide bed. Lannie tiptoed over to get a closer look.

Suddenly the figure shot upright. "Who's that?"

"Aaargh, Perrely! You've made me bite my tongue."

"Alanya!"

"Yeth, if I thurvive the heart attack you've given me."

Chapter 38: *Choir on the offensive*

"*UNTRAINED VILLAGERS? I don't believe it. Haven't they learnt the lesson of Berûvis, where they lost thousands of such people?*"

Bishop Shambor stared contemptuously across the reception chamber as he communicated with Mindbender Threndor in Herminar. Gelmion stood as always beside his chair. Shambor enjoyed keeping the arrogant incompetent dangling at his pleasure.

"*It seems not, your Radiance. Our spy tells us eight men and six women responded to the Ambon in Herminar. They have no armour or weapons, and as far as he can see they've been given none.*"

"*Hmmm...*" He pondered this conundrum. It sounded like the kind of move a young, inexperienced commander would make, trying to boost his numbers by any means possible. Shiván was young, but not inexperienced. He was as devious and unexpected as a snake. What was he up to now?

He'd been bottled up in that cleft in the Downs. He had to get out – which he was now doing. But moving northward, away from Darthane... Why?

Ah! Was he luring the *Gorelenyu* out into more favourable terrain, so the Dorbians could spearhead a recovery mission? That was it! This summoning of villagers was merely a cover. He'd move away from Herminar to more open country, expecting the Guards and the *Gorelenyu* to follow. Then he'd make his move.

Well, he wasn't going to catch Shambor out that way. Apart from losing their own greatest weapon, there was the Strongholder to be thought of. He daren't allow the *Gorelenyu* to slip through his fingers a second time.

"*Threndor, listen. The Guards can continue to shadow the rebels; and I'll direct the other troops coming from the Larwood to their current location. But the* Gorelenyu *stays in Herminar. It can be left to rest for a while. Is that clear?*"

"*Yes, your Radiance.*"

* * *

As they moved north and east of Herminar, the army gained a new lease of life free of Brakhól's constant pain. Garset knew the other leaders were as deeply relieved as he was; though Hastet, at least, shared his doubts about the Overguardian's latest scheme of summoning a choir. But it had got them out of that bottleneck and away from the tortured child — whom Shambor apparently didn't want to risk wandering about in open country.

The Guards were following them; and they'd been joined today by an infantry company that had probably been patrolling the eastern Larwood. But thank the One for the Dorbians! Released from the constraints of that narrow cleft, they had no trouble making the Bishop's forces keep their distance.

They had just reached Berick, a small village between Herminar and Gilmane, not far off the highway. The Dorbians had surrounded the village to keep the Guards out, much to the villagers' initial distress: but a rousing speech from Frengor had calmed their fears. Garset had always been a Hearth man, with little sympathy for the travelling priests; but he had to admit Frengor's charisma and high standing in the countryside was a great asset in their present situation.

Now Shiván was stepping out before them holding the Ambon. "Friends! I am Shiván *Aténnelor*, whom Frengor spoke of." There were cries of welcome from the crowd in the village square. Frengor had done his work well. "As you can see, I have the long-lost Ambon of Sûrilane. Today I am going to lift it up in your midst, calling for any of you who are good singers to join us!"

A rumble of surprise followed. "We need singers to strengthen us in our fight to overthrow the Usurper! Some have joined us already from other villages." He held an arm out towards a cluster of nineteen ordinary folk behind him. "Here, for instance, is Gerinor, from Herminar." A man stepped forward and bowed. "Arella from Orlest." A young lady shyly dipped her head. "And the others you can see with us."

He turned back to the crowd. "Shambor has a terrible weapon from Selmion." Good touch, Garset thought. Country folk were always suspicious of Selmion. "A poor, innocent child, whom he tortures, and then uses mindspeech to make everyone feel his pain!" Angry muttering from the villagers: Mindbenders were capable of anything. "That pain weakens us when we fight. But if we have enough singers praising the One, we can drown it out and rescue the child!

"I will raise the Ambon now. If you hear it calling *you*, then come!"
With both hands on the leather grips, Shiván thrust the Ambon
into the air. At once its pure trumpet call rang out over the village.
People gasped. Some involuntarily stepped back. And three women
and two men came charging up and clustered round Shiván, eagerly
reaching out to touch the Ambon.

Surrounded by wide eyes Shiván called out, "Are these your best
singers?"

"Yes!" came the astonished chorus. Garset, too, felt the familiar
awe in his heart. Singers. Every time. Never anyone else. At moments
like this his doubt melted away.

"But, your Lordship!" someone in the crowd shouted. A tall,
dark-haired man with a sharp nose and intelligent face. Well dressed,
too: Garset wondered if he was local nobility. He moved forward to
be better heard. "Why are you coming here, to Berick? And to Herminar and Orlest? We're just small villages, with only a few singers.
You should go to Gilmane!"

Shiván looked puzzled. "All right, er, I expect Gilmane is a bigger
place, but..."

"No, my Lord, it's not that," the man interrupted. "They're holding a *belangédey* there. Right now!"

Garset and Frengor gave simultaneous exclamations of delight.
The Overguardian stared at them. "A what?"

"A singing competition!" Frengor whispered. Amazement dawned
on Shiván's face. "An eisteddfod! Prince be praised!"

"There'll be hundreds of singers in Gilmane from all over the
north," the tall man continued. "If you need singers to stop these
Mindbenders' tricks, that's where you need to be!"

"Thank you, friend! Then that's where we'll go!"

* * *

They crested a hill and caught their first sight of Gilmane around
noon the next day. Shiván marvelled at its transformation. When
he'd last seen it on his way to Darthane several months ago, Gilmane had just been a medium-sized village on the highway. Now
there were tents in the fields for miles around, with a wooden stage
and a large cleared area just east of the houses.

Shiván brought the army to a halt, and asked Gwargif and Garset
to move their soldiers a little way back down the hill, out of sight of

the village to avoid unnecessary alarm. There they could hold off their pursuers, who were not far behind.

"We make wall here, stop dark people coming," Gwargif said with a wide smile.

Shiván grinned back. "Thank you, my friend. The Guards are not invited to this concert."

With a quick bark Gwargif trotted off. Garset and Hastet saluted.

Shiván continued towards Gilmane with his friends. The singers came too, their eyes widening as the sound of a rippling descant and heart-warming counterpoint reached them from the stage. They entered the village and made their way through side streets toward the focus of attention.

As they came out into the open area, they had to push their way through crowds of onlookers and rival singers — the different groups recognisable by their brightly coloured uniforms. There were exclamations of annoyance as they barged through. Finally three large men in plain green coats barred their way.

"Stop there!" the one on the left said. "No admittance to the front rows without tokens." He held out a hand.

Shiván surveyed him for a moment, then suddenly drew the Blade and pointed it at the man. It glittered in the light. "This is our token. The Blade of Darthane. Do you recognise it?"

The man froze, sudden doubt on his face. There were exclamations from those around.

"And this is our token!" Cârin declared. "The Ambon of Sûrilane. Do you recognise *that*?" He thrust it towards them, and all three men took a step back.

"Now let us through." Shiván sheathed the Blade and strode forward. The immediate crowd parted for them.

But getting the whole auditorium's attention was a different matter. The current choir was in full flood: making themselves heard was a forlorn hope. Yet they couldn't wait till whenever they finished.

He turned to Câr. "Raise the Ambon."

His friend gave him a wide-eyed stare, then gripped the sacred emblem with both hands and thrust it skyward.

The effect was like a thunderbolt from a clear sky. The Ambon let loose a mighty fanfare of trumpets, rising through the scale to hit the top note in mind-shivering purity.

The choir stopped in mid-note. Women screamed, and then were silent. The after-echo of the trumpets quivered in the air. The entire auditorium was still.

Then the singers came like a massive wave towards them. Shiván and Cârin pushed through to the centre of the open space, and in a moment they were pressed in by hundreds calling out and trying to reach the Ambon.

"*SILENCE!*" Garset bellowed at top parade-ground volume. The crowd fell quiet. While Cârin continued to hold the Ambon aloft, Shiván thrust his way to the stage, where he could be seen. There, to a hushed audience, he explained their mission and the need for singers. Frengor spoke after him, reassuring the crowd that these were indeed the promised Restorers of the Way, as shown by their possession of the long-lost Ambon; and that those who had responded to its call should consider themselves called by the One, to sing to the praise of his Light.

"Go and say goodbye to your families, or those you are staying with," Shiván told the new singers—some three hundred of them. "Then return in an hour, prepared to live rough for a week or two. Bring only as much as you can carry on your own back, including your tent if you have one."

Within the hour they were back. Shiván, Frengor, Cârin and Jomel led the way out of the auditorium, their footsteps dogged by a florid, perspiring man in a bright red tunic. "But you have ruined our *belangédey!*" he moaned. "How can we continue when you're stealing three quarters of the contestants? How? This contest was planned *months* ago—"

Cârin stopped and placed a firm hand on his chest. "Listen, friend. Either join our army and continue your contest there; or make do here with the hundred contestants you have left. Your choice."

The man's mouth opened a closed a few times, then he stood, woebegone, as Cârin caught up with Shiván and the new three hundred, on their way to rejoin the army south of the village.

They heard the fighting before they saw it: the clash of weapons mingling with snarls, howls and shouts. There were cries of alarm as the new recruits stopped on the road, many poised to run.

Câr raised the Ambon, and its heartening trumpet call rang out. "Don't be afraid!" Shiván called out, climbing on to a rock beside the road to be seen. "We're fighting enemies we've already defeated, and we'll defeat them again. You'll see Dorbians fighting: again I tell you, don't be afraid! They are our friends, and they're fighting for us. All you have to do is stand behind our soldiers and sing!"

They went forward slowly to the top of a small rise in the road where they could look down on the fighting. There was a buzz of anxious talk among the singers as many of them saw Dorbians—and a battle—for the first time. But the Dorbians were attacking the familiar grey of the Bishop's Guard. That reassured them.

"Now!" Shiván called out. "You all know the hymn, *God above all kings and powers*?" A wave of nods. "All right, pretend you're still in the *belangédey*—the contest! You have to sing that song the best you've ever sung it—and the Ambon will accompany you. Someone start!"

There was a pause, then a thickset blond young man with the centre parting of a kindler sang out in a clear tenor: "*God above all kings and powers...*"

In a moment three hundred and fifty voices joined him, all singing their respective parts. The Ambon took the descant, with multiple trumpets soaring effortlessly above the voices. A wave of glorious song surged out over the battlefield. Men shouted, Dorbians howled with joy, the attack was redoubled.

The grey cloaks lost impetus. Some tried to rally, but more broke before the force of the sudden attack. Suddenly they were fleeing for their lives, with the Dorbians pouring after them.

Chapter 39: *Song vs. torture*

JOMEL JOINED THE CHOIR. It seemed the obvious thing to do. She wasn't a fighter, and without Brakhól to care for she had nothing to do except pray. Which she did: often, with Frengor and his small group of priests. But she needed something to occupy her, and singing in this choir, with the Ambon's accompaniment, was thrilling. She didn't have a voice like the other well-trained *belan*; but she could keep a tune. Also, she admitted to herself, she enjoyed being with the younger singers. There were some good-looking men: but she kept her eyes off them. That was... over.

They'd stopped for a short rest break, and she was sitting against a tree trunk in a small patch of woodland by the highway, sipping chass and thinking about all that had happened.

Yesterday had been amazing. After their first victory near Gilmane the day before, they'd started early in the morning and marched down the Lômack highway towards Herminar. Three times the Bishop's Guards had tried to stop them, with help from green-coated infantry and some cavalry blue-coats who had come from patrolling the Larwood. And each time the choir and Ambon had sent them packing! The choir sang different songs—all stirring ones, praising the One's greatness—but the Ambon seemed to know them all, and played a heart-lifting accompaniment for each. She particularly loved *He holds me high*, where the Ambon's trumpets rippled up and down in an exhilarating counterpoint.

And in the evening they'd returned to the village of Berick, where that man had told them about the *belangédey*. He turned out, to everyone's amazement, to be the local Land Elder—Lord Merion! He was so different from the stuck-up Land Elders she knew—he mingled with his people and saw to their welfare. He was a Lightist, and the Ambon (and Frengor) had convinced him Shiván and his missing companions were truly the Restorers of the Way.

So he'd decided to help. They stayed overnight, and this morning two wagons of food had been waiting for them, plus another of general supplies including tent fabric, ropes, mallets, shovels, cooking utensils and a host of other valuable equipment—including several large jars of honey. A number of the singers had complained of sore throats last night after their all-day performance, and Lord Merion had given them the honey from his estate. Dissolved in warm water or milk, it made a soothing drink the singers found invaluable.

The Land Elder had promised to find more honey from around the district and send it to them later, along with regular food supplies. There was no doubt the One had called him to be their 'provider'. Jomel was learning that there was no limit to the ways in which the Lightists' God showed his love to those who put their trust in him.

Jomel glanced at the three wagons, standing nearby just off the highway. She knew what a relief they were to Shiván and Garset, trying to provide for the enlarged army. The Dorbians could scavenge on their own — though the leftover pickings of fruit and grain were slim — but the almost seven hundred Dûrians were a challenge, which was now solved.

All of it thanks to the One Creator God. *It's natural for me to say that now,* she thought. *He is truly my God, and Gadesh is nothing to me any more. How could I ever have wanted his approval?*

"Time to go, everyone!" Shiván called out, and Cârin raised the Ambon for a short trumpet blast. Jomel got to her feet and rejoined a couple of young women in the choir, who welcomed her. Soon they were chattering away as the army moved back on to the highway (which was otherwise deserted). The grûnet were re-hitched to the wagons, and they began the uphill trek to Herminar — which, with another small village, was situated on a small plateau at the top of the Herm Downs.

They kept following the highway's smooth ascent, and were approaching the crest where the plateau began when everyone stopped and gasped. Some clasped their heads and there were cries and screams as a wave of pain crashed over them. *Oh, no! They've started on Brakhól again...*

"Don't be afraid!" Jomel exclaimed to the choir women with her, who had started weeping and looking around anxiously.

"What *is* it?" Arella gasped.

"It's what the Overguardian told us about — the child, who the Mindbenders are torturing and making us feel his pain. Now we have to sing! To overcome the pain and help the army to fight!"

They stared at her doubtfully, but then Shiván's voice rang out: "Choir! Fight the pain with song! Now's when we need you to sing more than ever before! *God above all kings and powers*! He can take away the pain and help us rescue the poor child who's being tortured right here, just ahead of us. *Sing!*" he cried as another gust of anguish took their breath away.

A slightly quavery soprano started up further ahead, and Jomel and her companions joined in. Gradually the song gained in volume as the Ambon's descant encouraged others to ignore the pain and sing. The Light-filled music swelled to a grand paean of praise, and the pain began to falter before it. They crested the rise, and there in the distance were the houses of Herminar — with their army attacking the Bishop's Guards, who were blocking access to the village.

Suddenly the pain stopped, and everyone surged forward. Then they halted again, and the choir continued to sing for a long time while the Guards kept up a stubborn defence until at last the music became too much for them and they fled. "*After them! Recapture the child!*" Garset shouted from somewhere up front.

The choir started a rapid, up-beat song, but Jomel sat on the ground at the roadside and hugged her knees, waiting with her heart in her mouth. They had to rescue poor little Brakhól! They *had* to.

Half an hour later Shiván came, touched her shoulder, and said sadly, "They had fast horses. They got away."

She couldn't stop herself bursting into tears.

* * *

Brakhól cried out as his captor clutched a wound on his arm. He was sitting in front of the grey cloaked man on a horse, and they kept bouncing up and down as the horse ran away from the singing on the hill. But despite the pain, Brakhól's heart was singing too. He knew that music! He'd heard it in the camp with Shibán and Jomil. It was *their* music — and now it had forced the bad men to stop fighting and run away! It had stopped them from hurting him.

Shibán and Jomil are coming! Shibán and Jomil are coming! He repeated the magic words over and over to himself.

* * *

His heart mourning for Brakhól, Shiván had to deal with the situation as it was. The Mindbenders with Brakhól must have reached Darthane already, but the Guards were still streaming back to the city on foot, their dead and wounded abandoned. He told Gwargif to let them go. It would do no good to divide their forces. But the way to Darthane was now open, and Garset and Hastet agreed that with the choir and Ambon they were now strong enough to risk advancing to the city itself. Garset added that Shambor was obviously still short of unmindbent troops, otherwise there wouldn't be so few supporting the Guards — and it was the Guards who were most affected by their new weapon of choir and Ambon. They needed to take advantage of that while they could.

After a short break and a cold midmeal, they set off — Dorbians both in front and behind to guard against surprise attacks. But there were none. From Herminar the highway went downhill, and they made good progress. In the late afternoon they reached the north gate of Darthane unopposed. But the massive gatehouse dampened their confidence. It reared up before them, the closed gate at its foot small by comparison. The distant figures of red-caped City Guards stared down from above at their puny army. *Are we mad?* Shiván found himself thinking. *How are we ever going to get past* that?

After an impromptu war council, Gwargif sent his Dorbians to spread out and create a defensive line all along the wall from here to the Janulane gate — keeping out of bowshot of the City Guards. Shiván estimated the distance between the two gates at just short of a mile, or one and a half kilometres. Behind the Dorbians, in the centre, the choir started pitching their tents. Garset and his Pure Company took the eastward end near the north gate, while Hastet with the remnant of his own and Dolmet's companies took the westward end.

Then pain struck from within the city. Brakhól's torture had started again. It was not as strong from this greater distance, but formed a constant slow drip of hurt that wore people down. Shiván called the choir from their tents and cooking fires. They were tired, and with the pain eating away at them their song struggled to get going. Shiván called Jomel, Cârin with the Ambon, Frengor and other experienced individuals, and interspersed them with the choir to encourage them. Very slowly, with the Ambon's heartening influence, they hit their stride. They sang for an hour into the night; then the pain stopped.

People ate their daymeal and were preparing for sleep when, an hour later, it began again. The choir scrambled back together to sing. After an hour it stopped.

An hour later it started again…

* * *

"There are Dorbians outside the city!" Perrely exclaimed as she re-entered the apartment, her face alive with excitement and her hair mussed. "The legion has come!"

"Oh, how wonderful!" Danîsha exclaimed, her heart lifting. This was just the news they needed, cooped up here day after day.

Lannie's comment chimed in with hers: "Fantastic! If they're there, Shiván must be with them." Danîsha nodded, and Perrely's eyes brightened. "Yes!"

Perrely had found a small balcony on the north side of the Cathedral, and went out there often to get a breath of fresh air. A guard trailed behind her, of course: and only she was allowed to go. Danîsha longed to join her, but said nothing. It would only cause trouble.

But it was so good to have Lannie with them now! After she'd first broken into their apartment four nights ago, she'd found a back way the servants used, which was not guarded, only locked — and Harlon's master key opened it. She'd come last night and stayed over, sharing Perrely's bed, so she'd been with them all day.

Without warning an agonising pain struck Danîsha. She cried out, and at the same moment saw Perrely scream and double over. A deep hurt, like physical pain, pulsed through her. She and Perrely were weeping, they couldn't help it.

Lannie was also grimacing with the pain, but her eyes were hard. "I know what this is!" she exclaimed, then yelped as another shaft of agony hit them.

"Was it — the midmeal?" Danîsha gasped.

Perrely stumbled to a recliner and collapsed into it.

"No, this is not *our* pain," Lannie said. "*Aaagh!* I've felt something like it before, only —" she paused, gritting her teeth " — much worse. Remember, I told you about the Ambush?" They nodded, then cried out at another wave of agony. Danîsha clutched Teynel's comb in her pocket.

"Someone is being hurt — tortured — and we're feeling their pain. That's what happened at the Ambush. Shambor is doing this!"

Danîsha saw Perrely's eyes widen in horror, and she knew hers must be wide, too. "Shiván! And the Dorbians! He's trying to — hurt them."

"Yes. Which means—" She managed a grim smile. "Shiván must be winning."

Danîsha found some small comfort in that, hunched over as the pain continued. But if Shiván's army was suffering this, they needed prayer...

Later. When the hurting ended. If it did.

* * *

Everyone was worn out the next morning after a broken night. But there was no time to recover: soon after first light the alarm was given both in the east and the west: Bishop's Guards were charging the long line of their army from the city gates at either end. Fortunately the Dorbians were less affected by Brakhól's pain, and they immediately leapt up to engage the enemy.

Rubbing his eyes, Shiván called the choir out. It seemed to take forever for them to wake and stumble from their tents. He curbed his impatience. When they were finally lined up—some distance from the fighting on either side, thank the One—he called for silence.

"I know you're tired. Last night was terrible. But remember this: *your singing works!* We've seen it at Gilmane, all the way down the highway, again at Herminar—and even here, last night! Did you notice that the pain became less—wasn't as continuous—as the night went on?" There were a few tentative nods.

He opened his mouth to continue, but at that moment the pain hit them again, and everyone gasped.

"No time for—*aah!*—speeches! *Sing!* Sing with everything you've got, and we'll— break this pain! You can do it!"

"A little hesitant, but well said, Overguardian," Câr murmured with an approving nod. He stood beside Shiván, ready to raise the Ambon.

Shiván saw Jomel nodding at him from among the singers, and speaking to the ladies beside her. Thank the One for her! This choir had been her idea. She'd been a great asset ever since the Ambush.

One of the baritones started the lively song *All doors stand open*— and this time they picked it up quickly, the Ambon providing a scintillating counterpoint. The pain continued, but they'd learnt to phase it out. Shiván watched the fighting to the east and west: it had been agreed that he would stay in the centre to have an overview of both sides. Now the Dûrian troops had joined in at their respective gates, helping the Dorbians against the Guards' long-swords.

Three quarters of an hour later both skirmishes were over, and the Guards on either side had retreated back through the gates and into the city. The pain also stopped. The soldiers and warriors returned to their normal positions, many taking a drink or kindling a fire for a simple dawnmeal. Shiván sent up a prayer of thanks for Lord Merion: what a Godsend he had been, too. The Berick Land Elder had promised to arrange more food wagons from sympathetic merchants in Lômack as soon as possible.

He saw Garset approaching. "Congratulations, Captain! You sent those Guards packing."

"Yes, Overguardian. With the singing, their heart didn't seem to be in it." He touched his chest in a brief salute. "Apologies for any doubts you may have sensed in me earlier on. This choir was definitely the One's strategy."

"All doubts overlooked, Captain!" Cârin chipped in. "Seeing is believing with this Overguardian."

Garset gave the rebel sergeant a dark glance. Shiván knew he didn't appreciate Câr's levity. "Don't thank me," he said quickly. "Thank Jomel: it was her idea."

Garset's eyebrows shot up. "Really? There's more to that young lady than one would expect."

"Indeed there is."

Frengor came up and joined them. "All thanks to the One for Light-filled music!" he exclaimed, every wrinkle on his face beaming.

Garset nodded. "I was just saying the same to the Overguardian. But —" He paused, his face serious.

"Oh dear. We can't be complacent?" Frengor hazarded.

"No, we cannot. I don't want to spoil the moment, but we need to think ahead. Shambor is bound to have ordered reinforcements from the Grûzhack War. They may arrive any day now. He won't risk ordinary troops, there'd be too high a possibility that they would come over to us. They'll be Bishop's Guards. I know at least two legions of Guards were down south, one at Dhembis, the other at Leváris. I expect they're on their way here now."

Shiván hadn't forgotten that ever-present threat. "We have to trust that our Light-filled music, plus the Dorbians, will be enough to deal with them."

Garset nodded. "Yes, Overguardian, and it well may. But, may I ask, what is our long-term strategy? Are we still expecting the walls of Darthane to come down, as happened in your Book?"

"Yes, Garset. That's the plan I believe the One gave us."

"Josh-oo-ah," Cârin put in.

Shiván laughed. "You remember the name!"

"Of course. He was a Hero. Like you."

"Flattery will get you nowhere."

"Ah, Overguardian," Câr wheedled. "Just a few extra rations —?"

A sharp throat-clearing from Garset interrupted the banter.

With a twinkle in his eye Frengor cut in. "My priests and I have been praying for this outcome ever since you told us the story in the Larwood."

Garset wore a slight frown. "So how will the walls come down? Do we just stay here in front of the city and wait for it?"

"Not *just* that, my friend," Frengor corrected gently. "If that's what the One Creator God wants us to do, then it's a positive plan of action and we will follow it."

"But we'll also sing!" Shiván exclaimed. "Since seeing how effective the choir has been, I've started to feel more and more that singing is part of the One's plan — our 'long-term strategy', as you called it. I don't know how. I just know we have to keep singing."

"Is that what Josh-oo-ah did?" Cârin asked.

"Not quite. He had his people walk all the way around the city — which we can't do. We've done our best by covering the area between these two northern gates. And as they walked, the priests blew trumpets — there's our singing, with the Ambon! They did that for six days. On the seventh they walked round the city seven times, then as the trumpets sounded they gave a great shout: and the wall collapsed."

There was a pause as the three men digested this.

"Well," Frengor said, "if the trumpets in your Book correspond to our choir and the Ambon's trumpet, there's no question: we must sing and raise the Ambon for seven days!"

"It may not be that exact number of days," Shiván said. "But we just have to keep singing with the Ambon, trusting the One, and at the right time in his plan the walls will fall."

Garset nodded slowly. "I'll pass that on to Captain Hastet and our officers. They may not fully understand, but they trust you, Overguardian."

Shiván grinned. "So why not start now? The Guards haven't re-appeared, so let's have the whole army sing with the choir! I'll gather the choir again and we'll all sing together. That'll almost double its size! What do you say?"

Frengor grinned and Garset smiled his slow smile. "As you command, Overguardian."

"Ambon at the ready!" Câr exclaimed, standing to attention and clasping the Ambon's leather grips with both hands.

Shiván started the choir on a new song, and as they built it up with the Ambon's counterpoint the soldiers joined in. The song swelled, and the Ambon's music with it. Shiván, Cârin and Frengor were revelling in the sound, when the priest touched Shiván's arm.

"Do you hear that?" he shouted, pointing toward Darthane. Shiván frowned and concentrated on what he was hearing. Then it came to him, distant but unmistakeable: people in the city were singing as well!

"Praise the One!" he shouted, throwing his arms wide. Cârin and the choir members grinned at him. They'd heard it too.

The Guards made several more sallies from the two gates, but were beaten off each time. As the day wore on the waves of pain from Brakhól became less frequent and less intense, especially during the singing. The choir needed to rest more often—many were complaining of sore throats. But when they rested the Ambon kept playing and people in the city kept singing. Jomel and several helpers handed round the soothing honey drink.

By late afternoon Brakhól's pain ended and no more attacks came. The choir and Ambon rested, and a peaceful hush settled over the city.

* * *

Shambor sat at his *shey*-wood dining table, just off the reception room, wiping his brow. The terrible music had ended for now: he could think again. But his thoughts only led to a grim review of his current situation. That young snake Shiván had once more outwitted him: his Guards were weakened, and the *Gorelenyu*'s effectiveness was severely reduced with the Mindbenders torturing him having their concentration repeatedly broken. Who could have anticipated that a *choir* could wreak such havoc? Well, a choir plus the Ambon...

And then the people of the city joining in! It was open defiance, and in normal times he would have had the Guards out in force, arresting and torturing anyone they found singing. But he no longer had the manpower for that. The City Guard was a broken reed: they were probably singing themselves. He had only one Bishop's Guard legion left, and they needed all their dwindling strength to keep challenging the rebels.

He wiped a hand over his mouth. His two Guard legions from the Grûzhack War were on the way back, but it took time to reach Darthane from Dhembis and Leváris — and they'd both had to fight their way through the Grûzhack and take wide detours — as well as completing the last part of their journey on foot, since no horses could face the Dorbians. He expected — *hoped* — they'd be here in a few days.

No, there was no escaping it. This was the time he'd thought could never come, when all means of stopping Shiván had failed. A few more days of this, and the so-called Overguardian could simply knock on the city gate and it would be opened for him.

All means had failed... except one.

Sadly, with deep self-loathing and a searing pain in his heart, he made the inevitable decision.

Chapter 40: *Pain*

PERRELY CAME INTO THE APARTMENT to find Danîsha sitting at the dining table, sniffing at an array of steaming dishes. A special dinner had just been delivered, as Shambor had promised.

"Room service has improved!" Danîsha said. "What have we done to deserve this?"

"I don't know."

Danîsha gave her a sharp look. Perrely laid her green and gold shawl on one of the recliners and came to sit beside the older woman. "This does smell nice." She lifted a few lids. "Buttered *argis* sprouts — *sûlinar* — fried *delmiget* — and a nut loaf sprinkled with *ganáy*, the most expensive seasoning under the sky. Plus a light gold wine to wash it down." She shook her head. "Why?"

"I was hoping you could tell me, my dear."

"I have no idea. Shambor summoned me, and we had a most peculiar conversation. At the end he told me he'd arranged this special dinner for you and me." She shook her head. "Well. Let's enjoy it while we can. Pity Alanya's not with us."

"Yes. She's been a breath of fresh air. I hope she doesn't get caught, wandering all over the Cathedral like that while Shambor's searching for her."

Perrely smiled. "She's very careful." It had been good to see Alanya over the last couple of days, though her news about the Ambush had deeply saddened them.

They began helping themselves from the dishes, using blackwood serving spoons to fill the patterned Shildane dinnerware in front of them. Danîsha heaved a sigh. "I'm glad that awful pain has gone — which means they've stopped torturing whoever it was. Did you ask Shambor about that?"

"I did." Perrely was quiet for a moment, her eyes unfocused. "He told me it was an effect of the fighting outside the wall, which he and his Mindbenders felt and accidentally amplified so that others did, too; especially those sensitive to pain, like me."

"Nonsense! Alanya and I felt it as well. He can't claim we're all hyper-sensitive."

371

"I said you'd felt it, but he brushed that aside, saying you're a foreigner."

Danîsha snorted. "A convenient excuse."

Perrely looked at her. "I don't know what to think, Danîsha. Maybe Shambor was lying, though he's been quite straight with me until now. But he was strange tonight..."

"In what way?"

Perrely felt a frown gather on her forehead. "Well... It wasn't like the other times. He wasn't trying to impress me, or touch me. He didn't even ask me to sit down—though I sat anyway. He seemed terribly agitated, striding up and down, then suddenly coming and sitting on the edge of the recliner facing me, and leaning forward with such an... almost... *haunted* look on his face.

"He said he was sorry it had come to this. I asked, to what? He didn't answer. He said he deeply regretted that I was suffering in this way, and he wished he could prevent it, but he couldn't. He was so earnest, and his regret seemed completely genuine. It was as if he was suffering, not me. As though he'd done something terrible, and was desperately anxious for me to forgive him. I kept trying to ask what he thought I was suffering, but he talked over me." She paused to pour herself and Danîsha a goblet of wine from the crystal carafe. They both sipped, then spooned up more of the delicious meal.

Danîsha still looked sceptical. "Do you think you've had a good effect on him? That he's finally seeing the error of his ways?"

Perrely finished her mouthful of nut loaf and took another, deeper sip of the light, sparkling wine. She held the goblet up to the light. The wine was such a *rich* gold. A gold you could almost feel.

"No," she told Danîsha. "I don't think he was repenting." Anxiety shot through her. "A couple of times he begged me to try and understand. As if he was doing something dreadful to me. But he's done nothing dreadful—not yet. It was almost... as if he was *going* to do something, and was asking my forgiveness beforehand."

Her eyes filled with tears. She was feeling unusually alert, tense and fragile at the same time. The uncertainty about what Shambor had meant was like a dagger piercing her. But she was distracted by the light twinkling on the wine—so bright and clear—and the aromas of the food. They were separate and distinct: the mellow richness of the nut loaf, the sharp, spicy tang of the *ganáy*, the soothing blandness of the *delmiget*…

"My dear, you're frightening me!" Danîsha was sitting very straight, eyes wide, the wine goblet clasped tightly in her right hand. "You think Shambor is planning to do something to you? And apologising in ad—" She suddenly sneezed. Her breath wafted across Perrely's face.

Then she knew. Just the faintest whiff—but it instantly took her back to the alleyways of Berûvis. Bending over slumped figures with old Kindler Dorlion. 'Stinkies', those broken individuals were called—because the smell on their breath was much stronger. But this was the same. No doubt about it.

Teméyn.

"Danîsha! Put the wine down! We've been drugged!"

Danîsha leapt up, knocking her chair over, and threw the wine goblet into the nut loaf dish.

The door burst open and four Guards came striding in. Two grabbed Perrely and two Danîsha. They were marched struggling from the apartment.

* * *

Shambor's hand trembled as he lifted the goblet of neat *vardis* to his lips. He'd thrown aside his robe of office, and sat in a crumpled white tunic at his dining table. The gleaming expanse of *shey*-wood was bare of everything except a tray with the *vardis* decanter. He hadn't eaten. His mind was in turmoil.

So, it had come to this. Beyond all imagining.

He took another sip of the *vardis*, and coughed as the powerful liquor burnt its way down his throat. He seldom drank the strong stuff, but tonight was an exception. He didn't see how Shiván could possibly breach the massive walls and gates of the city, but he'd too often underestimated him. That forced him to his last resort.

Perrely.

Right now she and Danîsha were on their way to the torture chambers on the top floor of the Cathedral. The strong dose of teméyn in their meal was a necessary preparation, to heighten awareness and release their latent telepathy. He groaned and buried his head in his hands. The thought of Perrely—*his* Perrely—the only woman after Yestel whom he'd ever loved — being handed over to an unmindbent torturer immune to that Lightist singing, was tearing him apart.

Yet her pain, amplified as far as the singing allowed by his best Mindbenders, was the only weapon he had left. Perrely was not a *Gorelenyu* — her suffering would mainly affect those who knew and loved her. But that included Shiván.

At the same time the *Gorelenyu's* torture would continue, of course.

He hadn't had the courage to see her again. Everything was being organised by Mindbenders Threndor and Bardon, under his mental oversight. He'd instructed Jeld the torturer that her face was to be left untouched. He couldn't bear the thought of that winsome expression with the kindly purple eyes and forthright gaze being marred. Not that those eyes would ever look kindly on *him* again. He squeezed his own eyes shut, his hands clenching into fists against his forehead.

If only he could supervise the torture himself! Speak to her, explain, give her respite when she needed it. But that was out of the question. He himself would be as deeply affected by her suffering as Shiván. He only hoped he could continue running the country and two wars. On the other hand, Perrely's sufferings would be supplemented by those of Danîsha, who would be forced to watch the whole proceeding. That would not trouble him at all, but he knew it would trouble Shiván and probably his senior leaders.

He was raising his goblet for another sip of the *vardis*, when a long drawn-out scream pierced his mind like a razor-sharp longsword. He leapt, the liquor cascading over his tunic and the table. *Perrely!* The torture had begun. Everyone who knew her was sharing her pain.

She started uttering small, pitiful cries of agony, and Shambor found himself gasping in anguish. *Perrely, Perrely, my dear, beautiful Perrely! How can I do this to you?* Yet I have to survive. You understand that, don't you? I have no choice! I can't let your Shiván overthrow all I've built up for so many years. I want to give it to *you*! You won't be like Mama, and reject it? *Aah!* Perrely, I'm hurting with you. I love you! Forgive me — *Aaaah!* No, oh Gadesh, no...

* * *

Strapped down on the rough wooden table, her body racked with pain, Perrely could only cling to God. As each new agony bit into her flesh, she cried out for mercy and endurance. In the few moments of coherent thought between tortures, she realised she was being used as a weapon against Shiván. The Mindbender staring coldly at her face was projecting her pain. She pleaded with the Prince not to let her suffering influence Shiván—and to end it soon. At times she saw Danîsha strapped to a chair, her chalk-white face filled with horror, tears coursing down her cheeks as she saw all they were doing to her. She gasped out a silent prayer for Danîsha, too.

As her body was cut, a new, terrible fear darkened her mind. A fear that she would be so disfigured that Shiván would recoil in disgust when he saw her. *Oh God, don't let that happen! Don't let* Shiván *turn away from me!*

It went on and on, but the pain only increased. Her mind was a writhing cauldron of agony. She could no longer think. She could only see the suffering face of the Prince who'd died for her. Her pain was *his* pain. Every cut, every blow, every torment was happening to him, too. He was suffering with her, taking everything that was done to her on to himself. He would share every searing agony, right through to the end.

* * *

Brakhól screamed as the bad man cut his arm—again. It was hurting and hurting, and Shibán and Jomil were not coming! Why didn't they come?

Aaaagh! A distant cry of pain echoed in his mind. Another cry followed, from someone else. He screamed again as his leg was cut. *It wasn't only him—other people were being cut, too!* Shibán wouldn't let this go on—he would come! He was good, these men were bad—very, very bad.

Shibán! Jomil! Come quickly! Aaaah...

* * *

The horror of watching Perrely tortured threatened to overwhelm Danîsha's mind. Not even the massacre at Carreck Manor, when all her friends had been killed, could compare with this. Sitting in a dark room full of ghastly implements and machinery, with her head, arms and body strapped to a chair, unable to look away, jabbed with a sharp knife if she closed her eyes. And when her eyes were open, seeing Perrely's poor body being cut by the grim, thick-set torturer. Nothing could shut out the girl's screams and heart-rending whimpers.

Every nerve in her body was throbbing with Perrely's pain; her eyes flinched at every glint of light on the torturer's blades, every flicker of the fire where irons glowed dull red; her ears cringed at every swish of a knife, every dull *thunk* of a club. Perrely's cries pierced her like red-hot skewers. She knew she was experiencing things more acutely than normal, due to the drug. And those two grey-cloaked figures standing beside Perrely and herself seemed to be absorbing every response the two of them made.

Dear Lord, help me! Her right hand jerked against the restraints, trying to reach her pocket and Teynel's comb, her small comfort in times of distress.

She knew they were probably going easy on Perrely, at least to begin with: no deep wounds or parts dismembered; just blows, burns and superficial cuts in sensitive places. But those could be no less painful, and her heart felt the agony of every one of them.

The night wore on, and Danîsha's horror gave way to a growing anger. After the massacre she'd vowed to bring God's justice down on those responsible. Now, as she watched Perrely being deliberately mutilated, an iron resolve formed deep within her. If she ever escaped this monstrous room, she would never rest until Shambor and all his works were destroyed — or she died in the process. It was an Old Testament resolve. There was nothing of sweet, gentle compassion in it. Shambor was unutterably evil; he needed to be destroyed. Exterminated. Wiped out, as God had commanded the Israelites to wipe out the corrupt tribes infesting the promised land he'd given them.

She prayed for an opportunity to confront him.

* * *

A new anguish hit Shambor as he lay sprawled over the table, trying to blot out Perrely's agony. He sat up, his eyes widening. *Mama!* No, don't reject me, Mama! I wanted to be great for *you*. I didn't *want* to torture Perrely. I had no choice! Can't you understand? *Mother, no...!* Don't look at me like that. I love you! And I love Perrely. I never wanted to hurt either of you...

* * *

On the makeshift bed in Harlon's apartment, Lannie tossed and turned in a horrible nightmare. A great black bear had followed her into Perrely's bedroom. It had rushed past her and seized Perrely's head with both paws, and was trying to twist it off. Lannie was tugging frantically at the bear, trying to pull it away from the poor girl, who was screaming in pain...

She shot up on the pile of pillows. *It was true!* Perrely was in agony. She could hear the screams in her mind—yet she knew they were real. The pain was so exquisite that she began weeping, clutching her shoulders and rocking to and fro. *And 'Neesh!* Those were *her* cries...

Harlon came in with a lantern. Between sobs she told him. He lowered himself stiffly beside her, and they prayed for Perrely and Danîsha.

* * *

In a small, bare room on the Cathedral's fourth floor Gil heard Perrely's screams. Gelmion the mindbent slave shrugged them off: such things meant nothing to him. But a deep sadness fell on the inward Gil. Those screams would be tearing Shiván apart. Another scream—Danîsha, surely? Was Shambor really torturing 'Neesh? What did the sadistic bastard hope to get out of that?

Oh. Just pain. To hurt Shiván and his little army in every way he could. But why bother? They might look impressive out there on the plain with the Dorbians, but they could never breach the walls. He knew Shambor had recalled a number of crack units from the Grûzhack war. It wouldn't be long before they arrived, and then Shiván would be done for.

So much for the 'Restorers of the Way'.

And what about himself? Would he share their fate? Very likely.

He shuddered.

* * *

Out on the night-bound plain, the first scream crashed through Shiván's heart, bringing him leaping to his feet. *PERRELY! Aaaah, no! Perrely!* He dashed out of his tent. Where was she? Who was doing this to her?

There was no one there. Her heart-rending cries were in his own mind. But not his alone. Soldiers of the Pure Company were shouting questions. A lone wolf-voice began howling. Gwargif? Other Dorbians answered, until the ground resonated with their deep, mournful howls. Garset, Cârin and Jomel came running up. Shiván stumbled and sat down hard. *Perrely!* A black cloud of despair settled over his breaking heart as her whimpers churned his thoughts to shreds.

Cârin sat beside him, his eyes full of concern. Jomel was weeping and holding his hand. Garset patted Shiván's shoulder, pain and sympathy in his face. Then he hurried off to calm his men, who had also known Perrely and were feeling her suffering. As he left Gwargif trotted up and licked Shiván's cheek. His human-like eyes were full of sorrow. "Is Lady of Prayer and Lady of Song is being hurt! Dorbi weep with them." He sat down next to Cârin, raised his head, and added a long, drawn-out howl to the others from far and near.

Shiván's heart lurched. Yes, now he could feel it. Danîsha's pain was also mixed in with Perrely's. He didn't know how he knew, but he did. Poor, dear 'Neesh.

And Brakhól's misery was there too. No rest for anyone tonight.

Shiván sat hurting through the long hours of darkness, Jomel, Cârin and Gwargif beside him. The camp settled into an uneasy quiet. Shiván flinched whenever Perrely screamed, her pain burning into his mind.

A grey dawn lightened the eastern sky, and he stared at the towering walls of Darthane and the Cathedral crowning the hill beyond. Up in that Cathedral, sheltering behind those walls, that devil Shambor was using Perrely's suffering to try and break him. He would *not* succeed. Every particle of Shiván's being ached to leap to Perrely's rescue, to destroy those who were causing her such terrible pain — to end *all* such pain in Dûrion. But the walls stood in between.

Then they must come down! *Oh God, do a Jericho for us! Make those walls collapse, as you did for Joshua. Not just for Perrely – but for everyone in this suffering land.*

Gwargif and the Dorbians continued their deep, resonant howls.

———————————————

Chapter 41: *God above all kings and powers*

THE DAWN GAVE WAY to a still, bright day. Frengor and Garset came over to where Shiván was sitting, flanked by Jomel, Cârin and Gwargif.

"Shiván." Frengor squatted down in front of him, a wealth of empathy in his wise, brown eyes. "Would you like us to pray with you?"

"Yes—please." He pulled his mind away from Perrely. She was crying now; deep sobs of pain and exhaustion.

"Is Lady of Prayer is need us all speak to Shining One," Gwargif murmured.

"The wall must come down *quickly*," Shiván murmured, hearing the pain and weakness in his voice. "Let's pray for it… Jomel, keep them singing." She nodded. "They must sing— as much as they can. They mustn't let—this—stop them." He paused, his features contorting at a new wave of agony from Perrely. "It's time for this to end. Not just Perrely… All of Dûrion."

They prayed together, committing Perrely, Danîsha and Brakhól to the care of the One Creator God; and asking for his Light on their plan to follow the example of Joshua. Gwargif prayed in Dorbian— a strange, snuffly language. And Jomel prayed, too, in stumbling phrases, but with simple sincerity to a God she knew.

In the silence that followed Shiván felt a quiet peace well up in his heart, overlaying the unrelenting pain of Perrely's suffering. God was with them, and his everlasting arms were holding Perrely, Danîsha and Brakhól.

Then there were shouts from both gates, and they knew the Guards had resumed their attacks. Everyone dispersed, Garset and Gwargif to join their fighters; Cârin to fetch the Ambon; Jomel to gather the choir; and Frengor to mobilise his priests for prayer.

The morning wore on, and Shiván received reports from both gates that the Guard attacks were fiercer and more persistent, clearly strengthened by Perrely and Danîsha's pain. The toll of Dûrian and Dorbian casualties was high.

"Please, God," he murmured. "This can't carry on for long."

Through it all the choir kept on singing to the Ambon's clear and effortless accompaniment. Whenever there was a lull the army joined in; and voices from inside the city could be heard as well.

* * *

A city guard pacing the wall near the Lômack gate stopped suddenly and frowned, staring down. He called a comrade. "Look at this!"

"A crack in the masonry. So what?"

"A *deep* crack." He pulled a small knife from his belt, squatted down, and pushed the point a good couple of thumb-lengths into the jagged gap. "And it wasn't there yesterday."

"Oh, come on. Next thing you'll be saying the wall's going to collapse!"

His friend stood up again, giving him a dark look before resuming his patrol.

* * *

The torture of Perrely, Danîsha and Brakhól continued for four days. Somehow Shiván survived them — he didn't know how. It wore him down; and not only him, but also Garset, Frengor, Cârin, Jomel, and all who knew Perrely. By the evening of the fourth day Frengor's smile was rare; Garset's face had set into a grim mask; and Jomel's eyes were red-rimmed. Their suffering affected everyone else, and the choir struggled now to infuse hope and joy into their singing.

The Guards' attacks were more frequent now, and ferocious. Gwargif, Garset and Hastet reported ever greater losses.

It was the Ambon that kept them going. Its pure, unaffected praise of the One Creator God lifted their hearts in spite of themselves.

The fifth day dawned with sudden alarm as a new force of Guards was seen charging on foot down the western highway to join the attack on them from the Janulane gate. At the same time far larger numbers issued from the north gate. Desperate cries arose on both sides from the army as they struggled to hold off their enemies.

What they long feared had finally happened: Shambor's reinforcements had arrived.

At the same time Perrely's pain increased dramatically, and Shiván could hardly think. He sat down suddenly on the grass and clasped his head. Someone grabbed his arm, and he saw Jomel staring at him, red-eyed. "Shiván, what are we going to do? The choir are scared, some of them are trying to leave!"

With panic threatening to overwhelm him, Shiván cried out desperately to God. His tumbling thoughts gradually quieted. He knew God was there; and God knew what he needed. At last he heard a firm but calm voice: *"You've done everything. Now stand!"*

Yes! Now the way ahead was clear!

Ignoring Perrely's weary, heartbreaking whimpers, he leapt to his feet and yelled at the top of his voice, "LISTEN, *everyone!"* The milling choir members froze. Messengers standing by to take his orders leapt to attention. Cârin, holding the Ambon with one hand, grinned and snapped off a smart salute with the other.

"This is it! This is the time when God will intervene. Now we will sing as we've never sung before. We will *all* sing—choir, soldiers, citizens of Darthane, all who follow the One Creator God! We will sing a song that will echo down the centuries!" He swept his arm behind him. *"We will sing that wall into the ground!* The God above all kings and powers will do this. Now *SING!"*

To the messengers he rapped out, "Tell the commanders to stop fighting and *sing* when they hear the choir." They raced off.

Galvanised into action, the choir sang. A baritone gave the lead, and in a moment three hundred and fifty voices were singing *God above all kings and powers* with all the gusto they had. The Ambon responded in kind: trumpets soared and thundered in the richest, most varied counterpoint they'd heard.

Hundreds of other voices joined in, and the sound swelled as every member of the Restorers' army sang. The Guards at the gates faltered, their attack grinding to a halt. Distant voices from the city added their harmony.

Then the song deepened. Shiván exclaimed in delight as he realised that for the first time the Dorbians were singing! The profound, resonant bass of more than four thousand wolf-voices built the song to all-encompassing proportions, drowning out every other sound but that of the singers and the Ambon, whose trumpets rose in majestic descants above the harmony of over six thousand voices.

Whether it was by divine action, or an acoustic trick of the air and the silence, the music seemed to carry all over the city. They sang for an hour—maybe longer—song after song of resounding praise. Shiván felt he could sing forever to this glorious accompaniment. All the time the sound was growing. The bass deepened, as though an ensemble of huge brass instruments had joined the harmony, making the earth itself vibrate in praise.

Shiván suddenly realised that the earth *was* vibrating. A loud rumbling was growing in the air. They went on singing, watching with widening eyes as the solid wall of Darthane began to tremble. Stones and mortar from the gate tower came clattering to the ground. The red-capes on top were running about like ants trying to escape. A crack appeared, and spread rapidly down the front of the tower. A whole corner separated from the rest and slid with gathering speed down the wall. There was a resounding roar as it hit the ground, and clouds of dust billowed up. Through the haze they briefly saw the inner floors of the tower, the great wheels for raising the second gate, stairways with men running down them… Then the entire tower slowly folded in on itself, crumbled, and collapsed on to the battlements.

The ground continued to shake, and they continued to sing. Shiván felt tears in his eyes at the greatness of the One. He was indeed the God above all kings and powers.

Cracks appeared in the wall itself. They extended slowly at first, then quicker, until they were running like wildfire over the whole structure. The rumbling grew, and dust filled the air. By screwing up his eyes Shiván could make out the remnants of Shambor's garrison scrambling frantically for safety. A large segment of the parapet caved inward and disappeared. Then slowly, incredibly, with a deafening thunder the entire wall in front of them collapsed.

Chapter 42: *Victory defeated*

LANNIE AND BISHOP HARLON stood at the kitchen window of his apartment in the Cathedral. Lannie's eyes were wet; Perrely's pitiful cries still echoed in her mind. They both stared out across the walls of Darthane at the Restorers' army beyond. They were singing again—but somehow it was different now. More intensity, more conviction, more trumpets.

"It's beautiful!" Lannie murmured.

Then something new happened. The song became at once louder and deeper. "What are they doing?" she said.

"It's the Dorbians!" the Bishop exclaimed. "They're singing too!"

Below on Cathedral Hill many people had stopped to stare out over the wall. Voices rose on the still air. "The people are joining in again," Harlon said, joy in his eyes. "*God above all kings and powers. My favourite.*" He began to hum the tune. Soon they were both singing.

The volume of the sound increased. In all the streets of Darthane laid out below them people emerged from their houses and clustered together in crowds, their voices raised in song. Deep bass undertones made Lannie feel that a vast church organ was filling the air, the buildings, the very earth itself with a paean of praise to the God of all creation.

Time stood still while the whole of Darthane sang.

Suddenly Lannie pointed. "Look at the wall!" Dust was rising around it, and it was quivering. The soldiers manning the battlements were running to and fro. The *basso profundo* of the song had turned into a deep rumbling that filled the air. There was a crash of broken crockery behind them. They turned. A mug of chass had fallen from the table. They saw that the table itself was trembling. Small objects began falling off shelves.

The Cathedral itself suddenly shook, and many other objects came crashing down. A swathe of grand houses on the lower side of Cathedral Avenue crumbled and slid down to the street below, leaving a gaping wound in the hillside. Through the kitchen door they heard screams, frantic shouts, and running footsteps. Yet it never occurred to Lannie or Harlon to leave. Their eyes remained glued to the scene through the window. They continued singing with the crowds in the streets, their hearts caught up in the song and filled with the peace of God.

The tower above the Lômack Gate collapsed. "Dear Prince!" the Bishop exclaimed softly. The grand song went on, swelling beyond human voices. The more distant Janulane gatehouse crumbled and fell. Then the walls themselves began to subside. *It's impossible!* Lannie thought. *I can't be seeing this.* Yet whole sections of the wall, from the Janulane Gate in the west to the Galmanest Gate in the distant east, sank down into piles of broken masonry. The great northern aqueduct collapsed like a row of dominoes running outward from the city. Dust filled the air.

Tears were streaming down Harlon's face. "Praise to the One and only God!" he murmured. "He has vindicated himself today. All of Darthane has seen his greatness." '

Now the song ended, and a great cheer went up from citizens and the besieging army. Through the haze they could see people swarming over the masonry. Of Shambor's garrison, or his Guards, there was no sign. They watched as the people of Darthane greeted the incoming army with embraces and cries of joy. The Ambon's rallying call sounded, but neither of them had any urge to respond. Lannie realised it was summoning Shiván's Dûrian soldiers, who were streaming into Darthane while the Dorbians remained on guard outside, with the choir.

Eventually about two hundred infantrymen began moving up the hill towards the Cathedral, led by the Ambon. A vast crowd of Darthaners followed. As they approached the Cathedral Square, Bishop Harlon exclaimed in delight at his first view of Dûrion's ancient emblem. Lannie recognised one of the twins carrying it— where was the other?—and Shiván's tousled thatch beside him. She pointed Shiván out to Harlon.

Then she suddenly became aware that Perrely's cries had ceased. A moment later it dawned on her that this was the impossible opportunity she'd been praying for. She seized Harlon's arm. "Your Radiance! Now is our chance! Perrely's torture has stopped. Maybe in the chaos they've left her and Danîsha unguarded. We must find them, and set them free!"

He looked at her doubtfully. "My dear, you're a strong, active person. I'm afraid I'm a little beyond that. If you could bring them here—"

"No, no!" In her haste she was tugging him towards the door. "We discussed this, remember? You and Danîsha need to confront Shambor together. This could be our only chance! He may be trying to escape, or... or brewing some magic. We have to get to him as soon as possible..."

"The One have mercy on us," Harlon murmured.

"Wait!" Lannie dashed into her temporary bedroom and came back with a few necessities. She barged through the kitchen door and Harlon followed her, shaking his head. He locked the door behind them, pocketing the key.

They hurried through empty corridors towards the torture chambers Lannie had found on a previous excursion. Here and there a door stood open and personal belongings were strewn about. Below them in the Cathedral they could hear shouts and uproar.

They were approaching the servants' access passage that Lannie had found, when they both stopped in their tracks.

A terrible sound had broken out in the Cathedral. It sounded like a ghastly perversion of a bellaril. Both Lannie and the Bishop froze as bone-juddering discords crashed through their minds. All plans, all action disintegrated. They stood paralysed, their thoughts incoherent, their limbs unresponsive.

* * *

Gelmion stood with Mindbenders Threndor and Bardon at the imposing arched doorway of the Cathedral, flanked by eight Bishop's Guards. Bardon was holding Danîsha's bellaril. Gelmion watched with cold eyes as Shiván and his infantrymen entered the Cathedral Square. Cârin was there, holding the Ambon aloft. Some of the troops spread out into the square, while others started moving round the side of the building — no doubt to surround it. He looked at Bardon and nodded. The Mindbender began playing the bellaril.

Inside Gelmion's body, Gil cringed at the horrible sounds that proceeded from the instrument. Though Danîsha's songs had always stirred up unpleasant feelings in him, they were pure delight compared with this unholy cacophony.

But his reactions paled into insignificance when he saw the effect of the instrument on the Restorers' army. Shiván himself was some twenty paces away, Cârin beside him. As the bellaril began playing Shiván came to a sudden stop, his face contorted in horror.

The Ambon fell from Cârin's hands and crashed on to the paving stones, sliding a short way before lying still. Beside them Garset, Frengor and the rest of the army stood frozen.

Sorrow welled up Gil's mind. They'd come so close! It had been a truly heroic act, 'singing down' the walls of Darthane. Imprisoned in Gelmion's body, Gil had exulted. But capturing a Mindbender's city was one thing. Capturing the Mindbender was another matter altogether. With the power of the bellaril put to evil use, Shambor had turned their victory into defeat. Now he only needed to mindbend Shibán and the other leaders, and it would all be over.

The tones of the bellaril quietened slightly, and over it Gelmion gave his master's commands:

"Shibán and Garset, you will order your soldiers to wait while you lay down your weapons and enter the Cathedral. Frengor, Cârin and the Ambon will accompany you. Should you refuse, the bodies of Danîsha, Alanya and Perrely will be thrown out to you one by one."

Gelmion raised his hand. The music stopped. There was anger on the soldiers' faces, and the rasp of swords being drawn. Garset gave a sharp command, and the movement ceased.

"Do you refuse?" Gelmion asked in a cold voice.

Shibán, Garset and Frengor turned and spoke together. Another captain came pushing through the ranks to join them. The four of them held a lengthy discussion, with much vehement speech and many dark glances cast in Gelmion's direction. Gelmion waited stolidly. With the bellaril standing by, his master was in no hurry — unless the Dorbians turned up. Gil kept hoping against hope.

The Dorbians remained at their posts surrounding the city.

Finally Shibán turned back to Gelmion. "We'll come."

There was pain and resignation in his voice. He, Garset and Câr took off their swords and handed the weapons to the other captain, whose face was dark with anger. Garset then called out to the surrounding soldiers to remain on guard until they returned. The other officer repeated the command. Garset, Frengor, Shibán and Cârin came walking towards the Cathedral entrance, Cârin carrying the Ambon. Behind them the infantrymen shifted uneasily as they watched.

Gil's heart was a heavy stone within him.

* * *

The disintegrating music stopped. Harlon woke from a nightmare, and found himself standing in a strange corridor. Alanya was looking round with wide eyes beside him. The moment of disorientation passed, and he remembered that they had been on the way to find Danîsha and the girl Perrely.

"I don't know what *that* was, but praise the Prince it's stopped!" Alanya said in an unsteady voice. "Are you all right?"

"Just shaken. Shambor has found some new devilry. We'd better make haste."

They walked quickly down the corridor, Harlon limping a little. He hoped there wouldn't be too many more episodes like that.

Alanya led them through a maze of passages until she reached a narrow, unpainted door in a blank stone wall. She turned the handle, but it wouldn't open. She tried again, muttering in Inglish.

"This was unlocked last time!" she told Harlon. "Do you have the key of your kitchen door?"

He fumbled in the pocket of his robe and handed it to her. She twisted it about in the lock until there was a click.

"Praise the One it's a mother key," Harlon murmured.

Alanya grinned at him. "We call them master keys."

"Appropriate, in this place."

They entered a dark passageway. Along the left-hand side was a row of small doors, each with an opening covered by a metal grille in the top half. They peered through the nearest grille and saw a small room with blood on the floor and implements lying around, looking as though it had been used recently. But there was no sign of Perrely and Danîsha.

Then they heard voices from further down the passage.

Alanya turned to Harlon with a finger on her lips. He nodded, and they made their way quietly toward the sound. Harlon relaxed as the voices became clearer. It was two women talking to each other.

"...keep trusting the One," an older voice was saying as they reached the door. Harlon stopped. It couldn't be. But the likeness was incredible.

"He cannot intend us to die here like this," Danîsha continued. "*He* brought us here. *He* will get us out—somehow."

Alanya was looking through the grille. Only one person could do so at a time. A lighter voice came now, sounding weak and infinitely weary.

"I *do* trust him. I just can't think any more. You pray, Danîsha."

Alanya turned away from the grille, shock and pity in her face. She gestured to Harlon, and he bent to peer through the opening.

The sight that met his eyes made him want to weep. That such a scene should be possible in the Cathedral! In the High Hearth of Dûrion — built for the praise of God's love and mercy!

A flickering candle gave just enough light to reveal a sordid cell, full of the most horrible instruments, the floor stained with blood. Near him was a high-backed chair. He could see the side of Danîsha's head, clamped in a metal and leather contraption to the chair, her arms and legs also firmly attached. Facing her the girl Perrely lay strapped to a wooden table. His heart wept for her. Her tattered shift was stained crimson. Her face looked blue-grey, like watered milk, the eyes dark pools of suffering.

He turned away from the grille. He and Alanya stared at each other for a moment in mutual shock. Danîsha had started praying in short, halting sentences for the One's deliverance. Again, that voice!

Alanya recalled him. A faint smile touched her lips and she whispered, "Let's be the answer, shall we?"

* * *

Shiván and his three friends were escorted through the Cathedral by Gelmion and the Guards. In many places the ornate corridors and public rooms had suffered damage from the earthquake. Pictures and statuary lay smashed on the floor. Stained glass windows had shattered. They skirted one area where a section of the huge building had collapsed. Faint moans could be heard beyond the fallen masonry.

Shiván felt sick — both physically and emotionally. Their victory had been turned on its head. If only he'd brought the Dorbians into the city with him! But most of the Guards who'd come out of the Lômack gate had been killed when it collapsed; and it was pretty certain Shambor had no other forces in the city. He'd concluded they didn't need the extra protection. That left only the new arrivals from the west — so he'd left Gwargif behind to deal with them.

Also he'd wanted to avoid a panic in the city, which the sudden arrival of several thousand Dorbians might have caused... and so the excuses continued.

They climbed two wide, curving staircases to the second floor, and walked down a marble corridor to an imposing blackwood door. Gelmion plucked the chime. The door was opened by a tall young man with a solemn face and a white tunic spattered with masonry dust. He gestured them forward. They entered, followed by Gelmion and the Guards, who fanned out behind them.

The first thing Shiván saw was a plain wooden table in one corner. The side nearest him was dripping blood. A small figure was strapped to the table, uttering piteous little whimpers. Around him were scattered various instruments of torture. Two Mindbenders were standing over him, their cruel hands still for the moment. Shiván's heart went out to the helpless child.

A large figure in a dark blue robe with intricate silver embroidery was leaning against a blackwood desk not far from the torture table, a silver stole around his shoulders. Beyond the desk was a magnificent circular stained glass window that had somehow survived the earthquake. Light trees revealed a heavyset face that radiated authority. Suffragan Bishop Shambor dom Beldet.

A smile of triumph lit up the Bishop's face as they entered. "Ah! Here come the glorious conquerors. Welcome to the humble headquarters of your defeated foe. What are your terms of surrender?"

Shiván summoned up all the bravado he could muster. "You can't win, Shambor. If anything happens to us, the Dorbians will deal with you. I don't think your mind tricks will work on them."

"Perhaps not." Shambor advanced slowly towards them, menace in every step. A heavy fear settled on Shiván's heart. "But my mind tricks will work on *you*, won't they? And what will the Dorbians do when *you* order them to return home? I think they'll go, don't you?" His voice was soft and silky, his eyes hard.

"The Dorbians can 'smell' Light and darkness. They'll know if I'm mindbent."

"An expert in the Realm of the Mind, are you? But what about your friend Gelmion? For how many weeks was *he* mindbent, and you never knew? If I could make Gelmion 'smell' good to you, don't you think I can make *you* smell good to your Dorbian friends?"

Shambor stood in front of Shiván. His cold eyes surveyed him mockingly, his lips twisted in a cynical smile.

"Shambor, you think you've got the upper hand," Frengor declared. "But the One is about to do the last thing you expect."

The Mindruler laughed. "A delightfully empty threat. Visionary, your vision has failed you. Bardon, some music!"

The mind-numbing noise broke out behind Shiván, and his thoughts fell into chaos. Through a whirling kaleidoscope of pain, occasional sights and sounds registered as random fragments. Gelmion and the other Mindbender lowering Garset to the ground in front of him. Frengor and Cârin lying prone, their mouths forced open with a wooden implement. The sounds of a liquid pouring and someone half choking. An ominous smell that he couldn't place. Shambor bending over Frengor. Words spoken. And the agonising noise of the bellaril endlessly grinding down his inner being. At one point Garset, Frengor and Cârin seemed to get up and walk away. But the noise continued.

Then suddenly it stopped. He had no idea how long he'd been standing there, but it must have been an hour or more—his arms and legs were stiff. But as his eyes focused, despair settled over his heart. Shambor was facing him, leaning against the blackwood desk. Beside him stood Gelmion and three others. The Ambon was propped against the desk beside them. It took him a moment to realise that the others were his friends.

Garset, Frengor and Cârin stared at Shiván, faces cold and eyes blank.

Chapter 43: *Nightmare over*

DANÎSHA STOPPED IN MID-SENTENCE, her prayer unfinished, as she heard the door opening behind her. Had those fiends returned the back way?

Then Perrely exclaimed, "Alanya!" and her heart leapt.

"Yes, it's me," said Lannie's familiar voice. "And this is the Bishop of Dûrion. We've come to get you out of here."

"Your Radiance!" Perrely tried to move and a cry of pain escaped her as Lannie and a tall figure in a shabby blue house robe appeared.

"Lannie!" Danîsha cried in English. "Praise God!" She felt tears running down her cheeks.

Lannie smiled; but there was pain in her eyes. "No time to waste," she said briskly. "Shiván and his army are on the way. We must catch Shambor before he escapes. We all need a word with him."

A fierce anticipation flared up in Danîsha. During the long hours of Perrely's suffering God had shown her what to say to that ungodly worker of darkness, and like an Old Testament prophet she was burning to say it.

The Bishop turned, and Danîsha saw a tall man with a kindly, lined face. He stared at her intently for a moment, then smiled. He bent down to remove the straps binding her arms and legs, and undid the clasps on the contraption holding her head. Meanwhile Lannie was working on Perrely's bonds.

Bishop Harlon gave Danîsha a hand to help her out of the chair. "Thank you," she said as she struggled to her feet, her ankles numb from the straps.

Again that warm smile and intent look. "It's my privilege to assist a Restorer of the Way."

Danîsha went to help Alanya with Perrely. They eased her up into a sitting position, but she cried out with pain from the whip-lashes she'd received. Gently they lifted her and put her on her feet beside the table, supporting her till she recovered her balance. Then they both helped her put on the spare robe Lannie had brought.

Perrely stood leaning with her undamaged hand on the table, her face grey, eyes inward-looking.

"Can you walk?" Lannie asked anxiously.

"I must," she whispered.

"'Neesh, I think you should continue that prayer we interrupted." Instinctively Danîsha looked at the Bishop. His kindly eyes were full of concern. He came round the table to where the three of them were standing, and held one hand above Perrely's head, the other above Danîsha's. "Let's ask the One to renew our sisters' strength."

Danîsha's heart was warmed by the old man's prayer. It was brief and to the point, but radiated a simple trust in the living God. In the silence that followed she felt new energy flow into her. Perrely turned to look at Bishop Harlon, tears in her eyes. "Thank you, your Radiance." Her voice was stronger, and her face a little less washed out. "I think I can manage now."

"Right," said Lannie. "First stop, Shambor's reception room. That's where the Bishop thinks he'll be."

Danîsha nodded. "He will. Before those monsters left, the two Mindbenders told the torturer they had been summoned there."

"What about you, my dear?" said Harlon, looking anxiously at Perrely. "Can you bear seeing Shambor again?"

"Oh, yes." Perrely's dark-shadowed eyes met the Bishop's in a clear, uncompromising gaze. "I have things to say to Shambor dom Beldet."

Lannie suddenly said "*Hsst!*" Danîsha jumped, then froze like the others, listening. Her heart lurched as she heard the sound of footsteps approaching the main entrance to the torture cubicle. "They're coming back!" she blurted.

"Quick! Out the back way!" Lannie hissed.

Harlon and Danîsha supported Perrely as she hobbled slowly toward the rear door. Lannie stood by the door, her face creased in an anxious mask. The footsteps had almost reached them now. Perrely let go of Danîsha and grabbed the handle of the back door. She stood, panting.

"No, no— Keep going!" 'Neesh exclaimed.

But they were too late. With a creak the handle of the main door turned, and a figure entered. Danîsha grabbed a pair of tongs from a nearby table, ready to sell her life dearly if the newcomer touched Perrely again.

"Estaron!" the Bishop exclaimed.

There was a momentary tableau as they all stood staring at one another. Danîsha saw a tall, well-built young man in a white tunic, pale blue eyes in a strong face gravely regarding them. "Shambor's secretary," Harlon explained.

The young man inclined his head to the Bishop. "Your Radiance. I see you have preceded me. I learned that the torturer and Mind-benders had left, and I was coming to release the ladies Perrely and Danîsha." He bowed his head in turn to the two of them, and went up several notches in Danîsha's estimation. "And this must be the long-missing Lady Alanya." Another bow of the head.

"Yes, well, good to meet you," Lannie said. "But we can't hang around. Do you know where Shambor is? We need to speak to him."

The secretary's eyebrows rose; but if he found the request strange, he made no comment. "He is in his reception chamber, meeting with the Lord Shiván, Visionary Frengor and others."

"Then we'd better get there soon! Let's go."

"If I might suggest, it would be best to avoid the main door, which is guarded. I will take you by a back route to one of the side entrances."

"Oh! That's good," Danîsha exclaimed.

Harlon smiled. "Thank you, Estaron."

Estaron led them down the servants' passage at the back of the torture cubicles. Perrely gradually gained strength, and after a while was able to walk unaided. With frequent pauses for rest she negotiated the three servants' staircases down to the second floor. Her face was taut with pain, but she refused a longer break.

Down two side passages they reached a simple *colárre*-wood door. Estaron unlocked it, and they entered a narrow passage that immediately looked familiar to Danîsha. They passed an open door, through which came the rustles and squeaks of small animals. Danîsha glanced in, and winced at the sight of a blood-stained table with a box of small implements. She exchanged a glance with Lannie. This was where they had seen Shambor through the blaise. Bishop Harlon was shaking his head, pain in his eyes.

Estaron took them along a wider corridor to a palatial dining chamber. Now they could hear the sound of voices up ahead. They entered a waiting area dotted with occasional tables and recliners. Perrely limped along with her good hand on the wall, making for a door flanked by blue-and-silver wall hangings. The voices were coming from beyond it.

Suddenly the terrible, soul-destroying music broke out again. They all froze. Perrely toppled forward, her outstretched hand catching the back of a recliner and pivoting her towards it. She landed face down on the soft seat, then rolled slowly off on to the floor.

An hour passed...

* * *

Shiván stared in horror at his three friends. *Former* friends. Garset, Frengor and Cârin stared back, their faces impassive. Beside them Shambor leant casually against the blackwood desk, amusement on his heavy features. In the corner little Brakhól screamed, and pain wrung Shiván's heart.

It was over. Despite what they'd thought of as God's intervention in bringing the walls down. Despite all their prayers and suffering up to this point. Here, at the very last moment, they'd lost. He and Garset had banked on the Bible, the Dorbians, the choir and the Ambon to defeat Shambor. They hadn't. He had an answer to everything they tried. Despair threatened to overwhelm him.

Shambor laughed. "Face it, young Shiván. You've lost the war, you've lost your friends, and you've lost Perrely. That's what comes of taking on a Mindruler: you think you've won — and then you haven't. Very soon *you* will be mindbent, too. Your army, your instruments, your foreign friends, the Child, the Ambon — they all belong to me now. And so does Perrely." He paused. Shiván stared at the mocking face, and anger began to seethe under the despair.

The smile broadened. "Both the Dûrian Hearth and the Travelling Order will be under my control. The dear, hero-worshipping brothers will do anything Frengor tells them. Only gradually will it dawn on them that he's not quite the same — and by then new brothers will have joined who will be more... amenable. Meanwhile, with the *Gorelenyu* restored to its proper use, I shall soon defeat the Grûzhack.

"So you and your pathetic 'Restorers' have failed. It's all mine now, and I am stronger than ever. Say goodbye to your hopes and dreams, Shiván. You may have destroyed the walls of Darthane, but you'll never rule Dûrion, and you'll never see Perrely again."

Brakhól's torture intensified, and the child's agonised screams redoubled.

A clear voice cut through the noise. Everything came to a halt.

"You're wrong, Shambor. Shiván will see me now. And I'll *never* belong to you."

Perrely! Every eye turned to the frail figure leaning on Alanya's arm at the side entrance to the reception room. A lump formed in Shiván's throat at the sight of her. Her face was deathly white and slick with sweat; her neck and forearms were bleeding. Blood seeped from wounds on her scalp. One hand was a mangled wreck. Her breathing was ragged; she was obviously in the last stages of exhaustion. Yet the eyes in their dark circles that stared at Shambor were sharp and defiant.

"Perrely!" Shambor gaped at her, the blood draining from his face. "How — Who has done this to you? I'll have them — " She cut him off.

"You *liar!* You said you loved me, and *you* have done this to me. You wanted to lay the world at my feet, and you've mutilated and tortured me! You said you wouldn't harm my friends — but you've mindbent Gelmion, Garset, Frengor and Cârin! And now you're going to mindbend Shiván. Everything you've told me has been *lies!* My family — *you* gave the order for them to be killed, didn't you? You're nothing but a *liar* and a *murderer*." Her voice broke on the last word.

Shiván was in the firm grip of a burly Guard, or he would have been at her side in an instant. Shambor stood speechless.

* * *

Danîsha stepped forward from behind Perrely and Alanya, with a tall, elderly man in a blue robe beside her. Shiván blinked in amazement. This had to be Bishop Harlon — the true ruler of Dûrion! What was *he* doing with Danîsha? He was thrilled to see 'Neesh, but… she was different. There were new lines of pain on her face, her hair was greyer — and her eyes were twin points of sharpened steel.

She declared with steadily rising intensity, her fists clenched:

"Not by power, nor by strength, but by my Light, says the One Creator God."

Shambor stared at her, appalled. "What — That's not true! It's meaningless. Empty Lightist claptrap. It's a — "

Danîsha advanced on Shambor, pointing a finger at him:

"*Not* by power, *nor* by strength, but by *my Light*, says the One."

"—feeble excuse… those who have no power…" He couldn't breathe. He felt his eyes dilate with panic. *It was Mama!* She'd found him out at last.

"Not by power, nor by strength, but by my Light, says the One!"

"No! That's not— It doesn't work…"

"Listen to the One Creator God, you ruler of darkness! He says, *I am the Lord your God*—you shall have no other gods before me. *Not by power, nor by strength, but by my Light!"*

Shambor saw his dead mother's face, heard her voice. Her favourite saying crashed again and again into his consciousness. "*No, Mama!* I haven't been bad, I've tried to do good…"

Shiván blinked in shock. *Mama?* These two were in a different world.

Danîsha was standing right in front of Shambor, her finger pointing in his face:

"Not by power, nor by strength, but by my Light, says the One!"

Incredibly, tears began trickling down Shambor's cheeks. "No, Mama," he pleaded in a small, desperate voice. "*I* have power, too! Real power. I can show you…"

"Your power is *nothing.* This is the message of the living God and of His Son Prince Orrénne," Danîsha declared. "Your authority is cancelled. Your rule is over. Your abuses are ended. Dûrion shall be governed not by power, nor by strength, but by the Light of the One Creator God!"

Harlon stood beside Danîsha, his face filled with anguish.

The torture of Brakhól stopped, the Mindbenders stilled by their master's incapacity. The child continued to whimper softly.

Shambor's eyes were wide, his mouth slack. His mind was falling into chaos. He cried out, collapsed to his knees and clutched his head with both hands. "*No, Mama!*" he cried. "*I didn't mean it—*" He looked up at her, his pasty cheeks wet with tears. "*I'm sorry!*"

She said nothing.

He turned in desperation to the Bishop. "*Father!* I only wanted to please you!"

Shiván's dazed thoughts could hardly keep up. Harlon was Shambor's *father?*

"*I never meant to do all those bad things. I only wanted to make Dûrion a better place. You said you would trust me, and I just wanted* to please you! *But you* didn't *trust me! You kept on stopping me, telling me I was wrong –* "

Harlon shook his head. "Oh, Gari."

Shambor's voice rose to a strained falsetto, his face a mask of agony. "*I didn't mean to kill Mama! It was an accident! Everything went wrong... Ever since then... all wrong...*" He clasped his head in both hands.

A voice spoke in his mind. "*Gari.*"

The Strongholder! No! Dragged off to Selmion... Endless hopelessness... No no no no no... A dim recollection penetrated his screaming thoughts of how Mindbender Dhelgor had ended his pain. In a single, agile movement he leapt to his feet and on to the blackwood desk. He seized the Ambon leaning against it. With a mighty swing he smashed the circular stained glass window. As dusty daylight flooded the room, the ruler of Dûrion threw himself through the broken shards into the open air beyond.

Moments later, from three storeys below, came a distant medley of hundreds of voices crying out in shock and horror.

* * *

With a sound of rustling and several crashes every Mindbender and slave froze. A deathly hush fell on the reception room. Even Brakhól was silent. Gelmion, Garset, Frengor and Cârin stood unmoving with fixed expressions of dawning horror.

Lannie, Perrely and Shiván stared wide-eyed at the shattered window. Bishop Harlon ran to it and looked down.

He turned back to them, his face stricken. "He's dead. He was my son."

Danîsha hurried to him. "Your Radiance, I didn't know. I – "

Tears stood in his eyes as he laid a hand on her shoulder. "You spoke from God. Every word you said was true. He reached the end he deserved."

Danîsha nodded, then ran to comfort Brakhól and release him from the straps holding him to the table. Estaron helped her, then went with her as she took the sobbing child to find salve and bandages.

Shiván went to Perrely. Her knees had given way, and she was sitting propped against the wall. He stood in front of her, and she stared up at him fearfully, a wreck of her former self. He bent and very gently lifted her into his arms. She broke down and sobbed against his chest.

Shambor was dead. Every Mindbender, every spy, every Bishop's Guard throughout the country was frozen, stripped of their powers.

The nightmare was over.

Epilogue

UNABLE TO MOVE, GIL WATCHED Garset, Frengor and Cârin recover rapidly from the mindlock. They had been slaves for such a short time. Garset hurried out at once—no doubt to reassure the waiting army. Cârin went to pick up the Ambon, which had landed on the floor by the window, and began examining it carefully for damage. Shiván and Lannie were easing Perrely down on to a recliner. Bishop Harlon was sitting slumped on another chair, Frengor's hand on his shoulder. "You need to address the people," the priest said gently.

After settling Perrely, Lannie came over to Gil. She stared at his face for a long time, her expression sombre. "To think I once imagined you'd make a better Overguardian than Shiván." She shook her head. "So this is what your betrayal has come to. Your all-powerful master is dead. What will you do when you recover, I wonder? I suppose we'll have to look after you till then. But don't rely on me to hold your hand." She went back to Shiván and Perrely.

Gil's mind stared sadly after her. So, he'd lost Lannie for good. She couldn't know how his perspective had changed since Shambor revoked his autonomy. But even if she did, it wouldn't make any difference.

When he recovered from the mindlock he'd be free. But free to do what? All his options in this benighted land had led to dead ends. The future was a blank wall.

* * *

That evening Shiván, Alanya, Danîsha, Cârin, Garset and Frengor were gathered round the restored Bishop of Dûrion's ceremonial dining table. Perrely was lying on a nearby recliner, and Jomel was sitting next to her. Shiván held Brakhól on his lap, gently stroking his long black locks. The Cathedral staff had returned, and a simple meal was being served in Shambor's former apartment. Secretary Estaron had cleared the abominable animal storeroom and released its occupants.

"Gari never took easily to the way of humility and trust," Bishop Harlon told them. His eyes were red-rimmed as he related what he knew of Shambor's story. "Even as a young child, he wanted to control everything and everyone. Once my wife Mirélle…" He turned to Danîsha with a smile. "She looked and sounded very much like you, my dear. Anyway, Mirélle found Garion pulling the wings off an injured bird. Before she could say anything Gari looked up at her proudly and said, 'Look how strong I am, Mama! The bird can't fly away from me now.' Of course she was horrified, and gave him a thorough scolding. With hindsight I can see that this must have made a deep impression. Afterwards he was often sullen and secretive."

He heaved a deep sigh. "I confess he was a great disappointment to me. I was a young Kindler with high hopes for my son. Mirélle and I were unable to have other children, and we were too harsh with Gari. I can see that now. It turned him away from us. My duties as a Kindler kept me often out of the house, and the burden of discipline fell on Mirélle. It was a relief to us when we were able to send him to the Hearth School in Sûrilane. But… that was his undoing." The Bishop was silent for a long moment, staring at the red wine in his goblet.

"There he made friends with a Selmian lad, Barlesh. I don't believe that was an accident. Barlesh and his family were secret adherents of the Cult of Gadesh."

"Why secret?" Shiván asked.

"Oh, it was outlawed then. The Lightless cults could only operate secretly — until Shambor's Edict of Tolerance. Barlesh's family held private Gadeshite ceremonies around a shrine in their house. Garion was invited, and they began to talk to him about receiving 'personal powers' if he worshipped Gadesh. Well, you can imagine how that would inflame the imagination of a young lad on the threshold of puberty. He became an adherent — and later, some said, the youngest-ever devotee. At home during the school holidays he was increasingly unruly and overbearing. Mirélle went to Sûrilane one day while he was at home and made enquiries. She wrote all of this to me while she was there.

"I now realise she must have had a confrontation with Garion on her return. In retaliation he set fire to the house. I received an urgent message from neighbours the next day. When I arrived, there was nothing but a blackened shell." He drew a shuddering breath.

"At the time I thought both Mirélle and Garion had died in the blaze. I pulled my life together as best I could, and many years later was elected Bishop of Dûrion. When Shambor appeared on the scene some years after that, I had no suspicions. He didn't look or sound at all like my son. I now believe that he escaped from the fire that killed his mother, and was spirited away by the Gadeshites to Selmion. In fact it might have been a plot of the Strongholder's all along. At any rate, the Strongholder now had access to a bona fide ex-Lightist, the son of a Kindler, with all the background needed to make a credible Bishop of Dûrion. Meanwhile he was no doubt trained as a Mindbender in one of Selmion's temples.

"My election as Bishop must have been a delightful irony to the Strongholder. He was able to send back my own son to supplant me. A different appearance and a false identity were created for Garion: he became Shambor dom Beldet of Yarbiless. I've no doubt Beldet and his wife were handsomely rewarded — before suffering a fatal accident.

"In any case, Shambor appeared, studied law, and a few years later became Elder of Janulane. In that rôle he displayed such energy and efficiency that he attracted my attention. I invited him to Darthane for training as a Kindler; and a couple of years later appointed him my Bishop Suffragan.

"So." Harlon sighed and surveyed the table with a wan smile. "The rest you know. Shambor replaced me and took over full authority. But he could never bring himself to kill or mindbend me. For that, I suppose, I should be grateful. And also to all of you. Without you, my son would still be practising his abominations. My deepest thanks for everything you've gone through."

Frengor laid a hand on the old man's shoulder. Harlon bowed his head; his shoulders shook.

* * *

Two weeks later, Shiván sat beside Perrely on an open balcony in the Cathedral. It was bitterly cold, but clear and bright. They were warmly wrapped, and Perrely lay comfortably on a recliner. Brakhól was on Shiván's lap, swathed in layers of fur. They sat quietly enjoying one another's company.

So much had happened in the last two weeks: Bishop Harlon reinstated as ruling Bishop; Garset appointed Lord High Marshal of Dûrion — he'd left this morning to take over command in the Grûzhack War; the last pockets of Dûrian resistance dealt with — the

Dorbians had helped with that. Then the Grand Victory Celebration in the Cathedral yesterday...

Brakhól whimpered in Shiván's arms, and he gave him a gentle squeeze. "It's okay, little guy." He had a lot to recover from. At the moment he only trusted Shiván and Jomel.

Below them the whole of Darthane rejoiced. Comforted, Brakhól sat up straighter to watch what was going on. People danced in the streets to the sound of pipes and bellarils. In the Cathedral Square a great ambon had been set up with coloured ribbons radiating from it, like a maypole. Men and women wove an intricate pattern around it, leaping and singing. Jomel was one of them, dressed in a bright yellow outfit she'd found in one of Shambor's cupboards.

Even the Dorbians were welcomed — after all, these were *good* Dorbians, weren't they? They had helped to sing the walls down. Great grey shapes ran to and fro among the crowds, some carrying small children squealing with delight on their backs.

"I wonder if one of those is Gwargif?" Perrely said.

"Could be. He'd love nothing better." He leant forward for a better look. "Ah, but not today! I see an Englishwoman among the bellarists, with a big Dorbian sitting next to her. 'Neesh has found her friend again."

"We owe a lot to Gwargif."

"I know. And to you, and to Lannie, and Danîsha, and Garset, and me, and — "

"God."

He grinned. "Spot on." His smile faded as he looked to the west. Somewhere out there soldiers were still dying in the battle against superior Grûzhack weapons. And to the east... the looming menace of Selmion. As Frengor had said, by defeating Shambor they had declared war on the Strongholder — and on all the nations he controlled.

"God's seen us through all of this," he said quietly. "But it's not over yet."

* * *

In his study in the old royal palace of Orselm, capital of Selmion, a young man dressed in a plain white robe stared with hard eyes at the opposite wall as he mindspoke his subordinate. The Strongholder was not pleased. Those so-called 'Restorers' had done the unthinkable and killed a *Mindruler*. The entire Dûrian network was gone.

Of course, Shambor had been a flawed, unstable idiot; he should never have allowed him to continue in power after the fiasco that started the Grûzhack war.

Nevertheless those Restorers had set it all off; and they would pay the price. *No one* challenged the Strongholder and lived.

"Belyeru."

"Yes, Strongholder."

"Tell the cavalry to prepare for a major spring offensive. I want new recruits trained to take the place of those we lost in Dûrion. As soon as possible I want to see plans for the capture of the nearest Dûrian towns: Starmane, Astenar, Yarbiless. And over the winter I want more Gorelenye trained to replace the Grûzhack child. Do I make myself clear?"

"Yes, your Supremacy."

Did you enjoy this book?

*In the new world of publishing, word of mouth is often the most important factor in a story finding its readers. If you enjoyed this book, it would be fantastic if you would consider **rating** it and leaving a **review**. You can do so on **Amazon** or anywhere else the book is sold. Thank you so much!*

The story continues... Read on!

The Restorers of the Way have done the impossible, and set Dûrion free!

But only for a few short months as warfare is suspended during winter...

In the south the Grûzhack have come rampaging down from their mountain fastness with their terrible fire-weapons, and in spring will begin their unstoppable advance towards the Dûrian capital, Darthane.

And in the east the Strongholder, master of all mindbending, is preparing to strike a blow so devastating, so all-encompassing, that those who oppose him will be reduced to abject submission. *Can the Restorers and their Dûrian friends trust God do the **utterly** impossible?*

And if you haven't read the first book, now's the time!

Four unlikely strangers suddenly find themselves in an unknown country on an unknown world, their ears assaulted by the clash of swords on armour and the whizz of arrows...

Captured, enslaved, barely escaping, betrayed by one of their own, they are pursued across the country from one precarious refuge to the next by Mindruler Shambor dom Beldet.

Can the God they call upon overcome even the Mindruler's unimaginable powers? Are they themselves the long-awaited 'Restorers of the Way', who will set his tormented subjects free?

Both books can be found at your local Amazon store!

Visit *The Mindrulers* online!

For news about upcoming releases, special offers, author's comments and background insights, do visit:

https://www.facebook.com/pg/TheMindrulers/.

And for fascinating details, pictures, full-colour maps, descriptions of the Dûrian people and how they live, notes on the Dûrian language, and a wealth of information about the world of Malane, come and see us at:

https://www.themindrulers.com/.